I0628374

THE BEST OF DON WILCOX

VOLUME II

THE BEST OF DON WILCOX

VOLUME II

Don Wilcox

Edited by Von Rothenberger

Introduction by Mike Ashley

WILDSIDE PRESS

The Best of Don Wilcox Vol. II is copyright © 2017 by Von
Rothenberger. All rights reserved. Introduction copyright ©
2016 by Mike Ashley and used by permission of the author.
All photographs courtesy of Carolyn Ihde and used by permission.

Published by Wildside Press LLC.
www.wildsidepress.com

Contents

EDITOR'S PREFACE,
by Von Rothenberger

Don Wilcox (center) working as a typesetter for his hometown newspaper while in high school at Lucas, Kansas. (Circa 1920.)

"…Well, we took a poll of several thousand readers' comments and discovered that the ten most liked authors were (in order): 1. Don Wilcox; 2. William P. McGivern; 3. John York Cabot; 4. Nelson S. Bond; 5. David Wright O'Brien; 6. James Norman; 7. Edgar Rice Burroughs; 8. Robert Moore Williams; 9. David V. Reed; 10. Eando Binder…When you see any of those names heading a story—its good! And you can take your own word for it, because that's where the list comes from."

—*Fantastic Adventures* Magazine,
October 1941.

* * * *

I first became aware of teacher, artist, and writer Cleo Eldon "Don" Wilcox and his career as a successful science fiction/fantasy (hereafter referred to "sci-fi" or "sf&f") author when I moved to Lucas, Kansas in the fall of 2010. The population of Lucas is just short of 400 people, but over the past century the works of both local self-taught artists and other later artists moving into the town has earned the community an international reputation as a leading folk art center known as "The Grassroots Art Capital of Kansas."

I became acquainted with the head librarian at the Lucas Public Library, Carolyn Ihde, who showed me some of the stories done by her father, Don Wilcox, who had been born in Lucas. I was intrigued, as I had never heard of him before. I did some research and was astounded to discover how prolific he was, with dozens of stories published in the early to mid-20th Century, and that legendary science fiction writers such as Isaac Asimov, Ray Bradbury, Terry Carr, Robert Silverberg, and Lin Carter all mentioned him with respect.

And yet Don Wilcox is so unknown there has been debate in some sci-fi circles as to his actual existence.

The following illustrates perfectly how forgotten Don Wilcox had become. It is taken from the April 23, 2011 "comments section" for the *Visions of Paradise* blog, a sf&f eFanzine.com site, where I posed an certain question to the moderator of the blog:

> **Myself:** "Have read several of your postings with great interest, and you seem like the perfect person to pose this two-part question to: (1) What would the legacy of Don Wilcox be in the history of science fiction/fantasy writing, and (2) if one were to compile an anthology of his writings, who in your opinion would be perfect for penning the Foreword to such an anthology?."
>
> **Blog Moderator:** "I have never heard of a Don Wilcox in f&sf, nor does his name show up either at *Fantastic Fiction*, *Locus* or *Wikipedia*, nor in the contents pages of either *F&SF* or *Galaxy*. Even a general Google search turned up nothing. Is he a real person?"
>
> **Commentator #2:** "Don's name does show up in ISFDB (http://www.isfdb.org/cgi-bin/ea.cgi?872). I have not read any of his work. Most of his work appeared in the 40s."
>
> **Blog Moderator:** "That's a fairly extensive list of publications for somebody I've never heard of previously. Thanks, [Commentator #2]."
>
> **Commentator #2:** "I agree with you. It is rare to find an author I have never heard of let alone one who has written this much. From the comments on the Sony Reader Store site, it sounds like he was very popular in the 40s and early 50s. He does not appear to be reprinted in later years."

Even most of Don's hometown of Lucas did not remember that he was a published writer until the town's Grassroots Art Center hosted a

2002 Smithsonian Institution "Yesterday's Tomorrow's" traveling exhibit that included a tribute to Don and featured several magazines with his stories being displayed.

Don Wilcox as a baby.

When I saw the expanse of Don's published work, and also saw that while other writers of his generation were being rediscovered and celebrated he was not, I felt that this was a mistake, and that something had to be done to correct this oversight.

So I decided to give Don back the reputation I felt he deserved as an author, while at the same time presenting Don's works as a gift to his hometown in terms of a new kind of art to celebrate. The best way I saw to do that was to get an anthology of his work published.

I began to research Wilcox and uncover all he had written in the field of sf&f during that genre's golden age of the 1930s through the 1950s. The first thing I realized was that no one was quite sure what he wrote, as in several instances Wilcox's stories were published under a series of different pen names.

In due course I ran across articles referring to bibliographer, historian, and author Mike Ashley of England, and the work he had done in documenting and indexing the vast number of stories published in what were known as pulp magazines prior to the 1960s. Between Mike's work and information from the Wilcox family I arrived at a list of no less than 97 known published science fiction/fantasy stories written by Don—an impressive figure by anyone's standards.

Don Wilcox's daughter Carolyn and her cousin, Bruce Houghton, came up with original magazines containing about half of the stories. I found all but two of the rest on various websites that provided free downloads of the old magazines, now eagerly sought by fans and collectors alike. Then illness and other concerns halted work on the anthology for nearly two years.

In July 2013 I took up the project again by attempting to track down Mike Ashley in England—not an easy task even in the Internet era. Finding an address for him initially proved impossible, let alone an email address. After weeks of online research I at last ran across a 1996 interview that gave the name of Ashley's hometown, a village in Kent. Unfortunately, checking British phone and address directories proved fruitless.

A flash of inspiration in the end caused me to use Google Earth to locate the village library, to which I then wrote a letter, asking them to get in contact with him for me. Nine days after mailing that letter Ashley and I were corresponding by email, and the final two Wilcox stories also arrived via email courtesy of Mike, who had commissioned them during Don's final years. And so the final pieces of the anthology fell into place.

The stories for this two-volume set were selected from various stages throughout Don Wilcox's 53-year career and were chosen to represent that distinct Wilcox style for which he was known and respected by his peers in the sci-fi genre.

This project could not have been done without the participation, advice, and encouragement from Carolyn Ihde, Eric Abraham, Bruce Houghton, Mike Ashley, and Dr. Joe Hubbard. My thanks and gratitude go out to each and every one of them.

—Von Rothenberger

REDISCOVERING DON WILCOX, by Mike Ashley

When I first began collecting science-fiction magazines in earnest, back in the mid-1960s, I managed to acquire a fair size batch of the pulp issues of *Amazing Stories* when it was published by Ziff-Davis and edited by Raymond A. Palmer and later Howard Browne. I was already aware that the Palmer *Amazing* was not an especially sophisticated magazine, in fact quite the opposite. It went for sensationalism, with lurid covers, headline-grabbing story titles, and high-octane action fiction. So I wasn't looking for anything that would test the brain cells. John W. Campbell's *Astounding*, it most certainly wasn't.

Don Wilcox in 1951-1952.

But the magazine intrigued me, for several reasons, one of which was the contributors. Palmer had created a local, Chicago-based stable of writers. Some were known from their work elsewhere—Robert Bloch,

Robert Moore Williams, Nelson Bond—but most appeared predominantly, indeed some exclusively, in *Amazing Stories* and its companion *Fantastic Adventures*—William P. McGivern, Chester S. Geier, David Wright O'Brien, Berkeley Livingston and, of course, Don Wilcox. These authors contributed not only under their own names and a variety of personal pen names, but also under a family of house names, that is convenience names under which the works of several writers were hidden—names like Alexander Blade, Gerald Vance, P. F. Costello. To this day it is still not completely known who wrote what under these names and, as a result, the total output of these writers has not been identified.

It was this that got me interested and I began to undertake research. I read the stories trying to identify similarities in style, but that did not particularly help. I later learned that Ray Palmer and his assistant editors, notably Louis Sampliner and David Vern Reed, would edit the stories, sometimes excessively, to fit as many as possible into a house style. Even so, you can't completely eradicate a writer's style and I did start to find certain personalities amongst the work. But to be clear who wrote what, I needed to contact the writers. However, by the mid-1970s, when I started to do this, it was far from easy. There was certainly no internet to help track people down. Palmer's circle of writers had pretty much faded away in the 1950s. A few, like Robert Bloch and William P. McGivern, had moved on to fame and fortune, but most were no longer active.

One author I was especially keen to contact was Don Wilcox because his stories stood out. He was one of the more prolific contributors to the magazine and had a distinctive style, something the sub-editors couldn't mask. Although he occasionally wrote the formulaic fiction encouraged by Palmer, for the most part his stories had their own voice. The best known, quite rightly, is the one that established his name in the history of science fiction, "The Voyage That Lasted 600 Years" (*Amazing Stories*, October 1940) or, to give it Don's original and, to my mind, much better title, "Children of Space." It was the first to explore in detail the idea of a starship sent to a distant world on a journey where only the descendants of the original pioneers will survive. The story isn't a simple adventure but a sociological study. The captain of the ship is in suspended animation and wakes only every hundred years to check on developments, so witnesses the changes, mostly degenerative, amongst the humans. The story was almost rejected because Louis Sampliner felt it did not fit into the mould for the magazine, but Palmer saw the true merit of the story and accepted it.

*Don with his wife Helen and daughter Carolyn at the 1979
opening his art gallery in Sarasota, Florida*

"The Whispering Gorilla" (*Fantastic Adventures*, May 1940) was another that proved popular. A murdered man has his brain transplanted into a gorilla, but in Wilcox's hands this wasn't a simple ape-seeks-revenge story but something far more human. Assistant editor David Vern Reed liked the story and character and, with Wilcox's permission, wrote a sequel.

Then there were the Ebbtide Jones stories started early in his career and written under the pen name of Miles Shelton—a rather posh name for *Amazing Stories*, and in fact Wilcox's wife's maiden name—she was Helen Miles Shelton. Ebbtide Jones is an enterprising dealer in space junk. He has discovered a whirlpool in space where, because of gravitational forces, masses of space debris finds its way over time, and he makes use of whatever turns up.

One of my favourites, probably because it was the first story by Wilcox I read, was "The Giants of Mogo" (*Amazing Stories*, November 1947). Wilcox presents the seemingly implausible idea of mile-high giants living in a far distant star system, and who can't believe the midget humans who stumble on to their planet can have the intelligence to create spaceships. This first short novel is written rather like a fairy-tale and so soon lulls you into its concept and carries you along.

The idea of fairy tales must have appealed to Wilcox because some of his best stories, certainly his most atmospheric, were fantasies in *Fantastic Adventures*. A particular gem is "Mademoiselle Butterfly" (May 1942) about a femme fatale and her unusual pets. It's one of his more sinister stories. "The Land of Big Blue Apples" (May 1946), on the other hand, is more of a spoof, set on a fairy-tale Mars. Now and then Wilcox would produce an opening line which holds you spellbound. Take this one from "Rainbow of Death" (January 1942):

> Deep in the lavender mists that fill the caverns within the earth, the nine hundred and ninety-nine Servants of Death are laboring, even as they have labored through all of the earth's past and will continue to labor for an eternity of future time to come.

When I read that forty years or more ago it grabbed my attention and the story does not let you down.

These and much else made me determined to track down Don Wilcox. It took me several years. It wasn't until 1983, thanks to Will Murray and Ryerson Johnson, that I at last had Wilcox's address and made contact. It began an epistolary friendship that lasted for well over a decade. From the start I encountered a welcoming, friendly, very human individual who was happy to talk about his life and work and to share memories and experiences.

What I learned was that although Wilcox became friends with both editors Ray Palmer and Howard Browne, as well as many of the writers, especially William P. McGivern and David Wright O'Brien, he saw writing as a solitary dedication. "I was a loner in my writing habits," he told me. Though he didn't always write at home. There was a big dining room on the lower floor of the LaSalle Railway Station in Chicago which was half empty in the afternoon and he would sit there with his notebook or with pages spread out in front of him with notes and ideas for stories and characters and see what hatched. Other times he would take a stroll through the park or the zoo. It was while walking through Lincoln Park Zoo that he saw a gorilla watching the crowd and the idea for "The Whispering Gorilla" came to him. When Wilcox and his family lived at Lake Geneva, Wisconsin, Palmer would occasionally visit them. Wilcox recalled sharing a picnic table with Palmer. Palmer would read manuscripts whilst Wilcox plotted a story. But, as he told me, "I fear I was slightly tense, and perhaps only medium-warm as a friend." It seems that although Wilcox could join in with his colleagues he worked better on his own.

Maybe this had something to do with his background. He was not, after all, a native Chicagoan, and his training was as a teacher. I would hazard a guess that Wilcox may well have been one of the better educated of the Ziff-Davis writers.

He had been born in Lucas, Kansas on 29 August 1905. His father, Horace, worked as a bank cashier of the First National Bank in Lucas, where he later rose to the position of President. His mother's name was Docia. Don was christened Cleo Eldon Wilcox and was the second of what would be four children, with an elder sister (Zola) and a younger brother and sister (Marvin and Thelma). Don's father had been educated at the Kansas Christian College in Lincoln and graduated with a Bachelor of Science degree. Before entering employment at the bank, he became assistant principal at Lincoln High School.

Don rather followed in his father's footsteps. He graduated from the University of Kansas with an M.A. in sociology (hence the interest in "The Voyage That Lasted 600 Years"). He taught English, creative writing, sociology and history in several high schools as well as at Northwestern University and the University of Kansas. It was while teaching at Lucas High School that he met his future wife, Helen, and they were married in June 1929. Their daughter, Carolyn, was born in August 1937.

As early as 1932 he had turned his hand to writing, initially short plays for the high-school classes and then several feature articles for the *Kansas City Star*. By the late 1930s Don believed he might make a living from writing and took the risk of uprooting his family and moving to Chicago in 1938. He did the round of publishers, ending up at the back of the alphabet with Ziff-Davis and *Amazing Stories*. He had not previously taken any notice of science fiction, but felt he could give it a try. He had read about experiments on small animals by freezing them instantly with "liquid air" and then reviving them. A convict serving life had suggested it be tried on him. Don concocted a story around this which became "The Pit of Death." Palmer bought it for $90 and it appeared in the July 1939 *Amazing Stories*. Wilcox was on his way.

As he learned the ropes with Palmer he found he could sell one or two stories a month. Some, such as "Disciples of Destiny" (*Amazing Stories*, March-April 1942) and "The Eye of the World" (*Fantastic Adventures*, June-July 1949 as by Alexander Blade), were of novel length. All of those stories are collected in these seven volumes for the first time ever, providing a unique opportunity to read and explore the output of one of Palmer's more conscientious and dedicated writers. He also wrote for the other Ziff-Davis magazines *Mammoth Western* and *Mammoth Detective* and in total published over a hundred stories.

All good things come to an end, though. By the late 1940s Palmer had become fascinated by flying saucers and the Shaver Mystery, the latter a belief by Richard S. Shaver that the Earth was still under the malign influence of evil beings, which he called 'deros', which were descendants of an advanced race that used to live on the Earth in aeons past. Palmer established his own magazine *Fate* to explore UFOs and other phenomena. Howard Browne took over as editor and he wanted to change both *Amazing* and *Fantastic Adventures* into more sophisticated, possibly even slick, magazines. Wilcox, as one of the more adaptable contributors, continued to sell to Browne until 1952, but it was time to move on.

Thanks to a recommendation from Browne, Wilcox turned to television. He was introduced to Olga Druce, the producer of the TV series *Captain Video*. In those days *Captain Video* was broadcast live on a daily basis, so it not only ate up material, the scripts had to be written in such a way as to allow actors time to move between scenes and for the sponsors links to be incorporated. It took Don a while to pick up this process but in the end he produced a batch of twenty scripts for one particular story sequence. One factor that Wilcox noticed when he watched the production of the plays was how quickly scenes rushed past which, in a story, could be better savoured and he feared that viewers might be missing some of the material. After the experience Don found it less satisfying than writing stories. There was little if any feedback from viewers and the restrictions of the half-hour format was very limiting. By the end of the twenty episodes Don told me he was "utterly exhausted."

By then he found that he had also moved on from Ziff-Davis. For that matter, *Amazing Stories* and its new companion *Fantastic*, had also moved on. He wrote a few more stories for the magazines during the 1950s, but his last for a very long time was "The Smallest Moon" for *Boys' Life* in 1957. Browne tried to encourage Wilcox to write for John Campbell's *Astounding*, but by now Don had turned his thoughts to other activities.

Following a trip to Guatemala in 1958, Don developed, with the help of the American School foundation, a bi-lingual magazine for Spanish pupils. Called *Caminos*, it began in September 1959 and was used by many Spanish language classes in the United States. Don not only helped produce the magazine he wrote extensively for it and illustrated it, providing most of the covers for the next six years. In 1965 he became editor of *Opportunity News*, a newly established weekly magazine for Mexican-English migrant workers in Oregon. Two years later Don moved on again, and spent the next eight years, until his retirement in 1975, in public relations and editing for the Columbia-Presbyterian Medical Center in New York. After his retirement, when he settled in Sarasota, Florida, he returned to his love of painting, chiefly oil painting, producing many portraits.

It was in Sarasota that I at last tracked Don down in 1983 and I was delighted to be able to entice him back into writing and encourage his last two published stories. I put Don in touch with Robert M. Price who edited a number of little magazines, the chief one being *Crypt of Cthulhu*, dedicated to the work of H. P. Lovecraft. Price had developed several new publications, one of which was based on old-style space opera, called *Astro-Adventures*. Issue #8 (June 1989) included both an interview with Don that I conducted via our correspondence and a new story "Visit the Yo-Yo Falls." At that time I had also started a series of anthologies for the British publisher Robinson Books, including a sequence based on the myths and legends associated with King Arthur. For the second book in this series, *The Camelot Chronicles* (1992), Don brought together his passion for writing and art in an ingenious story, "Blueflow." This was his last published story and closes this set of books.

JULY 22 '91
(DON WILCOX)

Self portrait, late 1991.

To have known Don was a real delight. We lost touch in his final years after he and Helen moved back to Kansas to live with their daughter. He died at Lucas in March 2000, aged 94.

Most pulp fiction tends to be ephemeral. The old magazines crumble and fade, surviving in the hands of a few dedicated collectors. The wider world seldom gets a chance to savour most of the fiction except for the work of those few that outgrew the pulp world and established for themselves a wider literary heritage—writers like Raymond Chandler, Robert Bloch, Dashiell Hammett and Isaac Asimov. Even some of the greats, like Max Brand and Johnston McCulley, are fading in the collective memory, so it is always a moment to celebrate when the work of a great old pulpster is rediscovered and repackaged for a modern readership.

These stories capture a time and an age when our outlook on life was more free and unfettered by so many modern attitudes and restrictions. They were produced to entertain a primarily American public during the years leading up to and after the Second World War and, as such, they are escapist and pure fun.

As editor, Howard Browne told Wilcox, when he asked for some writing guidance, "Gimme Bang-Bang!" And that's what he got. Though, at times, a rather more unusual "Bang-Bang" than he might first have expected. These stories are full of surprises and can still deliver that thrill and excitement that they did all those years ago.

The gravestone of Don and his wife Helen in the Fairview Township Cemetery at Lucas, Kansas. Note his real name, Cleo Eldon Wilcox.

THE VOYAGE THAT
LASTED 600 YEARS

To open this set of stories we lead off with Wilcox's most critically-acclaimed and influential story. This was the first story ever published that introduced the concept of the generational starship, where succeeding generations continue to live on the same ship as it travels through space to a distant destination. Wilcox's idea has gone on to become its own distinct sub-genre of science fiction with hundreds of stories in books, movies, and television (such as the original Star Trek *series episode "For the World is Hollow and I have Touched the Sky").*

"One of the most interesting concepts is the generation starship, a vehicle which takes centuries and is crewed by generation after generation of persons born, educated, and trained on board... Don Wilcox's "The Voyage that Lasted 600 Years" *(*Amazing Stories, *October 1940) was, however, the first story to use this concept. His work is well-written, but has been virtually ignored—this is only its second known reprinting. Wilcox himself lived in the Chicago area for many years, teaching creative writing at Northwestern University. His work appeared infrequently in the science fiction field and then almost exclusively in Ziff-Davis publications.*"—Isaac Asimov, *from his introduction to* "The Voyage That Lasted 600 Years" *in* Isaac Asimov Presents the Best Science Fiction Firsts (1984).

"Once in a great while a writer sits down and does a yarn that he doesn't intend to sell, but which turns out to be a rare piece of science fiction, packed with real significance. An editor, in this case ourselves, decides it is what he has been looking for to break the monotony. Thus, in this issue you will find the most unusual story Don Wilcox has written to date. It is 'The Voyage That Lasted 600 Years,' *and we believe it to be the most significant piece we've had in months.*"—Raymond A. Palmer *in the editor's column* "The Observatory" *in* Amazing Stories *magazine, October 1940.*

*"Back in Chicago, back in the routine of work in the Trans-portation Building on South Dearborn, [*Amazing Stories *editor] Raymond A. Palmer learned that an unknown neophyte editor was being sent from New York to work with him... Soon we were to meet the first of these acquisitions, a funny, charming little guy named Louis Sampliner. He and I were destined to become friends, in spite of the fact that his first official act was to reject one of my stories.*

The story which Palmer handed to Sampliner to read, "The Voyage That Lasted 600 Years," *had been an interesting experiment for me in semi-sociological writing. I, the protagonist, was put aboard a space ship to guide future colonists on a 600-year voyage. I would emerge from my ice box every one hundred years to be sure the new generations were continuing on course. Sampliner rejected it because it didn't follow his rules of story writing. Possibly he never knew that I learned he had rejected it... If Louis Sampliner had succeeded in rejecting it, I would have tried to sell it elsewhere, though very possibly it would have been lost in the shuffle. Palmer, as he reported to me afterward, told Sampliner that he had been buying most of my stories and maybe he'd better take a look at it personally before returning it as a reject. The story was accepted and published and it has somehow stayed alive. Possibly a parallel comes up in readers' thoughts. That peril of overpopulation on the 600-year voyage! Are we now seeing the same for our Space Ship Earth?*

—Don Wilcox, *from his personal notes, 1989.*

CHAPTER I

THEY gave us a gala send-off, the kind that keeps your heart bobbing up at your tonsils.

"It's a long, long way to the Milky Way!" the voices sang out. The band thundered the chorus over and over. The golden trumpaphones blasted our eardrums wide open. Thousands of people clapped their hands in time.

There were thirty-three of us–that is, there was supposed to be. As it turned out, there were thirty-five.

We were a dazzling parade of red, white and blue uniforms. We marched up the gangplank by couples, every couple a man and wife, every couple young and strong, for the selection had been rigid.

Captain Sperry and his wife and I—I being the odd man—brought up the rear. Reporters and cameramen swarmed at our heels. The microphones stopped us. The band and the crowd hushed.

"This is Captain Sperry telling you good-by," the amplified voice boomed. "In behalf of the thirty-three, I thank you for your grand farewell. We'll remember this hour as our last contact with our beloved Earth."

The crowd held its breath. The mighty import of our mission struck through every heart.

"We go forth into space to live—and to die," the captain said gravely. "But *our children's children,* born in space and reared in the light of our vision, will carry on our great purpose. And in centuries to come, *your children's children* may set forth for the Robinello planets, knowing that you will find an American colony already planted there."

The captain gestured good-by and the multitude responded with a thunderous cheer. Nothing so daring as a six-century nonstop flight had ever been undertaken before.

An announcer nabbed me by the sleeve and barked into the microphone.

"And now one final word from Professor Gregory Grimstone, the one man who is supposed to live down through the six centuries of this historic flight and see the journey through to the end."

"Ladies and gentlemen," I choked, and the echo of my swallow blobbed back at me from distant walls, "as Keeper of the Traditions, I give you my word that the S. S. *Flashaway* shall carry your civilization through to the end, unsoiled and unblemished!"

A cheer stimulated me and I drew a deep breath for a burst of oratory. But Captain Sperry pulled at my other sleeve.

"That's all. We're set to slide out in two minutes."

The reporters scurried down the gangplank and made a center rush through the crowd. The band struck up. Motors roared sullenly.

One lone reporter who had missed out on the interviews blitzkrieged up and caught me by the coattail.

"Hold it, Butch. Just a coupla words so I can whip up a column of froth for the *Star*—Well, I'll be damned! If it ain't 'Crackdown' Grimstone!"

I scowled. The reporter before me was none other than Bill Broscoe, one of my former pupils at college and a star athlete. At heart I knew that Bill was a right guy, but I'd be the last to tell him so.

"Broscoe!" I snarled. "Tardy as usual. You finally flunked my history course, didn't you?"

"Now, Crackdown," he whined, "don't go hopping on me. I won that Thanksgiving game for you, remember?"

HE gazed at my red, white and blue uniform.

"So you're off for Robinello," he grinned.

"Son, this is my last minute on Earth, and *you* have to haunt me, of all people –"

"So you're the one that's taking the refrigerated sleeper, to wake up every hundred years –"

"And stir the fires of civilization among the crew—yes. Six hundred years from now when your bones have rotted, I'll still be carrying on."

"Still teaching 'em history? God forbid!" Broscoe grinned.

"I hope I have better luck than I did with you."

"Let 'em off easy on dates, Crackdown. Give them 1066 for William the Conqueror and 2066 for the *Flashaway* take-off. That's enough. Taking your wife, I suppose?"

At this impertinent question I gave Broscoe the cold eye.

"Pardon me," he said, suppressing a sly grin—proof enough that he had heard the devastating story about how I missed my wedding and got the air. "Faulty alarm clock, wasn't it? Too bad, Crackdown. And you always ragged me about being tardy!"

With this jibe Broscoe exploded into laughter. Some people have the damnedest notions about what constitutes humor. I backed into the entrance of the space ship uncomfortably. Broscoe followed.

Zzzzippp!

The automatic door cut past me. I jerked Broscoe through barely in time to keep him from being bisected.

"Tardy as usual, my friend!" I hooted. "You've missed your gang-plank! That makes you the first castaway in space."

We took off like a shooting star, and the last I saw of Bill Broscoe, he stood at a rear window cursing as he watched the earth and the moon fall away into the velvety black heavens. And the more I laughed at him, the madder he got. No sense of humor.

Was that the last time I ever saw him? Well, no, to be strictly honest I had one more unhappy glimpse of him.

It happened just before I packed myself away for my first one hundred years' sleep.

I had checked over the "Who's Who Aboard the Flashaway"—the official register—to make sure that I was thoroughly acquainted with everyone on board; for these sixteen couples were to be the great-grandparents of the next generation I would meet. Then I had promptly taken my leave of Captain Sperry and his wife, and gone directly to my refrigeration plant, where I was to suspend my life by instantaneous freezing.

I clicked the switches, and one of the two huge horizontal wheels—one in reserve, in the event of a breakdown—opened up for me like a door opening in the side of a gigantic doughnut, or better, a tubular merry-go-round. There was my nook waiting for me to crawl in.

Before I did so I took a backward glance toward the ballroom. The one-way glass partition, through which I could see but not be seen, gave me a clear view of the scene of merriment. The couples were dancing. The journey was off to a good start.

"A grand gang," I said to myself. No one doubted that the ship was equal to the six-hundred-year journey. The success would depend upon the people. Living and dying in this closely circumscribed world would put them to a severe test. All credit, I reflected, was due the planning committee for choosing such a congenial group.

"They're equal to it," I said optimistically. If their children would only prove as sturdy and adaptable as their parents, my job as Keeper of the Traditions would be simple.

BUT how, I asked myself, as I stepped into my life-suspension merry-go-round, would Bill Broscoe fit into this picture? Not a half bad guy. Still—

My final glance through the one-way glass partition slew me. Out of the throng I saw Bill Broscoe dancing past with a beautiful girl in his arms. The girl was Louise—my Louise—the girl I had been engaged to marry!

In a flash it came to me—but not about Bill. I forgot him on the spot. About Louise.

Bless her heart, she'd come to find me. She must have heard that I had signed up for the *Flashaway,* and she had come aboard, a stowaway, to forgive me for missing the wedding—to marry me! Now—

A warning click sounded, a lid closed over me, my refrigerator-merry-go-round whirled—blackness!

CHAPTER II
Babies, Just Babies

IN a moment—or so it seemed!—was again gazing into the light of the refrigerating room. The lid stood open.

A stimulating warmth circulated through my limbs. Perhaps the machine, I half consciously concluded, had made no more than a preliminary revolution.

I bounded out with a single thought. I must find Louise. We could still be married. For the present I would postpone my entrance into the ice. And since the machine had been equipped with two merry-go-round freezers as an emergency safeguard—ah! Happy thought perhaps Louise would be willing to undergo life suspension with me!

I stopped at the one-way glass partition, astonished to see no signs of dancing in the ballroom. I could scarcely see the ballroom, for it had been darkened.

Upon unlocking the door (the refrigerator room was my own private retreat) I was bewildered. An unaccountable change had come over everything. What it was, I couldn't determine at the moment. But the very air of the ballroom was different.

A few dim green light bulbs burned along the walls—enough to show me that the dancers had vanished. Had time enough elapsed for night to come on? My thoughts spun dizzily. Night, I reflected, would consist simply of turning off the lights and going to bed. It had been agreed in our plan that our twenty-four hour Earth day would be maintained for the sake of regularity.

But there was something more intangible that struck me. The furniture had been changed about, and the very walls seemed *older.* Something more than minutes had passed since I left this room.

Strangest of all, the windows were darkened.

In a groggy state of mind I approached one of the windows in hopes of catching a glimpse of the solar system. I was still puzzling over how much time might have elapsed. Here, at least, was a sign of very recent activity.

"Wet Paint" read the sign pinned to the window. The paint was still sticky. What the devil–

The ship, of course, was fully equipped for blind flying. But aside from the problems of navigation, the crew had anticipated enjoying a wonderland of stellar beauty through the portholes. Now, for some strange reason, every window had been painted opaque.

I listened. Slow measured steps were pacing in an adjacent hallway. Nearing the entrance, I stopped, halted by a shrill sound from somewhere overhead. It came from one of the residential quarters that gave on the ballroom balcony.

It was the unmistakable wail of a baby.

Then another baby's cry struck up; and a third, from somewhere across the balcony, joined the chorus. Time, indeed, must have passed since I left this roomful of dancers.

Now some irate voices of disturbed sleepers added rumbling basses to the symphony of wailings. Grumbles of "Shut that little devil up!" and poundings of fists on walls thundered through the empty ballroom. In a burst of inspiration I ran to the records room, where the ship's "Who's

Who" was kept.

THE door to the records room was locked, but the footsteps of some sleepless person I had heard now pounded down the dimly lighted hallway. I looked upon the aged man. I had never seen him before. He stopped at the sight of me; then snapping on a brighter light, came on confidently.

"Mr. Grimstone?" he said, extending his hand. "We've been expecting you. My name is William Broscoe –"

"Broscoe!"

"William Broscoe, the second. You knew my father, I believe."

I groaned and choked.

"And my mother," the old man continued, "always spoke very highly of you. I'm proud to be the first to greet you."

He politely overlooked the flush of purple that leaped into my face. For a moment nothing that I could say was intelligible.

He turned a key and we entered the records room. There I faced the inescapable fact. My full century had passed. The original crew of the *Flashaway* were long gone. A completely new generation was on the register.

Or, more accurately, three new generations: the children, the grandchildren, and the great-grandchildren of the generation I had known.

One hundred years had passed—and I had lain so completely suspended, owing to the freezing, that only a moment of my own life had been absorbed.

Eventually I was to get used to this; but on this first occasion I found it utterly shocking—even embarrassing. Only a few minutes ago, as my experience went, I was madly in love with Louise and had hopes of yet marrying her.

But now—well, the leather-bound "Who's Who" told all. Louise had been dead twenty years. Nearly thirty children now alive aboard the S. S. *Flashaway* could claim her as their great-grandmother. These carefully recorded pedigrees proved it.

And the patriarch of that fruitful tribe had been none other than Bill Broscoe, the fresh young athlete who had always been tardy for my history class. I gulped as if I were swallowing a baseball.

Broscoe—tardy! And I had missed my second chance to marry Louise—by a full century!

My fingers turned the pages of the register numbly. William Broscoe II misinterpreted my silence.

"I see you are quick to detect our trouble," he said, and the same deep conscientious concern showed in his expression that I had remembered in the face of his mother, upon our grim meeting after my alarm clock had failed and I had missed my own wedding.

Trouble? Trouble aboard the S. S. *Flashaway,* after all the careful advance planning we had done, and after all our array of budgeting and scheduling and vowing to stamp our systematic ways upon the oncoming generations? This, we had agreed, would be the world's most unique colonizing expedition; for every last trouble that might crop up on the six-hundred-year voyage had already been met and conquered by advance planning.

"They've tried to put off doing anything about it until your arrival," Broscoe said, observing respectfully that the charter invested in me the authority of passing upon all important policies. "But this very week three new babies arrived, which brings the trouble to a crisis. So the captain ordered a blackout of the heavens as an emergency measure."

"**H**EAVENS?" I grunted. "What have the heavens got to do with babies?"

"There's a difference of opinion on that. Maybe it depends upon how susceptible you are."

"Susceptible—to what?"

"The romantic malady."

I looked at the old man, much puzzled. He took me by the arm and led me toward the pilots' control room. Here were unpainted windows that revealed celestial glories beyond anything I had ever dreamed. Brilliant planets of varied hues gleamed through the blackness, while close at hand—almost close enough to touch—were numerous large moons, floating slowly past as we shot along our course.

"Some little show," the pilot grinned, "and it keeps getting better."

He proceeded to tell me just where we were and how few adjustments in the original time schedules he had had to make, and why this non-stop flight to Robinello would stand unequalled for centuries to come.

And I heard virtually nothing of what he said. I simply stood there, gazing at the unbelievable beauty of the skies. I was hypnotized, enthralled, shaken to the very roots. One emotion, one thought dominated me. I longed for Louise.

"The romantic malady, as I was saying," William Broscoe resumed, "may or may not be a factor in producing our large population. Personally, I think it's pure buncombe."

"Pure buncombe," I echoed, still thinking of Louise. If she and I had had moons like these—

"But nobody can tell Captain Dickinson anything…"

There was considerable clamor and wrangling that morning as the inhabitants awakened to find their heavens blacked out. Captain Dickinson was none too popular anyway. Fortunately for him, many of the people took their grouches out on the babies who had caused the disturbance in the night.

Families with babies were supposed to occupy the rear staterooms—but there weren't enough rear staterooms. Or rather, there were too many babies.

Soon the word went the rounds that the Keeper of the Traditions had returned to life. I was duly banqueted and toasted and treated to lengthy accounts of the events of the past hundred years. And during the next few days many of the older men and women would take me aside for private conferences and spill their worries into my ears.

CHAPTER III
Boredom

"WHAT'S the world coming to?" these granddaddies and grandmothers would ask. And before I could scratch my head for an answer, they would assure me that this expedition was headed straight for the rocks.

"It's all up with us. We've lost our grip on our original purposes. The Six-Hundred-Year Plan is nothing but a dead scrap of paper."

I'll admit things looked plenty black. And the more parlor conversations I was invited in on, the blacker things looked. I couldn't sleep nights.

"If our population keeps on increasing, we'll run out of food before we're halfway there," William Broscoe II repeatedly declared. "We've got to have a compulsory program of birth control. That's the only thing that will save us."

A delicate subject for parlor conversations, you think? This older generation didn't think so. I was astonished, and I'll admit I was a bit proud as well, to discover how deeply imbued these old graybeards were with *Flashaway* determination and patriotism. They had missed life in America by only one generation, and they were unquestionably the staunchest of flag wavers on board.

The younger generations were less outspoken, and for the first week I began to deplore their comparative lack of vision. They, the possessors of families, seemed to avoid these discussions about the oversupply of children.

"So you've come to check up on our American traditions. Professor Grimstone," they would say casually. "We've heard all about this great purpose of our forefathers, and I guess it's up to us to put it across. But gee whiz, Grimstone, we wish have see the earth! What's it like, anyhow?"

"Tell us some more about the earth..."

I told them about the earth. Yes, they had books galore, and movies and phonograph records, pictures and maps; but these things only excited their curiosity. They asked me questions by the thousands. Only after I had poured out several encyclopedia-loads of Earth memories did I begin to break through their masks.

Back of this constant questioning, I discovered, they were watching me. Perhaps they were wondering whether they were not being subjected to more rigid discipline here on shipboard than their cousins back on Earth. I tried to impress upon them that they were a chosen group, but this had little effect. It struck in their minds that *they* had had no choice in the matter.

More-ever, they were watching to see what I was going to do about the population problem, for they were not less aware of it than their elders.

Two weeks after my "return" we got down to business.

Captain Dickinson preferred to engineer the matter himself. He called an assembly in the movie auditorium. Almost everyone was present.

The program began with the picture of the Six-Hundred-Year Plan. Everyone knew the reels by heart. They had seen and hear them dozens of times, and were ready to snicker at the proper moments—such as when the stern old committee chairman, charging the unborn generations with their solemn obligations, was interrupted by a friendly fly on his nose.

W HEN the films were run through, Captain Dickinson took the rostrum, and with considerable bluster he called upon the Clerk of the Council to review the situation. The clerk read a report which went about as follows:

> To maintain stable population, it was agreed in the original Plan that families should average two children each. Hence the original 16 families would bring fourth approximately 32 children; and assuming that they were fairly evenly divided as to sex, they would eventually form 16 new families. These 16

families would, in turn, have an average of two children each—another generation of approximately 32.

By maintaining these averages, we were to have a total population, at any given time, of 32 children, 32 parents and 32 grandparents. The great-grandparents may be left out of account, for owing to the natural span of life they ordinarily die off before they accumulate in any great numbers.

The three living generations, then, of 32 each would give the Flashaway a constant active population of 96, or, roughly, 100 persons.

The Six-Hundred-Year Plan has allowed for some flexibility in these figures. It has established the safe maximum at 150 and the safe minimum at 75.

If our population shrinks below 75, it is dangerously small. If it shrinks to 50, a crisis is at hand.

But if it grows above 150, it is dangerously large; and if it reaches the 200 mark, as we all know, a crisis may be said to exist.

The clerk stopped for an impressive pause, marred only by the crying of a baby from some distant room.

"Now, coming down to the present-day facts, we are well aware that the population has been dangerously large for the past seven years—"

"Since we entered this section of the heavens," Captain Dickinson interspersed with a scowl.

"From the first year in space, the population plan has encountered some irregularities," the clerk continued. "To begin with, there were not sixteen couples, but seventeen. The seventeenth couple—" here the clerk shot a glance at William Broscoe—" did not belong to the original compact, and after their marriage they were not bound by the sacred traditions—"

"I object!" I shouted, challenging the eyes of the clerk and the captain squarely. Dickinson had written that report with a touch of malice. The clerk skipped over a sentence or two.

"But however the Broscoe family may have prospered and multiplied, our records show that nearly all the families of the present generation have exceeded the per-family quota."

At this point there was a slight disturbance in the rear of the auditorium. An anxious-looking young man entered and signaled to the doctor. The two went out together.

"*All* the families," the clerk amended. "Our population this week passed the two hundred mark. This concludes the report."

The captain opened the meeting for discussion, and the forum lasted far into the night. The demand for me to assist the Council with some legislation was general. There was also hearty sentiment against the captain's blacked-out heavens from young and old alike.

T HIS, I considered, was a good sign. The children craved the fun of watching the stars and planets; their elders desired to keep up their serious astronomical studies.

"Nothing is so important to the welfare of this expedition," I said to the Council on the following day, as we settled down to the job of thrashing out some legislation, "as to maintain our interests in the outside world. Population or no population, we must not become ingrown!"

I talked of new responsibilities, new challenges in the form of contests and campaigns, new leisure-time activities. The discussion went on for days.

"Back in my times—", I said for the hundredth time; but the captain laughed me down. My times and these times were as unlike as black and white, he declared.

"But the principle is the same!" I shouted. "We had population troubles, too."

They smiled as I referred to twenty-first century relief families who were overrun with children: I cited the fact that some industrialists who paid heavy taxes had considered giving every relief family an automobile as a measure to save themselves money in the long run; for they had discovered that relief families with cars had fewer children than those without.

"That's no help," Dickinson muttered. "You can't have cars on a space ship."

"You can play bridge," I retorted. "Bridge is an enemy of the birthrate too. Bridge, cars, movies, checkers—they all add up to the same thing. They lift you out of your animal natures—" The Councilmen threw up their hands. They had bridged and checkered themselves to death.

"Then try other things," I persisted. "You could produce your own movies and plays—organize a little theater—create some new drama—"

"What have we got to dramatize?" the captain replied sourly. "All the dramatic things happen on the earth."

This shocked me. Somehow it took all the starch out of this colossal adventure to hear the captain give up so easily.

"All our drama is second hand," he grumbled. "Our ship's course is cut and dried. Our world is bounded by walls. The only dramatic things that happen here are births and deaths."

A doctor broke in on our conference and seized the captain by the hand.

"Congratulations, Captain Dickinson, on the prize crop of the season! Your wife has just presented you with a fine set of triplets—three boys!"

That broke up the meeting. Captain Dickinson was so busy for the rest of the week that he forgot all about his official obligations. The problem of population limitation faded from his mind.

I wrote out my recommendations and gave them the weight of my dictatorial authority. I stressed the need for more birth control forums, and recommended that the heavens be made visible for further studies in astronomy and mathematics.

I was tempted to warn Captain Dickinson that the *Flashaway* might incur some serious dramas of its own-poverty, disease and the like—unless he got back on the track of the Six-Hundred-Year Plan in a hurry. But Dickinson was preoccupied with some family washings when I took my leave of him, and he seemed to have as much drama on his hands as he cared for.

I paid a final visit to each of the twenty-eight great-grandchildren of Louise, and returned to my ice.

CHAPTER IV
Revolt!

MY chief complaint against my merry-go-round freezer was that it didn't give me any rest. One whirl into blackness, and the next thing I knew I popped out of the open lid again with not so much as a minute's time to reorganize my thoughts.

Well, here it was, 2266—two hundred years since the take-off.

A glance through the one-way glass told me it was daytime in the ballroom.

As I turned the key in the lock I felt like a prize fighter on a vaudeville tour who, having just trounced the tough local strong man, steps back in the ring to take on his cousin.

A touch of a headache caught me as I reflected that there should be four more returns after this one—if all went according to plan. *Plan!* That word was destined to be trampled underfoot!

Oh, well (I took a deep optimistic breath) the *Flashaway* troubles would all be cleared up by now. Three generations would have passed. The population should be back to normal.

I swung the door open, stepped through, locked it after me.

For an instant I thought I had stepped in on a big movie "take"—a scene of a stricken multitude. The big ballroom was literally strewn with people—if creatures in such a deplorable state could be called people.

There was no movie camera. This was the real thing.

"Grimstone's come!" a hoarse voice cried out.

"Grimstone! Grimstone!" Others caught up the cry. Then—"Food! "Give us food! We're starving! For God's sake—"

The weird chorus gathered volume. I stood dazed, and for an instant I couldn't realize that I was looking upon the population of the *Flashaway.* Men, women and children of all ages and all states of desperation joined in the clamor. Some of them stumbled to their feet and came toward me, waving their arms weakly. But most of them hadn't the strength to rise. In that stunning moment an icy sweat came over me.

"Food! Food! We've been waiting for you, Grimstone. We've been holding on—"

The responsibility that was strapped to my shoulders suddenly weighed down like a locomotive. You see, I had originally taken my job more or less as a lark. That Six-Hundred-Year Plan had looked so airtight. I, the Keeper of the Traditions, would have a snap.

I had anticipated many a pleasant hour acquainting the oncoming generations with noble sentiments about George Washington; I had pictured myself filling the souls of my listeners by reciting the Gettysburg address and lecturing upon the mysteries of science.

But now those pretty bubbles burst on the spot, nor did they ever reform in the centuries to follow.

And as they burst, my vision cleared. My job had nothing to do with theories or textbooks or speeches. My job was simply to get to Robinello—to get there with enough living, able-bodied, sane human beings to start a colony.

Dull blue starlight sifted through the windows to highlight the big roomful of starved figures. The mass of pale blue faces stared at me. There were hundreds of them. Instinctively I shrank as the throng clustered around me, calling and pleading.

"One at a time!" I cried. "First I've got to find out what this is all about. Who's your spokesman?"

THEY designated a handsomely built, if undernourished, young man. I inquired his name and learned that he was Bob Sperry, a descendant of the original Captain Sperry.

"There are eight hundred of us now," Sperry said.

"Don't tell me the food has run out!"

"No, not that—but six hundred of us are not entitled to regular meals."

"Why not?"

Before the young spokesman could answer, the others burst out with an unintelligible clamor. Angry cries of "That damned Dickinson!" and "Guns!" and "They'll shoot us!" were all I could distinguish.

I quieted them and made Bob Sperry go on with his story. He calmly asserted that there was a very good reason that they shouldn't be fed, all sentiment aside; namely, because they had been born outside the quota. Here I began to catch a gleam of light.

"By Captain Dickinson's interpretation of the Plan," Sperry explained, "there shouldn't be more than two hundred of us altogether."

This Captain Dickinson, I learned, was a grandson of the one I had known.

Sperry continued, "Since there are eight hundred, he and his brother—his brother being Food Superintendent—launched an emergency measure a few months ago to save food. They divided the population into the two hundred, who had a right to be born, and the six hundred who had not."

So the six hundred starving persons before me were theoretically the excess population. The vigorous ancestry of the sixteen—no, seventeen—original couples, together with the excellent medical care that had reduced infant mortality and disease to the minimum, had wrecked the original population plan completely.

"What do you do for food? You must have *some* food!"

"We live on charity."

The throng again broke in with hostile words. Young Sperry's version was too gentle to do justice to their outraged stomachs. In fairness to the two hundred, however, Sperry explained that they shared whatever food they could spare with these, their less fortunate brothers, sisters and offspring.

Uncertain what should or could be alone, I gave the impatient crowd my promise to investigate at once. Bob Sperry and nine other men accompanied me.

The minute we were out of hearing of the ballroom, I gasped, "Good heavens, men, how is it that you and your six hundred haven't mobbed the storerooms long before this?"

"Dickinson and his brother have got the drop on us."

"Drop? What kind of drop?"

"Guns!"

I couldn't understand this. I had believed these new generations of the *Flashaway* to be relatively innocent of any knowledge of firearms.

"What kind of guns?"

"The same kind they use in our Earth—made movies—that make a loud noise and kill people by the hundreds."

"But there aren't any guns aboard! That is—"

I knew perfectly well that the only firearms the ship carried had been stored in my own refrigerator room, which no one could enter but myself. Before the voyage, one of the planning committee had jestingly suggested that if any serious trouble ever arose, I should be master of the situation by virtue of one hundred revolvers.

"They made their own guns," Sperry explained, "just like the ones in our movies and books."

INQUIRING whether any persons had been shot, I learned that three of their number, attempting a raid on the storerooms, had been killed.

"We heard three loud bangs, and found our men dead with bloody skulls."

Reaching the upper end of the central corridor, we arrived at the captain's headquarters.

The name of Captain Dickinson carried a bad flavor for me. A century before I had developed a distaste for a certain other Captain Dickinson, his grandfather. I resolved to swallow my prejudice. Then the door opened, and my resolve stuck in my throat. The former Captain Dickinson bad merely annoyed me; but this one I hated on sight.

"Well?" the captain roared at the eleven of us.

Well-uniformed and neatly groomed, he filled the doorway with an impressive bulk. In his right hand he gripped a revolver. The gleam of that weapon had a magical effect upon the men. They shrank back respectfully. Then the captain's cold eye lighted on me.

"Who are *you?*"

"Gregory Grimstone, Keeper of the Traditions."

The captain sent a quick glance toward his gun and repeated his "Well?"

For a moment I was fascinated by that intricately shaped piece of metal in his grip.

"Well!" I echoed. "If 'well' is the only reception you have to offer, I'll proceed with my official business. Call your Food Superintendent."

"Why?"

"Order him out! Have him feed the entire population without further delay!"

"We can't afford the food," the captain growled.

"We'll talk that over later, but we won't talk on empty stomachs. Order out your Food Superintendent!"

"Crawl back in your hole!" Dickinson snarled.

At that instant another bulky man stepped into view. He was almost the identical counterpart of the captain, but his uniform was that of the Food Superintendent. Showing his teeth with a sinister snarl, he took his place beside his brother. He too jerked his right hand up to flash a gleaming revolver. I caught one glimpse—and laughed in his face! I couldn't help it.

"You fellows are good!" I roared. "You're damned good actors! If you've held off the starving six hundred with nothing but those two dumb imitations of revolvers, you deserve an Academy award!"

The two Dickinson brothers went white.

Back of me came low mutterings from ten starving men.

"Imitations—dumb imitations—what the hell?"

Sperry and his nine comrades plunged with one accord. For the next ten minutes the captain's headquarters was simply a whirlpool of flying fists and hurtling bodies.

I have mentioned that these ten men were weak from lack of food. That fact was all that saved the Dickinson brothers; for ten minutes of lively exercise was all the ten men could endure, in spite of the circumstances.

BUT ten minutes left an impression.

The Dickinsons were the worst beaten-up men I have ever seen, and I have seen some bad ones in my time. When the news echoed through the ship, no one questioned the ethics of ten starved men attacking two overfed ones. Needless to say, before two hours passed, every hungry man, woman and child ate to his gizzard's content. And before another hour passed, some new officers were installed. The S. S. *Flashaway's* trouble was far from solved; but for the present the whole eight hundred were one big family picnic. Hope was restored, and the rejoicing lasted through many thousand miles of space.

There was considerable mystery about the guns. Surprisingly, the people had developed an awe of the movie guns as if they were instruments of magic.

Upon investigating, I was convinced that the captain and his brother had simply capitalized on this superstition. They had a sound enough motive for wanting to save food. But once their gun bluff had been established, they had become uncompromising oppressors. And when the occasion arose that their guns were challenged, they had simply crushed the skulls of their three attackers and faked the noises of explosions.

But now the firearms were dead. And so was the Dickinson regime.

But the menacing problem of too many mouths to feed still clung to the S. S. *Flashaway* like a hungry ghost determined to ride the ship to death.

Six full months passed before the needed reform was forged.

During that time everyone was allowed full rations. The famine had already taken its toll in weakened bodies, and seventeen persons—most of them young children—died. The doctors, released from the Dickinson regime, worked like Trojans to bring the rest back to health.

The reform measure that went into effect six months after my arrival consisted of outright sterilization.

The compulsory rule was sterilization for everyone except those born "within the quota"—and that quota, let me add, was narrowed down one half from Captain Dickinson's two hundred to the most eligible one hundred. The disqualified one hundred now joined the ranks of the six hundred.

And that was not all. By their own agreement, every within-the-quota family, responsible for bearing the *Flashaway's* future children, would undergo sterilization operations after the second child was born.

The seven hundred out-of-quota citizens, let it be said, were only too glad to submit to the simple sterilization measures in exchange for a right to live their normal lives. Yes, they were to have three squares a day. With an assured population decline in prospect for the coming century, this generous measure of food would not give out. Our surveys of the existing food supplies showed that these seven hundred could safely live their four-score years and die with full stomachs.

Looking back on that six months' work, I was fairly well satisfied that the doctors and the Council and I had done the fair, if drastic, thing. If I had planted seeds for further trouble with the Dickinson tribe, I was little concerned about it at the time.

My conscience was, in fact, clear except for one small matter. I was guilty of one slight act of partiality.

I incurred this guilt shortly before I returned to the ice. The doctors and I, looking down from the balcony into the ballroom, chanced to notice a young couple who were obviously very much in love.

THE young man was Bob Sperry, the handsome, clear-eyed descendant of the Flashaway's first and finest captain, the lad who had been the spokesman when I first came upon the starving mob.

The girl's name—and how it had clung in my mind!—was Louise Broscoe. Refreshingly beautiful, she reminded me for all the world of my own Louise (mine and Bill Broscoe's).

"It's a shame," one of the doctors commented, "that fine young blood like that has to fall outside the quota. But rules are rules."

With a shrug of the shoulders he had already dismissed the matter from his mind—until I handed him something I had scribbled on a piece of paper.

"We'll make this one exception," I said perfunctorily. "If any question ever arises, this statement relieves you doctors of all responsibility. This is my own special request."

CHAPTER V
Wedding Bells

ONE hundred years later my rash act came back to haunt me—and how! Bob Sperry had married Louise Broscoe, and the births of their two children had raised the unholy cry of "Favoritism!"

By the year 2366, Bob Sperry and Louise Broscoe were gone and almost forgotten. But the enmity against me, the Keeper of the Traditions who played favorites, had grown up into a monster of bitter hatred waiting to devour me.

It didn't take me long to discover this. My first contact after I emerged from the ice set the pace.

"Go tell your parents," I said to the gang of brats that were playing ball in the spacious ballroom, "that Grimstone has arrived."

Their evil little faces stared at me a moment, then they snorted.

"Faw! Faw! Faw!" and away they ran.

I stood in the big bleak room wondering what to make of their insults. On the balcony some of the parents craned over the railings at me.

"Greetings!" I cried. "I'm Grimstone, Keeper of the Traditions. I've just come –"

"Faw!" the men and women shouted at me. "Faw! Faw!"

No one could have made anything friendly out of those snarls. "Faw," to them, was simply a vocal manner of spitting poison.

Uncertain what this surly reception might lead to, I returned to my refrigerator room to procure one of the guns. Then I returned to the volley of catcalls and insults, determined to carry out my duties, come what might.

When I reached the forequarter of the ship, however, I found some less hostile citizens who gave me a civil welcome. Here I established myself for the extent of my 2366-67 sojourn, an honored guest of the Sperry family.

This, I told myself, was my reward for my favor to Bob Sperry and

Louise Broscoe a century ago. For here was their grandson, a fine up-standing gray-haired man of fifty, a splendid pilot and the father of a beautiful twenty-one year old daughter.

"Your name wouldn't be Louise by any chance?" I asked the girl as she showed me into the Sperry living room.

"Lora-Louise," the girl smiled. It was remarkable how she brought back memories of one of her ancestors of three centuries previous.

Her dark eyes flashed over me curiously. "So you are the man that we Sperries have to thank for being here!"

"You've heard about the quotas?" I asked.

"Of course. You're almost a god to our family."

"I must be a devil to some of the others," I said, recalling my reception of catcalls.

"Rogues!" the girl's father snorted, and he thereupon launched into a breezy account of the past century.

The sterilization program, he assured me, had worked—if anything, too well. The population was the lowest in *Flashaway* history. It stood at the dangerously low mark of *fifty!*

Besides the sterilization program, a disease epidemic had taken its toll. In addition three ugly murders, prompted by jealousies, had spotted the record.

And there had been one suicide.

As to the character of the population, Pilot Sperry declared gravely that there had been a turn for the worse.

"They fight each other like damned anarchists," he snorted.

T HE Dickinsons had made trouble for several generations. Now it was the Dickinsons against the Smiths; and these two factions included four-fifths of all the people. They were about evenly divided—twenty on each side and when they weren't actually fighting each other, they were "paw-ing" at each other.

These bellicose factions had one sentiment in common: they both despised the Sperry faction. And—here my guilt cropped up again—their hatred stemmed from my special favor of a century ago, without which there would be no Sperrys now. In view of the fact that the Sperry faction lived in the forequarter of the ship and held all the important of-fices, it was no wonder that the remaining forty citizens were jealous.

All of which gave me enough to worry about. On top of that, Lora-Louise's mother gave me one other angle of the set-up.

"The trouble between the Dickinsons and the Smiths has grown worse since Lora-Louise has become a young lady," Mrs. Sperry confided to me.

We were sitting in a breakfast nook. Amber starlight shone softly through the porthole, lighting the mother's steady imperturbable gray eyes.

"Most girls have married at eighteen or nineteen," her mother went on. "So far, Lora-Louise has refused to marry."

The worry in Mrs. Sperry's face was almost imperceptible, but I understood. I had checked over the "Who's Who" and I knew the seriousness of this population crisis. I also knew that there were four young unmarried men with no other prospects of wives except Lora-Louise.

"Have you any choice for her?" I asked.

"Since she must marry—and I know she *must*—I have urged her to make her own choice."

I could see that the ordeal of choosing had been postponed until my coming, in hopes that I might modify the rules. But I had no intention of doing so. The *Flaskaway* needed Lora-Louise. It needed the sort of children she would bear.

That week I saw the two husky Dickinson boys. Both were in their twenties. They stayed close together and bore an air of treachery and scheming. Rumor had it that they carried weapons made from table knives.

Everyone knew that my coming would bring the conflict to a head. Many thought I would try to force the girl to marry the older Smith— "Batch", as he was called in view of his bachelorhood. He was past thirty-five, the oldest of the four unmarried men.

But some argued otherwise. For Batch, though a splendid specimen physically, was slow of wit and speech. It was common knowledge that he was weak-minded.

For that reason, I might choose his younger cousin, "Smithy," a roly-poly overgrown boy of nineteen who spent his time bullying the younger children.

But if the Smiths and the Dickinsons could have their way about it, the Keeper of the Traditions should have no voice in the matter. Let me insist that Lora-Louise marry, said they; but whom she should marry was none of my business.

They preferred a fight as a means of settlement. A free-for-all between the two factions would be fine. A showdown of fists among the four contenders would be even better.

B EST of all would be a battle of knives that would eliminate all but one of the suitors. Not that either the Dickinsons or the Smiths needed to admit that was what they preferred; but their barbaric tastes were plain to see.

Barbarians! That's what they had become. They had sprung too far from their native civilization. Only the Sperry faction, isolated in their monasteries of control boards, physicians' laboratories and record rooms, kept alive the spark of civilization.

The Sperrys and their associates were human beings out of the twenty-first century. The Smiths and the Dickinsons had slipped. They might have come out of the Dark Ages.

What burned me up more than anything else was that obviously both the Smiths and the Dickinsons looked forward with sinister glee toward dragging Lora-Louise down from her height to their own barbaric levels.

One night I was awakened by the sharp ringing of the pilot's telephone. I heard the snap of a switch. An *emergency* signal flashed on throughout the ship.

Footsteps were pounding toward the ballroom. I slipped into a robe, seized my gun, made for the door.

"The Dickinsons are murdering up on them!" Pilot Sperry shouted to me from the door of the control room.

"I'll see about it," I snapped.

I bounded down the corridor. Sperry didn't follow. Whatever violence might occur from year to year within the hull of the *Flashaway,* the pilot's code demanded that he lock himself up at the controls and tend to his own business.

It was a free-for-all! Under the bright lights they were going to it, tooth and toenail.

Children screamed and clawed, women hurled dishes, old tottering granddaddies edged into the fracas to crack at each other with canes.

The appalling reason for it all showed in the center of the room-the roly-poly form of young "Smithy" Smith. Hacked and stabbed, his nightclothes ripped, he was a veritable mess of carnage.

I shouted for order. No one heard me, for in that instant a chase thundered on the balcony. Everything else stopped. All eyes turned on the three racing figures.

Batch Smith, fleeing in his white nightclothes, had less than five yards lead on the two Dickinsons. Batch was just smart enough to run when he was chased, not smart enough to know he couldn't possibly outrun the younger Dickinsons.

As they shot past blazing lights the Dickinsons' knives flashed. I could see that their hands were red with Smithy's blood.

"Stop!" I cried. "Stop or I'll *shoot!"*

If they heard, the words must have been meaningless. The younger

Dickinson gained ground. His brother darted back in the opposite direction, crouched, waited for his prey to come around the circular balcony.

"Dickinson! Stop or I'll shoot you dead!" I bellowed.

Batch Smith came on, his eyes white with terror. Crouched and waiting, the older Dickinson lifted his knife for the killing stroke.

I shot.

The crouched Dickinson fell in a heap. Over him tripped the racing form of Batch Smith, to sprawl headlong. The other Dickinson leaped over his brother and pounced down upon the fallen prey, knife upraised.

Another shot went home.

Young Dickinson writhed and came toppling down over the balcony rail. He lay where he fell, his bloody knife sticking up through the side of his neck.

IT was ugly business trying to restore order. However, the magic power of firearms, which had become only a dusty legend, now put teeth into every word I uttered.

The doctors were surprisingly efficient. After many hours of work behind closed doors, they released their verdicts to the waiting groups. The elder Dickinson, shot through the shoulder, would live. The younger Dickinson was dead. So was Smithy. But his cousin, Batch Smith, although too scared to walk back to his stateroom, was unhurt.

The rest of the day the doctors devoted to patching up the minor damages done in the free fight. Four-fifths of the *Flashaway* population were burdened with bandages, it seemed. For some time to come both the warring parties were considerably sobered over their losses. But most of all they were disgruntled because the fight had settled nothing.

The prize was still unclaimed. The two remaining contenders, backed by their respective factions, were at a bitter deadlock.

Nor had Lora-Louise's hatred for either the surviving Dickinson or Smith lessened in the slightest.

Never had a duty been more oppressive to me. I postponed my talk with Lora-Louise for several days, but I was determined that there should be no more fighting. She must choose.

We sat in an alcove next to the pilot's control room, looking out into the vast sky. Our ship, bounding at a terrific speed though it was, seemed to be hanging motionless in the tranquil star-dotted heavens.

"I must speak frankly," I said to the girl. "I hope you will do the same."

She looked at me steadily. Her dark eyes were perfectly frank, her full lips smiled with child-like simplicity.

"How old are you?" she asked.

"Twenty-eight," I answered. I'd been the youngest professor on the college faculty. "Or you might say three hundred and twenty-eight. Why?"

"How soon must you go back to your sleep?"

"Just as soon as you are happily married. That's why I must insist that you—"

Something very penetrating about her gaze made my words go weak. To think of forcing this lovely girl—so much like the Louise of my own century—to marry either the brutal Dickinson or the moronic Smith –

"Do you really want me to be *happily* married?" she asked.

I don't remember that any more words passed between us at the time.

A few days later she and I were married—and most happily!

The ceremony was brief. The entire Sperry faction and one representative from each of the two hostile factions were present. The aged captain of the ship, who had been too ineffectual in recent years to apply any discipline to the fighting factions, was still able with vigorous voice to pronounce us man and wife.

A year and a half later I took my leave.

I bid fond good-by to the "future captain of the *Flashaway*," who lay on a pillow kicking and squirming. He gurgled back at me. If the boasts and promises of the Sperry grandparents and their associates were to be taken at full value, this young prodigy of mine would in time become an accomplished pilot and a skilled doctor as well as a stern but wise captain.

Judging from his talents at the age of six months, I was convinced he showed promise of becoming Food Superintendent as well.

I left reluctantly but happily.

CHAPTER VI
The Final Crisis

THE year 2466 was one of the darkest in my life. I shall pass over it briefly.

The situation I found was all but hopeless.

The captain met me personally and conveyed me to his quarters without allowing the people to see me.

"Safer for everyone concerned," he muttered. I caught glimpses as we passed through the shadows. I seemed to be looking upon ruins.

Not until the captain had disclosed the events of the century did I understand how things could have come to such a deplorable state. And before he finished his story, I saw that I was helpless to right the wrongs.

"They've destroyed most everything," the hard-bitten old captain rasped. "And they haven't overlooked—*you*. They've destroyed you completely. *You are an ogre.*"

I wasn't clear on his meaning. Dimly in the back of my mind the hilarious farewell of four centuries ago still echoed.

"The *Flashaway* will go through!" I insisted.

"They destroyed all the books, phonograph records, movie films. They broke up clocks and bells and furniture—"

And I was supposed to carry this interspatial outpost of American civilization though *unblemished!* That was what I had promised so gayly four centuries ago.

"They even tried to break out the windows," the captain went on. "'Oxygen be damned!' they'd shout. They were mad. You couldn't tell them anything. If they could have got into this end of the ship, they'd have murdered us and smashed the control boards to hell."

I listened with bowed head.

"Your son tried like the devil to turn the tide. But God, what chance did he have? The dam had busted loose. They wanted to kill each other. They wanted to destroy each other's property and starve each other out. No captain in the world could have stopped either faction. They had to get it out of their systems..."

He shrugged helplessly. "Your son went down fighting ..." For a time I could hear no more. It seemed but minutes ago that I had taken leave of the little tot...

The war—if a mania of destruction and murder between two feuding factions could be called a war—had done one good thing, according to the captain. It had wiped the name of Dickinson from the records.

Later I turned through the musty pages to make sure. There were Smiths and Sperrys and a few other names still in the running, but no Dickinsons. Nor were there any Grimstones. My son had left no living descendants. To return to the captain's story, the war (he said) had degraded the bulk of the population almost to the level of savages. Perhaps the comparison is an insult to the savage. The instruments of knowledge and learning having been destroyed, beliefs gave way to superstitions, memories of past events degenerated into fanciful legends.

The rebound from the war brought a terrific superstitious terror concerning death. The survivors crawled into their shells, almost literally; the brutalities and treacheries of the past hung like storm clouds over their imaginations.

As year after year dropped away, the people told and retold the stories of destruction to their children. Gradually the legend twisted into a strange form in which all the guilt for the carnage *was placed upon me!*

I WAS the one who had started all the killing! I, the ogre, who slept in a cave somewhere in the rear of the ship, came out once upon a time and started all the trouble!

I, the Traditions Man, dealt death with a magic weapon; I cast the spell of killing upon the Smiths and the Dickinsons that kept them fighting until there was nothing left to fight for.

"But that was years ago," I protested to the captain. "Am I still an ogre?" I shuddered at the very thought.

"More than ever. Stories like that don't die out in a century. They grow bigger. You've become the symbol of evil. I've tried to talk the silly notion down, but it has been impossible. My own family is afraid of you."

I listened with sickening amazement. I was the Traditions Man; or rather, the "Traddy Man"—the bane of every child's life.

Parents, I was told, would warn them, "If you don't be good, the Traddy Man will come out of his cave and get you!"

And the Traddy Man, as every grown-up knew, could storm out of his cave without warning. He would come with a strange gleam in his eye. That was his evil will. When the bravest, strongest men would cross his path, he would hurl instant death at them. Then he would seize the most beautiful woman and marry her.

"Enough!" I said. "Call your people together. I'll dispel their false ideas—"

The captain shook his head wisely. He glanced at my gun.

"Don't force me to disobey your orders," he said. "I can believe you're not an ogre—but they won't. I know this generation. You don't. Frankly, I refuse to disturb the peace of this ship by telling the people you have come. Nor am I willing to terrorize my family by letting them see you."

For a long while I stared silently into space.

The captain dismissed a pilot from the control room and had me come in.

"You can see for yourself that we are straight on our course. You have already seen that all the supplies are holding up. You have seen that the population problem is well cared for. What more do you want?"

What more did I want! With the whole population of the *Flashaway* steeped in ignorance—immorality—superstition—savagery![1]

---

[1] Professor Grimstone is obviously astounded that his charges, with all the necessities of life on board their space ship, should have degenerated so completely. It must be remembered, however, that no other outside influence

Again the captain shook his head. "You want us to be like your friends of the twenty-first century. *We can't be.*"

He reached in his pocket and pulled out some bits of crumpled papers.

"Look. I save every scrap of reading matter. I learned to read from the primers and charts that your son's grandparents made. Before the destruction, I tried to read about the Earth-life. I still piece together these torn bits and study them. But I can't piece together the Earth-life that they tell about. All I really know is what I've seen and felt and breathed right here in my native *Flashaway* world.

"That's how it's bound to be with all of us. We can't get back to your notions about things. Your notions haven't any real truth for us. You don't belong to our world," the captain said with honest frankness.

"So I'm an outcast on my own ship!"

"That's putting it mildly. You're a menace and a troublemaker—an *ogre!* It's in their minds as tight as the bones in their skulls."

The most I could do was secure some promises from him before I went back to the ice. He promised to keep the ship on its course. He promised to do his utmost to fasten the necessary obligations upon those who would take over the helm.

"Straight relentless navigation!" We drank a toast to it. He didn't pretend to appreciate the purpose or the mission of the *Flashaway,* but he took my word for it that it would come to some good.

"To Robinello in 2666!" Another toast. Then he conducted me back, in utmost secrecy, to my refrigerator room.

I AWOKE to the year of 2566, keenly aware that I was not Gregory Grimstone, the respected Keeper of the Traditions. If I was anyone at all, I was the Traddy Man—the ogre.

But perhaps by this time—and I took hope with the thought—I had been completely forgotten.

ever entered the Flashaway in all its long voyage through space. In the space of centuries, the colonists progressed not one whit.

On a very much reduced scale, the Flashaway colonists are a more or less accurate mirror of a nation in transition. Sad but true it is that nations, like human beings, are born, wax into bright maturity, grow into comfortable middle age and ofttimes linger on until old age has impaired their usefulness.

In the relatively short time that man has been a thinking, building animal, many great empires—many great nations—have sprung from humble beginnings to grow powerful and then wane into oblivion, sometimes slowly, sometimes with tragic suddenness.

Grimstone, however, has failed to take the lessons of history into account through the mistaken conception that because the colonists' physical wants were taken care of, that was all they required to keep them healthy and contented.—Ed.

I tried to get through the length of the ship without being seen. I had watched through the one-way glass for several hours for a favorable opportunity, but the ship seemed to be in a continual state of daylight, and shabby-looking people roamed about as aimlessly as sheep in a meadow.

The few persons who saw me as I darted toward the captain's quarters shrieked as if they had been knifed. In their world there was no such thing—a strange person. I was the impossible, the unbelievable. My name, obviously, had been forgotten.

I found three men in the control room. After minutes of tension, during which they adjusted themselves to the shock of my coming, I succeeded in establishing speaking terms. Two of the men were Sperrys.

But at the very moment I should have been concerned with solidifying my friendship, I broke the calm with an excited outburst. My eye caught the position of the instruments and I leaped from my seat.

"How long have you been going *that way?*"

"Eight years!"

"Eight—" I glanced at the huge automatic chart overhead. It showed the long straight line of our centuries of flight with a tiny shepherd's crook at the end. Eight years ago we had turned back sharply.

"That's sixteen years lost, gentlemen!"

I tried to regain my poise. The three men before me were perfectly calm, to my astonishment. The two Sperry brothers glanced at each other. The third man, who had introduced himself as Smith, glared at me darkly.

"It's all right," I said. "We won't lose another minute. I know how to operate—"

"No, you don't!" Smith's voice was harsh and cold. I had started to reach for the controls. I hesitated. Three pairs of eyes were fixed on me.

"We know where we're going," one of the Sperrys said stubbornly. "We've got our own destination."

"This ship is bound for Robinello!" I snapped. "We've got to colonize. The Robinello planets are ours—America's. It's our job to clinch the claim and establish the initial settlement—"

"Who said so?"

"America!"

"When?" Smith's cold eyes tightened.

"Five hundred years ago."

"That doesn't mean a thing. Those people are all dead."

"I'm one of those people!" I growled. "And I'm not dead by a damned sight!"

"Then you're out on a limb."

"Limb or no limb, the plan goes through!" I clutched my gun. "We haven't come five hundred years in a straight line for nothing!"

"The plan is dead," one of the Sperrys snarled. "We've killed it."

HIS brother chimed in, "This is our ship and we're running it. We've studied the heavens and we're out on our own. We're through with this straight-line stuff. We're going to see the universe."

"You can't! You're bound for Robinello!" Smith stepped toward me, and his big teeth showed savagely.

"We had no part in that agreement. We're taking orders from no one. I've heard about you. You're the Traddy Man. Go back in your hole—and stay there!"

I brought my gun up slowly. "You've heard of me? Have you heard of my gun? Do you know that this weapon shoots men dead?"

Three pairs of eyes caught on the gleaming weapon. But three men stood their ground staunchly.

"I've heard about guns," Smith hissed. "Enough to know that you don't dare shoot in the control room—"

"I don't dare *miss!*"

I didn't want to kill the men. But I saw no other way out. Was there any other way? Three lives weren't going to stand between the *Flashaway* and her destination.

Seconds passed, with the four of us breathing hard. Eternity was about to descend on someone. Any of the three might have been splendid pioneers if they had been confronted with the job of building a colony. But in this moment, their lack of vision was as deadly as any deliberate sabotage. I focused my attack on the most troublesome man of the three.

"Smith, I'm giving you an order. Turn back before I count to ten or I'll kill you. One…two…three…"

Not the slightest move from anyone.

"Seven…eight…nine…"

Smith leaped at me—and fell dead at my feet.

The two Sperrys looked at the faint wisp of smoke from the weapon. I barked another sharp command, and one of the Sperrys marched to the controls and turned the ship back toward Robinello.

CHAPTER VII
Time Marches On

FOR a year I was with the Sperry brothers constantly, doing my utmost to bring them around to my way of thinking. At first I watched them like hawks. But they were not treacherous. Neither did they show any inclination to avenge Smith's death. Probably this was due to a suppressed hatred they had held toward him.

The Sperrys were the sort of men, being true children of space, who bided their time. That's what they were doing now. That was why I couldn't leave them and go back to my ice.

As sure as the *Flashaway* could cut through the heavens, those two men were counting the hours until I returned to my nest. The minute I was gone, they would turn back toward their own goal.

And so I continued to stay with them for a full year. If they contemplated killing me, they gave no indication. I presume I would have killed them with little hesitation, had I had no pilots whatsoever that I could entrust with the job of carrying on.

There were no other pilots, nor were there any youngsters old enough to break into service.

Night after night I fought the matter over in my mind. There was a full century to go. Perhaps one hundred and fifteen or twenty years. And no one except the two Sperrys and I had any serious conception of a destination!

These two pilots and I—*and one other,* whom I had never for a minute forgotten. If the *Flashaway* was to go through, it was up to me and *that one other—*

I marched back to the refrigerator room, people fleeing my path in terror. Inside the retreat I touched the switches that operated the auxiliary merry-go-round freezer. After a space of time the operation was complete.

Someone very beautiful stood smiling before me, looking not a minute older than when I had packed her away for safe-keeping two centuries before.

"Gregory," she breathed ecstatically. "Are my three centuries up already?"

"Only two of them, Lora-Louise." I took her in my arms. She looked up at me sharply and must have read the trouble in my eyes.

"They've all played out on us," I said quietly. "It's up to us now."

I discussed my plan with her and she approved.

One at a time we forced the Sperry brothers into the icy retreat, with repeated promises that they would emerge within a century. By that time Lora-Louise and I would be gone—but it was our expectation that our children and grandchildren would carry on.

And so the two of us, plus firearms, plus Lora-Louise's sense of humor, took over the running of the *Flashaway* for its final century.

As the years passed the native population grew to be less afraid of us.

Little by little a foggy glimmer of our vision filtered into their numbed minds.

THE year is now 2600. Thirty-three years have passed since Lora-Louise and I took over. I am now sixty-two, she is fifty-six. Or if you prefer, I am 562, she is 256. Our four children have grown up and married.

We have realized down through these long years that we would not live to see the journey completed. The Robinello planets have been visible for some time; but at our speed they are still sixty or eighty years away.

But something strange happened nine or ten months ago. It has changed the outlook for all of us—even me, the crusty old Keeper of the Traditions. A message reached us through our radio receiver!

IT WAS a human voice speaking in our own language. It had a fresh vibrant hum to it and a clear-cut enunciation. It shocked me to realize how sluggish our own brand of the King's English had become in the past five-and-a-half centuries.

"Calling the *S.S. Flashaway!*" it said.

"Calling the *S.S. Flashaway!* We are trying to locate you, *S.S. Flashaway.* Our instruments indicate that you are approaching. If you can hear us, will you give us your exact location?"

I snapped on the transmitter. "This is the *Flashaway.* Can you hear us?"

"Dimly. Where are you?"

"On our course. Who's calling?"

"This is the American colony on Robinello," came the answer. "American colony, Robinello, established in 2550—fifty years ago. We're waiting for you, *Flashaway.*"

"How the devil did you get there?" I may have sounded a bit crusty but I was too excited to know what I was saying.

"Modern space ships," came the answer. "We've cut the time from the earth to Robinello down to six years. Give us your location. We'll send a fast ship out to pick you up."

I gave them our location. That, as I said, was several months ago. Today we are receiving a radio call every five minutes as their ship approaches.

One of my sons, supervising the preparations, has just reported that all persons aboard are ready to transfer—including the Sperry brothers, who have emerged successfully from the ice. The eighty-five *Flashaway* natives are scared half to death and at the same time as eager as children going to a circus.

Lora-Louise has finished packing our boxes, bless her heart. That teasing smile she just gave me was because she noticed the "Who's Who Aboard the *Flashaway*" tucked snugly under my arm.

THE MAN WHO TURNED TO SMOKE

When bombs fall on Chungking, China during World War II a strange thing happens to cameraman Virgil Lamstead, and this 1942 tale of war immediately rises above the typical science fiction short story. True science fantasy of the highest caliber from the fertile imagination of Don Wilcox.

BOMBS were dropping over Chungking. They were blasting yellow rocks up in fountains of death.

I, Virgil Lamstead, an American cameraman, stood near the entrance of a public bomb shelter. I saw the stream of explosions coming straight toward me. If I kept on taking pictures I would be blown to bits. I grabbed my camera and the package of chemicals I had brought to leave at a laboratory. I ran down the shelter steps.

"Let me in!" I shouted in my best Chinese. Then I screamed it. *"Let me in!"*

An iron clank sounded against the din of bombs. The door was closed, locked. I was on the outside.

Then it happened, and there was no escape. The bomb explosion blew me high into the air.

"So this is death!"

It would have been, under ordinary circumstances. But once in ten million—or maybe ten billion—times, the forces of nature conspire to do strange things. *I turned into living smoke.*

At first I couldn't believe it. I was shooting up through a smudgy cloud of smoke, dirt, and debris. Broken rocks were flying past my body. My camera had been knocked out of my hands.

The package of chemicals was gone too. In fact, the chemicals and I had gone together. They had saved me—or changed me—or *was* this death?

It was not. It was some new amazing form of life. I was endowed with a completely altered body. I had the most curious sensations of fluffiness and weightlessness.

Yes, I had turned into living smoke. I wasn't exactly breathing. I was just rolling and swelling in the air. The big smoke cloud from the bomb explosion pressed against me as lightly as a baby's kiss.

I was still rising.

The smoke thinned around me and began spreading in all directions. *I began to spread too.*

Horrors! My arms and legs—if such they were—were trailing after me like pipe smoke.

As I floated over the Yangtze River I looked down and saw my gray reflection in the muddy waters. That puffy blotch of cloud was me.

Then I saw something else. Another squadron of bombers was coming over. Soon bombs rained down. I squirmed to get out of their path. Yes, I could move!

Though I climbed around rather sluggishly, I gradually succeeded in drawing what I called my arms and legs closer together. Soon I was such a compact wad of smoke that I felt crowded. I was no bigger than a rickshaw.

Then a bomb dropped *through* me squarely through what should have been my stomach.

"This ends me!" I thought.

FAR from it. The bomb made my smoky body spread out and I felt better, actually. What strange sensations of breeziness.

In a few minutes I learned. When the winds spread me too thin I could easily draw myself together. By growing smaller I changed my specific gravity. Then by taking advantage of the air currents I could move anywhere I desired.

By this time the raid was over, and people were filtering out of the hundreds of bomb shelters, bringing back their valuables and office supplies and shopping bags, to resume their day.

In many places over the city the fire fighters were working like Trojans to get the blazes under control. The helmeted firemen were still tearing through the streets aboard motors cars, and everywhere were volunteer bands of coolies. I floated over to see how they were doing.

I sifted down between some buildings to watch.

A Chinese boy who was on fire guard duty saw me. He jumped over a pile of rubbish and streaked down the hillside. I couldn't think what was wrong with him until I heard him whooping a fire alarm.

Some civilian firefighters heard him and came racing up the hillside carrying buckets of water. They manned a hand pump and turned a hose on me.

The cool water felt wonderful while it lasted, and I mentioned to myself then and there that I was going to spend my idle hours right down on the surface of the Yangtze to take advantage of those cool soothing sensations.

But now—well, I couldn't stand to see those people work so hard for nothing. I rose into the air and spread myself thin. The fire fighters muttered with grim satisfaction that they had made short work of that one. They ran on to the other blazes.

Now I felt very despondent.

Anyone would feel the same way if he found himself in my plight. For as matters appeared, I was doomed to a lonely life. If I'd try to mix with people I'd be sure to cause a fire alarm. For awhile I was very blue smoke.

I watched the other smoke clouds melting into the sky. I did some heavy thinking. Was there anything in the world I could do besides making a nuisance of myself? Did I have any chance to be useful?

I remembered what George Leahman had said after the first Chungking bombing we took in together. "Where there's smoke, there's fire."

I turned that over in my thoughts and grew bluer. "But at least I'm alive," I said to myself. "Not even a bomb could kill me now."

I was sure of that much, because one had gone through me. What a state to be in. Half dead, you might say. In fact, to all the people I had known I would be dead and gone. And still I might be doomed to live forever, since bullets couldn't—

I heard the cry of a girl beside a wrecked and burning building.

I knew that cry. It was the little nineteen-year-old Chinese girl that George Leahman and I had called Chestnut Eyes. She was an errand girl for the medical supplies department. I swooped down to her.

IN THAT moment I felt new powers. You will doubtless smile that I should mention a sensation of new powers at this particular juncture. But you can scarcely conceive of the extreme helplessness and clumsiness that had at first possessed me upon my transformation to smoke. And now, for the first time, I had a purpose looming vaguely before me, urging me to try my capacities to the hilt.

Yes, gradually I was gaining a much stronger control of my faculties of twisting and squirming and combating air currents.

Coming closer I saw the dangerous situation that surrounded Chestnut Eyes. The sight made me turn into little whirling eddies of smoke. She had been wounded. She lay near the burning house, sobbing with pain.

I swept down as swiftly as I could. The breeze I created only fanned the flames. That would never do.

I crowded close to the girl trying to blanket her with protection. Her clothes had been partially torn from her body; her left foot was losing blood from an ugly gash. Her eyes were nearly closed. Obviously she did not know the danger she was in. The flames licked the air within a few inches of her head.

Now I drew part of my smoky body over her face. I cut off her breathing. She fought for air. I hovered as tightly as I could between her and the fire. And then success began to reward my efforts. She turned instinctively away from the blaze.

I followed. I forced her to keep turning for air. Soon she was well away from the flames, breathing easily.

In a few moments the firemen came running up. The sight of smoke near her—for in my sympathy, I had lingered near her—had attracted them. They called for a stretcher. And so as I thinned into the upper air I knew she was being cared for, I had found one way, at least, of being useful.

Darkness came over Chungking.

Most of the fires had been soaked into smoldering heaps. The job of searching the wreckage for salvage and dead bodies would go on all night. I drifted back to the bomb shelter where I had been blown to smoke.

George Leahman was there. So was Bill Washmore. And several coolies *were there looking for me.*

Now I felt more helpless than at any time since the change.

"Don't be troubled about me!" I shouted it—but my shout was nothing they could hear. My efforts at speech didn't carry to them in the slightest. I wasted my smoky breath.

"Here's some scraps of his camera," Washmore said.

"I don't think so," said George. "He wouldn't run off from his camera."

"He might get blown off. Look."

"You're right, Bill. That was his camera. He's been blown to hell."

THEY kicked around over the stones and rubbish. They decided I might be under it. They got shovels and started digging. I tried to stop them. I coiled around them and threatened their eyes and nostrils with smoke.

"Can you imagine it? There's fire under this rock," George said. "What could it be?"

"We won't find Lam alive," said Bill. "But we'll keep looking. Anyway I've got nothing better to do. If it takes all day tomorrow what's the difference?"

"We'll find him," said George.

The way they said it tore my spirit to shreds. It's an awful thing to have to see a fellow's friends fighting for him that way, digging and sweating all the night through, even when they know he can't possibly be alive. I couldn't endure it. I drifted away.

The raids on Chunking came and went, and the millions of people that were threatened every time the planes hummed high, higher and higher over the city established themselves in the routine. It took a lot of courage to defy those savage air-birds.

Take Chestnut Eyes, for instance. She was a regular little dynamo of courage. When she wasn't busy on errands she would get groups of children together and teach them patriotic songs.

She made up a little catchy melody about the whistles that blew after the air-raid alarms were over. The tune began to spread, and soon thousands of people were singing it.

"Whooo-000-ooo—we're still fighting!"

That was the way it started, opening like the after-raid whistle. And when raids were over you would hear it all up and down the streets. Children would sing it, and so would the shopkeepers and merchants trudging back from their shelters, and the civilian street menders as they went to work clearing debris.

But Chestnut Eyes' most urgent job was to keep the medical supplies moving to all the branch stations. Before her foot had healed she was back at work sometimes using children to help her, but more often accepting the good-natured assistance of George Leahman and Bill Washmore. The three of them were often together after George and Bill had finished their news reports for the day.

Then came a fatal night when everything changed. Bill and George were to be transferred. They packed their goods, they said their farewells to Chestnut Eyes. And the three of them talked of me.

I had thought I was best forgotten; but now, as I listened, I knew my supposed tragedy had always been close to the surface.

"Virgil Lamstead left a few things," George said to Chestnut Eyes. "They're still in that shaky old stone laboratory, and now—they're yours—if you want them."

"He was a bit goofy about you, you know," Bill added.

The two newsmen got away safely, but that evening the bombings came. And Chestnut Eyes, who had gone straight to the old stone laboratory building, fell into a trap.

Or to be more accurate, the trap fell upon her. For she had failed to heed the warnings of a coming air raid. When a shower of bombs began dropping in that vicinity the jolt loosened the beams of the building and shook its walls and ceilings like an earthquake.

A WINDOW frame caught her, and a ton of debris rolled down to fasten her under it.

I tried to blow the dust away so she could breathe. It was awful to see her there trapped. What could I do? Nothing—not unless I could somehow at tract some rescue workers. She put up a valiant struggle until she succeeded in freeing herself, all except her ankle. But there she was caught in an unbreakable vise.

At that moment the fuller peril became evident. The wall hung above her like a tower of blocks. With every distant bomb-jolt it swayed. She saw, and then her eyes closed. Her lips were tight together and her fingers crushed into her cheeks....

The blasts were coming closer again. Inch by inch that shuddering wall was bending over. The countless tons of stone were actually swaying at the slightest pressure of the wind. Death was a certainty now, for I saw that this section of the city was completely deserted, and the vibrations of bombs were striding toward us.

Yes death was a certainty. But there was something in the room where Chestnut Eyes was trapped that jolted me to attention. My laboratory properties—*that package of chemicals*—that was it. It was my only chance.

For I remembered that these chemicals were the same as the ones I had had on that fatal day—

I rushed like a hurricane, hurled myself down the street toward a burning house. Here were flaming timbers and paper caught by the first bombs of the evening. I hurled myself in a gust of wind against the burning papers.

My excitement proved costly, for I extinguished three scraps of blazing debris before I succeeded. But in a few more seconds I managed to edge a few burning papers along the street and into the open door under the swaying wall.

And then, just as those tons of cold death spilled down toward Chestnut Eyes I did it. I touched the burning papers to the chemicals.

There was an explosive *pwoof*—then the hard crash of avalanching stones.

It was done now.

The impact of the falling wall shot me outward in all directions. Then everything was quiet, and the jolts of falling bombs had passed. I disentangled myself from a mass of bluish smoke—*smoke that was not me.*

"Are you there, Chestnut Eyes?" I asked in my own way of speaking.

"I—I seem to be *alive.* Yes, I'm still alive... And yet, I *can't* be... That wall fell on me. I must still be there, dead. These words I'm saying aren't real words... I'm only thinking—in another world. I didn't really hear someone call me Chestnut Eyes. I'm just—"

"Do you see another world around you?"

"I only see the same world—but through different eyes."

FOR moments she murmured bewilderedly, wafting along in a bluish smoky form, and I knew she was experiencing strange bodily sensations. Her emotions and thoughts, too, were possessed with an ooziness.

"What has happened to me?" she cried. "Who am I? What am I?"

Then I whispered to her that her life had been changed, that it had been the only way to save her.

I could sense that woeful feeling that enshrouded her. She spread her smoky arms over her head and face—or perhaps that was only as it seemed to me for her cloudy fluffiness was in a constant state of movement

"You were about to be killed Chestnut Eyes," I said to her over and over. "I couldn't let it happen. There were the chemicals—and I remembered how they had mixed with fire to change me... I hope you won't be too angry. Tell me, Chestnut Eyes, that you believe this will be better than final death."

On that point she made no response, as I was to remember long afterwards wondering if my action would prove an unkindness.

But now she began to exclaim in a lively manner, and her spirits lifted.

"You are Virgil Lamstead! I know you, of course—your manners, your voice—or do I *hear* a voice?" She added anxiously. "I'm not dreaming, am I? You are listening?"

"Every word is music, Chestnut Eyes."

"But you were killed. Bill and George, your American friends, told me—many days ago."

"Not killed—changed—transformed to *smoke*—*living* smoke—the same as you."

"Please, Virgil, if that were true—" She broke off and her confusion held her in silence for a moment. Then with a burst of eagerness she exclaimed, "But it is true. It was you that caused me to roll away from the flames—"

"Yes."

"You've been watching over me. I remember seeing you, and wondering about such a curious cloud of smoke. It was you that brought the firemen—"

"Of course. There, you do believe it's me. You see, we are not dead. We live! We are still able to help! This is our world—our civilization. It's turning to smoke, and we've turned with it. But even in the form of smoke we'll go on fighting. Won't we?"

"It's all so bewildering," Chestnut Eyes said plaintively. We had drifted over rooftops and were floating downward toward the surface of the river. It was so easy to float downgrade.

THE water's surface was so inviting. And Chestnut Eyes did look so relaxed coasting along beside me, as if this new steamy amorphous existence was the very self her war-weary soul craved.

I talked on, challenging her to see this new outlook on life as I saw it.

"We're the fumes of a great fight, Chestnut Eyes. We still have a part to play."

She was silent.

Then the whistle for all-clear sounded and in a moment Chinese children were bobbing out of shelters, singing their all-clear song.

"Whoooo! We're still fighting!" Chestnut Eyes gathered into a tighter knot of smoke, as if summoning her strength.

"Yes, Virgil," she said. "We have a part to play. Lead me on."

IT was several days later that we began to get wind of a spy ring operating on the outskirts of the city. We had been able to rise above the hills at night and see the hidden signal lights that directed Japanese scouts to this spy ring.

By daylight we followed the devious courses of those spies who were bold enough to show their faces. Among them was the traitorous Kong Wah, who appeared to be an armless beggar.

He carried a straw basket on his chest and went about pleading passionately for bread and gold. The sight of him wrung pity from many, who supposed him a war victim.

The stumps of arms that hung from Kong Wah's broad shoulders were covered with closed sleeves. No one actually saw those stumps of arms.

We followed Kong Wah. It was interesting to see what pains he took to make sure no one was following him. We were right over his head close enough to see the wicked light shining in his eyes.

He led us up the hillside, past the toiling gardeners tending their little two-by-four patches of beans on the terrace; past the plodding carpenters trying to make two damaged houses into one good one. Then we followed him across the heaps of rock that had separated that edge of Chungking from an ancient retreat of legendary Chinese gamblers.

We watched Kong Wah cross a perilously narrow ledge where one misstep would have sent him over a three-hundred-foot drop. But Kong Wah knew his way.

In a moment we were in the cave of Ho Lo and his spy ring. The legendary cave of gamblers was now a link in the Japanese gamble for empires.

We spread ourselves too thin to be noticed. Chestnut Eyes kept reminding herself that we were in no danger. There was already some smoke in the cave. Yellow oil lamps were burning in an inner room.

From a farther room came the intermittent screams of a boy being tortured.

A gang of eleven men—most of them Japanese—were lounging on benches or on the damp floor apparently paying no attention to the screaming of the boy. The baseness of the scene made Chestnut Eyes recoil.

T HIS man without arms made the twelfth. Presently a comrade removed his catch-basket, together with his outer shirt and the stubs of arms. Then Kong Wah's real arms were revealed, strapped tight to his body. The men unbound them.

"How have you fared?" Ho Lo asked, reaching into the basket.

The fakir laughed cynically. "I have wrung tears to flood the rivers."

"It's a pity you can't collect more gold and less tears."

"He's losing his touch," someone mocked. "We should chop his legs off." Everybody laughed.

The cries of the boy ceased.

"What's happened to our music? Didn't you have a torture record on?" this from Kong Wah.

"He's been on the frying pan long enough," said Ho Lo. "He ought to be ready to turn."

They brought the boy in, wired to the cross-bar of a frame of timbers. His fingers and toes were knotted together with wire behind his back, and a single strand of wire suspended him from the frame.

"Into their eyes and nostrils," I whispered to Chestnut Eyes.

We kept our snaky bodies spread thin, but drew our smoky fingers hick and hard into the eyes of the ring-leaders.

Ho Lo was shouting at the boy as they unwired him and set him on his feet. "Now, you turtle's egg, you son of a rich father, maybe you will go and find us the thousand gems we demand."

The wild eyed boy shook his head.

"Then you'll be tied up as before. And this time we'll hang weights to your belly... Or have you changed your mind?"

The boy's pain-racked face twitched. The tall Japanese leader, Joko-lo, a confederate of the Chinese traitors moved toward him with the wires, and the boy uttered no protest.

Then someone said to the Japanese, "What's the matter, Jokolo? Is this business getting your gall?

"There's nothing the matter."

"Your eyes are pouring tears, you fool. What's happened to your heart of steal?" the speaker accused.

Smoke in my eyes," said Jokolo.

And the traitorous Ho Lo echoed, "Smoke! I've got it too."

"Neither of you are the men you used to be," Kong Wah muttered. "Tears never—"

"Stop your nonsense. Give the boy some more—oooh!" Jokolo wailed and clawed at his eyes. "Where's the damn smoke coming from?"

"There's no smoke in here—no more than—eeegh!"

In a moment we had four of them fighting at the air like wild men. They darted for the entrance tunnel.

"So you fellows can't stand it," someone taunted. "You're walking out—"

The accused didn't wait to reply. They were out in the open air, and by this time Jokolo was shrieking, "I'm going blind. Blind, I tell you?"

Chestnut Eyes and I didn't let up the pressure for an instant.

Jokolo ran out into the open and stumbled over the cliff and went down—down—

THE three who had followed him were more careful. They stopped at the cliff's edge and looked down in awe. We released our grips on their eyes momentarily. They began to mumble superstitious sayings, and the rest of the gang, having followed to the door, wondered what dreadful mysteries were at work.

Together we suddenly renewed our attack on the traitorous Ho Lo. In a dizzy terrified instant he reeled to the cliff's edge. Three men tried to drag him back—and two of those three went over with him. Their cries faded into sickening whines as they fell—cut off by a dull crunch on the rocks far below.

In that moment the boy who had been tortured slipped out of the cave and raced off to freedom.

Immense relief was in the whisper of Chestnut Eyes.

"We've done it. He's away. And they'll never dare touch him again."

"They'll never have a chance," I replied.

I sent her on down to the Yangtze to wait for me on the cool waters. I would finish this house-cleaning before joining her....

Some days later I began to brood over the quietness of Chestnut Eyes. She continued to help me with the weird tasks that befell us through the stricken city. But I sometimes felt that I was losing touch with her. I began to ask myself again whether I had been cruel to spare her the relief of death.

I said to myself, "That spy ring was too much for her."

What might happen to her? Through long afternoons, floating high above the city, I would look down on Chungking funerals, wondering about my own existence—and hers. Whether we were slated for some death as strange as our new life I could not know.

It might be that a creature of smoke was destined to be wafted away on the breezes, diffusing into the air a little at a time, so gradually that not even his daydreams would be disturbed. When he became too scattered ever to collect himself together, that would be death. Or would it?

There was no one to ask, no books to consult, only a puzzle to leave hanging in the winds until the fatal time might come.

THESE thoughts made me wad myself into such a tense, tight cloud of smoke that I must have frightened Chestnut Eyes, as I floated down toward her.

She was hovering close to the ground at the edge of a rolling field of bay, and appeared to be preoccupied with chasing wisps of hollow straws. I must confess I was amazed to find her so far from the city and in such a state of idleness. The fact is, I had been looking for her for many hours. She observed in startled manner.

Is it you? Why are you that way?"

"What way?"

"All bound up so tightly, as if a hurricane wind were threatening you. Are you trying to turn into stone to resist some danger?"

"Precisely my feelings, Chestnut Eyes," I said. "These strange disconcerting feelings must have carried over from my old life, I think."

"I don't understand." She waved a gesture for me to settle down beside her.

"I used to wonder, in my philosophical hours, whether people don't live and have their being by virtue of a host of anxieties. The stronger and tenser the nerves, the surer the grip on life."

"Surely you don't mean that anxiety and nerve strain are good?"

"But they are good—at least within limits. Look over there and you'll see an example."

We watched an overzealous farmer driving four pigs down the road. "Is that man under any tension?"

"I don't know. He seems to be trying to keep the pigs in the road. Why?"

"The harder the job, the more his nerves have to exert. It's that exertion of his nerves that keeps him from being a scatter-brained fool."

"I don't know what you're driving at," said Chestnut Eyes.

"If someone tried to take those pigs away from him, he'd fight like a demon."

"That would be too bad," said Chestnut Eyes. "It would be like China's having to fight for what is already her own."

"Too bad, perhaps," I agreed, "but his life would suddenly have a lot more meaning. But suppose he were to go to the other extreme?"

"And refuse to fight?"

"Yes. Suppose *nothing* ever confronted him to make him pull his nerves together. Suppose he slipped into a state where he never had to exert himself."

"Then he would be delightfully relaxed," said Chestnut Eyes.

"Precisely like his pigs, I said. There would be no difference."

"Virgil, I've had enough of your supposings," said Chestnut Eyes. "If you want to talk about nerves, talk about nerves. If you want to talk about pigs, talk about pigs. But don't mix the two together."

"But the point is, here we are you and I, turned into forms that don't have to eat, or fear the cold, or endure pain or drive pigs—"

I WAS interrupted by some specks of color appearing on conspicuous points along Chungking's hill tops. The triangular lanterns were being hung on the crosspoles. That meant that a new Japanese air raid was on the way. It meant that the Jap planes had taken off from their bases far down the Yangtze.

"Lanterns, Chestnut Eyes."

She made no answer. Again she was chasing hollow straws along the ground playfully, forcing her smoky breath through them to hear them sing.

Her whimsies had never been more disturbing. Death was riding the skies. Tomorrow there would be more burials.

"Won't you come with me?" I asked.

"Where are you going?"

I summoned a determination that had been growing in me for many days. "I'm going *up.* "

"I'll stay—this time," she replied in a soft child-like manner.

I drifted away from her, and every whimsical word she had said clung to my thoughts. Had my warning struck home? Had I found her on the point of letting go, drifting away from it all? These reflections stung me and I coiled and humped into a smoky knot as I climbed into the skies. It was late afternoon. The city below me was winding up its day's trade before gathering up for a visit to the shelters.

I attained a high altitude by the time the lanterns on the hilltops changed.

Now they were round lanterns—the second warning. The bombers though still many miles away, were speeding onward.

The network of Chinese communication was at work, reporting every move and Chungking was making ready I could see the people hurrying like thousands of little ants, carrying huge baskets and bundles on their backs, moving in orderly lines to the cavern shelters of the hills.

In my own way, I was quivering, setting up a series of air currents around me. This was going to be a new test for me.

Now the planes came into view like little arrowheads of gnats so insignificant they appeared against the vast sky.

Again I climbed until at last I was nearly on a level with the leader of the squadron.

NOW it was a matter of seconds. My filmy body stretched out in two thin, almost transparent ribbons. The first big bomber plowed straight toward my station. I struggled to gain speed, as a man runs before leaping at a passing tram.

The roaring air vibrated through me. I had the sensation of being drawn into humming strings of a vast musical instrument. Propellers cut through me but somehow I caught on, even though I was spreading into countless tapering shreds.

Now I was speeding with the squadron and I seized to the bellies of a whole line of planes and clung like a long gaseous octopus. Through the tornado of whipping winds I rode as an invisible passenger.

I curled my myriads of tentacles around the planes searching in vain for an entrance. There was none. Not until the bomb hatches began to open.

That was the instant that my dangling branches folded, hissed up into the bombers' bellies. Was this a last *tour de force* that would amount to no more than a mad gesture? Was I pulling apart to be torn into nothingness?

Ah, but already I was achieving. In five different planes at once I succeeded in thrusting bunches of my smoky form past the line of bombs, up to the controls to gouge the eyes of the pilots. I gouged. At once the pilots in the several planes began to slap at their eyes. They snarled and cursed this strange something they couldn't understand. Two of them shot out of formation and swung through sharp curves.

Men with beastly faces were going mad from tortured eyes. And though my pressure against those orbs seemed an attack against stony, merciless things, I was getting results.

Two planes, cavorting as if piloted by blind men, came into a mid-air crash, then hurtled down, screaming through the air, leaving a comet-trail of flames behind them.

And they left me behind them, freeing my ribbon-like branches to slither into other bomb hatches.

Now I found eyes wild with fear. And I combed them mercilessly. The unaccountable crash of my first two victims had created a panic among the followers. By this time bombs were being dumped indiscriminately. And blinded pilots were shooting out in tangents heedless of their directions.

I slithered out of two planes in order to stay with the third. I rode it doggedly for an hour, far across the land, before I at last succeeded in achieving a crash into a mountainside.

Most of the night was gone before I found my way back. There was more tragic smoke over Chungking, but the tragedy was not unmixed. Around the wreckage of Japanese planes an assorted lot of Chinese had gathered, frankly mystified over why the planes had fallen, but nevertheless jubilant. It was good to see those grizzled old Chinese coolies, fire fighters with sinews of steel, standing around smiling through their sweat and grime.

Where was Chestnut Eyes?

ON EVERY clear day for the next two weeks I rose high above the city to gaze over the countryside. I wanted to go searching, but I couldn't possibly search in all, directions at once. My mood grew heavy.

And yet, I told myself, if it was her preference to spend her days idly chasing straws over the field, forgetting the turmoil of her past, that was surely her privilege.

And then one day I ventured into a so-called hospital—the hall of a once-wealthy home that was now lined with beds for the wounded.

I drifted in stealthily, for smoke is no welcome guest in such a place.

The doors at both ends of the hall were open. The attendants were trying to ventilate the place. Strangely, there was a thin little layer of smoke clinging to the floor and walls like the haze of a mirage.

Blue smoke—coiling, twisting, swirling in curious little eddies. A little yellow straw drifted along the floor, spun upward, and alighted on the bed of a patient. The injured man was no one I had ever seen before, apparently a patrolman who had weathered many raids, and taken a wound on the recent one.

The straw that lighted on his bedside caught his attention. The smoke-laden breezes seemed to be playing curious tricks for his amusement. By this, time I knew. And I too, had spread myself thin along the floors and walls. Chestnut Eyes whispered to me to listen. And so I heard the little song that vibrated through that bit of straw.

"Whoo-000-ooo! We're still fighting!"

The whistled bit of melody was not as distinct as one might have sung it, but it was unmistakable, for the straw was a flexible whistle capable of cunning effects when skillfully blown.

Again the little melodic message sounded.

The face of the Chinese fire-fighter lighted with hope. Perhaps he thought he was dreaming. But the bit of song—the melody that Chestnut Eyes had begun—was the music of courage in his ears.

The straw spun to the floor, swept along in what appeared to be an aimless course, and suddenly whirled upward again to alight beside the ear of another patient.

"Whoo-000-ooo! We're still fighting!"

THE SINGING SKULLS

The April 1945 cover illustration for Fantastic Adventures *magazine was created the month before by R. E. Epperley. It was then assigned to Don Wilcox, who was told "to write a story" about it. So Don wrote* The Singing Skulls, *a fantasy set in an underground city, where to be named the Festival Queen is to become the annual sacrifice. When one woman was named queen, the singing skulls rise to her defense.*

CHAPTER I

AMONG the vast red rock caverns, a ten-year-old child like Neeka could easily lose her way if she strayed too far from the underground city. Fortunately, Muriel had taken the little orphan under her wing. Muriel was nineteen.

"You must never come this far alone," Muriel would warn her as they explored new tunnels in search of food. "We're a long way from home."

"I'm tired, Muriel," the little girl complained. "Isn't there any shorter way home?"

So today they tried a shortcut. Soon the passage narrowed until the flames of their torches touched the red rock ceiling, and Muriel's flowing blonde hair sometimes brushed the walls.

They were about to turn back when a flickering red light appeared only a few yards ahead. At once their tunnel opened into a circular rock chamber. There, before a pit of sputtering yellow lava and red flame, stood a grizzled little old man.

"Who is he?" Neeka whispered. "S-s-sh!" Muriel held the child's hand. "We shouldn't have come here."

"How do you know?"

"My conscience tells me."

"My conscience doesn't tell me anything," the little child said innocently. "I want to stay and watch him."

For a long moment they lingered. Their eyes adjusted to the weird red flames. The details of this shadowy room became clear-cut. The little old man didn't see them. He was too busy puttering around the flames of the pit.

In his wrinkled red hand he held a long, crooked wire, heavy enough to stir the sputtering, lava as one, might stir a kettle of bubbling broth. He didn't mind the fumes that wafted up from the glowing coals.

"I've seen him once before," Muriel whispered. "He came to the festival last year. He's a hermit."

"He's talking to himself," said little Neeka. "What does it mean?"

"I wonder."

At that moment a liquid bubble rose out of the pit and floated upward, slowly, slowly, toward the domed ceiling. It glistened with running colors like a soap bubble, and it grew larger and larger until it was as big as a bucket.

Then—pop!

The bubble broke into a thousand splinters of light, and out of it fell—*a skull.*

The skull floated downward as slowly as the bubble had floated up. Its narrow jaws yawned and it gave forth a thin-voiced cry.

"Gheeeee-aaaah-gawwww-yup!"

It struck the surface of the lava, choked off, and sank.

"Oh!" Neeka cried out before Muriel could stop her. The old man turned. He came toward them slowly, dragging the wire with red hot end so that it made sparks beside his bare feet.

Muriel snatched up the two torches, handed one to Neeka, and started to run with her. They sprinted down the tunnel—

Clannnnk! A metal wall fell before them. Their escape was closed. A hidden mechanism, operated from a lever in the circular room, had made them prisoners.

Muriel caught a tense breath. She went back to face her captor. Her heart pounded. She felt as innocent and helpless as Neeka, even though she was the child's guardian.

"Must you be frightened?" The little old man spoke in a thin, cackling voice.

MURIEL couldn't answer. He was so strange in appearance, as if his half naked body had taken on the qualities of the lava pool. His face and shoulders and chest bore a thousand wrinkles, glowing like fire. His twisted locks of hair were like coiled ribbons of brass.

His eyes shone at her, deep and fierce and mysterious, under great eyebrows that were likewise twisted ribbons of brass, as were his whiskers. It was hard to guess whether he was scowling or smiling.

Another bubble floated up from the lava pool, and now a purplish-white skull floated down gently, and he, caught it on his fingertips and held it. Its jaw fell open and it began to cry like a dying animal.

Muriel was trying hard not to be frightened. But now she heard Neeka sobbing.

"Aren't you ashamed, scaring a little girl?"

"I have so few visitors. I didn't want you to run away so soon." There was something plaintive in the old man's voice. He looked at Neeka, disturbed by her crying, yet seemingly unaware that the whine of the skull was an unnatural thing that might frighten anyone.

"Is this your little sister?"

"She is Neeka," said Muriel. "I've taken her to be my child."

"Neeka—oh!" The brassy-whiskered old man tossed the skull deftly and caught it between the teeth. It ceased to cry. Then Neeka stopped her sobbing. The old man said, "Neeka—too bad, too bad. Does she know the tragedy of her parents?"

"S-s-sh! I try to protect her, so she'll never be reminded," Muriel said. She was surprised that this hermit should know all about the tribal happenings.

He repeated his words of sympathy. "Too bad, too bad. Twenty-five thousand of us *Dobberines,* and not one of us has the nerve to defy the Evil Heart Ceremony... Come here, little girl, let me talk with you."

He tossed the skull back into the sputtering pit and started toward Neeka, dragging the heavy wire, now hooked onto his metal belt.

Muriel stepped in his path, and he stopped before her. The cackle of his voice was harsh with impatience; "I'm not going to frighten her. Believe me, I know about her misfortunes. I could prove to her that her father was innocent. There was no reason to sacrifice him. Much less reason for her mother to commit—"

"Please!" Muriel cried. "Don't! I beg you, don't say any more to her." The little lava man's great eyebrows raised. He stared, silent, hurt.

"I was trying to help," he said slowly. "I have ways to *prove* what no one else knows. My skulls—"

"Please let us go," Muriel pleaded through tears that she couldn't hold back. Little Neeka's tragedy, her mother's suicide from grief after her father was sacrificed, must not be recalled to the child's mind. To Muriel, the happiness of Neeka meant more than anything. "Please—"

"Good-bye," the Lava Man said abruptly. He stalked to the lever, hooked it with the heavy wire. The latticed door across the tunnel lifted into the ceiling. "Come back if you ever need me... Good-bye."

As Muriel and Neeka hurried away, they heard the weird songs of the floating skulls fading in the distance.

CHAPTER II
Irlinza Needs Jewels

IRLINZA saw Muriel and Neeka returning to the city that day. She saw them approaching the footbridge at the rear of the palace. She touched a button to signal to the bridge guard. The bell tinkled, the guard jumped to his feet and obediently bent to the crank. The footbridge lifted so that no one could cross.

Irlinza, watching from the palace roof garden, laughed to see how much trouble she caused the two weary hikers. They were forced to take the long way around.

"Did you mean to do that?" a servant asked timidly. After all, Irlinza was only a luncheon guest. Her act was purely malicious.

"I have to amuse myself somehow," said Irlinza. "Why not amuse oneself at the expense of a 'nobody' like Muriel?"

"Is she a nobody, Miss Irlinza?" the servant asked submissively.

"Her father was a moss-gatherer."

"I've heard," said the servant, "that she may enter the Moss Festival beauty contest this year."

Irlinza mocked. "A sweet chance she'd have. The *Dobberking* doesn't even know her. And after all, he is the one who chooses."

"His royal workers vote, you know—

"Vote or no vote, the Dobberking makes the choice," Irlinza said emphatically. "That's why I'll be the queen again this year. Get me some more dessert."

Of the twenty-five thousand people in this cavernous world—the kingdom of the Dobberines—Irlinza was one of the most ambitious for wealth and royal privileges.

She was already a celebrity. She had won the beauty contest for the last two years. She had been the favorite luncheon guest of the young bachelor ruler known as the Dobberking.

Irlinza was twenty, a brunette of slinky curves. Her wardrobe was a subject of much gossip among the Dobberine women; Metal mesh was the standard material for wearing apparel for both men and women. But Irlinza also possessed dresses made of supple-bark products brought down from the storm-thrashed surface of this planet, high above the caverns.

Irlinza's eyelashes were so long and beautiful that the court poet continually wrote poems about them. But Irlinza never read these poems.

Reading was a bore to her. Besides, the flutter of her long lashes was for the Dobberking, not for any addle-brained poet.

The Dobberking had been in one of his frequent bad humors today. He had hurried away from lunch to take care of the affairs of state. Left to her own devices, Irlinza sat at the roof garden table, absent-mindedly gazing down the cavern valley to where Muriel and little Neeka found a place to leap across the narrow stream. Again she laughed, then her mind darted to the problem at hand.

"Neeka's jewels," Irlinza said to herself. Her eyes narrowed. "To-day—"

The servant was at her side.

"Did you call for something, Miss Irlinza?"

"Er—how soon does the Dobberking expect his royal workers to return?"

"In three or four days. Miss. Then the Moss Festival will begin at once. Are you already for the contest?"

IRLINZA didn't answer. Secretly, she was thinking of the new costume she expected to wear. Jewels—the cavern's finest. She watched little Neeka and her guardian climb the sloping path toward the farther side of the cavern city… Jewels… Three or four days.…

"I'll go now," said Irlinza. "But first, bring me the silver cheese-moss knife that the Dobberking was showing me."

"I'm not sure whether I should. Miss—"

"Bring it to me. I'll wait on the porch steps."

She sauntered to the front of the roof garden. Immediately before the palace was the sentry house carved in the outcropping rock ridge that formed the shape of a question mark. The dot-end of the question mark was a six-foot onyx stalagmite that had come to be used for a sacrifice post.

There was where Neeka's father had been tied, in last year's Evil Heart Ceremony, when the floods were rushing down.

Beyond the palace plaza lay the sprawling city on the upward slope of the cavern floor—a few thousand watertight clay mounds with glass windows. Most of the windows were lighted, at present; for it was mid-day, and thousands of torches burned.

Days and nights were a part of the Dobberine's well-ordered existence in this world of a thousand caves. Written legends traced the origin back to the habits of earlier ancestors who had lived on the outside of another planet called the earth. The red rock walls of Onyx City, the capitol, glowed with a profusion of torches through, the day time, and the waters of the subterranean streams chased noisily through the crevasses.

But at night the caverns were darkened, and the noisier streams were choked off for ten hours, to provide ideal conditions for sleep.

Only the lonely farmers—those moss-gatherers who lived apart in the various dark branch caves, could ignore the system of night and day. Many of them were said to sleep the greater half of their lives away. However, at such occasions as the annual Moss Festival or, later, the Evil Heart Ceremony, which came with the yearly rush of floods, all the population of these caverns gathered in to share the excitement of the city.

The servant met Irlinza on the porch steps. "I'm sorry, Miss. The Dobberking says the beautiful cheese-moss knife must be saved for the winner of the beauty contest."

"He's just being spiteful," she said angrily. "There's no reason he shouldn't give it to me now."

She wandered out across the palace plaza. Ubolt, the burly guard in the red and black chain-metal uniform, was sitting in his easy chair on the sentry house roof.

"What's new, my famous beauty?"

"If there's anything new, you should know it," she retorted.

IT WAS a fact that Ubolt, with his gift for gossip and time on his hands, kept a vulture's eye on the comings and goings of the kingdom. His station was an ideal vantage point. Carved out of the hook of the rocky question mark, it overlooked the palace plaza, the business streets and metal shops, the children's playgrounds, and the mound-shaped residences.

"I suppose you've picked out a costume for the contest?" said Ubolt.

"If I had, I wouldn't tell you," said Irlinza.

"Be sure to dazzle the Dobberking," said Ubolt. "When you walk off with the prize, you'll hear a big cheer from the top of this sentry house. That'll be me."

Irlinza threw a kiss to Ubolt and went on her way.

She crossed the town and came to the house of Neeka. It stood at the end of the street where the cavern floor and roof came together. She found the little girl playing along the narrow cliff path, watching the silver birds fly over.

"Neeka, my darling."

"Hello," said Neeka.

"I've come to see you, my dear. Do you remember me? I used to be a friend of your mother. She would often show me her beautiful beads and bracelets."

Neeka shook her head slowly. "I don't remember that."

"Who takes care of you these days, Neeka? Do you have any friends besides Muriel?… What a lovely old house… Is anyone at home?"

"What do you want?" Neeka faced her stubbornly.

"Come, sit down with me here on the step," Irlinza said, brushing the little girl's hair. "You are very charming. Some day I'd like to take you to the Dobberking's palace."

"I don't like palace people," Neeka said innocently. "Today someone raised the bridge so we couldn't get across."

"Oh, that's too bad."

"Muriel takes me on long walks," said the little girl. "We see wonderful sights. And we never tell anyone. You'd never guess the sights we see or the sounds we hear… Aren't you the lady who wins the beauty contests?"

Irlinza smiled. "Would you like for me to win again, Neeka? Think how beautiful I would look in your mother's jewels… Would you like for me to try them on?"

Diamonds, rubies, emeralds—beautiful necklaces, bracelets and tiaras—these were the pictures that floated through Irlinza's mind as she strove to win little Neeka's confidence.

"If you want to see the jewels," Neeka said simply, "you may come in. Muriel is trying them on right now."

Irlinza rose in surprise. "Muriel? Why?"

"She's going to wear them in the contest. I told her she could."

"What! Muriel *She—*"

"I think she's the most beautiful person in the world."

"Oh, Neeka, you poor little dear. Why, the Dobberking wouldn't even look at her."

Just then the door opened and Irlinza's jealous eyes beheld Muriel, dressed in a dazzling white party dress, bedecked with rubies and emeralds.

Now, Neeka, how do I—oh!" Muriel caught her breath to find Irlinza here on the porch. "Oh—hello."

"Well, *well.*" Irlinza drew herself up haughtily. She walked back and forth as if inspecting a model. "How *very* glamorous. And you, a moss-gatherer's daughter! What's the occasion? A wedding?"

"I was thinking of entering the contest—"

"Indeed!" Irlinza's lips curled in a cynical smile. "And do you think the Dobberking will be impressed by jewels—*borrowed* jewels?"

Little Neeka, bright-eyed, seized her opportunity. "But *you* came to borrow them yourself."

Irlinza's face tightened. She hated that meddlesome child.

No ten-year-old girl was going to cross her path. In a saccharine voice she said, "Isn't that *innocence* for you. Neeka thought I wanted to borrow the jewels."

"And didn't you?" Muriel was plainly puzzled.

"Certainly not," Irlinza lied. "I'd heard the rumor that you were going to enter the contest and I only wanted to make sure. You see I'll be much surer of winning if you do."

"I don't quite understand," said Muriel.

"The Dobberking hates jewelry. Irlinza's sarcastic smile played its full power upon the bewildered Muriel. "I do hope you'll wear lots of jewels in the contest."

CHAPTER III
The Moss Carnival

THE silver birds flew along the cavern ceilings migrating to new sources of food. Jaff, the fleet-footed young messenger of the royal palace, came running back to Onyx City with the news that the royal gatherers of cheese-moss were returning.

Through the night they came, several hundreds of them, the royal brigade of workmen. Their two-wheeled carts, heavily laden with heaps of cheese-moss as thick as sod, rumbled along the cavern thoroughfares. There would be food aplenty in storage when the annual floods rushed down through these subterranean chambers to wash the last of the old crop away. Cheese-moss was the most important item of the Dobberine diet.

The Festival began with the spectacle of a colorful parade and ended with the tense excitement of choosing the queen of beauty. Muriel was always thrilled by the gay pageantry of these occasions. Now, for the first time, her own beauty was a part of the parade.

She rode with nine other girls. Their float was decorated with moss blossoms—pink, white and yellow. Moving slowly through the crowds, she caught sight of her friends waving at her. Little Neeka's eyes danced with delight as she ran along beside the float.

"Be sure to win!" Neeka called.

Muriel nodded her head, smiling. She wouldn't win, of course. Not with Irlinza and other court favorites to compete against.

But it was fun being in the contest, if only for Neeka's sake. It had been Neeka's idea more than her own. This lovely white party dress, these jewels that hung lightly at her breasts, had, once been worn in this festival by Neeka's mother. Today amid the gaiety, a few spectators would recall the tragedy of last year's Evil Heart Ceremony.

Far across the crowd Muriel saw the little Lava Man. What an oddity. Of all these thousands of gaily dressed people, here was one who paid no attention to the parade. Half naked, he was lying on a red stone, like a lazy lizard that sleeps against a background of protective coloration. When the metal rhythm instruments began to beat a stirring band march, he didn't even look lip.

"Get back in line, Muriel."

Muriel winced. She was quite in line, she thought, as she glanced along the row of nine other girls.

It was Irlinza who had spoken. This was the third time since the parade began that Irlinza made an occasion to bawl her out. Graciously, Muriel said nothing.

The parade halted. One by one, the ten girls stepped down from the float, escorted by a uniformed official, and marched up the steps of the palace.

MURIEL was the last one in the line. Suddenly she realized that a great many people were gazing at her individually. Noskin, a brisk important little palace official with a face like a bird, batted his eyes twice. He touched his sash and bowed as if the Dobberking were passing. The unexpectedness of this gesture made Muriel smile.

Next, she caught the eye of Ubolt, the burly guard, who sat in his easy chair atop the sentry house. He had thrown a kiss to Irlinza when she passed. Now he stood and tossed kisses to Muriel with both hands.

Just as she was starting up the steps, Jaff, the royal messenger, slender and handsome and fiery-eyed, stopped her long enough to pin an ornament on her shoulder. This was slightly irregular. The official who was conducting her coughed with impatience. But the Dobberking himself was smiling down indulgently upon this little interruption.

It was a lovely ornament—an award that Jaff had once received as the champion foot racer of the tribe. Now it pressed cool against her shoulder, a miniature silver foot with wings.

"I'm giving you this for luck," Jaff said, smiling.

Giving it to her! An effusion of delight filled her—a quickening sense of popularity. The crowds were cheering as she, the last of the contestants, marched across the palace porch.

Nor did she fail to catch the gleam of interest from the Dobberking himself. He was a masterful young bachelor of thirty, short and stocky.

His solid head—wide cheekbones and heavy jaw—reminded her of a chunk of stone with two hot torchlights for eyes. The shining metal mesh of his ornamental vest seemed to swell as he drew a deep breath.

Muriel took her place in the line. She tried not to notice the jealous glance from Irlinza. She looked to the Crowds. How they were cheering! Her head swam with a strange dizziness. So many of them were applauding her, as if they loved her.

"You're going to win, Muriel!" came the shrill little voice of Neeka from the front of the crowd.

But no. Muriel didn't really want to win. This was enough—this dizzying sensation of being a part of the contest, being cheered, receiving favors—

She clutched the winged ornament at her shoulder. That had been the award of a champion.

Now the votes were being taken, according to the custom. The royal moss gatherers marched, single file, across the porch in front of the line of beauties. Each moss-gatherer whispered his vote to the Dobberking. No votes were recorded in writing. The Dobberking simply "remembered" whom his royal workers preferred.

T HE stocky, square-jawed Dobberking marched forward to announce the decision. He extended a hand, as he walked down the line of candidates. Irlinza started to step forward. But the Dobberking walked past her. Muriel saw the high color that leaped to her cheeks, saw her turn white with rage. But the Dobberking didn't notice.

He came straight to Muriel, took her by the hand, led her to the center of the porch. He lifted her to a pedestal that formed a part of the porch railing.

"Ladies and gentlemen of the Dobberine Kingdom, I give you, as the festival queen of the year—Muriel!"

The cheering was like the thunder of an approaching flood.

"Ladies and gentlemen," the ruler went on, "this is the first time that Muriel has competed in the festival contest, but from the acclaim you have given her, I know you hope it will not be the last time.

"To win this honor is also to win certain responsibilities. You all remember, the beauty queen plays her part in the Evil Heart Ceremony..."

The speech went on, but Muriel had ceased to hear anything. She was almost helpless against this sudden flood tide of popularity. She was the beauty queen! *She was the beauty queen—the queen—the queen—the queen—*

A skull! Her eyes grew wide. She was looking over the heads of the crowd. The little old Lava Man was watching her from a distance. He lifted one of his red arms to the level of his wrinkled, glowing shoulders. A skull appeared on his fingertips. A purplish-white skull.

But it didn't stay there. It came floating slowly over the head of the people, straight toward Muriel. Closer, closer, until it was near enough to touch.

She started to draw back, as if a bird floating slowly over the heads of the Dobberking didn't notice; he went on speaking. Neither did the crowd see it.

But it was real, it was there, it was singing to her, speaking words in a soft resonant voice.

"Muriei-l-l... Muriel-l-l... This honor-r-r. This honor-r-r... Do not let it defeat-t-t you-u-u."

The skull whirled twice around her head. Its jaws clicked like stones. It sailed back across the crowd, back to the little old man's fingertips, and disappeared. And Muriel, the Festival queen, was left, staring, speechless, oblivious to the thousands of Dobberines who were cheering for her.

CHAPTER IV
Rehearsal for Sacrifice

It WOULD have been wonderful being the beauty queen if there hadn't been so many complications.

Nothing like this had ever happened to Muriel before. Smiles from everyone. Praise from people she didn't even know. And gifts!

Just imagine buxom Aunt Friel coming home from her day's work at the palace, bringing a heaping tray of the finest cheese-moss, fruits and fish.

"Compliments to the queen of beauty," said Aunt Friel, bubbling over with pleasure and good humor, "from the palace servants."

"How lovely!" Muriel exclaimed. "I never dreamed this would happen to me."

"All you have to do is' stand up and be beautiful, and they pile the groceries right at your feet. It's the funniest way I ever heard of earning a free dinner." Aunty Friel laughed until she shook all over.

Little Neeka danced around with joyous excitement. "I'm going to be beautiful when I grow up too."

But Muriel tried not to be swept away by all this good fortune. Whenever she had a moment of quiet thought, the image of the singing skull came back to her, and she remembered its warning;

Could her good fortune last? She wondered. Through her school days, life had never been easy for her. Her home had been one of poverty. She had had to fight hard for her few successes.

When she had won certain scholastic honors, she had found herself very popular, but the popularity had never lasted. After all, she was Muriel, the daughter of a poor moss-gatherer. She couldn't dress in the finery that was required by the upper social levels. Her good times had been the simple times: gathering moss blossoms with her good friend Jaff, playing nurse-maid to little Neeka.

But now Neeka was hers to keep, and Neeka had been a child of wealth.

"I'm going to give you some jewels for your own," Neeka said. "They look so pretty on you."

"No, Neeka, you mustn't do that."

Muriel wondered. Should she accept a few? Would the people say she had attached herself to this child to get a share of her wealth? But no, they couldn't say that. It simply wasn't true.

THROUGH the streets came the town criers calling for volunteer laborers. Soon the floods would come. The last supplies of cheese-moss, left in stacks in distant caves, must be brought in at once. How many men and women would volunteer to help?

Muriel picked up a pair of work gloves and hurried out to the street. Here was a patriotic service she could perform.

"No, not you," said the crier. "You're the beauty queen."

"But I should help. My father and mother always helped with the cheese-moss harvest. They even made trips to the surface and braved the storms for supple-bark and fruit. They were proud to work with their hands."

"We can't accept you," the crier said. "It's not only that your hands are too beautiful; many good workmen might be distracted if the queen of beauty were along. Good-bye, Miss Muriel."

Curious incidents of this sort occurred almost every hour of the day. All at once Muriel was forced to assume a new personality. She couldn't dodge this wave of popularity?

A messenger from the Dobberking knocked at her door the day after the Festival. He, presented her with a slender blue-metal box.

"With the Dobberking compliments. A silver cheese-moss knife."

"Oh, how pretty." Muriel lifted the gleaming blade as if she were handling precious stones. "But I could never use it to gather cheese-moss. It's too bright and beautiful. Are you sure it's proper for me to accept it?"

The messenger laughed. "If you knew how much one of the other girls wanted it, you wouldn't hesitate."

"Irlinza?"

"How did you guess it? That sister wants everything. Most of all she wants the Dobberking. But since the contest, she's been in a rage."

"I'm sorry."

The messenger went on his way laughing to himself. But Muriel was sincere. For in a way she wished Irlinza had won.

She was still standing on the steps, holding the blue-metal box, when Jaff came running along the cliff path. As usual, he was on an official errand for the palace. But he took a moment to stop and look at her new gift.

"What a beauty of a knife?" It's a knockout, Muriel. Gee, I wish I could give you something nice like that."

"Why, Jaff, you gave me your own championship pin. That's the nicest gift I ever received in my life."

"Honest?" His large brown eyes were bright with boyish eagerness. "Do you really like it?"

"I'll wear it to all the ceremonies as long as I live," Muriel said.

"Gee, thanks. Well, I've got to hurry on. The Dobberking will be in a fever to know how much more cheese-moss is coming in."

Yes, Muriel would wear Jaff's winged pin at every public occasion. The Evil Heart Ceremony was just around the corner. She would wear it then. A shudder of uncertainty filled her whenever she thought of this occasion. It was the one tribal ritual that she had always dreaded—even before Neeka's father had fallen victim to it.

NOSKIN, the palace record keeper, was her next official visitor. He was knocking at everyone's door these days, collecting data for the Evil Heart Ceremony.

He was an important little man with a bird-like face and quick dark eyes. He walked in and made himself very much at home. He commented on the luxurious furniture that Neeka's parents had left. He was fascinated, too, by the sight of the silver moss-knife. Then he turned his attention to her. It wasn't easy for a face like his to smile, but he made an effort to accomplish the feat.

"I don't know why I should come here searching for Evil Heart evidence," he said. "Anyone knows that our new beauty is incapable of any evil. But you know how it is. We officials are paid by the number of calls we make. I'm canvassing every house."

"That must be dreadful," Muriel said.

"Why?"

"Because wherever you go, the people know you're looking for the most evil heart in the kingdom. Whenever you look at anyone, it makes that person wonder whether he may be sacrificed to the flood."

"No, no, no. You take it too seriously." He patted Muriel's hand. And being rather pleased with himself, he repeated, "You take it much too seriously," and patted her hand again. He moved his chair closer to hers. "Pleasant here, isn't it?"

She rose abruptly. "You were telling me about how you choose the most evil heart, Mr. Noskin."

"Yes, yes, yes." He quickly resumed his business-like manner. "It's very simple when you know how. I always put my prospect at ease by saying, 'How are your neighbors behaving? Do you have any neighbors that might be candidates for the sacrifice?' You'd be surprised what any man is willing to tell about his neighbor. Don't worry; I'll have a nice little bookful of evidence on tap when it comes for the crowd to make nominations."

He gathered up his record books. In the doorway he paused and Muriel saw that he was again practicing his smile on her.

"You're very timid. Miss Muriel. It wouldn't hurt you to make acquaintance of some of us influential officials. Now take someone like me. I'm not more than twice your age, and some people have actually said I'm handsome."

Muriel smiled with amusement in spite of herself. "Are you officials paid for the number of social calls you make?"

This may have angered Noskin, for he mumbled and floundered. Then abruptly he started off. On the porch steps he stopped, turned, took a letter from his pocket.

"I almost forgot to give you this," he said. "Ubolt, the guard, is probably waiting for you."

BEFORE the record keeper's sullen footsteps had echoed away, Muriel was hurrying down the long grade to the palace plaza. For the letter was an official notice to report for a rehearsal of the Evil Heart Ceremony.

"Where you been?" Ubolt called down from his sentry station. "The officials have already rehearsed. The show's over. You got left out, good-looking."

The accusation struck, sharp. Muriel didn't know how to answer. She couldn't explain that Noskin had tried to get friendly and almost forgotten his official business. No, that would never do.

"I'm sorry I'm late." Then a flash of hope came to her. "Do you mean I won't have to take part?"

"I mean nothing of the kind. There's only one person that ever has the honor of tying the victim to the post and that's the beauty queen. Come on, we'll go through your part of it right now."

He descended from his roof station, and invited Muriel to follow him into the sentry house. It gave Muriel a strange feeling to be coming into this place. All her life she had walked around this question mark shaped ridge of stone. This was the first time she had ever seen inside. Its hollow interior was like a curved stone. While the guard puttered around gathering together some ropes, she gazed out the wide, low window for a sentry's eye view of the city. The right corner of her view was blocked by the six-foot onyx stalagmite—the dot-end of the question mark—the death post for the Evil Heart victims.

SUDDENLY a horror gripped her. There was where Neeka's father had gone to his death. Within a few days Muriel would be forced to tie someone else to that post, to go to his death, and twenty-five thousand people would applaud her for her act.

"Are you listening to what I'm telling you?" Ubolt said harshly.

"I—I'm ill," said Muriel. "Please. I may not be able to—I'd like to be excused from taking part. Do you think the Dobberking would excuse me—"

"Aw, stop it!" Ubolt growled. "None of that weak-kneed stuff. The beauty queen always does the tie-up act. Now watch sharp what I'm telling you. See this rope?"

It was a thick, ten-foot fiber rope. Ubolt made her practice swinging the end of it.

"I don't know a thing about tying knots," she said.

"No woman knows how to tie a knot. But we have a way to take care of that. See this bucket of honey-glue? It's the same dope the valley folks use to seal their doors against the flood. All you have to do is swing the rope around the victim. It'll wrap around itself with a grab like a vise, see?"

"I—I guess so." Yes, she remembered, that was the way they had done with Neeka's father last year. Irlinza had officiated.

"Well, you'd better practice it once or twice."

"No… No… I'll be able to—please don't make me."

"Come on. You've got to be prepared. Sometimes you get a victim that squirms and hollers, and you have to whip that rope around in a hurry. Sometimes you get a victim that goes dizzy on you and falls away

in a dead faint with his tongue hangin' out—what the devil's the matter
with you, girl?"

"I—I—" Muriel reeled dizzily and fell to the floor in a faint.

CHAPTER V
Terrors of the Night

SUCH dreams! Such hideous hallucinations. Innocent people being
tied to the post. Innocent people with skulls for heads. Skulls, skulls,
skulls! Skulls that floated like bubbles; Skulls that sang. Skulls that whispered. Skulls that taunted, and growled and screamed. Yet all in dreams.
Muriel awoke in a cold sweat. She lay awake, listening for the faint signal bell from the plaza that announced the hour. The night was less than
half gone. She must restore her feverish body with sleep.

Neeka called to her through the darkness.

"Muriel, did you hear someone walking around the house?"

"No, dear. Go back to sleep."

For a little while Neeka was silent. Then, "Muriel, I heard someone."

"It was just your imagination, dear."

Then all was quiet. Soon the slow rhythmic breathing from Neeka's
room told Muriel that the child had gone back to sleep. Aunt Friel, too,
was sleeping peacefully.

As Muriel lay awake, the details of the frightening dream came back
to her. At once she wondered whether the dream skulls had been the
same skulls as those of the lava pit. No, there was a difference. It was
as if they were the distorted dream images of those real skulls from the
Lava Man.

But now she remembered that, at *the* last of the dream, skulls had
been dropping, one after another, with a rhythmic *crunch, crunch crunch.*
The rhythm of footsteps!

Yes, she *had* heard it. Neeka was right, there had been footsteps.
Slow, heavy ones that had woven into her dreams. Someone had been
prowling. Who? Why? Did she have any enemies?

One answer came clear. If there was someone in this kingdom who
knew he might be tied to the post by her in the forthcoming ceremony,
he might come intending to kill her. Cold terror shot through her heart.

Fear makes people do unaccountable things. Muriel now thought of
a weapon. She could get the silver knife, hide it under her pillow.

In the darkness, she crossed the living, room. She groped along the
wall. She knew the very spot, where it hung. The flat of her hand reached
out to press down upon the cool surface of the blade.

Even as she touched it, the blade *moved*. It lifted away from her touch. It was gone in the darkness.

Crunch, crunch, crunch. The swift heavy footsteps thumped across the dark room. The front door swung open, the prowler bolted put. Muriel's stifled scream gave him a burst of speed. He didn't bother to slam the door. He raced noisily out into the night.

Muriel bounded to the door, watched the shadow figure slip through a short alley and cut across to the cliff path. Only a fleet-footed person like Jaff would be able to overtake a man in the maze of tunnels along that path. Had he taken the one thing he wanted?

Muriel struck a torch. The knife was gone, all right. Whoever the thief was, she thought, wouldn't dare come back after narrowly escaping, detection. If only she had lighted a torch before going into the living room.

She hurried through the house to seek other evidences of plundering. None of the jewels had been touched. The silver knife was what' the thief wanted, and that was what he had taken.

SHE hastily dressed in street clothes. She made certain that Neeka and Aunt Friel were still sleeping. Then she slipped out of the house and ran down the long grade to the plaza to tell the sentry what had happened.

The night bell softly tinkled the hour, to break the plaza stillness. The faint sounds of chasing rivulets echoed dimly from distant caves.

"Guard!" Muriel called. "Guard! Where are you?"

Her own voice frightened her, echoing back from the ghostly white palace steps. She had never seen the city so empty.

Where was the guard? The roof station over the sentry house was not occupied. This was strange. Muriel knew that either Ubolt or one of the other guards was supposed to be always on duty.

Now someone within the palace brought a light to the front entrance and stared out to see who was calling.

"What's the matter, out there?"

The voice was familiar, but for a moment Muriel couldn't think whose it was. She talked rapidly, almost incoherently. She needed a guard to keep some mysterious marauder away.

When the man at the head of the steps replied, she realized she was talking with Noskin, the, record keeper. He was annoyed over being awakened.

"There are plenty of guards to take care of your troubles," Noskin growled. "Take your troubles to the sentry house and quit bothering the palace. Who are you, anyhow?"

"I'm Muriel." She ascended a few steps so that the torchlight revealed her face.

Noskin's anger melted. "Oh—*you!*"

"I'll try at the sentry house again," she said. "Sorry I wakened you."

"Not at all, not at all. Don't go away. I'll be back in a moment. I'll be delighted—delighted."

"No, thank you."

As she hurried back across the city alone, this conversation with Noskin kept disturbing her. She hadn't meant to be unkind. But her refusal of his courtesy must have angered him again. All in all, she doubted whether he could be relied upon to report this matter to the palace authorities. She would try to find Ubolt after the new day's torches were lighted.

The front door of her house was open. She couldn't remember whether she had left it that way.

Aunty Friel was slumbering peacefully. But Neeka—*where was Neeka?* She wasn't in her bed. She wasn't in the house. Muriel, with torchlight in hand, ran from one room to another.

"Neeka! Neeka! Where are you?" Aunt Friel roused up, and her sleepy face at once reflected Muriel's terror.

Two next door neighbors came over to see what the fuss was all about.

"I knew something was wrong when I heard that child's voice," one of them said. "But I didn't have the presence of mind to see what was up."

"You heard Neeka? Where? When? What did she say?"

"She was crying," said the neighbor. "It sounded like someone was taking her away in an awful hurry. They went south on the cliff path."

"What does this all mean?" Muriel gasped.

"It means," said Aunt Friel, "that our little Neeka has been kidnapped."

CHAPTER VI
Breakfast with the Dobberking

LOST child! Of all the terrors that beset the cavernous world of the Dobberines, none was so much dreaded as this. For the caves spread their hundreds of arms farther than any explorer knew, and in any cave there were literally thousands of places where a child might hide away and fall asleep.

"You know these tragedies are not uncommon, Miss Muriel," the

Dobberking said the following morning. "Only last year two children strayed away and stumbled into a pitfall."

"But this is *different,* your majesty." With tears in her eyes, Muriel pleaded her case to the Dobberking. "Neeka wasn't a child to stray away by herself. I *tell you she was kidnapped.*"

The Dobberking munched his cheese-moss breakfast thoughtfully. He looked out across the roof garden, southward along the dimly lighted valley. He was not in a good humor. His sleep had been disturbed. Grudgingly he had admitted her for this breakfast conference.

"Please, your majesty," Muriel tried to restrain her imploring voice. "If you'll allow some of your guards to question my neighbors, they will confirm what I have told you. They heard Neeka being led away. They heard her cry along the cliff path."

"My guards are all busy," said the stony-faced Dobberking. "This comes at a very bad time. The Evil Heart Ceremony must be ready. The flood may rush down on us any day. I have much oh my mind."

"Could you spare Jaff? I know he'd be glad to help me. He's so swift—"

"I'll need Jaff every minute to bring the weather reports from the surface."

"Yes, of course." Muriel wept softly. "Do you think they will kill her, your majesty?"

"Of course not. Nobody has any reason to harm her. It's absurd. I'm not convinced that she was kidnapped. I think you've been carried away by a case of nerves." The Dobberking looked at her with stern, cold eyes. "Listen to me, Muriel. The rumor came to me, before you won the contest, that you claim to have seen something very fanciful in the old Lava Man's cave—something about *skulls* that float around and sing."

"Oh!" These words struck her like an accusation of a crime. So that rumor had gone the rounds! Had Neeka told? No, it must have been Aunt Friel; for Muriel had never confided that strange happening to anyone else.

"You see," the Dobberking drove the cruel point home, "anything you think you've seen or heard is subject to some doubt. You're capable of having delusions. This kidnapping notion is just another of your silly fancies. The child will probably return before night."

MURIEL rose weak with anger. "So, you're not going to help me?"

"Young lady, I believe you failed to appear for the Evil Heart rehearsal recently."

"Oh, that was because I—"

"No excuses, please. Ubolt has already told me how you conducted yourself when he gave you a private rehearsal. You'd better pull yourself together. You've got to get over this faint-heartedness before the Ceremony. We intend to appease the Flood God with a perfect sacrifice."

"I understand."

"And while we're speaking of your conduct," the Dobberking drubbed his fingers on the table, "Noskin, my recorder, complains that you're not being too friendly to palace officials. In fact, you've been somewhat snobbish. This is not becoming a new beauty queen."

Uncontrollable emotions filled Muriel's throat. Without meaning to, she clutched the Dobberking's arm, clung to him as if she were drowning.

"I don't want to be the beauty queen," she cried. "I hate being the beauty queen. All I want is Neeka. I want Neeka!"

"Shut up, you little baby. You've *got* to be beauty queen." A strange light glittered in his eyes. He caught her by the shoulders, his cruel fingers tightened over her arms like a vise.

"You're the beauty queen because I said so. Understand? I *made* you the beauty queen."

Brutally he jerked her into his grasp, pressed his face against hers, forced his sensual kiss upon her. She tried to draw back, but she was too horrified to fight. It was a hideous thing for him to do, when her whole heart was crying for Neeka.

He flung her aside, then, and she fell to the floor. For a few moments she lay there, listening to the guttural laugh with which he taunted her.

The servant who had witnessed this scene from his station now helped her to her feet and led her away.

CHAPTER VII

Irlinza Bestows a Favor

V OLUNTEER groups scoured the valleys. Jaff, before leaving for his day's journey, had stopped by to give Muriel what comfort he could.

"I'll tell every moss-gatherer I meet," he promised. "Take heart, Muriel. We'll pick up her trail."

"Do you believe me, Jaff, when I tell you she must have been kidnapped? She would never stray away."

"I believe whatever you say," said Jaff. "But why should anyone do it? If the jewels haven't been touched, there must be some reason. Is there anyone you suspect?"

"Irlinza," said Muriel. "I don't dare accuse her, because she's a favorite of the Dobberking. Already he refuses to help me."

Jaff shook his head slowly. "A person in Irlinza's, position wouldn't dare do such a thing."

"You're so unsuspecting, Jaff. Do you remember the silver knife the Dobberking gave me?"

"Of course."

"I was told that Irlinza wanted it. She tried to get it before the contest. Does it mean anything to you that it disappeared last night? About an hour before Neeka was taken away, someone entered the house and took that knife."

"Did you tell the Dobberking this?"

"I tried to. He wouldn't listen. He thinks that I have delusions. 'A case of nerves,' he says, and lets it go at that." Jaff frowned. "You say someone entered your house an hour before the kidnapping?"

"Yes. Neeka had heard the footsteps. I was afraid. I went to get the knife. The room was dark, but I knew exactly where I had hung the knife on the wall. Just as I placed my hand over it, someone drew it away. He rushed out of the house with it. I saw his shadowy form as he ran through the alley across to the cliff path. Then he as gone."

"You're sure it was a man?"

"From his size and the weight of his footsteps I'm sure."

"And then you went to the palace to report, and when you came back—"

"Neeka had been taken away," Muriel held back her tears.

"I'll think it over every minute I'm gone," Jaff said. "You let the others do the searching. You get some rest. And don't be too suspicious of Irlinza. I'll tell, you why. I happen to know that she has gone out of her way to bestow a favor on you. She has organized a search party."

"Irlinza is doing that for me?" Muriel was doubting her own ears.

"She didn't want it known," Jaff said. "Many people are that way about kindnesses they do. But it's true. She's already sent five servants out on an expedition to scour the southern caverns. So take courage, Muriel. And remember, you're a champion."

MURIEL smiled, and the tears came to her eyes as Jaff kissed her. As soon as he was gone, she went to her room and pinned his winged badge of championship on her shoulder. Somehow it comforted her.

Then she looked out to the cliff path, for she could hear the voice of Aunt Friel calling. Aunt Friel was also on the search.

"Neeka! Neeka! Where are you, Neeka? I've got something for you."

It was heartbreaking and yet comical. Buxom Aunt Friel was carrying a tray of food that she had brought from the palace, and her plaintive call attracted a flock of silver birds. They fluttered down like a gang of thieves; they snatched at the food and almost upset the tray and Aunt Friel as well, which would have been a sizable upset.

"Go way, go way!" she cried, waving her free arm. "Go find Neeka and I'll give you all the dinner you want." She edged along the narrow cliff tottering like a fat lady on a tight rope, and her calls for Neeka soon blended with the other echoes from farther down the valley.

Muriel couldn't rest. She couldn't stay in her room. The neighbors who came in to comfort her did all that could be done. But Muriel's mind was tortured with thoughts of Dobberking's cruel rebuke, and with the awful uncertainty of Irlinza.

"You'd better stay here and rest," her neighbors advised.

"I must see Irlinza," said Muriel. "I'm going to her house."

"You'll quarrel with her if you do. She's not a person to be trusted."

"That's what I intend to find out."

W HEN one suspects that an enemy has done him a favor, it does something to one's heart it melts the steel coating that one has built around it. The hardness is always quick to dissolve if the heart is steeped in grief, as Muriel's was this morning.

Two acquaintances stopped her as she was crossing the city, both to tell her, in strictest confidence, that they had heard her rival, Irlinza, had sent out a party of servants to help with the search.

Irlinza was watching from her oval window as Muriel approached. Muriel tried to see a certain tenderness in Irlinza's somewhat dissipated eyes with their long dark lashes. She was undoubtedly an attractive girl. For the first time Muriel stopped to wonder what brutality she may have suffered at the hands of the Dobberking during the past two years of her great popularity.

"Come in, Muriel," Irlinza said as she opened the door. "I'm so sorry about what's happened."

"I came to thank you," Muriel said, "for the generous thing you've done."

"You've heard? It's the least I could do."

"Somehow I feel that I should apologize because—" Muriel groped for words. Just why did she feel apologetic toward Irlinza? "Because I've misjudged you so."

Irlinza received this sentiment, with a smile and a careless remark. She made Muriel comfortable and brought her a drink. "We all make mistakes. But I think I can tell you something that will help you. That's why I'm glad you've come. I know you have a great deal of trouble on your hands. And it isn't all Neeka. Part of it is the Dobberking."

"Oh—you've talked with him?"

"I just returned from there," said Irlinza. "Let me begin with a question. *Do you believe in dreams?*"

"Why—I—I don't know."

"Well, you mustn't. It's a dangerous habit. It's dangerous to believe in the things you dream while asleep. And far more dangerous to believe what you dream when you're awake."

"I—I don't understand."

"You will," said Irlinza confidently.

"I've heard about your experience down in the cave of the Lava Man. Yes, I got it straight from your dear Aunt. She was in quite a talkative and friendly mood one night. Not that I meant to pry."

"She shouldn't have told. That was our secret—Neeka's and mine."

"The Dobberking got it all. That's why he understands you. That's why you must take advice. You mustn't believe that any such fanciful thing ever happened."

"But it did. Neeka and I both *saw* it. There were skulls singing—"

"I can't help you if you talk that way. You're holding onto a delusion, Muriel. A *delusion*. Irlinza tapped her glass on the table to emphasize each syllable of the word. "Now let me ask you, what did Ubolt say to you last night when you came down to the plaza to announce that your silver knife had been stolen?"

"I didn't find Ubolt," said Muriel. "I called, but he wasn't at his sentry post."

"Another delusion," said Irlinza. "He *was* there."

"Oh, but he couldn't have been."

"I tell you, Ubolt was at his post," Irlinza insisted. Any of a dozen people at the palace will tell you so. He saw you walk by, he heard you call, and *he answered you.* But you acted like you didn't see him and walked on past."

Muriel was trembling. This conversation had brought her to the point that she hardly believed her own senses. "What are you trying to tell me, Irlinza?"

"Simply that your whole story about hearing footsteps and feeling knives slip out of your hand, and hearing Neeka's cry fading along the cliff path are more of the same thing. They're all in your mind. If Neeka has strayed away it's probably because she got tired of your wrought up nerves. I hope it's nothing worse than that. If so, she'll probably be back in a few days.

A knock sounded at the door.

For a moment Irlinza was plainly disconcerted. She didn't know what that knock might mean. But she recovered herself at once, and with supreme poise she said, "Who knows, maybe that's the news that Neeka has already returned."

"Is Muriel here?" came a familiar voice from the front door. It was Aunty Friel. "I want to see Muriel at once."

Muriel crossed toward the door. Irlinza was responding in an uncertain voice. "You seem alarmed. Is there anything wrong?"

"Maybe murder," said Aunty Friel, "but Muriel didn't do it. They can't say she did."

Muriel's heart stopped beating. Her words come breathlessly. "Aunt Friel! Has she been found? Is she dead?"

"Of course she isn't dead." It was Irlinza who answered; then, as if she had caught herself speaking out of turn, she stepped back.

Aunt Friel took Muriel by the hand. "No, she hasn't been found. But I've got to talk with you in private. They can't say these things about you."

Muriel gave Irlinza a parting glance. There was a hint of a strange smile on Irlinza's face. Perhaps it was only her amusement at Aunt Friel. Many persons smiled at Aunty's comical manners.

But Aunt Friel was never more serious than now. She led Muriel away from the plaza toward the chasm where the noisy river all but swallowed up her words.

"They can't say you did it, Muriel. But that's what they are saying. It's spreading all over the city. They say you've planned the whole thing. They say your schemes were laid before you ever became Neeka's guardian. You had your eyes on her mother's wealth—especially after your home was lost in the flood."

"No," Muriel cried. It was true that she and her aunt had moved in, but only after the insistence of the friends of Neeka's parents.

"You wanted her jewels."

"No, no, no."

"But you've waited, they say, until you won all this new popularity, before taking the awful chance—"

"What chance?"

"To get rid of Neeka. To murder her for her wealth."

Suddenly Muriel's pounding heart turned to steel. "Where did this story come from?"

"I—I don't know."

"Did it come from the palace?"

"I guess it did. That's where I first heard it."

Muriel turned and started down the chasm path. She was walking fast, almost running. Aunt Friel couldn't possibly keep up.

"Where are you going, Muriel?"

Muriel called back, just loud enough to hear herself above the chasm stream.

"They can't say those things about me. I never dreamed of murdering anyone. I couldn't. Not unless it was—"

"What did you say?" Aunty Friel called after her.

"I don't commit murders and I don't have delusions. But I've seen floating skulls and I've heard them sing. No one can tell me different. I'm going to see them again right now."

CHAPTER VIII
If Muriel Were to Murder

AFTER a long walk Muriel found the right cave. She wound through the narrow passage, where the flames of her torch touched the red rock ceiling and her flowing blonde hair brushed the walls.

But her visit was doomed to disappointment. The latticed gate was down. There was no way to get through.

She placed the torch back of a rock, and when it's light was no longer in her eyes she could begin to see a little of the lava chamber at the end of the tunnel. Flames were leaping. The lava bubbles were floating upward, bursting with a fine spray of light, and frequently the purplish-white form of a skull could be seen floating downward.

They could be heard continuously. If one were to pass this tunnel casually, he might think the weird noises were simply the fantastic echoes of some babbling subterranean river. But as Muriel listened, she began to catch what she had caught before—the clearly defined singing tones and the babble of distinct syllables.

"Waaaat—cannn—thaaaaa—tooooooo…"

Sometimes she could almost distinguish a series of chanted words. But other skull voices would come in over the one she was trying to listen to; or the sputtering of flames would drown out the consonant sounds.

She had watched the scene for several minutes before she made anything out of the dark form lying beside the lava pit. Now she saw, by the leaping flames, that it was the Lava Man lying there asleep.

"Hello!" she called. "Helloooooo!"

He didn't stir. She called again and again. It was hopeless. Like many of the moss-gatherers who lived away from the city, he probably slept like dead for hours on end.

Once her call apparently attracted one of the skulls, for it started to float out into the tunnel toward her. This frightened her so that she fell silent. How long would she have to wait before he came to life? Hunger and fatigue were on her. She knew where she could find some cheese-moss. A little food, a little rest, perhaps a bit of sleep....

When Muriel awoke, it was with the feeling that the skulls had been whispering to her. She saw three of them drifting back from the lattice gate as she arose. By the lava pit the little old man was still sleeping. Muriel's torch had almost burned away. It was high time to start back to the city unless she could find another light.

"Maybe I can overtake a search party," she thought.

Whether it was due to her rest or to something the skulls had chanted to her, Muriel might never know; but the odd fact was that her thoughts began to click, one, two, three. Everything was coming to her, crystal clear.

As she hiked along, she talked to herself.

"Muriel, they've trapped you," she said slowly. "The skull that warned you was right. This good fortune has brought evil down on your head... Evil... *Evil!*"

THE awful word echoed in her ears.

The Evil Heart Ceremony.... Whom would they choose for the sacrifice? They would choose someone whose evil doings inflamed their imaginations.

Would they choose some poor moss-gatherer? No. Would they choose some metal worker or tradesman who was comparatively unknown? No.

They would choose someone who had recently risen to the pinnacle of popularity—and slipped! Someone whose spectacular rise to fame could be interlocked with a criminal scheme. *Someone who had borrowed jewels to become the beauty queen, and then, intoxicated by her success, had committed murder.*

"The story is already spreading like fire," Muriel said to herself. "By the time I get back to Onyx City someone will be believing it—unless little Neeka can be found alive."

But where did Irlinza fit into this pattern? Was she now a friend who might be counted upon to help turn the tide of this false rumor? Os had she herself started it?

Before Muriel got back to the Onyx Cave she was to learn that her worst fears were justified.

Twice she came within listening range of search parties. Their conversation was highly revealing. A few of the searchers had come out from the city within the past hour, and they brought the knockout story.

"Yes, the circumstantial evidence all points to Muriel as the murderer of Neeka," they would say. "If the body isn't found, the Dobberking will have an easy time deciding who is to be sacrificed."

Muriel's torch had gone out. She sat in the darkness, watching the party move on through the canyon, listening to their ceaseless call of "Nee-eeka! Nee-eeka!"

The steel in Muriel's heart hardened. This was no time for despair. If she yielded before the awful tragedy that was engulfing her, she would be deserting Neeka. For Neeka's sake she must fight. For Neeka might still be alive.

She might be waiting within some cavern prison, sobbing her little heart out, wondering why Muriel didn't come for her.

"It's a trap," she said aloud. "It's a deadly net woven out of jealousy. And it's meant to catch me and Neeka—and Neeka's jewels and property. It's a net and the only way I can escape it *is to cut my way out.*"

She repeated these words slowly, desperately. Then she added, "With a knife."

The steel was welding to a deadly hardness in her heart. What she had been subjected to in these recent hours—the Dobberking's brutality, Irlinza's wily deceptions, the treachery of spreading rumors—flooded through her with the heat of fire, transforming her soft nerves into the toughest steel mesh.

There would be a way to fight this trap. No matter if it cost her her own life. There would be a way. She must think, plan, act.

ANOTHER party passed along within her hearing, and one of the voices struck through her like an electric shock. It was Irlinza. This was Irlinza's rescue party, but they were not calling out for Neeka. They were too much engrossed in their own conversation.

"The Evil Heart Ceremony always follows the same pattern," Irlinza was saying. "When the time comes for the accusing speeches, I'll be ready."

Yes, the routine of the Ceremony, thought Muriel, would give Irlinza every opportunity to win. For the crowds would be excited, and any dramatic accusation would sway them.

The Dobberking would be the one to decide, in the analysis. But in the first place, there would be a call for nominations from the crowd, and at such a time any number of persons might be nominated. It was a common thing for a man to nominate his worst enemy. However, unless he could make a speech that would ignite the hatred of the crowd against that enemy, he usually failed in his purpose.

Once the nominations were made, it was up to Noskin, the record keeper, to check over the evidence against the most prominent candidates. Then—while a crowd waited in awful suspense—he would whisper his recommendation to the Dobberking.

The final steps, then, would be the Dobberking's announcement of the victim. Whether the Dobberking would always choose the person that Noskin recommended was a secret that no one but he and Noskin would ever know. But as Muriel rehearsed these steps in her mind she saw clearly which step was the key to her fate: it was the speech. That fate was already in the making. For the words of Irlinza that she had just overheard were unmistakable. *"When the time comes for the accusing speeches, I'll be ready."*

Muriel sprang to her feet. The steel of her heart had spread to every nerve of her body. She ran swiftly, silently, along the dark cavern path toward the lights of the rescue party that had just passed.

Now she slackened her pace. Again she could hear the voice of Irlinza. She stopped, and her keen eyes searched the contour of the walls ahead, picking out the hiding places. She dare not approach much closer to the party, for fear the swish of pebbles under her feet would cause them to turn.

The light of five torches was in her face. The shadows of her hand against the rock wavered as the five torch bearers moved along. She needed one of those torches. But more to the point, she needed one of those persons bearing the torches—needed that person *alone*—within the reach of her own clutching fingers—fingers that could choke a soft throat like Irlinza's.

She skipped silently along to the next biding place, and the next, and the next.

"Listen!" one of the four servants said. "What did I hear?"

Deadly silence, except for distant echoes of underground streams.

"Nee-eeka!... Nee-eeka!" The servant wasted his voice on several calls. He turned to Irlinza. "Do you think she would come this far?"

Irlinza answered impatiently. "Just keep on searching. That's the only way. I'll leave you to your own devices. Yell your throats out if you want to, but don't think you'll hear any answers. Someday someone will find her skeleton in the bottom of a chasm, and then we'll know that Muriel got rid of her, just as I said."

"Aren't you coming with us, Irlinza?"

"I'll have to go back now. The Dobberking wants me to run over my speech. You keep searching, and remember, I'll reward you well if you find her body."

Irlinza turned back, and then the party went on.

MURIEL crouched low among the rocks. The light of Irlinza's torch came close, causing the black shadows to bob and bend and turn along the dim red rocks.

Irlinza passed within seven feet of Muriel. Her face was a study. The lips slightly curled in a smile of deceit, her eyes with their long lashes, narrowed against the light.

"The knife!" Muriel's lips formed the words. She held her breath, waited, watched. Yes, it was the same silver moss knife that the Dobberking had given her. The scroll design on the handle could not be mistaken. And now the blade of the knife hung at Irlinza's side.

Muriel stalked her prey. With soft, soundless footsteps she kept pace, hardly ten yards back. Twice she dodged, when Irlinza looked back over her shoulder to make sure the rescue party was moving along.

Then Irlinza slowed her pace, watching furtively from the corner of her eyes, as if half aware that someone among these dark walls might be watching her. She kicked at a pebble, then bent down casually to pick it up.

Muriel bounded toward her. The beat of footsteps caused Irlinza to whirl about. Muriel leaped forward with one swift sure purpose. That knife—it was hers—hers to *use*—

Irlinza reached for it, too, and their fingers locked over the handle. The torch jumped from Irlinza's hand. For an instant the struggle froze.

Irlinza's eyes flashed hatred. "What's the matter with you?"

"You took Neeka! Where is she?"

"Don't shriek at me, you little fool!"

"Where is she? You'll pay—" The breathless words were lost in a furious match of strength- against strength. Muriel's full force wrenched at the knife, tore it free, hurled it into the air. I fell to the path where, catching the light of the torch, it lay like a slice of red fire.

MURIEL paid dearly for that split second of throwing the knife. Irlinza caught her by her long flowing hair, jerked her off her balance, threw her to the ground. She tried to spring up. She fought at the tight fingers in her hair. Irlinza reached for the torch.

"Beauty queen!" Irlinza sneered.

"We'll see."

The torch fluttered as Irlinza's arm swung down. The blaze barely touched the ends of Muriel's blonde hair. *Slap!*

Muriel struck out the blaze. She rolled, and Irlinza rolled with her. They were off the path. Their struggling bodies struck a wall rock. The torch tumbled away. They were engulfed in the shadows.

But there was that slice of red light—the silver knife. Muriel's heart thumped-like bouncing stones. A stone was in her hand, then, and that hand was free to strike. It lifted.

The light caught it. Irlinza's arm batted against it. The stone humped across the path and plummeted into the chasm beyond.

Again they were rolling, biting, pulling hair, slapping. Toward the chasm. Away from it. Back again. It was a horrible see-saw.

Then Muriel's fingers were tightening on the soft throat. Irlinza was gasping hard.

"Where is Neeka?" Muriel cried. "Where? What did you do with her?"

"Let me up," came Irlinza's sullen snarl.

"Where is she? I'll choke the very life out of you if you don't tell. I'll—"

The knife! Muriel's hand swept it up, her arm lifted it. Its reflected light flashed over Irlinza's terror-filled eyes.

"I'll count to five," Muriel said. "If you refuse to tell me about Neeka, I swear I'll plunge this knife through your black heart... One... Two... Three... Four...."

Irlinza screamed. She must have seen what Muriel saw—a purplish white skull hanging in the air. It had seemingly materialized before their eyes. It was whining within three feet of their ears, louder, louder.

"Nnnn nnnn nnnnaa." It's tone was that of a hurt animal. The word came clearer. "Nnnoo...nnooo...no! No. Murrrielll, do not killlll."

CHAPTER IX
The Voice of Conscience

"WILL you follow meee, Murielll?" said the skull in a soft, weird, chant. This was no delusion. Even Irlinza knew that. The faint white glow from the floating object fascinated her. Muriel saw her shrink when it moved past her.

The enchanting invitation was more persuasive than any command. Muriel followed. Once she looked back to see Irlinza disheveled and temporarily defeated. The ex-beauty queen picked up the torch and started off toward the city without a word.

"Forgettt about Irlinnnza," the skull sang. Its voice was a feminine voice, Muriel thought, though it was low-pitched and rich with resonance. At once she felt confident that it was friendly.

It led her back to the chamber of Lava Man. The gate was open. The little brass whiskered old man was wide awake, puttering around the flames with a long wire. The wrinkles of his red face twisted into a smile at the sight of her.

"Welcome, welcome, Miss Muriel. I am very proud to have a beauty queen as my guest."

Muriel felt not at all like a beauty queen. She felt like a fighter who had just won—and almost lost—the hardest physical combat of her life. She glanced at her torn sleeves, her soiled skirt and dusty shoes. Only the knife at her belt had come through, the combat shining.

"You told me that if I ever wanted to see you I might come back."

"Do you think it is me you need talk to with so much as your own conscience?"

Muriel trembled at the thought. "My conscience? What would it tell me now?"

The purplish-white skull that had led her back to the cave—undoubtedly the same skull that had come to her many days ago during the Moss festival—now began to speak again.

"I say to you—" it's words were drawn out in a singing resonance, soft, yet accusing voice, "that you must beware of knives."

"What does this mean?" Muriel turned to the old man in alarm. "Is this my conscience?"

"Does it sound like your conscience—or the conscience of someone else?" the old man asked. "Hasn't it been with you all along? Haven't you heard it in your dreams?"

Again the purplish-white skull was hovering close to her, offering its whispers. Accusations, warnings, exhortations. *So this was her conscience!*

"You almost murderrrred." It drew out the awful word. "You might have murderrrred. If it hadn't been for me, you would have murrrdered."

"Oh. I don't want to be haunted by you," Muriel cried. "Don't talk to me."

"You'd rather hear the conscience of some of the others, perhaps?" the old man suggested.

A HOST of skulls burst out of their lava bubbles, and the cavern became a pandemonium of singing. Wails, harsh laughter, guttural growls, and the high-voiced shrieking of unbelievably hideous consciences—all of these mixed their voices in a terrifying concert.

Once she distinguished the heavy thundering words that somehow reminded her of Ubolt's thumping footsteps. The voice was accusing someone of entering houses and stealing.

Once she heard the rasping of an ugly, spiteful voice. The long-jawed skull somehow reminded her of the pointed face of a bird—or of Noskin. But what this conscience might be accusing Noskin of was more than she could catch. Too many other weird sounds came in upon it.

Could this light, sweet-toned singing be the voice of Neeka's conscience? If so, did it mean that Neeka was still alive?

"Can you hear the conscience of Neeka's parents?" the little old man asked. "No, I'm afraid they're too faint. Against all these others, the voices of the dead are not easily distinguished. But if you can make them out you'll find them much like Neeka's—with an unusual sweetness. You see, they haven't worn themselves hoarse accusing their owners."

These voices eluded her, for now she was hearing the rasping feminine conscience that kept calling, "You are a liar, a cheat, a kidnaper, a murderer." Over and over again, in a tone that connoted jealousy, avarice, and uncontrolled ambition. "You are a liar...a murderer."

Muriel caught the implication of this conscience—unquestionably Irlinza's. It was trying to tell Irlinza what she was becoming. It was trying to swerve her from her course of action.

"Does Irlinza hear these words?" she asked.

The little old man shook his head sadly. "Most people don't listen to their consciences. Irlinza? My dear, her conscience has been shrieking at her for years without the least bit of effect."

A ray of hope came to Muriel out of all this bedlam. "These voices— they tell so much," she was pleading. "Can't they be used to tell the people that I am not too terribly guilty?"

The little old man looked at her sympathetically. But his words were not words of hope. "The Dobberines have their beliefs and traditions. I am a Dobberine. I have never used my knowledge to destroy any tribal ceremonies."

CHAPTER X

The Evil Heart Ceremony

THE storms were thrashing on the surface of the planet. Messengers came down the trails every few hours to report the weather to the palace. The people hurried to store their last gatherings of moss in their clay homes. Honey-glue was being prepared in the valley homes to be used on the wedge-shaped doors as protection against the rush of water.

The hour for the Ceremony was twice pushed ahead, owing to new reports of conditions overhead. Then, several hours ahead of the scheduled time, the palace bells rang, and the people gathered in from far and near.

The Evil Heart Ceremony! What a time of excitement this occasion always was; but never more than this year. For the swift rumors of evil deeds had rung like shrill bells all through the Dobberine world.

Moss-gatherers from the hinterlands came down to the plaza, gawking and staring, wondering which of the beautiful faces of the many lovely girls might be that of the ill-fated beauty queen. Some of them, the parents of beloved children, were incensed to a fighting rage over what they had heard.

"She waited until she'd got to be beauty queen," they would say, "and then she took full advantage of the little child. Killed her, most likely. Anyway, got her out of the way somehow. That's the way, when folks get mad for jewels and riches. They lose their judgment. It's a clear case."

The bells rang almost constantly for an hour, and by that time the plaza crowd had swelled to thousands. Many hundreds would continue to stray into the city from remote places as the Ceremony proceeded. Muriel, walking along the outskirts of the crowd, kept watching the trails for the appearance of Jaff.

But it was quite uncertain whether Jaff would arrive for the ceremony. If the danger of the flood was too imminent, he would wait until all the other messengers had come in; for he was the swiftest runner and would eventually make the announcement that would send all these people scurrying to their water-proof homes.

But might Jaff not come back for the Ceremony before his last official message? No, Muriel was hoping for the impossible. In fact, it was her lingering hope that he might have found Neeka that kept tantalizing her.

"We are gathered to nominate a candidate for sacrifice," the Dobberking shouted through the huge metal horn. The crowd quieted and gathered in closer. "Any Dobberine has the privilege of making nominations."

The meeting moved swiftly. For once, these nominations took less than an hour. In times past they had been known to require as much as a day. For if there was no victim in sight whose evil deeds had struck through the hearts of many people, a great number of "spite" nominations could be expected.

At last Irlinza rose to make her nomination. She did not stop halfway up the palace steps, as most of the speakers had done. She ascended to the porch and spoke through the metal megaphone usually reserved for the Dobberking himself.

Her speech was brief—so much so that it was over before Muriel had recovered from the shock of the hundreds of faces that turned to stare at her.

"Is there any doubt," Irlinza concluded, "that we should choose for the sacrifice the one who has set this abominable example of social climbing—who has cast good judgment to the winds—who has forgotten every law of personal and property rights in her passion to get her hands on the riches of an innocent little girl? I nominate Muriel, the beauty queen."

THE words "beauty queen" were drawn out in a tone of high sarcasm that brought down a tremendous ovation. The cheering was a mass brutality, barely under organized control. It was the fever of a vast, unwieldy crowd, ready to descend with the full force of its latent sadism upon a single victim.

The throngs that surrounded Muriel turned to her and began to make way, as if she had already been chosen. She was almost bound to start walking forward, under public pressure.

Technically, the selection was not yet official. It was never official until the Dobberking made his announcement. Some whisperings within Muriel's hearing expressed this uncertainty. Would the Dobberking coincide in the public choice?

Now Noskin went through the officious routine of reading off the names and numbers of a number of laws that had been violated by the chief candidates for the sacrifice.

Meanwhile, Muriel looked again for Jaff. But Jaff did not come. It must be that the signs of the coming flood were too near for him to break away from his vital post somewhere overhead.

Each time that Muriel looked around she would see the little old Lava Man, sitting way back in one lonely corner, near the valley house of some friend who would probably give him shelter when the headwaters came.

"He's taking no interest in these proceedings," Muriel thought. "And he doesn't have a single skull in sight."

But she was remembering, in her courageous heart, the strongest advice that her own conscience had sung to her: that she must not fail the traditions. Whatever was expected of her as a Dobberine, *that she must do.*

Now Noskin whispered to the Dobberking. Absolute quiet reigned over the crowd.

The Dobberking nodded and rose to address the multitude.

"All evidence of evil deeds has pointed to one candidate. The sacrifice will be made by the beauty queen, Muriel. Muriel will come forward."

The crowd made way, and Muriel walked down to the front of the audience. When she came to the six-foot stalagmite—the point of the curved ridge of stone—she turned and faced the silent crowd.

"It is customary," the Dobberking called out, "for the beauty queen to officiate at this point of the ceremony. The victim must be tied to the stone pillar, and the beauty queen is supposed to tie the knot. However, in this case I must call upon the former queen of beauty—"

In a clear voice, Muriel interrupted this announcement with a statement that shocked every ear that could hear it.

"I am the queen of beauty. I have the right to tie myself to the post. I insist upon my right as a Dobberine—

The rope, its ends saturated with honey-glue, was brought to Muriel. Swinging its ends deftly, she managed to make the strands catch. The honey-glue fastened with the strength of a knot. She had tied herself to the pillar.

CHAPTER XI
Sacrifice to the Hood

MANY Dobberines would long remember that picture. One of Muriel's forearms, not quite caught within the bonds of rope, was crossed over her breast. Her fingers clung to the winged ornament on her shoulder which Jaff had given her on another public; occasion only a few short days ago.

But at once the picture became more complicated than anyone had anticipated. A purplish-white skull seemed to have formed out of the air. At least it looked like a skull to all who could see it hanging there. No one saw where it came from. It attracted a thousand whispered speculations, and before the officials were through consulting over its strange appearance, a second skull formed out of thin air to join it. Then a third.

The thousands of onlookers were almost unaware of the low rumbling sounds of the approaching flood. As a rule, the first echoes of thundering water from the caverns overhead would start the audience scurrying for shelters. But this sight of skulls was too tantalizing. There must be a meaning.

Ubolt paced back and forth impatiently, and Noskin, trying to exchange a word with him, was brushed aside. Irlinza came down the steps, followed by a number of the palace royalty, and they crowded around the lower end of the sentry ridge, demanding of each other that someone do something.

"I saw one of those before," Irlinza said, within Muriel's hearing. "The girl is bewitched. It's a good thing we're getting rid of her."

But now the crowd broke a path for the little old Lava Man. There were a few, among the audience of thousands, whose hopes were struck with fire at the sight of him; for in the years past, a few had heard tales of these mysteries or had even experienced, in secret, the revelations of these conscience voices of which the old man was obviously the guardian.

"Who is he?" Ubolt muttered.

"Let him talk," Irlinza said. "Find out what's at the bottom of all this."

So, before a wide-eyed audience, the Lava Man was allowed to speak. He was even provided with a megaphone. He pointed to the cluster of skulls—six of them were now floating in an eight foot orbit around Muriel's head—and he identified them to the audience as *consciences.*

"My life in the Lava Pit is more interesting than anyone can imagine," he said, "for I have the privilege of listening to the consciences of any of you. Can you hear the singing voices of these skulls? Listen to that beautiful soprano hum. That is the conscience of little Neeka."

Most of the crowd could not hear, but those who were close enough caught the sweetly spoken words. "Do something nice for Muriel... Something nice for Muriel... For Muriel...."

"And listen," said the Lava Man, "to the conscience of Noskin. It talks loud enough you'd think he could hear it, but he seldom does."

A HARSH voice called out wisps of accusations, dimmed by the uproar among the ranks of the palace crowd. "Is it right?... Is it right?... Is it right to take money...for lying about the evil deeds...of the people?"

The Dobberking was marching down the palace steps now. He had been left out of this show, and he probably intended stopping it before his conscience was revealed. But halfway down, he turned back. He caught sight of one very important messenger coming down the trail on a dead run. From somewhere overhead the rush of floods was echoing. The crowds began to break away.

"Wait!" the Lava Man cried. "You must hear the conscience of Ubolt, and the Dobberking, and above all, Irlinza."

Ubolt's guttural conscience could be heard by the ears that were tuned to the approaching flood roar. "Ubolt, you live by making trouble... Trouble, Ubolt... Gossip... Lies... Intrigues... Are you going to help Irlinza with a murder?"

Then Irlinza's shrill, distraught wail came from another skull, clamoring above the uproar of the crowd. "Listen to me, Irlinza. I am your conscience... You haven't murdered her yet... Release her!... Release her before it it's too late!"

At that, Muriel broke her terrified silence. She cried out to the palace crowd, and her accusing eyes shot at Irlinza like arrows. "That's your conscience, Irlinza. Listen to it. It's telling you not to murder Neeka—"

Her words were swallowed up in the tumult. This was unheard of, unprecedented. How did a person, bound to the stake for a sacrifice, dare to make accusations at her accused.

"It's a trick!" Irlinza screamed, white with rage. "All these skulls are cheap magic. But they won't win you your freedom. You're tied. The flood—"

The flood was coming. The last messenger, Jaff, raced down to the plaza, and bounded up the palace steps. At the sight of him, hundreds of persons had already begun to run for shelter. Now the Dobberking shouted his final announcement, bells began to ring, the whole plaza became one wide outspreading of people.

Jaff came down to Muriel, so breathless that he couldn't say a word. But he saw that she was clutching the winged ornament.

"Good-bye, Jaff." Her lips formed the words. His heart was pounding too hard for him to accept any such resignation. He flew at the ropes, tried to tear them to shreds.

"Get him away from there," Ubolt shouted. Three guards whirled to the task. Jaff was struck down. He bounded up. They were on him with knives, then, and he was forced back to the farther side of the plaza. Some messenger friend tried to reason with him. It would not do to break up the sacrifice to the Flood Gods. He must control himself, even as Muriel herself had done so admirably.

T HE first headwaters rushed through a channel on the Onyx City level. They were less than a mile away. A flood-tide coming down fast, pounding, thrashing, dashing into every nook and crevice that wasn't sealed.

The plaza had cleared. All across the slope the inhabitants of the Dobberine kingdom watched through their glass windows.

. In the sentry house three figures huddled close, tense with the excitement of the oncoming flood. Ubolt and Irlinza were laughing. The

Dobberking, having chosen this station rather than the palace, was not in a good humor. The recent voices of the skulls had struck deep. He would have plenty of music to face, from their revelations, after this flood was over. Even if he could prove that there was nothing to their words, that it was a cheap magic trick to try to save Muriel—

They opened the sentry house door to admit a fourth party—Noskin. He had changed his mind the last minute, and as they closed the door after him, the water struck against it with a terrific thud. But the sentry house was a rock to stand against any force—

Except the force of shrill vibrations emitted by singing skulls.

For within the view of the thousands of Dobberines, safe in their sealed homes, fully ten skulls had gathered around the post of sacrifice. From the movement of their jaws, one could imagine that they were singing at the tops of their voices.

Muriel, the only person left against the rising flood, heard their weird song above the pounding of waters.

Their vibrations rang against the stone, and abruptly a huge chunk of it broke away.

It fell with a rip and a roar and an echo through the hollow lower end of the question-mark ridge of stone.

The effect was two-fold. It sent the sacrifice post reeling down toward the water. It opened the lower end of the natural tunnel that formed a part of the sentry house.

Muriel caught a quick glimpse of the sentry house window—the upper bulge of the question mark. Those four faces at the window saw her falling. They saw her ropes slip loose. *But they did not see that the lower end of their own shelter had broken open.*

Therefore they did not see that the little prisoner hidden within that end of the ridge, was revealed, not only to the eyes of Neeka but also to thousands of Dobberines.

One house nearby dared to open its sealed door at that moment. Jaff came bounding out, splashing knee-deep in the first rush of waters.

"Come on, Muriel!" he cried.

Muriel looked for the skulls. All but one had now disappeared and that one was fading. But it called to her, in the familiar voice of her own conscience. "Run, Muriel. The Flood Gods have spoken!"

Already Jaff had gathered the frightened little Neeka into his arms.

In the moment the three of them were safely behind the sealed door of, the nearby house. It was their turn to look out at the wall of water that now came plunging down to engulf the whole valley.

"It's rushing into the Sentry House by the back door," Jaff said.

Little Neeka was hugging Muriel for all she was worth. "I knew you'd come all the time," she said. "One of the skulls from that funny old man's cave kept whispering to me that sometime you'd find me."

Muriel was weeping with joy.

But now the spectacle of the flood threatened to block their view. They knew that a few days of outer darkness would have to close over them before they could carry lights out into the open cavern again.

The last thing they saw, before the waters dashed over the window, was the boiling rush of the flood, striking its deadly blow at the sentry house, hurling its occupants out into roaring sea.

"Some thousands of people saw that happen," said Muriel. "I wonder what they'll think?"

"I'll bet they wonder if we can miss the sacrifice for three or four years, to make up for those four people," said Neeka innocently.

"One of those four was the Dobberking," said Jaff. "I've a hunch we'll do without the sacrifice for a long time to come.

THE LAND OF BIG BLUE APPLES

1946's The Land of Big Blue Apples *is a intentionally tongue-in-cheek science fantasy farce that permanently cemented for its author the nickname "Don 'The Madman' Wilcox". An American falls for a Martian posing as an university cheerleader and, together with his elderly uncle, joins her on a fairy tale Mars, where in an immense forest the apples grow big and blue and the people have horns for catching them as they fall. Throw in poachers from another planet, a violent case of "naggie-madness", and the immortal line "*The Earth Man is good to look at,*" *and you have a science fantasy tour-de-force from a true master of the genre.*

CHAPTER I

"TO THE most attractive drum majorette that ever twirled a baton—"
Joe Banker reached for the silver loving cup.
"—in behalf of the Chamber of Commerce of the City of Bellrap—"
His short arms swung in a full gesture toward the main street crowd.
"—I do present this token of our highest esteem. Take a bow, Miss Londeen!"
She didn't take a bow. But she smiled as only Donna Londeen could smile, and little Joe Banker thought, "What a dame, what a dame! Wait until she finds my note in the cup."
Her shapely pink hands (six-fingered hands, Joe noted for the first time) embraced the loving cup. This was the climax of the Bellrap City Festival, and the main street crowd gave with a mighty cheer. Bellrap City—where everyone knew everyone—and yet here was a stranger walking off with the honors.
Who was Donna Londeen?
The newspapers had referred to her as the niece of Uncle Jim Keller who owned a small chicken farm at the edge of town. She had been staying with Mr. and Mrs. Keller for several weeks, the papers said. But this was the first time she had been seen in public. She had been tak-

ing "twirling" lessons in private, to compete in today's drum majorette contest.

"What a dame!" Joe Banker wasn't the only young bachelor who sighed for a date with her. But he considered that his chances were better than anyone else's. He was the master of ceremonies today. He was the city clerk every day. He was handsome. He was a dynamo of energy and good nature.

Furthermore, he was, now and then, original—and that goes a long way with any girl. Who but Joe Banker would think of putting a note in the loving cup? He could hardly wait till she read it. It contained a very important question.

"She's not so tall, after all," Joe thought. He was consoling himself. He happened to be the shortest man in the male quartet that sang at Sunday night concerts and Friday night box suppers.

The shortest, the handsomest, and unquestionably the most aggressive.

Donna Londeen wasn't so tall. It was the two-foot blue fur shako she wore on her head that made her look tall. Also the high blue fur epaulets.

Whoever saw such a striking uniform, with proud epaulets built up to a height of ten or twelve inches over each shoulder?

Whoever saw such an interesting face, with such bright purple eyes and such dangerous curves of eyebrows? Dangerous curves of lips, too. And if one's eyes strayed beyond the beauty of her face, as Joe's did, there were still other dangerous curves.

"One moment. Miss Londeen, don't go 'way," Joe sang into the mike in his rich tenor, "Would you be so kind as to remove your shako?... Oh, I beg your pardon, I didn't mean to make you blush, but if you would please remove your hat—"

"I'd rather not, Mr. Banker."

WHAT an accent! Joe had listened to the soft coo of Southern girls of many and varied accents that time he had gone down to New Orleans to the Mardi Gras. But never had he heard any weird twisting of sounds to match this. He persisted:

"The judges are curious to know, Miss Londeen, whether the winner is a blonde, a brunette, or a redhead. If you'll kindly remove your shako and take a deep bow—"

She shook her head, now blushing violently.

So she wanted to play coy, thought Joe. He began to mock her. She shook her head, *no*. He shook his head, *yes*. And the crowd loved it, and cheered and shouted. "Stay with her, Joe!"

"Knock it off!"

Playfully Joe gave her high blut hat a push. Her blushing, smiling face went white with anger. As the shako toppled, it revealed her oddly colored hair. But that wasn't what amazed Joe and several hundred spectators.

She had horns!

Extending up through her thick lush hair was a pinkish white horn rooted right above her left ear. Another grew from the top of her head. And a third from the right side of her head, just above her right ear.

The unbalanced shako clung to the points of the horns. She grabbed for it, jerked it down over her forehead. She thrust the loving cup back into Joe's hands. She whirled and ran to the edge of the stage.

"Wait! Come back!" Joe started after her. "I'm sorry. Miss Londeen. Come back… Help me, someone."

She bounded off the stage, to run through the thinnest ranks of the crowd. A policeman made a pass at her.

"Carry on. Mayor," Joe shouted back at Mayor Smith. "I'll—"

He gestured with the loving cup. He had goods to deliver. He sprang from the stage to the street and ran into the crowd.

For a moment it looked as if the policeman had stopped her. (Though he later remarked, "If she wanted to run away, I guess she had a right to, and I figure it wasn't too dignified of Joe Banker to run after her that way, the darned wolf.")

The policeman seized her by the shoulder, gently but firmly. He gripped the high shoulders of the uniform, where the epaulets were built up to a height of ten or twelve inches. She tore out of his hands. The epaulets tore loose, and horns poked through—*two sharp-pointed pinkish white horns growing out of each shoulder!*

She ran like the wind. She covered a shoulder with one hand, held her high hat on with the other. She never looked back at the gaping crowd. She missed seeing the shame-faced policeman, who glared at his scratched and bleeding hands, muttering, "Darn, she's got sharp shoulders!"

She ran out of the crowd and into a drug store.

She ran back to a side door that led into a hotel lobby.

Joe whirled through the drug store entrance and called to her as she disappeared beyond. He dashed the length of the room, collided with a waiter and turned a tray of refreshments into an ice cream geyser, with the waiter underneath.

He bounded into the hotel lobby. His high-hatted quarry ducked into the adjoining telegraph office. He followed. He was gaining on her. Two more bounds and he would overtake her.

But he dropped the folded paper from the loving cup. He dodged back to recover it. The employees in the telegraph office stared at him. One of them said sarcastically, *"Mr. Banker, what is the matter with you? Lose something?"*

"Not yet," Joe snapped back. He strode out the front door, looked both ways, saw Donna Londeen jumping into a taxi half a block down the street.

There was no other taxi. At once a number of excited persons gathered around him, hounding him with questions.

"Did she get away?"

"Who on earth is she?"

"Was she a blonde or a brunette, Joe?"

"By George, I didn't *notice—that,"* said Joe. "Or did I?"

"It was purple!"

"Purple!" Joe echoed. "By George, it was, I remember."

"What are ya gonna do with the cup, Joe?"

"By George and by Joe, I'm gonna *deliver* it."

CHAPTER II

AT THE edge of town the old barn stood black against the moonlit sky. Joe could hear the voices again, old Uncle Keller's and his wife's, and then that sweet weird voice of Donna Londeen. They were helping her carry her baggage out to the barn—of all places.

"She must have a car in there," Joe thought, "or a plane."

But when they opened the doors and switched on a dim ceiling light, he saw that it was some sort of rocket ship. It was a slender, cigar-shaped craft, almost as long as the 75-foot barn. It was bright yellow, decorated with straight row of blue apples painted along the side from nose to tail. Joe slipped along the fence for a better view. What a craft!

"The blue apple rocket boat," he said to himself. "Now where could that have come from? Where on earth do they grow blue apples?"

Where *on earth?* He reflected that he should perhaps take in more territory. A space ship—a beautiful girl with six-fingered hands, purple hair, and seven pinkish-white horns growing out of her head and shoulders—what did it all add up to?

"By George and by Joe," he said breathlessly. "She's about to take off. Wherever she came from, she's heading for home, bag and baggage."

He looked up into the vast moonlit sky and wondered how it felt to leap through it in a rocket ship. What a thrill that must be.

Old Jim Keller was loading the luggage into the ship. Mrs. Keller was kissing Donna Londeen good-bye and making a sob scene out of it. Donna, magnificent in a glittering space suit and a fan-shaped head-dress that adorned her horns and flowed down over her shoulders, was talking sweetly, telling the Kellers how grateful she was for all the hospitality.

"I wish I could come back some day," she said. "But I mustn't promise. One never knows."

"You forgot something, Donna," Mrs. Keller said. "You were going to call the lady who gave you the twirling lessons and tell her good-bye."

"Do you think I dare?" said Donna. "I've heard that the parade officials have been looking for me. I wouldn't want them to find out—"

She and Mrs. Keller hurried back to the house to make the call.

Joe looked, at the sky, at the ship, at the silver loving cup in his hand. He muttered darkly to himself, "I told the boys I'd deliver this prize... Hmm."

He took a notebook from his pocket and scribbled a message:

"Mr. and Mrs. Keller. Please tell the boys at the city hall I'll be back as soon as I deliver a loving cup. I'll keep an account of my expenses and present a bill to the city when I return. I can't state in advance whether this errand will take me to Africa, the North Pole, or the Moon, but I promise to deliver. In the meantime, tell the boys to carry on.—Joe Banker."

HE SPRINTED across the potato patch to the mailbox at the corner. He wrapped the note around a rock, fastened it with a rubber band, and dropped it in the box. He sprinted back to the barn.

He heard the screen door of the house close. They would be coming back. He had no time to lose. If only Jim Keller didn't block his way... Ah, the passage seemed to be clear.

Under the dim light in the ceiling of what had once been a dairy barn, he slipped along the walk back of the stanchions. For a moment he had to set the loving cup down while he climbed over a gate. The yellow gleam of the brightly colored ship excited him. The oval-shaped door was open. He darted through the row of stanchions, over the feed rack, and into the ship.

He hesitated for a moment at the long aisle offering a narrow passage either to the right or the left. The floor was pleasantly soft to his dusty shoes, the sleek lines of red light along the ceiling a few inches above his head were a delight to his eyes.

"Who'd have thought it?" he mumbled in awe. "And all this hunk of wonderland hidden away in Jim Keller's barn—oh-oh!"

"Who's there?" Jim Keller barked.

Joe had taken five steps to the right, away from the ship's control cabin, and there stood Keller, straightening up from packing the last box, tall and skinny in his overalls and brown woolen shirt. He looked both fierce and scared, his bright little eyes blazing under brownish-red beetle brows. He dropped the rope he had been using on the boxes and gave an angry puff at his corncob pipe.

He came at Joe, snarling. His duty was plain. He must bounce this intruder before the ship took off.

"Out! Git out! *Git!*"

"Not so fast, Uncle." Joe didn't want a clash of fists, but he saw to it that his hands were free for any emergency. He had laid the silver loving cup somewhere. "I'm here on city business. I've come to deliver—"

"I know all about it. I was in the crowd when you made your speech, grinnin' like an ape every time you looked at the winner. Well, you had your chance then. But you had to git smart and knock her hat off and let everyone see she had horns."

"But I didn't know—"

"All right, git off. This boat don't need a city clerk—*nulp!*"

Uncle Keller choked off as Joe caught him over the mouth. "Pardon me, Uncle, I don't want to hurt you. But you've got to quiet down and listen to me."

For a moment Uncle Keller tried to twist out of Joe's grip. But the struggle endangered his precious corncob pipe, so he relaxed, "All right, I won't holler," he whispered. "What's your game?"

Joe, releasing him, decided to risk a confidence.

"I'm going with this ship. I don't know where it's going, but *I'm going.*"

"That's a rash thing to do, young man. Have you thought it over?… S-s-sh. Here they come back. She's all set to take off. In about twenty seconds. You'd better—"

"I'm hiding right here. And don't you say a word." Joe dived into the mass of soft packing among the light luggage. "See that you keep a straight face on the way out."

The voices were just outside the airlocks now. Donna repeated her goodbye to Mrs. Keller. She called goodbye to Mr. Keller, and was a bit puzzled that she received no answer.

"He must have gone on about his chores," said Mrs. Keller. "He hates goodbyes."

This puzzled Joe. From his hiding place he could see Uncle Keller still standing there in the aisle staring at his corncob pipe, scowling.

Donna could be heard stepping into the ship. A switch snapped, hydraulic levers swished, the airlocks were closing.

"You'd better get out, Uncle," Joe whispered. "She's closing up."

Uncle Keller looked down at him, "Move over," he said. "We're on our way to Mars."

CHAPTER III

THE shock of taking off began with a roar of rocket motors. For just a split second Joe thought, "Oh-oh, the whole town will come out to see what exploded. They'll hear that I'm off for Mars, to deliver a silver—"

WHAMMMMMMM!

When Joe Banker woke up, several hours later, he looked up into the pretty face of Donna Londeen. She was bandaging his left wrist. Her smile was disturbing.

"Think he'll live?" Uncle Keller asked between puffs on his corncob pipe.

"His eyes are open," Donna said in her sweet, weird voice. "But I think he knows not a thing. He is so dizzy."

"I know everything," Joe growled. "What's the meaning of all these bandages? Where am I?"

"In my rocket ship. You took a nasty jolt, both of you."

"Didn't bother me none," said Uncle Keller. "I'm tough. But these city clerks—"

"Don't worry about me," said Joe. He was fascinated by Donna's purple hair that cascaded over her shoulders among the horns.

"Didn't bother me none," Uncle Keller repeated. "'cept for breakin' my pipe stem. But I always carry an extra."

"You mischief boys, playing stowaway," Donna teased. "Why not tell me you want to go to my planet? I am delighted to bring home two living souvenirs."

"I'm no souvenir," said Uncle Keller. "I'm a free citizen and a Democrat."

"That'll cut a lot of ice with the Martians," Joe said sarcastically.

"Two souvenirs," Donna laughed, looking out into the blackness of space. Was she planning to sell her trophies over a bargain counter when she got home? "Two live ones—one short and one tall—"

"Who's short?" Joe Banker barked. "Just because Uncle Keller happens to be built like a bean pole—"

"One tough one," Donna continued, "and one tender—"

"Who's tender, darn it?" Joe growled. "Not me... Ouch! Easy on that wrist, lady."

The blackness of space was' everywhere outside the ship. The earth and the moon had been left far behind. The motors hummed so evenly you forgot you were moving at high speed.

Gradually the sun shifted. The bright dot of Mars, nearly straight ahead, grew larger.

THE beautiful girl with the seven horns and the purple hair spent her hours at the controls. She was studying languages, between times, and was not to be bothered.

Sometimes she gave Joe and Uncle Keller lessons in her own native tongue. It was surprisingly like English, a fact which fascinated Joe. She urged them to study from her books. They would go obediently to the observation nook at the rear of the ship and work for awhile. But soon they would fall to talking.

"What on earth are you smoking, Uncle Keller?" Joe asked, looking up from his book.

"Paper. And it don't taste healthy. But I been clean outa smokin' for two hours."

"Well, don't start burning the ship down."

"This was somethin' in your handwritin'—somethin' I found on the floor."

Joe searched his pockets. "H-m-m. I know. Darn it, you're burning up the note that I wrote to Donna asking her for a date."

"That's what it smokes like." Uncle Keller gave a sour puff.

"Well, anyway I got my date without the note. Mars—think of it! I've got a hunch she likes me. Uncle."

"Maybe so, for a souvenir."

"I fell at first sight, or did I tell you that before?"

"Fifteen times. You're goofy, Joe. When you saw her horns you shoulda chased the other way."

Joe didn't like the way Uncle Keller was throwing cold water. He got up and paced the floor, annoyed.

"Let me ask you. What did you and your missus do when she first arrived and asked to stay with you."

Uncle Keller tapped his pipe and frowned. "To be right honest, we took a fancy to her the minute we laid eyes on her. The horns was stickin' up in plain sight, but the way she had her fancy hair ornaments and veils all woven around, it sorta took your breath.

"The first thing Mom whispered was 'Goodness, ain't she perty!'"

"There you are!" said Joe.

"But fallin' in love with her—well, tell you, son, it won't work."

The space ship rocketed on through the black mysterious sky, and the two men fell silent.

Little does a guy realize, when he gets that feeling that he'd follow a gal anywhere in the world, how much travel he may be bargaining for. Or how much adventure.

Mars loomed up like a great white moon. Donna Londeen shared a meal of synthetic foods with her two passengers. Then she returned to the controls.

Keller at six of the little food cubes with great relish. Joe warned him, "Concentrated stuff, Uncle. She said each cube equals two blue apples. You've eaten twelve apples."

"Blue apples? Never heard of 'em. Maybe they're small, like plums."

"Maybe they're large," said Joe. "Cast your eyes at the plastic icebox down the aisle."

Uncle Keller's eyes widened. The icebox specimen was as large as a grapefruit. It was a soft-skinned fruit, deep blue.

"Twelve?" Uncle Keller put a hand to his midsection. "Confidentially, Joe, I've got a stomach-ache."

THEY landed on Mars in the darkness, a little before the dawn of a Martian day.

A half hour before they swooped down upon the planet's vast, shadowy surface, Donna gave a little lecture.

She was much too attractive, Joe thought. Her horns were brightly polished. Her lovely purple hair fell in waves over her bare shoulders. She wore an abbreviated sport costume that would have attracted attention on a tennis court or a bathing beach. The red and white striped flowing gauntlets that hung from her wrists matched her striped, high-heeled pumps.

"You are not souvenirs to be sold over the counter. You are free men as long as you behave yourselves. But do not tell anyone I have a space ship." She was deadly serious. "It was a gift from someone on another planet. Hardly anyone knows I have it. My people are not interested in the languages of other planets. They would not approve of space ships. That is why I land in the dark."

Joe and Uncle Keller stared at each other. They had imagined her people to be a race of planet-hopping scientists.

"Scientists? No, you will find my race of Martians rather primitive."

They sailed down into a world of dark tree tops. It looked as if the branches would reach up and scrape the hide off the ship.... Zwinnng!... Zwimingl... Zwinnng!... The counter motors had been retarding their speed for the past hour or more But these last moments were the dizziest.

Uncle Keller, still regretting his twelve-apple dinner, fell into Joe's arms.

"So you're tough, are you?" Joe muttered.

"I need a smoke," Keller replied weakly.

"If she smashes into those trees we'll all smoke."

Within two miles of the wide, silvery river, the bluff of a hill loomed. The slope was bare of trees for the space of a hundred yards. Donna landed the ship neatly. There was a grating sound.

Zwinngll… Zwinnnng… Zwuppp! It came to a stop.

Donna looked at her passengers. "How many are still alive?"

"Just one," said Joe. "Poor old Uncle just now died in my arms."

"I ain't dead," groaned Uncle Keller. "I only need a smoke."

Donna operated a lever to throw a beam of light along the crest of the hill. A wide concealed door in the sloping ground folded open. Rows of green lights revealed a deep cavern hangar.

"Don't remember anything you see, my friends," said Donna. "This is my little secret."

The ship eased into the hangar.

"There are two things worrying me," said Joe. "First, how are you going to account for your absence?"

"I shall say I was Up North," said Donna.

"What's up north?"

"In the Apple Forest Nobody knows. Nobody asks. When you say Up North, with a capital U and a capital N, that is where anyone has been when he does not wish to tell. What is your other worry?"

"How are you going to explain *us?*"

"That is not easy," said Donna. "To be safe, I must hide you… Here we are. Are you ready to step out?"

"Step out?" said Joe grinning. "I've come thousands of miles just to step out with you. But poor Uncle, I think he passed out… Didn't you. Uncle Keller?"

"I been Up North," said Uncle Keller.

They gathered up a few, things in the haste and confusion and light-headedness of arriving on a new planet. Uncle Keller took his loop of rope but shook his head when Joe offered to fill his pockets with food cubes. Joe couldn't think where he had put the silver loving cup. He decided he would come back for it later. Just now he was eager to bound outside.

CHAPTER IV

MARS!

Mars! The light gravity made Joe feel as weightless as popcorn in the popper. It was exciting to run out on the hillside and try out his new legs.

"Come this way, Joe. You and Uncle mustn't be seen."

Gray dawn was over the land. Donna led the way through the forest of black tree trunks. The sweet air was exhilarating. Joe simply had to run. He bounded like a deer over every root or log or clump of grass. When they came to a ravine, he picked Donna up in his arms and leaped across with her. He felt much too good. He'd bet he could jump over that ravine backwards.

"Just watch me!" His foot slipped on a fallen apple, and he sat down in the mud.

"Do it again," Donna laughed. "Uncle Keller did not see you."

Joe got up, rubbing his hip. "It's a thrill to set foot on Martian soil, as the saying goes.... Coming, Uncle Keller?"

"I hear animals," said Keller, pausing with a hand to his ear. "It sounded like an elephant steppin' in the mud."

"Me," said Joe.

"Naw, this was somethin' else. Hear that kerthump? There's another one... By crackies, I hear 'em from all directions."

"You are in the land of falling apples," said Donna. "They ripen and fall constantly. In Mars there is no finer food."

"Don't mention food," Uncle Keller put a hand to his stomach.

"The river bluff is just ahead. There I will hide you in a cave above the village... Are you coming, Uncle?"

Ker-thump!

Uncle Keller wasn't coming. A big blue apple had smacked him on the back of the head and knocked him down.

"What a peaceful expression," said Joe. "See his lips puff. He's dreaming he's having a smoke."

"Quick, Joe. Someone is coming. Can you carry him? We must make a run for it."

CHAPTER V

DONNA caught Joe's hand and almost jerked him off his feet. He ran back with her and gathered up Uncle Keller, who still sat on the ground, muttering at the apple that had struck him.

"Come! Hide!" Donna exclaimed. "We should not be seen here."

The three of them dodged behind a large tall tree trunk. The Martian who had sauntered into view came nearer. It was the celebrated chef, Ruffledeen. Donna knew him well.

"He prepares the finest foods in the forest," she whispered. "I wonder why he is here... Look."

Ruffledeen picked up a fallen apple and threw it toward a treetop. He repeated this act. Was he trying to hit that *orange* apple?

Each tree, as Donna had explained, had one orange apple near the top. *Orange apples were poison.* Usually they did not fall, except during wind or rain storms.

"By George, he's trying to bring down that poison one," Joe whispered.

"S-s-sh."

Ruffledeen came closer, trying for the orange apples of nearer trees. He did not know he was being observed.

He was dressed in short, puffy pantaloons and a workman's yellow jacket.

He was eight horned. (Joe realized at once that he preferred seven horns, because of Donna). He looked like a walking picket fence. Joe was impressed by his lumpy whiskers which resembled a bunch of purple grapes.

As he sauntered closer, a blue apple fell. One of his horns caught it neatly. Now Joe realized for the first time that *people who live in the land of falling apples need horns.*

He reached up and removed it, took a bite or two, and threw it away.

Then suddenly he looked in their direction and his purple eyebrows jumped at the sight of Uncle Keller, who failed to pull his neck in.

He came over, then, and it was a strained greeting. He stared at Joe and Uncle Keller. He was embarrassed, it was plain. So was Donna. She made a gesture toward her two companions. She spoke in her Martian tongue, most of which Joe understood.

"Ruffledeen, I will ask you to say nothing about my hornless friends."

"I will say nothing." Ruffledeen's eyes shifted toward a treetop and back to Donna. "You will say nothing."

HE WALKED away. Donna looked after him wonderingly. Between them a temporary bargain of silence had been sealed. Yet neither knew what the other was, up to.

"We must hurry on," she said to Joe. "At the hangar I received a message from my sister. One of my friends desires to see me at once."

"A friend with horns, I suppose," Joe said, growing warm at the temples.

"No." Donna hesitated, uncertain whether to confide. "It is my scientist friend from Venus."

"Oh, that bird from Venus!" Joe Banker was stung with jealousy. She seemed fond of mentioning him.

Along the rocky bluff was a small cave, not easily seen from the slope below. Between it and the river were the unpainted mound-shaped wooden structures that comprised the village.

"In this cave you two will be comfortable until I return," Donna said…. "You will like it here—I hope."

Then she left them, bewildered and stung, and hurried away.

A few hours later a gruesome event took place in this part of the Martian forest. A Martian girl was killed. And by a twist of fate, Joe Banker was involved. It was a cruel ordeal for a newcomer to this land.

Before it happened, Joe was beginning to like Mars. In their cave he and Uncle Keller made themselves comfortable. They first had the trouble of chasing a *naggie* out. The *naggies,* as Donna had told them, were the chief animals of this region, slow moving sheep-like beasts, as sure-footed as any mountain goats.

"Don't smell like a goat, though," Uncle Keller observed. "Don't, smell bad, in fact."

Uncle had slapped the naggie's mane and caught a handful of loose white wool. With a burst of inspiration, he, packed the wool in his pipe, lit it, and began to smoke. A peaceful smile spread over his face.

"By crackies, better'n the best tobacco I ever tasted."

Then he laid down the pipe and dashed out of the cave.

"Gotta find that goat, Joe," he called back. "Gotta lay in a supply of smokin'."

JOE laughed. Lazily he stretched out on the cave floor to watch the forest village. People were out under the trees, gathering food, working with tools, or tending children. He had brought binoculars from the ship. Whenever he saw a pretty girl he thought, "Maybe that's Donna's sister."

Everyone had horns—six, seven or more—occasionally as many as ten or twelve. Often the horns were loaded with fallen apples. People carried them with no more concern than Joe carried chewing gum in his pocket. When a person grew hungry, the food was there.

Uncle Keller came back with his overall pockets full of naggie wool. He tossed two blue apples to Joe.

"I'm still off my feed. What do they taste like?"

"Yummie! Not like apples or food cubes. They're more like a swiss steak and sweet potatoes and all the trimmings. From now on I'm on a blue apple diet."

From somewhere down the valley a long, weird scream sounded.

"Yee-eek!"

It was the terrorized voice of a girl. She was approaching the village on a dead run. A gang of boys were after her, shouting wildly.

She ran straight into the village of mound-shaped houses. The swift-footed lads were right on her heels. She dodged from one row of buildings to another. She bumped into a child as she rounded one corner. The child fell, crying, and the mother came to the open door in time to see the wild chase.

"Yee-eek!" the girl cried. She leaped over an outdoor fireplace, she hurdled a pile of dead timbers, she almost ran into two of the boys. They dived toward her, heads down, their sharp-pointed horns aimed with deadly intent. She sprang like a deer and cleared them.

Now she cut a straight course along the foot of the cliff. She passed beneath the cave, and Joe saw her wild, panicky expression. Her purple hair was streaming like flames around her horns.

Against the vertical barrier of rock, she was surrounded. Eight of the young huskies gathered in a semicircle, moved toward her slowly. They bent their heads forward, so that their horns became a trap of deadly spears, closing in.

Her back was against the wall. She looked for a chance to leap out of the circle. But the other seven youths outside, held their heads high. Whichever way she might leap, they would catch her on their horns.

They meant to kill her. Joe was convinced. He glanced toward the village. Housewives and laborers were running out to see the excitement.

"Stay out of it!" Uncle Keller warned.

"How can I?" Joe snatched up the coil of rope. "She might be Donna's sister!"

He clambered to the upper edge of the rocky cliff. He tied a slipknot in the rope as he ran. He reached a jutting stone straight above the point where the girl was trapped.

He hooked a foot under a root, leaned forward almost farther than he dared. They were right below him, about twenty-five feet down. The girl wasn't screaming, now. She was stricken silent with terror.

The gang of eight closed in, bending for the kill. Their deadly horns were within seven feet—six feet—five—and they sprang!

Joe's loop of rope fell true, over the girl's head and shoulders, to tighten around her waist.

He hoisted. His new strength against the light Martian gravity was in his favor. He drew up. She screamed like mad. Her pursuers straightened. Who was this hornless man spoiling their game?

"A demon!" they cried in Martian. "A hornless one!"

The villagers, coming on the run, shouted and swore. Did they want to see her killed?

Joe hesitated. For a moment she hung high in the air, eighteen or twenty feet above her pursuers.

Then she took her fate in her own hand. With a violent twist of her head she slashed at the rope that held her. The central horn of her head was sharp like a knife blade.

She slashed with insane fury. She severed the rope and fell.

Joe, frozen with amazement, watched her descend.

"The horns!" he gasped.

She fell on them—three sets of sharp-pointed horns on the heads of three boys. Their pink tips speared clean through her body. She hung there and her scream died away.

Then their Martian shout broke out afresh. "A demon! A hornless one!"

CHAPTER VI

"QUICK, Uncle! We've gotta get out!"

Joe's shout was superfluous. Uncle Keller had seen everything. He had already snatched the binoculars. Now he grabbed the rope that Joe was about to discard, and joined Joe in flight.

With Martian gravity to help and any number of horned Martians to inspire them, they ran six times faster than the best dash record of Bellrap, U.S.A.

They headed eastward, toward that part of the forest where they had originally landed. For several minutes they couldn't tell whether they were being pursued. They were above the long winding ledge, the Martians were below it. At every break along the way Joe expected to, see dozens of horned men surging through to the upper level.

But, happily, his, expectations were not fulfilled.

Thirty minutes later, in a deep, sheltered recess among the rocks, they stopped to catch their breath. They were not being followed, after all.

Why not?

Before they could catch their breath to talk it over they were frozen into silence by the sound of voices from somewhere beyond.

"Martian hangmen, most likely," said Uncle Keller. He was scared white. Not that he considered Joe guilty of man-slaughter in the recent ordeal. The girl had caused her own death, of course. But when people shout, "Demon!" in a strange country you don't feel like waiting around to argue your innocence.

"Hs-s-sh! There they are. By George! They're hornless!"

Joe stared. The two men dressed in tan work clothes, were lazying in the sunshine on a table rock, halfway down the cliff, near a slow-burning fire. It was plain that they knew nothing of the recent incident of the girl, and cared less. They might have been camping here for days.

One of them was lying on his back, looking up at the steamy clouds with a contented, if somewhat evil, countenance. His face reminded Joe of a rabbit. The, other, a huge tousled man with scarred hands, was leaning on one elbow, idly polishing something that looked like a Martian horn. Joe could have tossed a pebble between the two men.

"Come away," Uncle Keller whispered. "They might be Americans. Listen! They're speaking English—sort of."

"Come away. You're already up to your ears in trouble."

Joe knew that. But he couldn't help staring....

"I don't like their faces," Uncle Keller whispered.

"I don't like their accent," said Joe. "It's like nothing I ever heard before.

"And they *don't* have horns."

U NCLE KELLER was becoming acclimated to the way of the Apple Forest, Joe observed. He was already more suspicious of persons who didn't have horns than persons who did.

"I suppose you're even suspicious of us," said Joe sarcastically.

"Dern right. We're outsiders. We got no business bein' here. Much less, fallin' in love with perty girls, or messin'with savage murder parties."

A ground squirrel, skipping along the top of the ledge, caused a small pebble to drop. It struck the iron kettle on the fire. Ping!

The tousled man with the scarred hands sprang up, thrusting the horn inside his shirt, and grabbed a small black pistol from his pocket. His eyes combed the cliff.

He growled, "I thought you was keepin' watch."

"I am," said the rabbit faced one. "Put your artillery away."

Joe, watching every move, was still too much confused by his own recent scare to analyze what was going on here. But Uncle Keller, more wary than ever, saw no-good in these hornless men.

"I told you they was mischief makers," Uncle Keller whispered, "Men don't jump and grab their guns unless they're expectin' trouble."

"But they do have horns!" Joe exclaimed under his breath. *"Removable horns.* See, over there by the wall."

THERE were three sets of head and shoulder harnesses. The single horn which Scar Hands was polishing had been removed from one of these sets. From the tan color of each harness, and its head-and-shoulder-shaped contour, it was easy to guess that a set was to be worn as a deception. A hornless man thus might appear to be a native.

"Let's stick around," said Joe. "I want to see what these phonies are up to."

"Three sets of horns and only two men," said Uncle Keller. "Maybe they carry a spare."

For the next hour Joe was torn between two courses of action. He wanted to steal down the cliff for better eavesdropping. He wanted to scout back to the cave to see if Donna had returned. But neither seemed safe, Uncle Keller persuaded him to stay in his present hiding place.

Together they got one big earful. There was to be a festival soon. The people were only waiting for the popular Donna Londeen to return from some mysterious visit "Up North."

They needed her approval—and her Uncle's—before they gave the new young judge from "Up North" the authority to preside in this region.

Part of this discussion was carried on in such quiet voices that Joe couldn't hear. Then, too, there were numerous mysterious allusions. The big man would speak in the Apple Forest language part of the time. Joe could understand a part of this. He had studied it on the ship and had caught its similarities to English.

The men fell into a dispute over the laws. Donna Londeen was involved. One declared that she could be required to choose a husband at the Festival. The other said she couldn't. They finally agreed that it depended on whether her uncle, Londeenoko, ran the festival or someone else.

"Anyway," said Rabbit Face, "She will choose, this time. The people are gonna force her into it. She's been runnin' off to other lands and they're afraid they'll lose her."

"I look for a fight if she does choose," said Scar Hands. "These Horn Folks ain't gonna like her choice."

That remark shot through Joe like ice.

Hours later, with a new daylight dawning over the Apple Forest, Joe was n deep turmoil.

He and Uncle Keller had slipped back to their cave above the village, and he had slept—but feverishly.

"I'm in a devil of a stew," he admitted. "I follow a girl through thousands of miles of space. Then she hides me here and walks off and forgets me. And now—"

"Now you're actin' like a chicken with its head off."

"Now I hear that she's got to choose a husband, and I know darned well who it will be."

"Who?"

"That Venus scientist she's always talking about."

"How do you know?"

"From what those yeggs said yesterday. They said the people aren't going to like her choice. That means she's going to choose someone without horns. That must mean him."

"Too bad," said Uncle Keller. She ought to choose someone with horns."

Joe whirled angrily. "But I don't have horns."

"You figure she oughta choose you?"

"I didn't come to Mars for the joyride."

"Hmm." Uncle Keller puffed at his wool-filled pipe. "If you married her, what do you figure your children would look like?"

"Do you have to bring that up?" Joe snarled.

"Can't you just see those youngsters of yours goin' to school an' knockin' the other kids down with their horns and scarin' the teacher into the corner?"

"Shut up."

"An' when they git into high school they could play football. They'd be perty good at that—if they didn't ram into the goal post."

"Stop it!" Joe shouted.

"All right, you get sensible," said Uncle Keller. "You and she are two different breeds of humans, an' if you start mixin' up its gonna get complicated."

Joe slept some more, and dreamt. When he awoke, Donna Londeen stood before him.

CHAPTER VII

"**H**ELLO, Mr. Earth Man," said Donna, smiling. Her face was radiant, catching the pink sunlight. The flowing silky gauntlets rustled at her wrists as she reached her hand out to him. But he didn't notice.

"Am I dreaming?" he said, coming slowly to his feet.

"You were sleeping very soundly," said Donna. "I hated to disturb you, but I have only a few minutes to talk to you."

He was conscious that his hair was tousled and his clothes were unpressed from being slept in. Hotel accommodations in this cave were nothing to brag about. Here was his chance to complain to the management.

"You don't by any chance have a cave with hot and cold running water, and a mattress, do you?"

At a small pool of water among the rocks near the cave entrance, he washed. She watched him as he combed his blonde hair.

"The Earth Man is good to look at," she said. "Does he ever smile?... What is the matter, Joe?"

Again she offered her hand to him. This time he took it, and, they walked back to the cave together.

"Where did Uncle Keller go?" he asked.

"Out to get more naggie wool for his pipe. He is such a funny creature. When I lived at his house on the Earth, he and his wife were very friendly to me. They were the first Earth people I ever knew and they taught me so much. I will always like Earth people when I think of them."

They sat down together. Joe avoided her smiling eyes.

"I didn't think you liked Earth people," he said. "I thought you preferred Venus people."

"You are in a very strange mood," said Donna. "Is it because your cave does not have a barber shop and a swimming pool? After I have gone you may walk to the river and have a swim. Then you will feel better."

"I don't dare. I can't cross the village without being seen."

"Today there is no one in the village," said Donna. "Everyone has gone to the Festival, three miles down the river."

"Festival!" Joe perked up. "That's my chance to present the cup—oh-oh!" He stopped, crestfallen. The Festival of the Horn Folk! That would be the occasion those two yeggs were talking about, where Donna would be forced to choose her husband.

"What is the matter, Joe?" She placed a hand on his shoulder.

He turned toward her, clutched her bare shoulders with a savage impulse that he thought was jealousy. He wanted to crush her. Then he was kissing her; and for a long moment his head swam with the pleasure of knowing her lips, of finding their answer to his own. She did not draw away from him, and when he looked into her eyes, her pretty face was serious.

"I'm crazy about you, Donna," he whispered tensely. "I've been half mad about you since the first time I saw you. You must have known. That's why I couldn't let you get away from me. That's why I came here... Say something, Donna. Don't just stare at me that way."

HE WAS holding her close. As if in answer to his words, she bowed her head slowly against his chest. The three horns of her head brushed gently across his face. She bowed deeper until the sharp points stroked under his chin, to press against his throat.

Was that her answer to his feverish declaration of love?

She moved away from him slowly. She rose to stand like a goddess, her majestic head high, her firm breasts outlined within the close fitting stripes of her brief costume.

"After the Festival is over," she said softly, "I may be able to take you and Uncle Keller back to your homes. I cannot promise now. It depends."

It depends! Joe breathed hard. So she did not know whom she would marry! Or did she mean that she and her future husband were undecided whether to go to the Earth on their honeymoon?

"I assume," she added, "that you *will* want to go back soon?"

He looked at her sharply. Had she already heard of his ill-fated effort to rescue the screaming girl?

She took her leave again, to hurry away to the Festival. He called to Uncle Keller. This time they would not stay and wait. They would follow!

The festival grounds were under tall trees, well spaced, with trimmed trunks. The wide arm of branches formed a high ceiling of lush green foliage.

Joe and Uncle Keller followed a winding ravine to avoid the crowds.

"I never figured you'd dare walk this close to danger," said Uncle Keller. "What did she say when you told her about the girl and the rope?"

"I never told her," Joe admitted. "It's something I want to forget. Do you think it'll fly back in my face the first time I meet someone?"

"I think Donna would have warned you to skip the country."

"That's what I was afraid of," said Joe. "And I don't want to miss the Festival. Especially if she *chooses.*"

"Ugh. I hope you ain't got any ideas."

"I just want to see what the bird looks like that can walk off with her."

T HE very young boys with half developed horns were chasing around an arena, warming up for this game. Through a thicket Joe and Uncle Keller could see the whole arena.

The judge was there, on an elevated platform built between tree trunks. He and Londeenoko stood glaring at each other, snarling.

The judge had come to run the festival, and Londeenoko challenged his right to do it.

Their quarrel drew a crowd. Everyone in Donna's village knew that

Londeenoko, a thick, crusty sharp mustached old gentleman with seven reddish horns, was bombastic enough to knock the young judge off the stage if he didn't like the way things went.

But the young judge was a stubborn number. He had the greater advantage. The office of judge carried great esteem.

Mobar wore the customary green face paint and a bold-striped judge's robe. His judgely dignity and charm captivated many. Although he was a newcomer among their people, having come from "Up North," he seemed well on his way to being accepted as their new leader.

The former judge had been Donna's late father. His administration of justice had won great popularity. Now his surviving brother, Londeenoko, was reluctant to accept this young upstart, Mobar, as a worthy successor.

"Give him a chance," people kept shouting from the crowd.

Londeenoko was at last forced to bow to pressure. He was the father of nineteen children, the grandfather of an uncounted number of grandchildren. This tribe knew how to band together against the crusty old man's will. It had become their habit to consider, as a matter of course, that he was in the wrong whenever he got into an argument.

"I concede the power to Mobar," Londeenoko called out at last. "Never before have we accepted a judge from Up North. But I refuse to be accused of being so prejudiced in favor of my brother that I cannot accept another judge. Let us give Mobar a chance."

The crowd cheered with a weird, half laughing, "Yo-yo-yo-yo!"

Then the two men on the elevated platform gave the sign of friendship. Each in turn bowed to the other, touching his sharp horns against the other's chest *gently,* thus proving that all feeling of malice were set aside.

It was Mobar's turn to speak. Joe, watching from his hiding place, could not read the young judge's expression. The squares of green paint over that dignitary's face were a part of his official protection.

"I wish to honor the brother of the late judge." With his robed arm he made a gracious gesture toward Londeenoko. "I hereby appoint him my assistant, and ask him to take over the active management of this Festival."

I T WAS a clever stroke, almost sly in its psychological effect. Londeenoko took a deep proud breath and held his head high. His tribal relatives who had just thrown him overboard in favor of this newcomer could see, now, that he was still a big and important man. He would remain on the stage to run the Festival.

"If at any time you need any assistance in making decisions," the young judge added in his precise Martian tongue, "my judgment is at your service."

This took a little wind out of Londeenoko's sails. But he gave a gruff laugh to treat it as a joke.

Then a messenger arrived with a call for the judge to come elsewhere. The judge frowned as the message was whispered to him. He bowed to the crowd and excused himself.

"I shall leave you temporarily," he said. "A matter beyond the next village requires my attention."

Joe, watching everything through the thicket, went tense. "Did you hear that, Uncle?"

"I heard, but I didn't get it. What's up?"

"I'm not dead certain, but I think they're on our trail."

"On account of that girl you didn't rescue," Uncle Keller grunted. "I dunno what we've got ourselves into, but I figure that act of kindness is gonna cost us."

Donna had joined the crowd, and wherever she went people greeted her and told her they had missed her. They wished her father could still be here, running the show as he used to do. And some of them would say, "I am sure you will make your choice this season."

"Do not be too sure," Donna would answer.

"Oh, but you must. The young men are impatient to know who it will be. Have you decided?"

"Wait and see."

"It will be some handsome man with ten or twelve horns, let us hope."

"Wait and see." Then smiling with embarrassment, she would hurry away from them.

Once Joe heard someone ask her if it might not be the new judge. She seemed a bit startled.

"I do not believe he would enter the contest," she said.

"And if he does?"

"Please do not ask me to think of any other judge except my own father," she said. "Come, let us watch the games."

There were all kinds of contests involving apple-throwing and naggie-chasing. The small boys fought with their horns, and two clowns, who were really officials, interceded whenever there was a danger of an injury. These clowns wore false faces representing naggies.

Between the games they kept the crowd laughing. One of them turned a flip-flop and landed on his head, or rather, his horns—so that he stuck in the ground. He kicked like an animal in a trap. The other clown ran circles around shouting for the crowd to come and help. Then with a nimble handspring the stranded clown whirled to his feet.

Before the feast, the young men chose partners. For this event the girls gathered in the center of the arena, and their heroes took turns throwing apples at the group. A tall handsome ten-horned man wound up like a baseball pitcher. When he let fly with the blue apple, several of the girls bent forward to try to catch it on their horns. He had lots of girl friends.

The bashful boy could hardly be persuaded to take his turn. He tried deliberately to miss the whole group. But when the apple fell on the horns of the most beautiful girl, he flushed with pleasure as the spectators cheered.

IT WAS during the feast that the exciting announcement was called out by Londeenoko.

"The big event will take place immediately after the feast. Ten young ladies will enter the choosing ceremony."

Joe and Uncle Keller could see the many faces that turned to Donna. Everyone wondered whether she would be one of the ten. Soon they guessed the answer. Her pretty little sister carried a message to Londeenoko, and when he looked across to her and smiled, everyone knew that he had won his point. Donna would enter the choosing ceremony.

"I'll see you later," Joe whispered as he ducked away.

"Where you goin'?"

Uncle Keller got no reply. Joe was off on another foot-race—a race against time.

He followed the curve of the river. That was the trail he knew. He took no chance of being seen by anyone who might have remained in the village. If only he could find one of those two men with the artificial horns—Rabbit Face or Scar Hands!

Breathless, he drew up at the hiding place where he and Uncle Keller had listened to the two hornless plotters. Neither of the men was to be seen now. But someone else was there—someone he had not seen before. Luck was with him. This stranger wore a harness over his head and shoulders—an eight-horned harness. So here was the *third* member of the gang who were passing themselves off as native Martians.

The man was hastily dressing in a naggie wool suit. The jersey fitted tightly around his neck, hiding the harness that held the horns. Joe had no time to wonder who this man was or what he was planning. Ten swift bounds brought Joe to the ledge overhanging the shelf on which the man was working. For a moment Joe waited, the loop of rope ready. If the fellow would just step this way a trifle—there!

The rope fell true—over the arms and down to the ankles. Joe yanked up on it like a fisherman with the biggest catch of his life. The fellow whirled off his feet, strung up by the noose.

It was but the work of a moment to secure the rope to a small tree, and the captive was left dangling a few feet above the shelf.

"Gollies, he's the best inter-planetary cusser I ever heard," Joe thought. He raced down over the rocks to the shelf. He worked under the handicap of flying fists, and a broadcast of profanity. It was a supreme achievement for Joe to hold his own tongue during this operation, but he didn't want this mystery man to know that he spoke English.

"My friends will tie a stone to you and throw you in the river," the fellow threatened.

He must have repeated the threat in several languages, Joe guessed. His snarling voice still echoed in Joe's ears two minutes later as Joe raced away. But the friends had not appeared, and the fellow was left hanging by his feet.

Most important of all, Joe now wore a handsome set of horns.

"By George and by Joe, I'm a native Martian," he said to himself;

CHAPTER VIII

SEVEN candidates for the hand of the beautiful Donna Londeen stood in line under a tall and graceful blue apple tree and one of them was Joe Banker, the city clerk of Bellrap, U.S.A.

Two of the candidates were broad-shouldered twelve-horned men—husky young giants with three horns on each shoulder and six over their heads.

The tallest of all the candidates was a dark-skinned boyish fellow with eleven horns. He wore a yellow jersey and long naggie-wool trousers. Beside him Joe must have looked very short. But Joe chose to stand next to him, heedless of the jibes, for a very, definite reason. Joe, too, was wearing a jersey.

A close-fitting jersey with a high neck had been necessary as a covering for the harness over any deceiver's head and shoulders. It was well enough for Martians who grew their own horns to strut around with naked chests and shoulders. But if one is obliged to conceal straps across the chest and under the armpits, a borrowed naggie-wool jersey is a convenience.

Even so, Joe knew that he was in great danger of being discovered. The tall fellow looked down on his head. And while the band which curved over his skull had been camouflaged with patches of hair between horns, that hair did not match his own. It matched the black hair of the man who had been left dangling by his feet from a rope.

"What is the delay?" one of the candidates asked. "Where are the officials?"

"They were called to the ravine by someone who saw a demon," said the tall eleven-horned fellow.

"A demon?" Joe gulped. "What kind of demon?"

"A hornless one," said Axloff, the tall boyish fellow. "He may be the one who participated in the recent killing of a 'naggie' girl."

Joe swallowed hard. What did this mean? Had they caught Uncle Keller? Surely he would never stick his neck out of yonder thicket to be seen.

"He was a hornless demon who blows smoke," Axloff continued. "They discovered him in the thicket setting fire to a tube in his mouth!"

"The corncob pipe!"

"Joe blurted the words in English before he could catch himself. Axloff looked at him strangely. "What did you say?"

The chills raced through Joe's spine. His first impulse was to break and run.

"Stay in line, my friend," Axloff snapped at him.

But a moment later the word passed around that the demon with the fire in his mouth had been struck to the ground by the powerful Londeenoko.

"They've beaten Uncle Keller!" Joe thought. "They've struck him. And where was I? Out chasing down a pair of horns so I can compete for Donna—when anyone knows that I haven't a chance. I'm a heel!"

He started to edge away from the line of candidates.

Axloff caught him by the arm. "Come back in line, my friend."

"I'll come back soon," said Joe. He tried to pull away from the tall fellow.

"Stand where you are—unless you want to deal the cruelest insult to Donna."

"What do you mean?" Joe asked.

"Have you forgotten the code of the choosing ceremony? We men walk forth in this arena—Why? Because we hope to win this girl. Here we stand in a line. If one of us should change his mind and walk away, to her it is a slap to be remembered for life."

JOE stood tense, looking up at Axloff.

These words of counsel were sound. He was angry at himself for what he had almost done. He would stand fast. For now he realized how much Donna meant to him. For the present Uncle Keller would have to fight his own battle.

Then the further report came. To some extent it subdued his wrought-up feelings.

"The beautiful Donna interceded for the demon," came the news, to be relayed from mouth to mouth through the throngs. "She asked Londeenoko to have him imprisoned in the dry well. After the Festival is over, they will call him to account."

"On with the Festival!" the crowd began to clamor. "On with the Festival!"

The seven candidates were made to parade twice around the arena. They were fair game for the spectators, who cheered for their favorites and shouted all manner of insults at the others.

"Who is that little, short one in the naggie-wool garments?" they would yell. "He must have grown up on orange-colored apples. Where did he come from?"

On the second march around the crowd, Joe became the target for so many jibes that he wondered whether they guessed he was an imposter. A general yell had spread along the line, particularly among the younger boys.

"Where did little eight-horns come from?"

The tall angular eleven-horned candidate, Axloff, stopped to glare at some of these hecklers. He shouted back an answer in defense of Joe.

"Little eight-horns came from Up North. Any complaints?"

He bent his head forward so that his eleven horns pointed straight toward the loudest of them.

The effect was gratifying. Joe heard no more heckling.

"Thank you, Axloff," Joe said in Martian. "If Donna should not choose me, I hope she will choose you."

"She could do worse," said Axloff. His remark earned a series of stony glares from the others. Especially from the two husky twelve-horns. They had frowned on any signs of fraternizing within this line of rivals.

Donna walked slowly to the center of the arena. She was the tenth and last of the girls to choose a husband today. Joe wondered how many of his six companions were left over from the previous events, and how many had waited for this particular choosing.

Above all, Joe wondered what had become of the hornless Venus scientist. Was he here, among these seven? Not unless he, too, was wearing artificial horns. Could it be that this tall, boyish Axloff was the Venus man? Hardly. His horns were too convincing. His diction, too, was precise Martian.

THE sound of the weird musical notes from wooden pipe's—the official signal for each event—beautiful Donna Londeen walked slowly toward the candidates. You could hear the low whispering of the spectators. They watched every move as she extended her greeting of friendship to each of seven men.

She bowed to each, barely touching the horns of her head to their chests. When she came to Joe, the last in line, she gave a surprised gasp.

"You? But how—?"

She glanced quickly at the barely perceptible outlines of the harness that curved over his head. She suppressed a smile as her sharp eyes caught the patchwork effect of his hair.

"Thank you for coming," she whispered. "But you must not be disappointed...if...when...but, thank you."

There was no time to clarify her message. No time for him to ask about Uncle Keller. The other six candidates were waiting impatiently for her to address them. The two husky twelve-horns exchanged suspicious nudges.

She stood before the seven of them, extending her six-fingered hands in a gracious gesture of appreciation. Her eyes avoided Joe as she spoke:

"My very great thanks to each of you for engaging in this contest. I shall become the wife of the one among you who wins. I wish to each of you good luck."

She started away. She glanced back, as if uncertain whether everyone was there that she had expected. She crossed the arena to the elevated platform.

"The Venus man!" Joe thought. "I'll bet a thousand dollars I left him hanging, head down, from the cliff. If she knew, she would never forgive me."

In that moment Joe felt the arrows of conscience as never before. This was dead wrong, for him to steal his way into the ranks. If her heart had gone to someone else, what business did he have to be here? Her whole life depended upon the choice of this hour.

"Do not stand there dreaming," Axloff called back at him. "March with us."

Joe marched as if in a trance. Never in his life had he felt such an emotion of deliberate guilt. He looked at Donna, standing there on the high platform beside her Uncle. He tried to guess her thoughts.

"I've got to take these horns back!" he said to himself. "I've got to let that Venus guy have his chance."

That was all he could think about for the next several minutes.

HE FOLLOWED the line of candidates through a routine of difficult feats. At Donna's order he took his turn at lifting weights, leaping over hurdles, turning handsprings and hornsprings. The harness on his head and shoulders held firm! Apparently no one suspected his horns were not his own.

Through one contest after another he held his own. But his thoughts were elsewhere. All the time he kept asking himself questions.

Could he be sure that the hanging man *was* the Venus scientist? What other hornless persons might there be in this land besides Uncle Keller and himself? And the mysterious rabbit-faced man and the man with the scarred hands? And the man hanging over the cliff, who may or may not have been their friend?

Donna had not told much of her escapades to other planets. Now, as Joe recalled her chance remarks, he could bring to mind only two acquaintances of hers from lands beyond Mars.

One of these was the Martian scientist, who had first interested her in other worlds and had made her a gift of his space ship while he carried on his research and experiments here on Mars. He was the one she mentioned most often.

The other was an adventurer of Mercury, who had taken a fancy to her while she was there, and had once followed her all the way back to Mars in his own ship. She had barely mentioned him. Joe did not know whether he was here now, or on Mercury.

Both of these men were, according to his impressions, hornless human creatures more or less related to Earth man—for this breed had undoubtedly found its way around the planets at some time in the historical past.

Casually, Donna had mentioned three or four different Martian friends, favorites of her uncle, Londeenoko. Two of these, Joe guessed, were the twelve-horned men now leading the line of contestants in a tightly fought apple throwing contest.

"Your turn, Axloff," one of them said. "Beat my record if you can."

Axloff weighed three apples in his hand. He was allowed three trials. The platform was about thirty yards away, and there Donna stood, waiting, her head bent forward. Her horns were the target.

Three apples now hung on her shoulder horns. None of the contestants had succeeded in hanging one on her head horns. The center horn carried the highest score.

AXLOFF hurled an apple. It missed. The twelve-horns gave a low laugh. Axloff wound up for his second trial and let fly.

The apple caught squarely on the left horn of her head. The crowd cheered. Axloff's third and last trial! The apple flew to the right horn of her head and barely hung there. The crowd went wild. The twelve-horned men muttered sarcasms as Axloff retired to the line.

"Your turn, little Eight Horn," said Axloff. "Good luck."

Joe winked and clicked his tongue. He had been the pitcher for the South Side Wildcats in his day. He stepped up, weighed three big blue apples in his hand, rolled two of them to the ground, and whammed out with the third.

It was straight and fast, but high. Donna waited, motionless. It sailed over the point of the middle horn, barely grazing it. Donna's purple hair waved with the wind. Her head moved a trifle, and the last apple that Axloff had hung on her head fell off and bounced from the platform in two halves.

Crusty old Londeenoko's eyebrows jumped. He was agitated over the way these contests were going. He had already shown a definite preference for one of the twelve-horned huskies.

He marched across to her from the farther side of the platform, lifted his heavy hand and barked a sharp warning.

"But I did not mean to move, Uncle," Donna replied.

"Do not let it happen again," he growled.

Donna stood motionless, her head bowed, waiting. Joe's second shot came, as straight as an arrow. It struck the central horn squarely. It hung to the crest of her head as if it had grown there.

The crowd burst into a panic of cheering, and Joe caught an enthusiastic slap on his back. Axloff's.

"You will win on that one, friend! Throw away your third shot!"

But old Londeenoko didn't like it. Again he came thudding across the platform, his sashes fluttering. No one could hear the warning he called to Donna. But a moment later everyone heard him bellow like a wounded bull. Joe's third apple went wild and caught him in the solar plexus.

CHAPTER IX

EVERYONE thought that "Little Eight-Horn from Up North" had won.

But Londeenoko had other ideas. He waved his arms for silence. In a thunderous voice he proclaimed, "Foul! Foul!"

Arguments ensued among officials and spectators. Londeenoko's nineteen sons and daughters and their numerous children protested that grandpa was playing favorites. The young judge, they declared, would have to come back and settle the arguments. Someone was dispatched to find him.

Others, including Axloff, declared that the rules provided for emergencies such as these. It would be necessary only to devise additional contests of skill or daring to determine which of the leading contenders should win.

"The *leading* contenders!" one of the twelve-horns echoed sarcastically. "I suppose that lets us out."

And while the quarrels mounted in fury, Joe slipped away unnoticed, to do what he thought was the only honest thing to do: Give the Venus scientist a chance to take his place.

It was a hard, exhausting run, coming on top of all the strenuous games. Steaming with perspiration, Joe clambered up the trail he had previously followed along the top of the cliff. Before he reached the village he saw three men coming in his direction along the trail below.

Of the three, only one was obviously hornless. But on closer approach, Joe knew that none of these men possessed horns of his own. The three were the non-Martians that Joe had come to know as Rabbit Face, Scar Hands, and "Black Hair."

It was Black Hair whom Joe had left hanging. It was Black Hair's head and shoulder harness that now supplied Joe with his eight horns. It was those black patches of hair now adorning his own blonde head between horns that had worried him all through the contests.

Joe stopped, breathing hard, waiting for them to come within earshot. He grew feverish at the thought of what he was about to do. It was a bitter pill—to concede that this black-haired man whose horns he wore, must be the Venus scientist in love with Donna. It was doubly bitter because Rabbit Face and Scar Hands were his companions.

"Three tough yeggs," Joe thought. "I wish I wasn't so darned honest."

But the flash of disappointment which he thought he had once seen in Donna's face when she surveyed the seven candidates drove him to go through with his plan.

"Hi, down there," he yelled over the cliff to the path below.

THE three men stopped abruptly and looked up.

"There is the man!" Black Hair exclaimed. "Those are my horns.

That is my garment."

"I want to explain—" Joe's speech was out-shouted by a bellow from Rabbit Face, who started climbing up the face of the cliff like a sure-footed naggie.

"Thief! Come here! You are ours now!"

"Wait. Don't be sore. Let me explain," Joe yelled. "I made a mistake. I'm sorry."

"Sorry?" Black Hair echoed with a sneer. "Off with those horns before my men thrash you!"

"Don't rush me!" Joe warned savagely. "I'll make everything right if you'll listen. Don't rush me!"

His warning failed to impress Rabbit Face, who bounded up over the elevation like a hound after a rabbit. He came straight at Joe—in time to catch a flying fist, *kerpop*, on the left jaw. He staggered and almost fell over the cliff. Joe caught him by his hair and harness and jerked him back.

"I told you not to rush me." He walked the wobbly rabbit-faced man to a niche where erosion had formed a natural slide of loose earth. There Joe allowed him to roll down to his less ambitious companions. Joe, dusting his hands, repeated, "Sorry, gentlemen, but if you'll let me explain—"

Scar Hands helped Rabbit Face to his feet while their black-haired leader said, "All right. Let us hear what a thief can explain. Talk fast."

"I know who you are, now," said. Joe. "I didn't realize when I roped you that you were the Venus scientist. I apologize."

"Huh?" said Black Hair. His two companions gave a questioning look. One of them nudged Black Hair and said, "How did he find out, boss, that you are the Venus scientist?"

Joe sensed their impatience to know what he meant to do about it. He continued.

"As soon as I saw my mistake, I realized that you're the one Donna really loves. She isn't interested in any of the rest of us. *You* should have been in the choosing ceremony instead of me."

Black Hair nodded with a savage sidewise movement of his head. "I agree with you there—Yes, I agree. But—"

"All right, you still have a chance," Joe said. "I'm about to win the contest. I've brought your horns back so you can take my place. It isn't too late. Think what it means to Donna.

J OE started to unstrap the harness.

But curiosity caused him to hesitate. The three men went into a pow-wow of whispers. Joe waited. He sat on a stone at the cliff's edge, looking down on them. Something was in the air. Was it possible that Black Hair didn't want to compete for Donna's hand?

Black Hair looked up and spoke deliberately. "An exceedingly noble gesture, my good man. What is your name?"

"Joe Banker."

"Where are you from?"

"Bellrap, U.S.A., the Earth. I'm the Bellrap City Clerk."

"Hm-m. Inter-planetary exploiters are becoming quite thick around here. Much too thick! Are you in love with Donna Londeen?"

"To put it mildly, I'm nuts about her."

"Do you think the two of you are well matched?"

"Perfectly," said Joe. What was he driving at? Was he going to be noble and magnanimous too? "Perfectly—Except—"

"Except for the horns?"

"Yes," said Joe. "If it wasn't for her horns—"

"I have a suggestion, young man. You have recognized me as the scientist from Venus. Let me suggest that a few experiments might prove that these forest folk would be as healthy and happy *without horns*. Have you considered the possibilities of an experiment?"

Joe was all ears. Might there be some simple way out of his difficulty?

"If you are winning the contests," said Black Hair, "the judge and the elders are sure to listen to you. Gather four or five of them together and propose a dehorning experiment."

"Dehorning?" The suggestion struck chills through Joe. It sounded inhumane, somehow. And still, coming from a scientist—

"Dehorn only twenty or thirty at the start," Black Hair continued. "Wait until you see the effects before you decide how and when to dehorn Donna. The judge and the elders will listen to you."

Joe considered. If he could go back and win the final events, would Londeenoko give him a break in the interests of science? As a newcomer to Mars it was impossible to know whether this venture might catch on. But it sounded worth a try.

"This means," said Joe, "that you're willing for me to keep this set of horns until I've put myself across?

The three men held another brief whispered pow-wow. Then, "All right, Mr. Banker, return them later. We will see that you do. But be sure to sell the dehorning idea. It was your own idea, you know."

"Mine? Did I think of that myself?"

"A very brilliant idea, Mr. Banker. Congratulations."

All the way back to the arena Joe kept relating this conversation to himself, trying to remember just when and how he had originated the de-horning scheme. If he, should succeed in putting it over with, a bang—if he should start a new fashion in Apple Forest—wouldn't that be one to tell the boys back at Bellrap!

He arrived at the arena just as Donna's candidates were being called together for the announcement of-another event.

CHAPTER X

T HIS would be a human whirligig, to be operated by *horn-power*.

"Fortunately we have a prisoner who will serve as the victim for this event," Londeenoko explained. "The competition will be open to the four of you with the highest scores."

"Correction, my dear uncle," said Donna. "The rules say only the two highest shall compete in these additional events."

After another savage argument with his relatives, Londeenoko was forced to bow to the established tradition, though it hurt him to have to leave the two twelve-horned huskies out of the game. They and the other three competitors were now through. The decision lay between Axloff and Joe.

"This game is cruel," Donna said aside to Joe. "There were other alternatives, but Uncle Londeenoko and the officials insisted that a certain prisoner should be punished, the sooner the better. Do you understand what this implies, Joe?"

Not knowing what the human whirligig consisted of, Joe was in the dark. But he had his guess as to who the victim might be.

While the mechanics prepared the whirling beams on a horizontal shaft between two trees, the crowd recessed for an hour of feasting. The multitude of horns had collected a multitude of falling apples. For those who preferred more expensive delicacies, Ruffledeen's finest pies and tarts were sold. A corps of boys passed through the crowd with trays, tempting the buyers with the magic name of Ruffledeen.

During this repast, Joe found himself surrounded by three or four elderly men of affairs. Londeenoko himself paid Joe the respect of looking in on this group. A little later the young judge arrived to rejoin the crowd, impressive in his freshly painted green face and stuffy costume.

This was Joe's chance to spring his big idea, to sound out these gentlemen on the subject of dehorning.

"Gentlemen, if a candidate from Up North may be privileged to propose a plan *in the interests of science*—"

Joe paused, trying to read the expressions of the four or five faces around him. The word *science,* had not brought the warm response he had hoped for.

"—I suggest that it would be useful to know what would happen to a growing child—or an adult—*if his horns were to be removed."*

Cold silence. Everyone was eyeing him. No one responded. He went on:

"A few boys and girls could be dehorned, to begin with. Different methods might be tried. If the experiment has no ill effects, it might become an established practice."

More silence. Glances exchanged. The young judge spoke one sharp word.

"Why?"

Joe gulped. Why should horns be removed? When you came right down to it, his only reason was that in case a hornless man wanted to marry a horned girl—

But he didn't dare say this. Already these men were scrutinizing him with suspicious scowls. Somehow the argument didn't sound half as good as before.

"Why?" the young judge repeated sternly. "Why should anyone want to lose his proudest possession?"

Joe floundered. "Well—I only thought—that is, in the interests of *science—"*

T HE weird musical notes of the wooden signal tubes sounded, to Joe's immense relief. He backed away from the staring group and hurried along to the elevated platform.

Sure enough. Uncle Keller was there.

Poor Uncle Keller! What would the folks back in Bellrap say if they saw him now? Even his pigs and chickens would hardly recognize him. That prison well must have been full of dried apple dust. His overalls were bluer than ever, and his face and hands were smeared with what might have been blue chalk dust.

If the blue dust had been inflammable, Uncle Keller would have blown up. For again there was a fire burning in the "tube in his mouth."

Indeed, this cob pipe was such an attraction to boys and girls and even grown-ups that the famous chef, Ruffledeen, seemed to be looking on with envy. Londeenoko was nettled to find himself distracted from the impending event. Those gentle puffs! Those swirling rings of smoke! That fragrance of burning naggie wool.

"I'm outa smokin' again," Uncle Keller said, chiefly for Donna's benefit, for he didn't attempt to speak much Martian. "Down in the well

I kept wishin' a naggie would fall in, to keep me company and fill my pipe."

"What are you smoking now?" Donna asked.

"A bit of naggie wool garment I chopped out of the judge's robe when he wasn't lookin'. When he turns around you'll see.... Say, whaddya reckon they're gonna do with me?"

Before answering, Donna glanced at Joe, who was stationed nearby. She put a hand on Uncle Keller's shoulder. The officials and spectators around her were growing angry. What was she saying to this culprit—this spy—this demon who blew fire?

"They will hurt you, Uncle," she said. "There is nothing I can do until the choosing contest is finished. I have already antagonized my uncle Londeenoko. I dare not say any more until I know which man will be my husband."

Uncle Keller's beady little eyes shone fiercely. He looked from Joe to the tall, eleven-horned boyish Axloff.

"You mean it's gonna be one of those two?"

"Yes, Uncle."

"Then can't we fix it so you'll get the tall handsome guy with the horns?"

"He is wonderfully nice," said Donna, "but it is Joe that I love. I have loved him since the day he chased me with the silver loving cup."

Uncle Keller suffered a wobbling of the Adam's apple and his voice sounded strangely sentimental. "Well, then, if it's Joe Banker you love, let's fix it—"

"Poor Uncle!" Donna patted his dusty cheek. "Do you not realize that my fate must now be decided by a *contest of brutality?* Whichever one succeeds in hurting you worse will win me."

Uncle Keller's lips tightened. "Then, by crackies, you see to it that young Joe gives me hell!"

W HEN the second signal notes sounded, Uncle Keller was tied to the end of the sixteen-foot whirligig. It was a crude one-man Ferris wheel without seats—a pair of parallel beams fixed to turn on a horizontal axis between tree trunks. Uncle Keller's hands and feet were tied to the cross-bar between one end of the beams, a short log was attached to the other end as a crude balancing arrangement.

Uncle Keller was a little heavier than the weight at the other end. Thus, when the whirligig was at rest, he hung straight down. His long bent body, tied up by wrists and ankles, hung limply at a height of seven or eight feet above the ground.

One of the officials took a running jump and struck Uncle Keller with his horns. This caused the whirligig to start spinning, and the lone passenger began a series of most uncomfortable Ferris-wheel whirls.

"Pick up my pipe!" he yelled as he raced through the air.

But an official, no respecter of pipes, kicked it off the grounds. That was only the beginning of Uncle Keller's tortures.

"The two candidates will be judged by the energy with which they punish this hornless foreigner," Londeenoko called out to the crowd. Then, evidently realizing that a justification for such cruelty was needed, he added, "Let me remind you that this foreign demon was caught spying on our Festival. We do not know what damage he might do if allowed to go unpunished.

"But are these two candidates patriotic enough to punish him severely? We may well wonder, for one of them is a stranger from Up North, and the other is an outlander from a village below the river.

"You have your instructions, candidates. You may proceed."

Axloff stood back to give Joe the first run. They were to take turns "running under" their victim. Joe ran and made a long leap, his horns striking Uncle Keller across the seat of his dusty trousers.

Joe looked back at the blue dust cloud to see Uncle Keller whirling up through a swift arc. As he swung over and down, Axloff ran under him, struck with his horns, and added speed to the whirl.

Around again, and Joe again crashed in, to add impetus. Smack!... smack!...smack!...In a moment the one-man Ferris wheel was whirling so fast that it made four or five revolutions to each smack of horns.

The higher the speed, the more perilous the operation. Joe knew that if he ran under a shade too soon, there was danger of inflicting serious wounds.

Smack!...smack!...smack!

Axloff was trying to be humane about it, too, Joe noted. He was not going to insult Donna by putting on a poor show of energy. But he was trying to strike at an angle that would prevent any serious hooking by the points of his tall, sharp horns.

Some of the noisy spectators called for more brutality. "Tear him up! Spike him in the back!"

I T WAS a horrifying demonstration. At best neither of the candidates could avoid inflicting much torture. Sometimes Joe missed his calculations and knifed at the shoulders or the small of the back. Once Axloff's thrust ripped an overall leg down to the ankle. The victim's clothing was being cut to shreds. Drops of blood began to fly.

"How much can the old man stand?" Axloff said to Joe on the sly as they circled back for another round. And the next time around, "Why do we do it? The judge isn't watching."

Joe saw, then, that Judge Mobar, Londeenoko, and a few other top officials had gone into a huddle, as if to discuss something urgent. What? Could it be the dehorning idea?

While the whirligig went on, the conference of the leaders was swiftly spread into a whispering campaign among the whole crowd. Something was in the air. Some mysterious news was spreading, and as rapidly as the people heard it they turned to stare at Joe.

Now their eyes were following his every move.

Smack...! Smack...! Smack...!

Not an outcry from Uncle Keller. Was the fellow unconscious?

Joe wondered. Should he try to strike harder, to win, to bring this hideous whirligig ordeal to an end? Tilting his horns at the safest angle, again he dashed under.

Flop!

His shoulder fastening broke. The harness suddenly went loose over his right shoulder and flopped off the top of his head.

He stopped so abruptly that Uncle Keller almost struck him on the next whirl.

As he grabbed for his loosened horns, he heard Lon Londeenoko's commanding bellow.

"There! Just as I said. Look at him!"

The crowd was gaping. Axloff stopped to gaze. Donna sprang forward from her seat on the platform, put her fingers to her lips. Londeenoko pointed down, and his broad mustached face twitched with anger, gathering breath for a roar.

Above the sound of the whirligig spinning on its axle, the murmurs of amazement from the crowd rose to a sullen thunder.

"A demon!"

"A hornless one!"

"Another spy!"

"An imposter!"

"A foreigner—a hornless foreigner!"

Some half grown boy shrieked, *"He is the one who roped the 'naggie' girl!"*

Then Londeenoko bellowed in a way that welded the whole crowd into a dangerous mob.

"He is the one who would have us *cut our horns off.* Yes, my people, that is the very plan he has proposed—to have *us remove our horns!* There he stands! No wonder he has such ideas! He has no horns of his own. *He* is *a freak—a hornless demon!"*

The crowd spilled out into the arena, drawn by the magnetism of this excitement. Londeenoko, however, motioned them to stay back. With a dramatic whirl, his sashes fluttering, he clapped his six-fingered hands together as a signal.

"Boys! Boys! I want twenty boys!"

At once, forty or more youths came running up from the ranks of the spectators. Joe saw them begin to form a trap of horns, the same circular spear trap that had gathered around the runaway girl by the cliff.

"Run, Joe!" Donna cried. "It's the *ring of death*. Run for your life!"

CHAPTER XI

JOE leaped to catch the whirligig. He jerked a horn out of the harness that now dangled over his chest. He used it like a knife. The cords that bound Uncle Keller popped from the strokes of Joe's slashing arm! Poor Uncle Keller fell to the ground—not dead but groggy from pain and loss of blood.

Joe dropped to his feet and gathered the helpless, bleeding friend into his arms. Above the tumult he heard Donna's weird, terrified cry.

"Run, Joe! Run!"

Joe dodged ahead of the circle that was trying to close around him. Two young men raced across to block his escape. With Uncle Keller in his arms, he whirled at one of them, and Uncle Keller's long legs swung out like a baseball bat to knock the fellow flat. With one hand Joe grabbed the next assailant by the horns, jerked him forward, dodging his headlong stagger.

Ten minutes later the two "hornless demons" were out of hearing of Festival, slogging along through a marsh near the river.

"Still alive, Uncle?"

"I need a smoke," said Uncle Keller weakly; "And I could use a couple gallons of horse liniment… Let me do my own runnin' now, Joe. I'm too heavy for you to carry. Besides, you'd better git on ahead. They were plenty powerful mad at you when you broke away. I heard everything."

"I'll carry you," said Joe. He knew Uncle Keller was in no shape to walk, and might be laid up for days. "It's easier to throw them off the trail with one set of tracks than two, anyway. It's an old trick I learned when I was a Boy Scout."

"The way you socked that one guy with an apple did me good."

"I used to be the pitcher for the South Side Wildcats."

"And those last three kids that tried to run in front of you—you hollered like thunder at 'em and they beat it! By crackles, that did me good!"

"I used to be the tenor in the quartet," Joe laughed.

When darkness came over the apple forest they made camp on a grassy knoll somewhere many miles down the river. The low steady roar of the Silver Falls was barely audible. Close around them were the ceaseless sounds of failing apples.

Uncle Keller, bandaged and patched and somewhat restored, murmured that these were peaceful sounds to sleep by, and he doubted whether he would wake up for forty-eight hours. Privately, Joe was worried for fear the old mail might never wake up. It would be a tough pull, to live after the ordeal he had gone through.

But Uncle Jim Keller was tough. After many hours of sleep, he took nourishment and grew talkative and began to complain over losing his pipe. Joe decided he was on the mend.

THEY were too near one of the river villages to make a permanent camp here. When a searching party came too near, Uncle Keller awakened Joe out of a nap and they broke up camp in a hurry.

"Let's make some more tracks, Joe."

Another day, another camp.

There was nothing to do but eat and sleep and keep out of sight. Uncle Keller was coming back, slowly. He slept seven or eight hours out of every ten, which was all to the good.

But he complained about his troubled dreams. "I keep dreamin' about those boys that circled that girl with their horns, and finally got her when she fell. Sometimes I dream it's me instead of the girl. And sometimes it's you, Joe. And there I am, whirlin' on the whirligig, an' everything's dizzy and blurry, an' I keep faintin'."

"What are we going to do, Uncle?"

"Die in exile, I reckon. We've got no way back to the Earth. An' you've cooked your goose with Donna and all her people—for life."

"Don't rub it in," said Joe.

Another day, another camp, and another dream.

"You know what I been, dreamin' lately?" said Uncle Keller. "You was married to her, living back in Bellrap, U.S.A. You had three half grown kids, with seven horns apiece, and when the mayor came for dinner he mistook one of 'em for a hat rack—"

"Cut it out!"

"An' when the minister's big fat wife came and greeted you folks and started to hug your wife, the way she hugs everyone, her double chin got hooked on Donna's shoulder an' she let out an awful holler—"

"Stop it!"

Another day, and still another camp. They were moving deeper and deeper into the uncharted forest of big blue apples. With them went the strange feeling that someone was following them. That was Joe's dream—that they were always about to be overtaken.

"What are we going to do, Uncle?"

"Stop and live out our days, I reckon.... I know where there's a space ship, Joe. It's hid in a hillside—"

"Uncle Keller, you wouldn't!"

"I never said nothin'." Uncle Keller munched innocently at a shiny blue apple.

"After all the damage I've done to Donna," Joe mumbled, "I'd be the worst heel in the world if I ever—"

"Quit kickin' yourself in the face. It gives me the back-ache," Uncle Keller growled.

"Besides, that space ship wasn't exactly hers. It belonged to the Venus scientist she was always talking about. I'll bet a hundred dollars he has stolen her away from Axloff, by now, in spite of the choosing ceremony. Axloff was too easy-going. But that Venus scientist was the sort of guy who would steal whatever he wanted. There's something phony about that guy."

"You think so?"

"By now, he and Donna are probably honeymooning around the rings of Saturn."

Uncle Keller tossed the apple aside, and turned, with difficulty, to rest his lame hips on softer grass.

"You know something, Joe? I can't figure out why you think a perty girl like Donna would want to marry a guy with white hair and long white whiskers."

"Who's got white hair and long white whiskers?"

"The Venus scientist."

"Huh? Who says so?"

"That's what Donna always told my wife an' me when she was stayin' with us back at Bellrap."

"White hair! Whiskers! Are you nuts, or am I?... Ye gods, then *I've never seen the Venus scientist!*"

"Of course you haven't."

"Then who the devil was that *black-haired guy* I stole the horns from?"

"How do I know who you steal from?"

Something was screwy, Joe realized. He began to pace back and forth. His anger and confusion mounted. "When I went back and found that black-haired guy, I apologized to him—*apologized,* mind you—because I'd figured out that he was Donna's scientist boy-friend."

"And he admitted it?"

"Not only that. He sprung this plan for dehorning the natives as a scientific experiment. He told me it was all my idea and I should go ahead and promote it."

"Hmph."

Joe was blazing with anger. "Is that all you can say? *Hmph?"*

"Sonny boy, it looks to me like you've walked into somethin'."

CHAPTER XII

J OE stopped pacing and stared at Uncle Keller, studied him from head to foot, wondering how soon the poor fellow would be well enough to move under his own power. He couldn't be left here in the forest alone. But Joe was breathing hard with ire and lust for revenge. Did he dare go back and settle a score or two—or die in the attempt?

A rustling sound from a nearby thicket caused him and Uncle Keller to turn.

A Martian was approaching them—a stately horned man with a yellow workman's jacket and puffy pantaloons. In one hand he carried an orange-colored apple, in the other, what appeared to be a small loaf of bread.

Joe recognized him at once. But he courteously introduced himself as he advanced.

"I am Ruffledeen, the well known chef of Apple Forest. I have seen you before. Do you remember me?"

"We remember," said Joe. "What do you want?"

"Would you care to try my latest cake?"

He offered the loaf to Joe, who stood with arms folded. A suspicious offer, to say the least. What sort of man offers you a cake with one hand while he holds a poison apple with the other?

"I'm not very hungry," said Joe, "thanking you just the same... No, Uncle Keller is not very hungry either."

"I just et," said Uncle Keller.

"My cakes are very famous," said Ruffledeen, not in the least disturbed by this cool reception. He came a little closer. His wavy purple whiskers, shining in the thin shafts of sunlight, again reminded Joe of a bunch of purple grapes. He continued, "This is my latest creation."

He fairly forced the loaf into Joe's hands. Joe scowled. It was incredible that this man should have wandered into these depths of the forest by accident.

"What brings you here?"

"I often walk through the trees," said Ruffledeen. "I enjoy the peace of the trees. Sometimes I meet people and if I think they are in trouble I tell them."

"That's a laugh," Joe snorted. "I'm already up to my neck in trouble. Anything you might tell me couldn't make any difference."

"That is bad," said Ruffledeen. "Sometimes people are so deep in trouble that they will eat the orange-colored apple."

"I've thought of that all by myself, pal," said Joe, with a hint of desperation that made Uncle Keller wince.

"But I did not offer you the orange apple. I have given you the cake. Will you give your sick friend a part of it?"

J OE broke the loaf and handed half of it down to Uncle Keller, who lay resting on an elbow. There was an awkward pause. Uncle Keller sniffed at the cake. It smelled delicious. But he stalled, his glances shifting from Joe to Ruffledeen to the poison apple.

Joe acted as if he were going to take a bite, then he too stalled, taking refuge in a bit of friendly conversation.

"You must be tired, Ruffledeen. Do you want to sit down with us?… No?… Er—you mentioned a warning of new trouble? Go ahead, give us the worst."

"Very well," said Ruffledeen. From his expressionless face he might have been discussing the balmy weather instead of an approaching storm. "Some unknown criminals are entering the villages every night to seize some unsuspecting native."

"Kidnappers, huh?"

"Horn removers."

"Horn removers!"

"When I left the last village, *thirty-five persons had already been dehorned.* You two foreigners are being sought for these nightly crimes. New search parties are being organized. *You will be killed on sight.* "

"We—? Ye gods! That black-haired, lying scoundrel—that double-crossing hornless four-flusher!" Joe was on fire with the passion of revenge. He tightened his fists, and the cake twisted into a doughy mass in his hands. It contained something hard, but at the moment Joe was too enraged to notice such trifles as cakes. "By George and by Joe, there'll be murder!"

"Careful! My cake!" Ruffledeen warned. "I have baked it especially—"

"The cake!" Joe snorted. Then recovering his manners, "Yes, the cake. Thank you so much... Does Donna Londeen believe I am guilty of this dehorning stunt?"

"She knows," said Ruffledeen, "that you proposed the idea to the leaders. That was a mistake."

"Then she believes—"

"I cannot say what she believes. I cannot say whether her uncle believes that she herself may be involved. I can only say that she wants to see you."

Ruffledeen began to walk away as slowly and mysteriously as he had come. He gave a definite warning, however, that he was not to be followed. He made them agree.

Joe called after him. "You say she wants to see me? Wait! Tell her where to find me!"

"It might cost her life if she tried," Ruffledeen moved on, his back now turned to Joe.

"Tell her I'll come back and find her—very soon—as soon as Uncle Keller doesn't need me. And if she isn't already married, tell her not to marry that black-haired devil. Tell her to marry Axloff—"

"Perhaps I will tell her where I last saw you," said Ruffledeen; "if you like my cake."

"Of course we'll like your cake," Joe called. "We'll eat every bit of it! Won't we Uncle?"

Ruffledeen looked back once, again before he disappeared. Joe and Uncle Keller were eating their cake.

"It's a good cake, so far," said Uncle Keller, smacking his lips. "Oh-oh, what's this? I just bit into somethin' hard."

CHAPTER XIII

J OE turned to Uncle Jim Keller. "I bit into something, too. That chef must" make his cakes out of rocks... Well by George and by Joe, look at this." His worried look changed to a boyish grin. *"It's the bowl of your corncob pipe."*

"Eh? By crackles," Uncle Keller's bright black eyes shone under beetle brows. "I've just bit into a *pipe stem.* Now how do ya reckon—?"

"Ruffledeen the chef must have rescued it for you at the Festival."

"He's gone to a lot of trouble, followin' us around the forest. But anyhow we're saved."

Joe scowled. "Saved? How do you figure that? There's a bounty on our scalps."

"Don't worry, son. I've got my pipe. I'll have a good smoke an' dream our way outa trouble."

"You and your pipe dreams! I'll rely on footwork, in this strange country. Come on, we're moving."

"Hey ain't we gonna wait an' see if Donna comes?" Uncle Keller whined.

"With any kind of luck, we'll meet her half way. Come on, Uncle. We're breaking camp."

"Now be reasonable. I just got my pipe filled."

But Joe gathered up Uncle Keller in his arms and strode off in the direction that Ruffledeen had gone. Uncle Keller thought he felt well enough to walk. But Joe preferred to lose no time. The light gravity of Mars gave him strength and speed to spare. And the cake he had just eaten was full of quick energy.

"Son," said Uncle Keller, "you're headin' back to the river, square into danger."

"Scared?" said Joe.

"We'll run into a thousand Martians with ten or twelve horns apiece and git ourselves horn-jabbed into human pincushions."

"Lost your nerve?"

"No, but I'm proud," said Uncle Keller. "If Donna Londeen carts my dead body back to the Earth, I want the Bellrap citizens to know it's me, not some fancy Martian mince-meat. Where we goin'?"

"To overtake Ruffledeen. He must be a friend or he wouldn't have brought your pipe. I'll make him lead us to Donna."

"Stop!" Uncle Keller demanded. "These trees are drippin' blood. Look at my hand."

Joe stopped. On the back of Uncle Keller's hand was a drop of blood. It had fallen from somewhere overhead. Joe looked up into the trees. He squinted....

"Whatcha lookin' at, son?" Uncle Keller squirmed to his feet, and stood, a bit wobbly, looking up through the branches loaded with apples.

In this strange land, where big blue apples were constantly ripening and falling with an almost rhythmic thump...thump...thump...upon the ground or upon the horns of unconcerned natives, and where one lone orange-colored poison apple could be seen near the top of every tree, and where the natives had purple hair and six fingered hands and several horns on their heads and shoulders, it might seem that visitors from Earth should not be surprised at any other odd sights. But here Joe and Uncle Keller stood, near a thicket along the bank of a small stream, staring up into a tall blue-apple tree.

Forty feet above them a Martian hung between two branches. Blood was dripping from his head. He had just been dehorned. He hung motionless, and to all intents and purposes appeared dead.

CHAPTER XIV

A SMALL pool of blood on the ground revealed that the man had occupied his high perch only a few minutes.

"How in blazes did he git up there?" Uncle Keller mumbled.

Joe frowned. For a moment he stood, his fists planted on his hips. He studied the tree from trunk to topmost branch, calculating the difficulties that any dehorning party would have climbing up. A fight out on those high branches would have been perilous. But there were no signs that anyone had fallen.

"Do you reckon they chased him up," Uncle Keller asked, "an' gave him the business when they got him out on the limb?... I don't git it."

"He's alive!" Joe muttered. "I saw him move." He shouted, *"Hi, up there!"*

"Hsssh!" Uncle Keller flung his hands up for silence. He whispered, "Great guns, Joe, you'll have us murdered in no time. How far away d'ya reckon his dehorners are? Right over the bank, most likely. That job's fresh from the ax."

"Too neat for an ax," said Joe calmly. Then he called again, in his best Martian accent. "Hold on, up there. I'll come up and help you."

The Martian, a typical villager in a soiled red workman's suit, turned his bloody head and tried to look down. He uttered the one word, "Come!"

The tree would have been a tough climb on the Earth. But Joe's lithe muscles, aided by the comparative weightlessness that he enjoyed on Mars, made him equal to the feat. All the way up, his thoughts whirled with conjecture. How? How had this job been accomplished? Had a machine hurled this victim? Surely no team of men could have thrown him to this height.

Nine horns had been removed. There were three bloodless stumps on each shoulder, three on the crest of the head. But the saw had evidently slipped, gouging his head and the flesh of his shoulders in several places. The fellow's locks of purple hair were matted with blood and sweat. His face was tight with pain.

"Do not let me fall," he begged. He was too badly injured to try to help himself. He looked down forty feet to the pool of blood on, the ground, and acted as if he would fall from dizziness.

It was hard for Joe, astride the branch, to administer first aid. But he stuck to his job. Then, with the aid of his rope he lowered the man from one branch to another, and at last to the ground.

"Where are they?" Uncle Keller's Martian accent was faulty.

The victim shrugged. He thought the question referred to his horns. "Off," he said, pointing to his head.

"Where are the guys that chopped 'em off?" said Uncle Keller, lapsing into his own brand of English. "I'll bet they're hidin' along this crick, layin' fer us."

"Off," the Martian repeated sadly. "Gone. The masked men attacked me with saws. I fought! They seized me. They flew with me. Then I saw them without their masks. They wanted my horns. They got them."

"*Flew* with you?" Joe echoed, his face a question mark.

"It was horrible. My horns—I was so proud of them! I cannot talk about it. But—thank you. I will go now—this way." He barely fought off a faint, then, slowly, he began to walk.

"You're in bad shape," said Joe. "We'll tag along."

T HE three of them followed the bank of the stream. Night came on and they kept trudging, with the aid of torches. The bandaged man declared that he must reach the Silver River. The waters would heal him.

"I need you," Joe said to him over and over. "You must tell me who did this thing to you."

"I will talk after I have reached the healing waters."

"If you would only rest—"

"Let us hurry on," the Martian said.

Uncle Keller grew weak, and Joe was obliged to carry him. This pace was slow and cautious. Joe's eyes grew blurry, watching for trouble from every black shadow of every tree trunk. Before morning Uncle Keller dropped out. He would follow at his own speed, he promised. And Joe understood. Exhaustion had overtaken the old fellow. He would undoubtedly sleep before he tried to finish the Journey.

From then on, Joe carried the Martian—carried him in a sitting position to keep him from complaining of the dreadful pains in his head and shoulders.

"We will reach the healing waters soon after dawn," the Martian said. "But for you I would have died from loss of blood. I owe my life to you."

"You, in turn, will save my life," said Joe. "You will tell your people that I am not the man who removes horns."

"Tell my people?"

"Yes. Otherwise they are going to kill me for what I haven't done."

"But I—I cannot *face* my people, now that I have no horns. I *cannot!*"

"You'll have to! It's the least you can do. Promise me that you will."

The Martian drew a painful breath. "I will talk after I reach the healing waters."

The pink light of morning came at last. A soft cloud of mist could be seen across the clearing by the river. The low roar of the falls came from that direction. The tributary that Joe followed circled to the west of the Silver Falls village and joined the river two miles downstream. Uncle Keller might find his way here by daylight without being seen.

The Martian bathed in the shallow side of the great bend. He ate a little, and slept. Joe waited. Would the man fulfill his half of the bargain when he awoke? Or would he be in the mood to kill every hornless foreigner?

JOE lay on his stomach, his head propped in his hands. He almost dozed. From a distance the soft sounds of falling apples, like the lightest patter of, raindrops, lulled him to unconsciousness.

The grass rustled. The Martian was rising slowly. Joe sprang to his feet, stood squarely before the man whose life he had saved. The poor fellow passed his hands over his head and shoulders to convince himself that the awful happening was no dream. For a moment Joe thought he would weep. He bowed his bandaged head, closed his eyes.

"Now I know how Donna would feel if she were ever deprived of her horns," Joe said to himself. "And to think—I had wished it—so I could marry her! Why did I dare fall in love? Uncle Keller warned me…"

In that moment Joe knew the pain of having to fight when you're already beaten.

"Courage," he said to the Martian. "You've lost your horns, but you're still alive. Let me tell you a secret. There *are* such things as *imitation horns.*"

"Imitation?" The Martian's eyes lifted slowly.

"I've seen them. In fact, I've worn them, a whole set. They strap on with a harness, and you smear grease paint around your shoulders and ears so the harness won't show. When you get fixed up, no one will know the difference."

The Martian's eyes glowed. He pressed Joe on the arm. "You have already befriended me. If you can find horns for me, I will do anything you ask."

Joe's face set with a fighting determination. "There's only one thing I have to fight for now. It's that other hornless man—the one we left behind. If you can fix things so we won't be killed—so I'll have a chance to get him back to his home—that, and clear the decks for a certain girl—

"What would you have *me* do?"

"Get well, so you can tell them—"

Plop!

An orange-colored apple struck the ground within fifteen feet of them. It burst with a spout of reddish liquid.

"Where the devil did that come from?" Joe muttered. The nearest tree was several yards away.

"Quick! Take me from here!" the Martian cried.

Joe swung him off his feet and bore him away. They ran downstream. This gave them the advantage of a wider clearing between the river and the forest.

"What are we running from?" Joe said, slackening his pace, now that he had failed to sight any danger.

"Do you not know of *naggie madness?*" said the Martian. "Let me down. We are out of danger now. But it is lucky the poison apple did not burst upon us."

Joe mounted a stone and looked back over the terrain. "I don't see anyone."

"Someone was there. Someone threw the apple."

"What if we'd been hit? Are those poison apples sudden death?"

"Not death but *madness.* Have you never seen a naggie gone mad from eating one? It runs in all directions at once and smashes into trees."

"I saw a girl that acted like that one time," said Joe reflectively. "They spoke of her as a 'naggie girl.' She was running like wild. A bunch of young fellows were chasing her, and I think they meant to kill her."

"Of course they did," said the Martian. "When anyone gets the madness of the naggie, *he must be killed.* Nothing less than the Ring of Death will serve, if you become a 'naggie man.'"

Joe understood, at last, the mystery of the girl he had tried to rescue on that first memorable day. So it was madness that had caused her to cut the rope and fall to her death on the waiting horns—a madness that came from contact with the wrong kind of apple.

The Martian stood beside Joe, gazing across to the bank of trees. No one could be seen, yet both men knew that an enemy was closing in. Poison apples don't roll across the clearing by accident.

"We've got to walk into the village at once," said Joe. "You've got to tell them who attacked you—"

"But not until you get horns for me."

"We can't wait for that. We'll go at once."

"No. The *horns*—"

Slash!

A spear plunged through the Martian's side, just above the left hip.

CHAPTER XV

"THE horns!" the Martian repeated.

Joe would always remember that moment of pride and glory in the Martian's gesture toward his high head, imagining the horns that would be replaced, according to Joe's promise.

The expression went sick all at once, as the spear whizzed up from the river bank to plunge through him.

The Martian stumbled forward, clutching his side. Miraculously, he recovered his balance and ran to the riverbank. Joe saw him dodge a flying rock, then plunge over the bank, hugging the spear as he dived, aiming it.

A shrill cry rang out. The Martian had caught someone on that same spear.

Joe leaped to the bank and saw. It was that foreigner Rabbit Face, who had caught the spear-head through the heart. The handle broke. The dehorned Martian, with the broken stub plugged through his side, backed away and sank down against the sloping earth, still watching. Blood spurted from the rabbit-faced man's mouth. His cry choked off. His eyelids fell, and he was dead.

"Rabbit Face!" Joe muttered. "What the hell was *his* game?"

"He was one of the gang who took my horns," the Martian said. "Another had scarred hands. And there were others."

"Talk fast," said Joe breathlessly. The Martian's life was ebbing away. Tell me everything. Tell me—"

"They flew over in a house."

"A house?"

"A house with wings and a roar."

"A plane or a rocket ship! Go on."

"They meant to tie me to a tree…as they have done to others… But I fought… It was then that the flying house appeared, and stopped near me… When they took me in, I saw…"

"Yes, go on. Go on!"

"I saw their faces without masks. I saw the piles of horns they have gathered into their flying house, like bundles of wood. We flew. When they finished with me they immediately dropped me from high in the air, and I fell to the forest. But the fall did not kill me, and you found me."

"Was there a black-haired man?" Joe asked anxiously.

"The leader...and I recognized him... His color...*changed...*"

"What do you mean? Who was he? Speak up! Tell me!"

"From another world... *His color...changed...*"

That was the last. The Martian died in Joe's arms.

TWO dead men at Joe's feet. One, a man born to wear horns with pride, and Joe looked upon him with tenderness. The other, a hornless fellow whose schemes Joe was beginning to understand. He and his friends, from "another world" were here to gather horns as ivory traders might gather elephant tusks.

But Joe was also aware that at least two other men had had a share in this attack, for he had caught a fleeting glimpse of their retreat down the river a moment after Rabbit-Face was killed. He doubted whether either was Scar-Hands or Black-Hair. They were two of the assistants—with horns—although the horns might have been imitation.

Later, as Joe related the whole fracas to Uncle Keller, he theorized that these two who raced away could well have been Martians, somehow forced into Black-Hair's game. For it seemed likely that men with a flying ship could have done their killing with guns or rays, if they had wished.

"But instead, what did they do? They resorted to such Martian devices as poison apples and spears."

"That means," said Uncle Keller, "that they figured to shift the blame."

"And with a few Martian stooges already lined up, doing their dirty work, they'll get away with it. That makes it all the harder to deal with. These spear-throwing apple-throwing people won't have any conception of what a clever enemy they're up against."

Joe and Uncle Keller were trudging back into the forest slowly, thoughtfully. "Did you have any hankerin' to stay and bury your Martian friend?" Uncle Keller asked.

"I wouldn't have dared," Joe admitted. "The natives came thick and fast within five minutes after Rabbit-Face let out that awful death cry."

"I heard it myself. By crackies, I was scared it was you, Joe."

"That's no compliment to my voice." Joe grinned. "Remember, I sing first tenor in the Bellrap quartet."

"I figured you were practicin' grand opery," Uncle Keller chuckled.

As they tramped along, they did their best to keep up a gay front. But it wasn't easy.

"We're like a couple of convicts slated for the chair," said Joe. "The one guy that might have saved us has got himself bumped off, and we're trying to be cheerful about it."

Uncle Keller was philosophical. It was something to know, who your enemies were.

"I always figured if I was gonna be hanged, I'd rather be hanged in the daylight than in the dark."

"So you won't miss out on the show, I suppose," Joe mumbled.

"Yeah. An' so I'll know who to haunt when I get to be a ghost."

"Well, you can haunt a black-haired, smart looking fellow of medium height, who speaks good English, like all of these men-about-planets. He's probably from Mercury. He flies some sort of ship, and has a crew of helpers—"

"And is as tricky as the devil, pinnin' this whole dehornin' scheme on us."

"But the Martian told me one thing about him, right at the last, that I can't figure out," said Joe. "Something about his *changing color.*"

They pondered this mystifying remark. Uncle Keller had a theory.

"It means he turns yellow. He's a coward."

"That might be right if we were on the Earth," said Joe. "But turning yellow doesn't mean anything to a Martian."

"Why not?"

"Because it's just an expression. An American expression."

Uncle Keller couldn't get that through his head. He argued stubbornly.

"I figure if a guy's yellow, he's yellow, whether he's an Earth man or a Martian or a Mercurochrome."

"You mean a Mercurian."

"I mean a yellow guy is a coward, in any language," said Uncle Keller.

Joe had his own theory that the color change was from white to black; that the black-haired scoundrel from Mercury, and the white-haired scientist from Venus might be the same person. He had never seen Donna's scientist friend. But wasn't it a reasonable guess that a man skillful enough to disguise himself in a harness of horns might also disguise himself in white hair and whiskers?

"I've got it doped out," said Joe confidently. "It's like this—"

But Joe's theory blew up before he could tell it. For at that moment, as they walked over the crest of a wooded hill, they looked down on the camp of the Venus scientist. Donna and her sister were there. So were Axloff and a few others. But the dominant figure was the white-haired scientist himself. He was not Black-Hair. He was like no one Joe had ever seen before.

CHAPTER XVI

DONNA was more than cordial. She was genuinely joyful. She came running, calling so eagerly that everyone knew these were the two Earth friends she had lost.

"It is so good to see you, Joe. I was afraid you had fallen into wrong hands... And you, Uncle Keller, you are able to walk. You look strong. I am so glad."

The scientist's guards approached, putting away their weapons as they came. Axloff extended the warmest of welcomes to Joe. He was the same handsome, boyish eleven-horned rival that had competed with Joe for Donna's hand. Yet, as before, Joe felt the sincerity of his friendship.

"To you, Uncle Keller," said Axloff, "I apologize for striking you so hard with my horns."

"I reckon you had to do it," said Uncle Keller philosophically. "One guy's meat's another guy's poison, they say."

Axloff scowled, trying to decipher the maxim. "Poison? What we did to you is not to be compared to poison. Have you ever seen the naggie leap from its four hoofs when it tasted poison?"

"I saw some gal run when she was naggie-crazy," said Uncle Keller.

"Then you know how dreadful it is. We brought no such harm to you, bumping you with horns."

"Well, nothin' to make me run, if that's what you mean. By crackies, I couldn't even walk. But I'm gettin' spry again."

"Big news," said Donna. "I have learned that Axloff is the son of my scientist from Venus."

Joe's jaw dropped. He looked from the tall eleven-horned young stalwart across to the hornless white-haired man.

"You'd better say that again. I didn't quite catch it."

"Do not frown so," Donna laughed.

"It is true. Axloff, *who has eleven horns,* is the son of Axotello, *who has no* horns. And I am told that Axloff's mother had no horns."

Joe stared blankly. "How is that possible?"

Donna held up her hands. "Do not ask me to explain such mysteries. That will be for Axotello, whose business is to puzzle over the strangeness of the universe. He is forever writing his scientific observations, but never reading any conclusions aloud. Come, you must meet Axotello now."

Then Joe and Uncle Keller found themselves being introduced to one of the boldest scientists of the interplanetary world of science.

H E WAS tall—as tall as Axloff minus the horns. His face was broad, with a massive white forehead beneath flowing waves of white hair. His features might have belonged to a dignified judge or a minister on the Earth. His eyes, however, were related to the cat family, Joe decided—the eyes of a lynx or a leopard—large, amber-colored eyes partially covered by the straight upper lids. His white whiskers, clean-trimmed like a Southern colonel's, only emphasized the breadth of his face.

In spite of white hair and whiskers he was, above all, youthful.

Joe, shaking the man's strong, solid hand, felt a return of that emotion which had swept through him before. He was jealous. This was the man who had befriended Donna and made her a gift of a space ship—the man she had hastened to see, on her return to this planet.

And with the sudden wave of jealousy, Joe also felt himself dwarfed. Physically, he was perhaps the shortest man of the group—

But one remark from Axloff reminded him that he had already made his mark as a tough, hard-fighting champion.

"This is the Earth man, father, who fought me to the finish in the festival competitions," Axloff said.

"I am most proud to welcome you to my camp," said Axotello. "And may I compliment the good judgment of your Earth city in choosing Donna for honors. You have presented a silver cup to her, I believe."

"I'm going to present it. That is—" Joe grinned, slightly confused, "I came along to Mars for that purpose. I figured it should be done in public."

Uncle Keller chimed in, "Joe hankers for an audience whenever he does anything."

The scientist smiled and the others laughed, more at Uncle's manner and accent than his words.

"What's more," said Uncle Keller, "Joe's the Bellrap city clerk, and I'm the clerk's clerk, and we figure Bellrap can do with some free advertisin'. Ring the bells for Bellrap, that's our motto—"

"S-s-sh! You and I are talking too much," said Joe. At the same time, amid his confusion, he was asking himself, "Now where did I leave that silver loving cup? Somewhere in Donna's space ship, or—"

"Come this way, Joe," said Donna. "You and Uncle must join Axloff and his father in a feast Ruffledeen has prepared."

J OE feasted, but he felt uncomfortable—as if he had been plunged into a convention of Donna's boyfriends. However, the dinner became a rollicking affair. Troubles, the scientist said, could be met later. Now was the time for merriment and song. Uncle Keller furnished much of the merriment, Joe his share of the song.

Ruffledeen walked past the camp.

The scientist nodded to the chef as he passed. Ruffledeen may not have noticed. Like a stray cat he cast curious sidewise glances. Someone called a compliment to him. His feast was perfect. He did not respond. He only stroked his wavy purple whiskers and walked on.

To his assistant cooks he spoke in private. Presently they gathered up their portable kitchen and followed him out of camp.

No one was surprised at this. In fact, no one but Joe seemed to pay any attention. For it was Ruffledeen's mysterious way to cook for anyone he wished, as long as he wished. There was no contract between him and the Venus scientist. On another day he might be found serving his fancy dishes to the people of any river village, or to the young judge from "Up North," or to Donna's hardboiled old uncle, Londeenoko.

Joe watched the purple-whiskered chef wander away, followed by his two assistants. As often before, Ruffledeen was carrying a poison apple. It seemed to be his favorite habit.

"Will he come back?" Joe asked, looking from Donna to Axloff, and then to the wise-eyed Axotello.

"Who knows?" said Axotello. "Who cares? We never lack for food in this bountiful forest."

His handsome, eleven-horned son said, "No, father, we never lack. But some of us are better equipped to catch our food than others."

Axotello smiled faintly. "My son never ceases to enjoy his advantage of having horns. He is always afraid a falling apple will injure me. For my part, I do not mind the thump of the largest blue apple. My head is hard. The only apple I fear is the orange-colored one. And I would fear it even if I had horns. But I never sit beneath it. I leave that to my careless son."

Axloff looked up, then, and to his chagrin, discovered he was sitting directly beneath one of the dread fruit. He moved, and everyone laughed.

They laughed more, a moment later, when a large blue apple dropped and struck his father squarely on the head, and upset him from his seat.

"It is your turn to move," Axloff laughed.

"No," said the scientist, quietly amused. "The laws of chances will not put another apple directly above my crown—"

He was looking straight up, and his words broke off abruptly. Everyone looked up. Joe saw, through an opening between leafy branches, what all the others saw. He heard the low steady roar.

"What a bird!" Uncle Keller mumbled.

It was a black metal object flying above the forest tops, below the clouds. It was shaped like a narrow oblong tube with triangular wings tight against its sides.

"That's no bird," said Joe. "That's the flying house that took our Martian friend for a ride."

CHAPTER XVII

WITHIN a few minutes the scientist's camp was on the move. By late afternoon it was established in a deeper and darker part of the valley, not easily observed from overhead.

Axotello was not convinced that the ship portended any harm for him. He had made no enemies. But he preferred to carry on his work out of sight. Off and on, through the years, he had carried out experiments in this land. By keeping off the well beaten trails along the river, he had seldom been molested.

But now it was well known that a band of horn thieves were at work. Joe and Donna, as well as Ruffledeen had seen the evidences with their own eyes.

The scientist listened to these reports with great interest. If a Mercury gang had come to Mars to pillage, there might be great trouble in store.

But Axotello himself did not say, "Let us get together and fight these desperadoes and put a stop to their ugly game."

Instead, ostrich-like, he buried his head deeper in the sand of his own private interests. "Let us move," he said, "into deeper shadows. I do not want to be annoyed by spies from the air while I proceed with my studies."

A little distance from the new camp, Joe rested under an overhanging cliff, free from falling apples. Exhausted from many continuous hours without sleep, he slept heavily until evening.

When he awoke, Donna was beside him, smiling at him.

Joe rubbed his eyes, yawned and grinned. "This is a pleasant surprise."

"A herd of naggies were grazing along this ravine," said Donna. "I did not want them to wake you."

Joe took her hand. Love is like that, he decided. You think of little courtesies, things you wouldn't think of ordinarily.

"Did Uncle Keller get some rest?" He asked.

"He snored like a broken-down space ship," Donna laughed. "But now he is at his usual occupation, smoking his pipe, filled with the wool of the naggie. He is also writing in a notebook. See him over there?"

Joe nodded. Uncle was keeping a record of all expenses, real or imagined, which the Mars adventure had entailed. He had some fanciful notion of presenting a bill to the city of Bellrap, if he ever got back.

"There he sits," Joe said, pointing to a clump of trees beyond the camp. "He thinks the Bellrap treasury will pay for all our hours and discomforts, because I'm the city clerk—"

"And he calls himself the clerk's clerk. But why should Bellrap pay—"

"Because I came on official business. That silver cup. I intend to make a public presentation. If I had it here now I'd—"

"Where is it?"

"I put it—er—let me see—" Joe almost remembered. But something else attracted his attention. "Donna, you're carrying a gun!"

"Yes, a ray weapon. A gift from the Venus Scientist."

Joe felt a wave of warmth sweep through his face and neck. "Donna, I wish you wouldn't—I mean—well, he's a nice fellow and all that, but I wish he wouldn't give you so many gifts."

"You Earth men are funny," Donna laughed. "He is my friend, and if there is trouble from Mercury men, I should not be helpless. You should have a gun too. I would not want you to be helpless."

SHE patted his arm as if to calm his ruffled spirits. But Joe rose now, and straightened to his full height. Not that he was tall. Once she had called him short, and in fact he was slightly under average height. But he felt tall, and stood tall, and he wasn't going to have anyone call him helpless.

"I can help myself," he asserted.

"Then why do you not help yourself?" she said, and rose to stand beside him.

"I will," he snapped. "I'll tackle these damned desperados single handed, if necessary. I'll show your people who's making the trouble. I'll—"

"You will help yourself," Donna repeated.

Then he took her in his arms and held her, fiercely, possessively. "I'll help myself," he echoed, and then he was thinking only of her.

He kissed her. Her large purple eyes did not close, but watched him intently as his lips blended with hers. He took strength and boldness from her in that prolonged moment.

"I am going to marry you, Donna," he said tensely.

Donna nodded and spoke almost without breath. "I know it, Joe. I've known it since—since you won me at the Festival?"

"Did I win you? But I was forced to run out—"

"You won me," said Donna. "Axloff knew that you won me, no matter how the Festival ended. He knew that my heart went to you. But you must win me again, Joe. You must clear your own name and mine, with my people."

Joe's head was swimming. "If I can, Donna—"

"If you can, then I will marry you—in my heart."

"In your heart! What do you mean by that?"

Donna's eyes filled with tears, and she tried to bury her head in his shoulder, without touching him with her horns.

"How can we marry, except in our hearts," she sobbed softly, "when I have horns and you have none. Where would we live? Who would our friends be?"

He kissed her forehead and her eyelids. Then he shook her by the shoulders, and again he spoke fiercely.

"I intend to win you. Donna, whether I can ever marry you or not."

Uncle Keller, pipe in mouth, came limping down the ravine, clinging to the wooly neck of a naggie. In the soft twilight, Joe could have imagined it was a white sheep, except for the three perpendicular horns across the top of its head.

On one of the beast's horns an apple barely clung. It looked *yellowish* as the naggie moved through a shaft of light.

"A poison one!" Donna gasped. Then she screamed. "Uncle! Let it alone!"

But Uncle Keller was too intent on his purpose to hear. He succeeded in cornering the naggie and was jerking a handful of "smoking" from its wooly neck, when the beast turned and rammed at him.

The poison apple burst and spilled its orange liquid over Uncle's bare arms.

"Well, by crackies!" Uncle muttered to himself, giving an angry puff on his pipe. "Shower bath without a towel."

CHAPTER XVIII

DONNA gripped the ray gun and moved silently down the slope. Joe was right back of her. She stopped, shuddering, and leaned close to him. She handed him the gun.

"You'll have to do it, Joe," she said.

"Make it quick, before he knows we're here."

"Donna, I couldn't. I simply couldn't," Joe whispered.

"You've got to. It is the easiest way for him. In another, moment he will be a mad animal—"

"Let me get a rope and tie him."

"What rope would hold him? You would only prolong his suffering. Besides, he will have crashed into trees before you could get a rope. There he goes—no, not yet. Please—"

Joe moved a step closer and took aim.

Uncle Keller came up the ravine slowly and stopped in the thin shaft of sunlight to examine his drenched hands. He shook the broken bits of orange-colored apple flesh from his wrists. He held his handful of naggie wool up to see whether it had been damaged.

The ray gun in Joe's hand steadied toward the gaunt old man's heart, but the handful of naggie wool momentarily confounded Joe's aim.

"Go ahead," Donna whispered, choking on her own words.

"Wait till he puts his hands down."

"Go on and shoot. The ray will sweep him clean."

"If I don't—"

"The villagers will get him on their horns. You couldn't let a poor, limping old man race against the Ring of Death. Here, I'll do it."

"I'll do it," said Joe. His aim was sure, now. He pressed at the trigger, but not quite hard enough. Then Uncle Keller looked up and saw the two of them.

"Hey, up there!" he called. "Look at this mess o' poison on my hands. That derned naggie—*Joe! Are you aimin' somethin' at me?*"

Joe lowered the gun. He looked to Donna. Tears were streaming from her eyes.

"Not now," she whispered. "Wait till he flies into madness. But *why doesn't he?* ... Wait, Joe, there's something strange...."

They escorted the bewildered Uncle Keller to Axotello. Here, indeed was a case for a scientist's investigation. For as the minutes passed, he exhibited no symptons of becoming a "naggie man."

"By thunder, Joe, you had me half scared for a minute," he said, chuckling. "When I seen that gun pointin' toward my midsection, you looked almost like you meant business."

Joe couldn't say a word.

THE scientist proceeded to fill a test tube from the liquid that he carefully washed from Uncle's arms and wrists, and some minutes later, when he fed a spoonful of it to a stray naggie, the beast went mad and stormed off into the forest like a cyclone. But Uncle Keller was not affected.

"I can't figure what the fuss is all about," said Uncle Keller innocently.

"We do not understand why you have not contracted naggie madness," said Axotello.

"Me? Oh, I'm tough," said Uncle Keller. "I never git nothin' like that. Never had the measles or mumps or—"

"I will keep you here under observation," said the scientist.

Through the night Donna and Joe tramped together through miles of forest, toward the east. Over and over they pondered the strangeness of the day's events. And whenever they came back to Uncle Keller's narrow escape from death, they were struck by dread terrors of what might have been.

By morning they reached the bluff where Donna's space ship was hidden. Within a few minutes they were cruising west, high over the land of big blue apples.

"Please sit down back there," Donna said. "A space ship pilot should not allow herself to be kissed while the ship is in motion."

"Pardon me," said Joe. "I forgot we were in motion."

From their elevation the whole forest land was spread out below them like a vast map. Yellow sunlight and blue shadows highlighted the ridges along either side of the winding Silver River. The falls could be discerned. Farther downstream were the clearings, paralleling the river like cow paths. Joe identified the bend where the dehorned Martian and Rabbit-Face had met death from the same spear.

Up and down the river the small villages could be seen—mound-shaped houses peeking out like patches of toadstools in a garden of ferns.

"Sooner or later," said Joe, "we'll see a big black bird sailing over those tree tops."

"That metal bird may see us first," Donna remarked.

Joe's plan of action was simple. He would force Black-Hair to confess his guilt in public.

"This ray gun will do the trick," Joe declared.

O N THE night's hike to the ship he had practiced. It was a unique weapon. On a steady aim, its ray could cut a circular hole, two inches in diameter, through an apple a hundred yards away, and leave the apple hanging.

His plan was simple. He would spot the black-metal ship and trail it until it stopped. Then he would wait in hiding until he could catch Black-Hair and Scar-Hands on the ground.

"I'll march them in front of your uncle Londeenoko, and Mobar the judge, and all the villagers we can gather in."

"And suppose Black-Hair and Scar-Hands refuse to march?" said Donna. "Will you shoot them down?"

"They'll march," Joe declared. "I have a hunch Black-Hair is a coward. The dying Martian spoke of his changing color."

"He may be smart enough to know you won't kill him. A dead man can't confess."

"With this gun I could plug holes through his arm. I could remove his fingers, one, two, three, four, five—"

"I hope he doesn't kill you, Joe. He could do it you know, and be a hero. For the dehorning crimes happen to be on your head, not his."

Joe drew a deep breath. "If only we could catch him in the act. If—"

"If only we could have some authority like Londeenoko or Mobar the judge *with* us *when* we catch him... But on one point I must correct you, Joe. If Black-Hair is who I think he is, he is not a coward. What does he look like?"

In answer, Joe took pencil and paper and began to sketch. Donna, holding the ship at the lowest air cruising speed, drove down toward the tree tops within a half mile of the river. She was a clever pilot, and dared to skim so low that the morning shadows of the tallest trees flicked across the windows of the ship.

Joe finished his sketch. He turned it upside down.

"I remember him best the way he looked when I hung him by his feet and jerked his horns off... Well, how does he look to you? Pretty fancy sketch, huh?"

Donna's lips tightened. "I hate him," she said.

"Then he is someone you know?"

"Too well. He tried to force his friendship on me when I made my trip to Mercury. He was a national hero in the interplanetary colony at that time. He had done some exploring in his ship, *The Black Comet*, and they called him the Black Cometeer. I was introduced to him at one of the Colony parties—"

"And you fell for him?" The warmth of Joe's forehead betrayed his quick jealousy.

"At first, Joe, I was a bit overwhelmed," Donna admitted. "But soon I began to suspect him. He had falsified some of his claims. He had held back some valuable information that he owed his government. You see, his secret commercial schemes were already forming."

"Have you seen him often?"

"Only once, here on Mars. He followed me back and came to see me when my father was still living. Father was the judge, and it did not take him long to discover that this dashing Black Cometeer meant to steal from Mars. He even invited father to join him. Father quietly persuaded him to leave the planet. But he must, have returned recently with this vicious plan. He is evidently stealing horns for the Interplanetary ivory trade."

"He's clever," said Joe. "Aside from you and the scientist's party, there are probably no people on Mars who do not believe that I started this wave of horn thievery."

"He is clever," said Donna. "And he will not easily take on the color of a coward."

ONE of the instruments in the control panel had been humming a faint musical note. Now it swelled to an insistent volume. It was the metal detector. The black-metal ship was being approached.

After a series of switchbacks, they knew the exact spot beneath the leafy forest branches where it was concealed. It was an hour's work to find a suitable hiding place for their own ship within easy walking distance of the Black Comet.

"No telling how many villagers have seen us by this time," said Joe. "They seemed to be on the move all along the river this morning. But their seeing us won't make any difference if we can march that black-haired cometeer to justice."

Joe had sketched a rough map of the region from the air. As soon as they left the ship the map became indispensable. The clearing a mile to the south was familiar.

"That's where the spear deaths took place yesterday morning!" Joe exclaimed. "The river is just beyond."

"It is also where we saw villagers gathering this morning," said Donna. Then she pressed Joe's hand in a gesture of restraint. "Look!"

A long line of villagers with spears was moving out into the forest from a river trail.

From a clump of bushes Joe and Donna watched.

"I have counted three hundred," Donna whispered, and still more are coming."

The long line moved swiftly, stealthily, single file, its members spaced about thirty yards apart. It passed at a distance of a quarter of a mile from their hiding place. It began to circle. Soon Joe knew that a huge trap of spears and horns was being formed.

"They expect to find the dehorners inside the circle," said Joe. "They'll gradually close in, like hunters on a round-up."

Donna trembled against Joe's shoulder. "It is the largest Ring of Death I ever saw. They must know that they are about to enclose the black-metal ship."

"Then they'll enclose the Black Cometeer," Joe said, "also Scar-Hands and all the rest of the gang."

"But our ship they will not enclose!" Donna exclaimed. "Luck was with us when we hid it."

"But what about us?"

"We are already enclosed," said Donna. "We will soon find ourselves at the center of the ring."

"Face to face with the Cometeer," said Joe, "I *hope.*"

CHAPTER XIX

THE ray pistol shot noiselessly. A spray of leafy bushes fell over with a quiet swish. The bolt of disintegration had cut the stalks like a hot steel blade through candles.

"Our camouflage," Joe whispered. Then seeing that Donna did not know the word, he added, "We will disguise ourselves as bushes."

Donna smiled. "If you had not shaved in camp yesterday, more bushes would not be needed."

They cloaked themselves in the bushes of shrubbery. They ran and walked and crept, by turns, taking advantage of every screen the forest provided. Within a few minutes they were nearing the center of the guarded area, and not once had they been seen.

Joe knew it was a race against time and chance. If the dehorners, working somewhere within the circle got wind that a great Ring of Death was closing in, they would leap to their ship and fly off.

A naggie path cut across a bit of open meadow. The wide patch of blue sky was what Joe had been looking for.

"A ship could find its way through that opening," Donna observed.

"Then it's in that, ravine where the stream curves into the cliff," Joe said.

A moment later they were feasting their eyes on the famous Black Comet. Its blue-black metal sides shone where patches of sunlight filtered through the overhanging trees. It was set with its nose toward the meadow clearing. Its plastic windows revealed the gleam of its interior trappings.

"I don't hear anyone," Donna whispered. "But they must have left someone on guard... Joe, where are you going?"

"Inside. You'd better wait here."

He held the ray pistol ready. He slipped from one tree to the next. He discarded his shoulder covering of shrubbery as he neared the final curve of the ravine. He stood in the ship's shadow, then, and braced his hand against its cool polished side.

The open airlocks awaited him. Three quiet steps. The brilliant lights of the interior dazzled his eyes. He clung to the handrail and paused, on the third step. The smell of machinery mingled with an odor slightly reminiscent of a butcher ship. Looking back into the passenger compartment, he saw the horns.

There were five or six bundles of them, stacked like faggots, lying on a mat on the floor. A spot of sunlight through the window highlighted them, and in their varied shades of pink and white they gleamed.

The sight was breathtaking. More than five hundred persons must have been dehorned to make such a pile. This outrage could grow into a permanent strife between planets.

A barely audible snore sounded from the control cabin. Joe moved forward a few steps until he saw the strange peaceful face of a hornless man—a Mercurian, no doubt—lying asleep beside the controls.

The keys that dangled from the man's fingertips gave Joe his cue. It was plain that those keys would fit the slots in the control panel.

Another low snore.

J OE slipped the keys from the sleeper's hand. He crept back to the airlocks. He heard a stirring and groaning. But he was away, now, keys pocketed, ray pistol on the alert, and nothing could stop him.

"You keep the keys," he said to Donna as they hurried on. "I might run into a bullet or a flash of disintegration. But if you can tell your uncle what I've seen—"

"And if the ship cannot get away—"

"We'll have them, by George!"

They camouflaged themselves again and chanced a view from a hilltop. The villagers with, spears were a long way off, as yet. They could be seen plodding along, jabbing at clumps of bushes and searching among the crags and other natural hiding places. In an hour or less they would close in, and when they did so, they meant to have a gang of dehorning criminals cornered.

"I can see Uncle Londeenoko pacing," said Donna, "trying to hurry them along."

"If I thought he would listen to reason, I'd have you go to him," said Joe.

"He will listen to reason when we make the criminals confess, not before. I will stay with you."

They moved cautiously down into the next wooded valley. The mischief makers would be between here and the nearest river village, un-aware that they were being surrounded. It was the logical place for them to work, just over the hill from their parked ship, near enough to the river trail to kidnap new victims. For many a curious Martian would gravitate toward the scene of yesterday's killing, a short distance down the river.

"Watch everything," Joe warned. He was growing tense. "If they catch one hint that these woods are being combed, they'll by-pass us and make for their ship."

It would have been a surer bet to hide near the Black Comet and wait till the larger circle brought them in. But the hope of catching them in the act drove Joe on.

"We are on the right trail," said Donna. "Listen!"

A muffled cry came from a victim tied to the trunk of a tree. It was a half grown boy. His horns were gone. Bandages had been slapped over his mouth to keep him from shouting. But his choked cry could be heard faintly.

Another one! A Martian girl in her adolescence was bound to the very next tree. Her clothing was torn, her hair was in sad disarray, her eyes were tear-filled. She had ceased to struggle or try to call.

A third, a fourth, and a fifth! All of them were gagged so they couldn't cry an alarm.

"We can't take time to release them yet," Donna warned, "The gang must be just ahead."

She and Joe ran, then, and the beat of their footsteps mingled with the thump of falling apples. They ran back of the line of victims.

A sixth victim was an old man, whose scalp had been gashed. Donna knew him.

"Free him, Joe. He may die before we get back to him."

Joe slashed with his knife. "Which way are the masked men?" he demanded.

THE bewildered old man wasn't sure. Released, he slumped, and lay at the foot of the tree, feeling his hornless head, weeping.

A seventh victim, and an eighth. Then no more.

"Which way did they go?" Donna cried. "We will capture them."

The seventh victim nodded ahead, the eighth victim indicated that he thought they had gone back. Now the line of victims had run out. And no gang could be seen in any direction.

But over the rise, several yards beyond, the spear-men appeared, closing in with their Ring of Death.

"The gang must be hiding down in that thicket," said Joe, "or else we've followed the line the wrong way."

"Come!" Donna called.

Now free of all camouflage, they retraced their steps on the run, cutting back toward the first victim they had found.

Joe slashed the bonds of the sobbing boy, and jerked the bandages off his mouth.

"Which way did they go? Have you seen them lately?"

"I could hear them," said the boy. "But they stayed back of these trees, out of my sight. I could hear them gathering up the loose horns."

"Which way?" Donna cried.

"*That* way, I think. Or *that* way."

They ran back to the girl with the tear-filled eyes, to set her free.

"Tell us—"

BUT Donna's demand was checked by an unexpected outburst of vicious temper. The girl, gathering her torn clothes about her, pointed at Joe.

"You did it!" she wailed. "I know you without your mask. I saw you at the Festival—"

"Quiet, you idiot!" Donna caught the girl's face in her hands and shook her. "If you can't tell us where they went, don't talk. They must be here—"

"They must have slipped through our fingers," Joe said. "To the ship!"

They ran to the crest of the rise. A line of spear-men was marching toward them. *The Black Comet* had already been passed, and no doubt a number of men had stayed to guard it.

"We are trapped," said Donna.

"Not as long as I have this!" Joe jerked his pistol.

"Do not shoot them, Joe." She caught his free hand, and they backed away from the advancing line.

Joe spoke through clenched teeth. "I could melt those spears right out of their hands."

"No, Joe. It is too dangerous. If you cost them one finger or the tip of one horn—"

Swish! A brown spear came through the air, straight like a bullet.

Joe shot at it. Whether by luck or good marksmanship, the disintegration ray caught it and dissolved it in the air.

Thirty or forty Martians must have seen it pass into nothingness.

Another spear started through the air. With less luck than before, Joe nevertheless shot the point off. Then with crisscrossing strokes, the ray cut it into a dozen pieces. The advancing Martians saw the scraps fall to the ground. Several of the men stopped in their tracks.

But one flank of a dozen or more, being ordered to charge, lowered their heads and came forward on a run.

"Stop!" Donna cried. "Stop! We are not the ones!"

They would not have stopped, however, but for Joe's swift work with the pistol. The disintegration ray sliced through the base of five small trees. The timbers twisted and toppled to form a barricade of branches.

The Martians stopped abruptly. They began to back away. For any weapon capable of dropping trees to the ground might conceivably play havoc with men's horns, or arms or legs.

This momentary halt gave Donna her chance to call out, "We know who you are looking for. We are looking for them too. Let us join you."

"You are Donna Londeen!" one of the spear-men answered. "Your uncle, Londeenoko, does not deny that you may be assisting with these crimes."

"My uncle should know better," Donna flung back at them. "Let your circle close in, and you will find the criminals you are searching somewhere in that ravine. They have made victims of eight more of our people."

"Eight more! You had better be right or it will be bad for you. March ahead of us," the spokesman ordered. "We will hold our spears until we have talked with Londeenoko."

Ten minutes later the circle closed in from all sides, to become a wall of spears and horns around the newly released victims.

The round-up was complete, then. But oddly, it had netted no one but Joe and Donna.

CHAPTER XX

LONDEENOKO'S voice was heavy with anger. For two or three minutes he simply roared without saying anything. His massive face grew red with rage. He paced around within the ring, and Joe and Donna kept turning to face him.

Joe still held his gun. More than a dozen times in the past few minutes he had felled branches of apples or whole trees in the paths of Martians who showed too much eagerness to hang him on their spears.

The effect had been noteworthy. Although he was a marked man, well remembered from the festival, they were inclined to treat him with respect. Although he was, from all appearances, their prisoner, they preferred to keep their distance. No one volunteered to walk into the center of the ring and take his gun away.

The eight dehorned Martians were now being treated for injuries outside the circle, and were the objects of much attention. Some of the spear-men were urging them to step forth and identify Donna and Joe as *the* horn thieves. But these victims were too dazed or humiliated or just plain mad to agree on anything. Amid the wrangling, their immediate testimony came to nothing.

It took the hard-boiled, red-faced Londeenoko to weld the mob spirit of these several hundred angry men into a swift, if ruthless, legal action. Unquestionably, they believed this hornless man deserved to be perforated with spears or horns. But first, he deserved to be duly convicted.

Londeenoko's roar gradually became more distinct. Then Joe realized he was raving more at Donna than himself.

"…such a disgrace! It is criminal beyond words! And to think that your own father was the most honored judge we ever knew. What would he say if he knew his own daughter had betrayed us—"

"Stop!" Joe shouted. "You can't say those things to her."

"Who says I can't?"

"You are not the judge," Joe said savagely. "If you were, you might want to hear the truth. You might listen—"

J OE'S voice was lost in the angry uproar. Three spears came flying through the air. One went wild over Joe's head. Another made Donna dodge, and even so, it thumped through her horns. The third would have struck through her breast if Joe hadn't caught it with a ray from his pistol. With phenomenal accuracy he took it, and it was gone.

Londeenoko roared for order, and he marched twice around the circle to give, the spear throwers his best tongue lashing.

Then he came back to Donna and Joe.

"Your crimes will cease from this hour," he said. "After all we have seen, after all the horrible evidence you have created against yourselves, there is nothing to do but order the two of you to be put to death at once."

"Suppose we refuse to die," Joe snarled.

"At one word from me, the spears will strike you from all directions."

Joe breathed fire. "Are you so sure? With one sweep of my weapon there will be no spears. *And there will be no men!*"

"You are not that swift."

"Shall I show you?"

But Donna cried, "No, Joe. Don't kill them. Make them listen. Tell them that if they kill us they will not end this trouble. The horn thieving will go right on."

Londeenoko's eyebrows jumped. "So you admit your gang is so highly organized—"

"We admit nothing," Joe snapped, "except that we know who the horn thief is. I'll bring him and his gang to you if you give me a chance."

The half grown boy, recently dehorned, squeaked his comment to this boast.

"Give him a chance, and I will help him, because he set me free."

It was a small, piping voice, but it weighed heavily, in that moment, against the roar of Londeenoko. The big, crusty man hesitated. The boy happened to be one of his many grandchildren. If there was one thing that Londeenoko tried to avoid it was an argument from his children and grandchildren. They had a way of banding together and upsetting his firmest decisions.

"We will hold court here and now," Londeenoko growled. "I will appoint my officers—"

"Here comes the judge!" Someone shouted.

Judge Mobar, attended by one servant, came stalking up through a thicket from the direction of the river. The circle broke to make a place for him.

As usual, he was a dramatic figure in his official robe, wearing the overlapping squares of bright green paint on his face. His eyes were depths of darkness. His dark hair was bushy over his ears. His horns were highly polished.

Three apples hung upon his horns, and this might have been taken to signify that he had come on a long jaunt through the forest.

The young judge took command immediately.

His servant escorted him across to Londeenoko, who gave him the dignified greeting befitting any judge.

"I did not know you were in this part of the valley," Londeenoko said, half apologetically.

"I see that you have captured the foreigner who is known to have proposed our most horrible crime wave," said the judge. "I trust you did not intend to let him escape."

"No verdict has been reached," said Londeenoko.

"Verdict? Do you imply," the young judge said sharply, "that you would have held court without me?"

LONDEENOKO showed his fighting face. "You were absent when we organized the ring of spears, Mobar. How were we to know that you had not returned to your land 'Up North'? No one has seen you recently—"

"Spare me your excuses," Mobar said. His young face was hard. The green squares on his cheeks and forehead, bright in the sunlight, gave him a metallic cast. It was difficult for anyone to defy him, if only from his stern mouth and deep eyes. "As you see, I am here at the time I am needed. We will proceed with the case."

Judge Mobar seemingly had won out over Londeenoko, as usual.

Yet some whispers around the circle were evidence that Londeenoko's sharp thrust had hit home. It had reminded the crowd that Mobar was comparatively new and not well known. He had come as an itinerant judge, from "Up North"—that mysterious realm of the unknown, from which anyone might be said to come if he did not wish to tell precisely where he had been.

To Joe, Mobar said, "Step forward, you. Another step... There... Now answer my questions. Where do you come from?"

Joe looked to Donna. She nodded for him to go ahead and answer.

"From another planet called the Earth."

"What is your business?"

"I am the city clerk of Bellrap."

"Bellrap? What is Bellrap?"

Joe had to explain the nature of his Earth city and the duties of a city clerk. He admitted that he came in a ship that could travel through space, and that another Earthman was with him, but he did not mention Donna.

"We have already surrounded the ship," Londeenoko interrupted, much to the judge's obvious discomfort. "We have stationed guards and have bound the sleeping man who occupied this ship."

The judge scowled deeply. "Were any evidences found to explain these dehorning crimes?"

Someone replied that stacks of horns had been discovered in the ship.

"I will examine the ship myself in a few minutes," said the judge. "What do you call this weapon that you hold?"

"A ray pistol," said Joe.

"Did you bring it from the Earth?"

"No."

"Where did you get it?"

"I borrowed it."

"It came from another planet, you will admit?"

"Yes."

"Then you will also admit that you have friends from other planets who are helping you with your dehorning crimes."

"I will not. I am not engaged in any dehorning crimes."

"Will you show us how the ray gun operates?" said Mobar. "There is a heap of fallen apples against that tree trunk. Shoot at them."

JOE shot into the heap. With a slight turn of his wrist, he disintegrated six or seven apples and cut holes through others. He sliced a niche four-fifths of the way through the tree trunk. The tree trembled and a shower of apples fell.

Then he held the gun, as harmless as a cob-pipe, in his hands, and waited for the agitated judge to proceed.

"This demonstration proves," said Mobar, "that this Earth man is equipped to slice horns off our heads. You admit this, do you not?"

Joe admitted it, but he added, "Look, Judge, if I were slicing your horns off, I would never go to the trouble of tying you to a tree. You know that all of these victims have been bound. And the jobs look like they've been done with a meat cleaver or a hack saw. Now if I were do-ing it—well, step out, Judge and I'll show you how easy it would be if I were using—"

"Silence!" Mobar snapped. "There will be no further demonstra-tions. Where did the gun come from? From your Earth?"

Again Donna nodded for him to go ahead and answer, so Joe said, "Venus."

Mobar turned to his servant. "Examine the gun and see if the Earth man is telling the truth—"

The servant approached to take the gun. Joe hesitated.

"Let him examine it," Donna advised.

Joe looked at the servant's extended hands. They were caked with a layer of yellow mud. They had apparently been dipped in the slime of the nearby ravine recently, for they were not dry between the fingers.

Those mysterious hands waited for the weapon. Joe started to hand it over, when—

Plop!

An over-ripe apple fell and struck one of the hands, scoured a patch of yellow mud away, to reveal that *scars marked the flesh of that hand.*

Joe took two backward steps. He gripped the ray gun firmly.

"Get away from me, Scar-Hands!" he barked. "Stand where you are, everyone. You want to know who the real horn thief is, don't you?"

"Yes!" Londeenoko shouted above dozens of others.

"Well, I'm telling you right now, because he's right in this circle, wearing artificial horns. He is—"

Smack!

The poison apple, thrown by someone Joe did not see, struck him squarely on the back of the head. He felt a stinging sensation. Almost instantly he went naggie-mad.

CHAPTER XXI

JOE knew he was mad. A hundred wild impulses struck him at once. The strongest impulse was to knock down a tree. Any man, woman, or naggie would crash into a tree, Joe remembered, when seized by naggie-madness. And that was his uncontrollable desire.

Joe crashed into the first tree he saw. He struck it hard with his left shoulder. The trunk cracked off its base and the whole tree fell. (Joe forgot that previously he had almost cut the tree down with his gun.)

Now all the men around him knew he was naggie-mad, and he was fully aware of it. But he was nonetheless mad. The heat of the naggie poison circulated through his body like wild fire.

Donna called to him in a shrill terrified voice. She wanted him to run.

He wanted to run, but there were so many other things he wanted to do at the same time. He wanted to clip Londeenoko's mustache off. So, with his deadly accurate ray gun, he clipped the mustache off.

The men were hastily forming three concentric circles, and the innermost was a small, fierce circle of lowered heads with deadly horns that all pointed at him. It was moving toward him. He wanted to play leap frog over it, and over the second and third circles, too. But first he wanted to trim Scar-Hands' toenails. So he shot in that direction.

"I didn't know you could dance," he yelled at Scar-Hands. "Dance some more!... That's wonderful. More! More! Dance till your horns flop off!"

Then he wanted to give Mobar a haircut where the hair was too puffy around his ears. He wanted to see how black that hair was under the wig. So he shot in that direction. Not all of his aims were perfect. He was too full of mad, wild impulses to care about the results.

"Let the chips fall where they may!" he yelled, clipping another lock of Mobar's hair. "Turn your face, you green-faced checkerboard. I'll trim your profile. I'll change your color, like the Martian said."

He remembered clipping a niche along one side of Mobar's face. And while he still was obsessed by the desire to draw the outline of the judge's features, it seemed high time for him to move. The spears were coming at him.

"Let the lady out!" he screamed.

But Donna was already on the outside of the third ring, he discovered. Where she was, he wanted to be. So he played leap-frog over the three rings.

A flying spear ripped under his left arm, tearing the flesh. A pin-prick. What did he care for flying spears? He cleared the last barrier of men, cutting two spears out of the air. The men ducked and fell to the ground to avoid the unseen ray of his gun. A spray of foliage showered from a tree caught in its path.

He ran at Donna as if to strike her with his head.

"L-O-O-K O-U-T!" he yelled, in a weird, wild voice.

THE brambles a few yards beyond would be a sticky place for her to land if he knocked her off her feet. Why not land in them himself? He leaped over her head. His strength, increased by the light gravity of Mars, had never been so great as now.

He sank into the brambles, but came up with a bound and broke into a dead run. The scratches burned his arms and legs, and the torn flesh in his side smarted in the wind. But these were nothing to the explosive fire that filled his whole body—naggie madness!

He was all of the planet's mad men rolled into one.

He was all of the swiftest footracers of Mars, rolled into one.

He was a bulldozer with invisible wings. If he dodged trees instead of smashing at them headfirst, it was only because he was looking for bigger game.

He whirled when a spear slid along the ground near his feet. He saw them coming, no longer with spears, but with most determined horns. He pointed the pistol over his right shoulder, and shot a zigzag line through the overhead branches as he ran. A green shower fell to the path in his wake. His pursuers found themselves in a tangle.

Long before he reached the river he had outdistanced them, all but one.

He still held his gun. It could destroy anything. Persons? Of course. Trees? The very largest. The river? Perhaps.

What of the powerful waterfalls? Could he cut it into pieces with the disintegration ray?

He dodged tree and rocks, he leaped bushes, he followed the river to the falls. He wished the people of Bellrap could see him now—the strongest, wildest, maddest creature that ever lived! The freest, the least controlled. He was Joe Banker, the "naggie-man" of Mars!

He looked back. Donna dodged behind a tree. She alone had followed him all this distance. He could see the line of her pink shoulder, the green-and-white stripes of her abbreviated sport costume.

So she was still following him.

She would see him disintegrate the waterfalls.

He shot the ray at the falls, but nothing happened. He could see the line that marked the penetration of the ray, but the water filled it instantly.

The gun was no good.

"It's no good! No good!" Joe yelled, and he threw the gun to the ground.

HE WOULD fight the waterfalls with his bare hands. The falls were powerful, but so was he. He would show them!

He climbed up on a rock, and made ready to dive. He looked back. He knew Donna was screaming at him, not to do it. That was because she didn't understand. He was an Earth man. He liked a fair fight.

But there was better rock than this to dive from, so he climbed down and went to it. Then he discovered a still taller one. He clambered up its steep sides. The scratches and prickles and torn flesh were nothing to the fire that burned inside him. He was naggie-mad. He made ready to dive.

But suppose he should encounter a huge fish—with horns! He should have his gun.

Donna had the gun now.

That was all right. Let her come along. If they met a huge fish with horns, she could collect the souvenirs.

"You go first!" he shouted to her. She began to back away. Maybe she didn't hear.

"Ladies first!" he yelled at the top of his voice.

She was running away. He would have to catch her and throw her in. Then he would plunge in after her.

Whenever the clouds hung heavy or the breezes blew strong through the forest of falling apples, the villagers chased for shelter. They ran no risks of being struck by an orange-colored apple. It was well known that poison apples frequently fell during rains or windstorms.

Now the clouds had gathered, and the horned pursuers took heed and gave up their chase for today.

Consequently, only Donna saw Joe going through his horrible antics. She alone followed the wild trail of his comings and goings.

That he was in terrific physical torment, she did not doubt. He was completely unpredictable. Any new chance impulse might set him off on a new tangent.

When he failed to overtake Donna to throw her in the river, he threw a log in, instead. It splashed beautifully, and darted over the falls, and he yelled, "There you go, Donna!"

Then, "I'll catch up with you!" and he threw another log in. "There goes Joe Banker! He used to sing tenor in the Bellrap quartet!"

Joe turned and ran, then, crashed into a tree. The blow was a knock-out. He passed out cold.

CHAPTER XXII

DONNA was carrying him. A falling apple had awakened him. The wind was whipping the trees. The low rumble was not thunder, but apples thumping down the slopes and filling the ravines.

He was a heavy load for her, and she was having a hard climb against the wind. Darkness was coming on. Her horns were loaded with apples, all of them. She hadn't taken time to rid herself of the extra weight.

A wild exultation filled Joe's heart. He awakened laughing.

"I never would have believed it. I love being mad if it earns me this! Let me carry you awhile."

"Quiet," said Donna. Her eyes were wide, frightened. "Do not squirm. I will take you back to the ship. You were stunned by a hard blow. I do not know whether you were seriously injured, but I—"

"Injured! I feel wonderful. Let me carry you!"

"Do not shout. If the villagers hear you they will kill you."

Joe gave forth a shout that would have put the loudest roar of Londeenoko to shame. He shouted because he was happy. He was with Donna.

"Just let them try to kill me for that!"

"They could do it, and they may."

"Impossible. I'm too happy to be killed. Hooo-whoopie!"

Donna ran with him. Often she looked back through the falling apples and spattering raindrops to see whether any Ring of Death was following. Suddenly she stumbled on a rolling apple and fell. Her arms released him.

He scrambled to his feet, yelling. "So you want to play!" He grabbed all the apples and began throwing them at her.

She lowered her horns to catch the first volley—her instinctive self-protection. At the same time, she ran backward, watching his every move.

He stooped to pick up an armload of apples. He looked up to see that she was running away. He threw at her. He threw at everything, the trees, the clouds, the village a mile away, the falling raindrops. Then he raced after her, but she was swift.

She still had the gun, and now she played his game of cutting down branches as she ran, to obstruct his path. When she felled a tree, he shouted gleefully.

"Now we'll play. I'll throw the whole darned tree at you and see if I can knock you down!"

But it was a heavy tree and he couldn't lift it. So he kicked it. Then he grabbed his foot, and gave a howl of pain, laughing at the same time.

DONNA was far ahead of him, descending a ravine that Joe remembered. Her space ship would be there. Maybe she would enter to escape the storm. The rain was growing heavier.

He heard the click of the airlocks. He sprinted down the bank.

"Wait for me. It's raining!"

A spotlight turned on him. He liked that. He stopped to wash his hands in it. It looked so warm in the thick darkness, and his hands were wet and cold.

The spotlight moved. Joe moved to keep up with it. It was shining from the side of the ship. The ship was moving. Joe ran and tried to keep abreast. The ship leaped ahead a short distance, then waited. Then hopped again.

"So you want to play games!" Joe yelled. "Just give me a chance to climb aboard."

Donna gave him no such chance. But she was playing a game, all right. She was leading him back to the camp of the Venus scientist.

It was almost morning. The rain had ceased.

Ruffledeen the chef and Axotello the scientist were holding a conference around the fire. Uncle Keller was snoring gently on the soft camp bed nearby. A wide canvas roof had been hung high among the trees to protect Ruffledeen's camp kitchen.

The fire was low. Two lights hung from posts to enable Ruffledeen to sort through his pack of recipes. He and the scientist were comparing notes. For many of the special cakes on the chef's list there were corresponding records in the scientist's file.

"Formula number 327," the scientist would say, "was an attempt to lengthen life."

"I have fed more than nine hundred cakes from this formula to old men and women of this forest."

"Yes, here is a record of their ages at death!" And the scientist would review the periods of feeding, and compare their average length of life to that of a similar group not treated to such cakes.

Later, "Formula 420 was our experiment in altering the shapes of horns from straight spikes to graceful curves."

"These cakes were fed to infants," said Ruffledeen. "We have also given many to expectant mothers; but I think the results have been negative."

This was frequently Ruffledeen's comment, or that of the scientist. They could not hope for success with the great majority of their feeding experiments. For one or two successful experiments, dozens or hundreds might end in failure. But the one or two might prove a boon to the whole population.

Uncle Keller ceased to snore and began to stir.

"Shall we give him another round?" asked Ruffledeen.

"A warm drink first, then more questions," said the scientist.

UNCLE KELLER was not in the best mood. He had been subjected to endless questioning since his recent encounter with the poison apple.

"I ain't slept a wink," he complained.

"I will bake a cake to help you sleep soon," said Ruffledeen. "But first, Axotello wishes you to remember some more of the foods you eat on the Earth."

"Yes," said the scientist, "Go on with your list, please."

"What did I end with?" said Uncle Keller.

"You named thirteen kinds of pies, including apple pies. You stated that you have eaten no blue apples before you came here, but that red apples are common and yellow apples are not unknown. This statement may be the key to our problem. Were your yellow apples anything like our poison apples? Maybe you have grown up with a resistance to poison."

Uncle Keller shook his head. There was more difference than he could explain. On the Earth anyone would be a fool to call a yellow apple poison.

When Axotello tried to pin him down to the probable differences in chemical content, Uncle lost his temper.

"Stop it! I don't like scientific words. How do I know but what you're callin' me names behind my back?"

The scientist smiled and told him to go back to bed and finish his night's sleep. This Uncle Keller gladly did.

"The next logical move, Ruffledeen," said the scientist, pacing back and forth in front of the fire, "is to experiment with the other Earth man."

"How?" Ruffledeen asked.

"We will break a poison apple over him," said Axotello. "If he does not become naggie-mad, we will know that Earth man's diet holds the secret."

Ruffledeen produced a poison apple from his stores and sat by the fire polishing it.

"And suppose," said Ruffledeen, "that the other Earth man does go naggie-mad?"

"Then he will simply become one of our unsuccessful experiments. Too bad, of course. He is an alert young man. I have high hopes that he will be immune—"

"Someone is coming over the hill," said Ruffledeen.

In the early morning twilight they saw the silhouettes of the two running figures, several yards apart. "Donna!" the scientist exclaimed. "She is running from someone. Quick, my gun! Guards, where are you?"

The camp came to life almost before the echo of Axotello's voice had faded. Wet branches were falling from the trees along the ridge, being shot down by a disintegration ray gun in Donna's hand. Her pursuer was hurdling these barriers like a deer.

"It is Joe!" Axloff cried, running up to join his father. "Joe! Donna! What is happening?"

It was Donna who cried, "Don't shoot him, Axloff. Only catch him *and* tie him. He is crazy from a poison apple:"

CHAPTER XXIII

JOE heard the commotion in camp. He shrieked with laughter to hear them say he was naggie-crazy. He already knew it. He had known it since yesterday. Were they just now finding it out?

So they meant to catch him and tie him, did they?

"Bring your stoutest chains, Axloff!" Joe shouted, "No rope will hold me!"

The confusion from the camp annoyed him, so he leaped a high thicket and cut a course in front of Donna. She was forced to run in another direction. The camp was left behind.

On the third hill beyond camp he overtook her.

"Whew! You run too fast!" he said, with a laugh that was almost a bray. "I can keep up with your ship as long as it jumps like a frog, but I can't keep up with you. You don't have to point that gun at me, Donna. I already love you. I'm going to marry you as soon as I remove your horns.... Here, stand right up against this tree. It will only take a minute."

Joe, please! Please let me go! You don't know what you're doing. You're out of your head.... Oh, why did I not shoot you?"

"Cause I'm too good looking," said Joe. He guffawed. "If you want me shot, let me do the dirty work."

He tossed her gun over his shoulder. His hand flashed back, tearing a strip from his water-soaked shirt. He bound her hands behind the tree.

He bound her feet with a twisted piece of his sleeve. With the remainder of the shirt he made a band around the trunk above her head to include her three head-horns, tying them back securely.

"You don't happen to have a saw, do you, madam?" he said, smiling happily. He wiped the sweat from his eyes.

From his trouser pocket he brought forth a sturdy pocket knife.

Donna was eyeing him steadily. "Listen to me, Joe. Do you know that I am trying to save your life? Do you understand that?"

"Remind me to give you a quarter," said Joe. He whetted the knife on the palm of his hand. "Plain or fancy, madam?"

"Joe, you are naggie-crazy. By all the rules, I should have killed you. But I thought I could exhaust you, making you follow along with the ship. You'll die in a few hours, Joe, at the rate you're burning up your life. If you could only control yourself—make yourself rest—give Axotello a chance to help you. By now he may know why Uncle Keller didn't go crazy. Please, Joe, listen to me."

"You're trying to stop my fun. I want to cut your horns off."

"Kiss me, Joe," she said desperately. She was at the end of her wits. "Kiss me, Joe!"

"Ha, ha, ha! So you want to play games. One kiss for each horn I remove. Here we go."

He began to wield the knife. He muttered that the handle was too sharp and the blade was too dull, and he had just as well turn it end for end. So he did. He tapped her horns with the handle and gripped the blade until he noticed blood was dripping from his hand.

"Darned knife's no good," he said. "Hold it for me while I go get a saw."

"All right," said Donna. "The scientist has a saw among his tools. I will wait."

He placed the open knife in her bound hands. Then he scampered away, bounding like a deer.

THEY caught him at noon. It took the whole camp to do it, and as matters turned out, Ruffledeen became the key man. It was one of his sleepcakes, more than the pit-fall trap, that turned the trick.

But almost everyone helped, and the suggestions by Uncle Keller were invaluable.

"Let Donna act as a decoy," Uncle insisted. "Set a beartrap in the path, and cover it over. Then put Donna on the other side of it."

"I am afraid," said Axloff, "that he will pay no attention to Donna, being crazy."

"He's not that crazy," said Uncle Keller.

Donna had freed herself and hurried back to camp, and was urging Axotello to do something.

Joe could be heard carrying on his mad antics beyond the hill. He had forgotten about Donna's horns and was now engaged in a fight with her space ship, beating its metal nose with a timber.

"He cannot hurt anything," Axotello said. "As long as he is bumping around up there we can work on a trap. But if he starts back to the village we must overtake him, or they will slay him."

THE scientist's swift workers grabbed their spades, ran to the appointed spot, and made the loose dirt fly. Everyone helped, and they soon had a deep pitfall in the path. Uncle Keller marveled. On the Earth such a task would have taken all day.

Ruffledeen, who had hastened to make a triple-potency sleep-cake, came trudging up the grade to see what the "bear-trap" looked like. By this time it was covered, and looked like a part of the path, surrounded by a wide scattering of fresh earth.

The chef got down on his hands and knees to convince himself that there was a covered pit. Someone shouted at him to come away.

Then Axloff yelled, "Quiet! Here they come!"

The mad chase came over the hill, Donna well in the lead. She had attracted Joe's attention, according to plan, and was running straight down the path toward the camp. Joe was gaining on her, shouting again that he wanted her horns.

She leaped over the pitfall, slackened her pace, looked back to see what would happen.

Joe came on. Ruffledeen drew back out of his way. But Joe didn't fall through.

Instead, he stopped on the path within three feet of the hidden spot. His mad merry glance took in the scattered dirt. Then he gave Ruffledeen a push. Ruffledeen went down in a shower of dirt.

Joe enjoyed this effect. It was interesting to see the chef surprised and hear him yell for help. Joe sat down and dangled his feet over the edge of the pit and watched the show.

No one else seemed to be around. Actually, the others were watching anxiously from concealment, wondering what the mad man would do next.

He was in the mood to rest, so he sat there, calling down to the imprisoned chef. He had always been attracted by Ruffledeen's wavy purple whiskers.

"You should eat more of my cakes and you might have purple whiskers," said Ruffledeen. "I have one cake down here. Will you come down and join me?"

"Why don't you run back to camp and bake some more," said Joe, "and we'll have a party."

"But I am down here," said the chef. "Let me take your place till you come back."

Joe leaped down. After a superhuman struggle, he managed to get Ruffledeen out. Then he ate the one cake while he waited.

He never knew how long he waited, because he went to sleep. When he awakened, he was bound so tightly to a tree he could hardly breathe.

CHAPTER XXIV

"**B**OW! Bow-wow!" he yelled. "Bow-*wow-wowrr!*"

Uncle Keller and Donna emerged from a camp shelter and sauntered toward him.

"Poor guy," said Uncle. "I doubt if he'll ever come out of it."

"Bow-wow!" said Joe.

"He must think he's a naggie or somethin'," said Uncle Keller.

"I'm the bark of this tree!" Joe yelled at them. Then he laughed a choked laugh under the handicap of his bonds. "So you don't like the bark of this tree? Well, I refuse to be the sap. Cut me loose from here."

"Take it easy, Joe."

"Cut me loose. I have an important engagement."

"You are right, Joe," said Donna. "The scientist will come here to see you this afternoon. He wishes to try certain foods—"

"I have a singing engagement," said Joe. "Ladies and gentlemen— and Uncle Jim Keller, please take your seats for the concert. The guest star of our afternoon program is none other than the renowned tenor, Joe Banker, of Bellrap, U.S.A. Applause, please.... Thank you."

Joe sang for two hours. His concert rambled from popular songs to classics and opera, and ended with the Star Spangled Banner.

Almost everyone in camp gathered around to listen.

He sang some quartet numbers, first announcing that, unfortunately, the other three members of the quartet could not be present. On one of these songs Uncle Keller found himself growing sentimental. The old Earth times seemed so far away and long ago. But when Uncle chimed in on a strain of the *Old Oaken Bucket*, the concert came to a dead stop, and Joe said, "Someone drop an apple on the bald-headed row and stop that snoring!"

The scientist decided to wait until Joe calmed down before trying to plan his diet. Donna urged the listeners from the camp to go back to their work.

"We will leave you now, Joe," she said. "I will see you after you have rested. Uncle Keller will stay with you.

So Joe concluded his concert with the Star Spangled Banner, and to his satisfaction everyone stood attentively—not because they knew it was proper, but because the song thrilled them.

Soon Joe was alone with Uncle Keller.

"Ropes hurt you much, Joe?"

"Ropes insult me," said Joe. "I told them nothing but chains would hold me. I could break these ropes if I wanted to."

"Relax, Joe."

"Don't you believe it? I'll break them just to show you. Watch me."

"Relax! Relax! You'll skin yourself alive."

"Relax!" Joe mocked. "If you were full of fire like I am, you'd uproot this tree, and turn it into a battle-ram, and bust up the camp—Say, that's an idea!"

Joe strained his muscles against his bonds.

"If I was you," Uncle Keller began. Then he shook his head, and mumbled, "Naw, you wouldn't listen."

H E SETTLED down against the foot of a tree and refused to look at Joe. He puffed calmly at his pipe.

"If you were me—what?" Joe was curious.

"I'd light a pipe an' have a good smoke and quiet my nerves."

"Give me your pipe," said Joe.

Uncle Keller rose slowly. "This naggie-wool makes a right good smoke," he said. "I reckon I can spare you a puff."

He put the pipe between Joe's teeth, and Joe smoked.

"It's awful," Joe said. "I don't see how you endure it…. Wait, not so fast. I didn't say I was through. Let me finish this pipeful."

When he finished, he said, "I'll be honest about it. Uncle Keller. That wasn't bad. Fill'er up again."

He smoked another pipeful, and another. Uncle Keller watched him suspiciously.

"I like it," said Joe. "It's good medicine."

Uncle Keller, tapping the pipe, paused to look Joe in the eye.

"You like it, huh? Maybe you ain't so crazy as I thought."

"I'm not crazy at all," said Joe.

"Son, you're as looney as a flea-bit flea."

"Not any more. I'm well."

"Since when?"

"Since I smoked that naggie wool."

CHAPTER XXV

Uncle KELLER thought he would have to swing his fists at two of the camp guards before they would agree to let him interrupt. The scientist and Ruffledeen were working up a new cake recipe.

Finally Uncle Keller succeeded in breaking in on the scientist's study, although he was almost too angry to talk.

Fortunately, the scientist could understand his brand of English. But the news Uncle announced struck with a shock.

"How do you know he is cured?"

"Because he talks horse-sense, the same as me," said Uncle. "No baloney."

"What does he say?"

"Well, first he said that naggie-wool makes good smokin'—and that's as wise a statement as anyone could make. I don't figure a judge could improve on that."

"Go on."

"Well, next he began rememberin' things, hopin' he didn't do too much' damage while he was off his nut."

"That is good," said the scientist.

"What else?"

"Right away he was all hot and bothered for fear he'd chopped off Donna's horns. He was in a stew for me to send her around so he could be sure he hadn't—"

"Did you?"

"He said he'd go crazy if he didn't see her right away—and I didn't want that to happen—so—"

Donna and Joe appeared, silhouetted on the hilltop, coming down the trail arm in arm. Five minutes later Joe and Ruffledeen were joking over the tea party that they didn't have down in the bear trap. Fifteen minutes later, Joe's cuts and bruises were being treated. The guards prepared a bed for him and he was made to lie down and rest.

He fell asleep slowly. His overtaxed muscles and nerves gradually relaxed. He could hear the excited discussions over the merits of smoking naggie wool. He listened until he heard the scientist declare that Uncle Keller was the hero of the hour for his wonderful discovery.

"You have done what we scientists with all our formulas failed to do," said Axotello.

Uncle Keller said modestly, "It was a pleasure. I like to share my smokin'."

And Joe, smiling, fell asleep.

Later, he learned that Axotello's studies had found a scientific justification for the miraculous cure. The potent poison of orange-colored apples penetrated through the skin of any man. But not through the wool of the naggie. (That beast was affected only when he ate some of the poison.)

Naggie wool was found to possess marvelous properties of poison resistance.

TWO days later, a multitude of horned Martians gathered at the edge of a village between the cliff and the river.

Uncle Keller and Joe went by taxi—the most exclusive taxi in the land—Donna Londeen's space ship. For by now the rumors had traveled far and wide that she was a flier of ships. She could no longer keep it a secret.

"Joe and I will just stay in the ship while you attend the meetings," said Uncle.

Donna laughed. "Since when have Bellrap citizens become so bashful. This may be your chance to 'Ring the Bell for Bellrap.' The people will want to see you."

"How well I remember," said Uncle Keller. "They want to make mince meat out of us for a lot of horn thievin' that Mercury bird got away with."

"Or did he get away with it?" Joe asked. Flashes of memory from his siege of madness kept tantalizing him. "It seems to me I combed someone's hair with that ray gun when I first went wild. I can't quite remember who."

"It was Judge Mobar," said Donna, "and your aim was perfect. Don't you remember what you did to him?"

"Did I—did I *change his color?*"

"His color and his shape," said Donna.

The facts began to dawn on Joe. A few minutes later he was standing on the cliff before one of the largest crowds of homed Martians ever assembled.

Londeenoko stood beside him, addressing the crowd.

"I have the honor to present our guest from another planet, Joe Banker. He is the man who exposed the criminal who called himself Judge Mobar."

"Who, me?" Joe blushed with pleasure.

"As a token of our appreciation, we present you with the trophies of your good deed."

LONDEENOKO motioned to two attendants. They marched forward, bearing the gifts. Londeenoko took the head-and-shoulder harness containing the artificial horns.

"Here is the apparatus which the Black Cometeer used to disguise himself as one of us. There were several sets of these, used by his helpers. But this is the one he wore—the one which fell apart when Joe Banker fired a ray gun over his left ear."

"Who, me?" Joe began to grin.

"And this," said Londeenoko, taking from the hands of the other attendant a rubber mask marked with bright green squares, "is the false face which the Black Cometeer wore, with the official markings of a judge. The slit across the left temple is the result of the most excellent marksmanship on the part of Joe Banker."

"That's one." Joe smiled all over his face. He stole a glance at Donna. She was flushed with pleasure.

"These were the devices," Londeenoko went on, "by which a desperado from Mercury carried out his acts of cruelty. When hundreds of you spearmen joined in a vast Ring of Death, he and his gang had no trouble in slipping through, pretending they were helping with the search. And yet, at that very moment, their ship, the Black Comet, was hidden only a short distance away, filled with stolen horns. That ship—"

Londeenoko drew a deep breath. His numerous grand-children in the crowd, he noted, were watching him anxiously.

"That ship is to be left in my care, I am proud to say. I am sure my niece Donna will gladly teach me to operate it."

A chorus of shouts greeted this announcement. But from a certain undercurrent of whispers, Joe knew that it wouldn't be long before the old gentleman's grandchildren would take possession of the infamous Black Comet.

Before Londeenoko completed his speech, Joe learned new and startling things about the Mercury desperado. A few years earlier the Black Cometeer had undertaken his first piracy. Soon after his first visit to the apple forest, he had learned the value of the Martian's horns as a commercial product.

"He intended to raise *crops of horns* on Mercury," Londeenoko charged. "And for this purpose he kidnapped several newly married couples from our forest and took them back to Mercury. He confessed this crime yesterday before he died from the numerous horn-punctures."

An audible hiss came up from the crowd.

"But I also learned, from his deathbed confession, that his kidnapping scheme turned out badly. The children who were born on Mercury to these horned couples *did not have horns.*"

"Why not?" Joe blurted. He almost jumped out of his shoes. Then his face went red, for everyone was staring at him, and they were amused. He began to back away.

At this moment the scientist walked forward, and Londeenoko beckoned to him.

"Here, my people, is the famous scientist of Venus, who may be able to explain the mystery of our horns."

After being duly presented and received, the handsome amber-eyed scientist began to shuffle through his papers. Something was missing. The last page of his conclusion on the horn theory was gone.

He looked around at the circle of guests assembled here above the crowd, and his penetrating gaze froze upon Uncle Keller.

Uncle, according to his habit, was totaling his expenses.

"What do you have there?" the scientist said.

"Huh?" said Uncle. "This is just an old scrap of paper I picked up with some foreign writin' on it. I was figurin' up a bill—"

"My document! Please!"

U NCLE gave up the valued paper without any fuss. He felt a glow of importance, as the scientist began reading. Beside him, Axloff, sitting with Donna's sister, gave him a smile and a wink.

"…and so, in view of the evidence," Axotello read, "one must conclude that all *human infants possess the capacity to grow horns.* If the environmental factors are favorable during infancy, the horns will develop. If not—"

"What on Earth is he saying?" Joe whispered.

"Nothing *on Earth."* Donna replied. The scientist held up the paper and gestured toward it as he commented. "In other words, my friends of Apple Forest, the children born in this region will develop horns, whether the parents have horns or not. And children born in other lands do not develop horns, whether their parents have horns or not.

"Londeenoko has just told you of the horned couples who were kidnapped and taken to Mercury, whose children, born there, remain hornless. Let me add an illustration of my own:

"When my wife and I arrived on this planet for the first time, she was expecting a child within a few days. After the child was born, we discovered that it was developing horns, like any native of this realm. The shock led to my wife's death. I too was stunned. But now I understand that it was a natural and inevitable development. This apple-falling environment produces horns. And my son, Axloff, living among you, has been proud to possess his eleven horns.

"My theory is not complete," Axotello concluded. "I am not yet ready to prove that it is the result of a blue-apple diet for nursing mothers. I cannot prove that the perpetual sound of falling apples upon infant eardrums may not have an effect. I shall gladly devote my remaining days to the perfection of these theories..."

BEFORE the scientist had finished, the people of apple land were glowing with a collective pride. They were the only people in the world whom Nature had blessed with beautiful horns. They applauded the hornless scientist for his assurance.

Londeenoko now turned to Joe, and asked him to stand again before the crowd.

"Joe Banker, rumor has it that you came to our land to make a public presentation of a gift."

Joe, filled with a chestful of importance, gestured to Donna.

"Ladies and gentlemen, I have the honor, in behalf of the Chamber of Commerce of Bellrap, U.S.A., the Earth, to present—wait a minute! *Uncle Keller!*"

"Huh?"

"Where did we put that silver loving cup?"

"We? Don't ask me about that. I ain't seen it since the day of the Bellrap Parade."

Joe snapped his fingers. "By George and by Joe, I just now remembered where I left it. I was crawling over a feed rack in your barn. Uncle, and here was this space ship all lighted up. I laid the cup down and forgot to pick it up. I left it there in the hay."

"Well, by crackies!" Uncle Keller chuckled. "I'll bet the old hens is layin' eggs in it every day."

"Ladies and gentlemen," Joe called out, "the presentation of Donna Londeen's gift must be postponed, owing to a technical difficulty. I'll have to wait until I get back to the Earth—if I ever do—and I sure hope I do!"

The meeting ended, a few minutes later, and Joe turned to look for Donna. Where was she? Not with Axotello or Axloff. Not with her sister. Had she gone down to some of her friends in the crowd, or returned to her space ship alone?

He was detained by throngs of villagers who wanted to meet him as a friend and a hero. They were shaking his hands eagerly, and smiling at him. As soon as possible he broke away and hurried back to the ship.

Donna had left a note for him with one of the four guards stationed at the airlocks.

"Dear Joe: I did not know you were so anxious to go back to the Earth. I had hoped…but please take my ship and go. Never mind the silver cup. I will always remember that you meant well.—Donna."

CHAPTER XXVI

"*SHE'll always remember!*" he exclaimed. Then, to the guard, "Where is she? Which way did she go?"

"She has given you your order," the guard snapped. "She said you knew enough about the ship to run it. Get in and go."

The guard started to usher him in.

"Stop it! I'm not going!"

"Yes you are!" The big guard glared down at him. Two others lowered their heads to press their horns against his ribs, forced him into the air locks.

He was on the verge of swinging his fists. "By George, you won't get away with this. I'm not going—"

"She said you were eager to return," the big guard growled.

"But not without her," Joe snapped. "When I go it'll be on a honeymoon, and I'm gonna tell her so. Now let me out or I'll—"

"Joe!" It was the soft voice of Donna, calling from inside the ship.

"Donna! What's the gag?"

"Joe, I only wanted to hear that—that word—*honeymoon.*"

For a moment Joe was speechless. He began to smile. Donna came to him, took his hand in both of hers. With a nod, she dismissed the guards. They sauntered away, chuckling.

"You still want to marry me, Joe—horns and all?"

"I love your horns," he breathed. "I can hardly wait till you march in the Easter parade back home in Bellrap. You'll be the queen of them all."

He took her in his arms and kissed her. He was still holding her when they heard limping steps approaching from somewhere outside the ship.

"It's Uncle Keller," said Joe. He'll be here in a minute."

"Joe, when we are married—"

"Yes, Donna?"

"We will have children?"

"Yes, dear."

"I wonder—shall they be born on Earth, or here in the Apple Forest?"

Joe smiled and shook her by the shoulders and then by the shoulderhorns. "Maybe some of each, dear. We'll discuss that later."

Uncle Keller, limping up the steps into the ship, seemed to be in a great hurry.

"Donna! Joe! Can you taxi me back to Earth for a couple o' weeks? I gotta lotta work to attend to."

"What kind of work?" said Joe.

"Orders to fill. I'm in business! Gonna bring civilization to this apple forest! Won't Bellrap be proud of me?"

"And your wife, too," said Donna. "What is this new business?"

"Corn-cob pipes. I already got seventeen hundred orders."

CONFESSIONS OF A MECHANICAL MAN

By BUZZ-BOLT ATOMCRACKER

In 1947 Don Wilcox created a story with a true science fiction background—the autobiographical tale of a robot's life—that featured a murder mystery with traces of film noir. It was published under the strangest of the many pseudonyms associated with Don, though this time there was an understandable reason for the odd pen name.

"...the other day a mechanical man walked into our office and handed us a manuscript. "There's my story," he said. "Take it or leave it." Then he walked out, buzzing and clicking. Now, if he'll come in again, we'll give him a check for the story—because we took it! We think it's a very nice piece of work, and maybe Mr. Buzz-Bolt will find he'll make a lot of friends with his first story, Confessions of a Mechanical Man.*"—Raymond A. Palmer in the editor's column "The Observatory",* Amazing Stories, *May 1947.*

DEAR MR. PALMER:

I am a robot looking for a job and I wonder whether you can use me in your office.

What are you blinking about? I expect blinks and stares from most people, but I thought the editor of *AMAZING STORIES* would be just the guy to understand. Wait till you see me. I have a satin-silver forehead and a chromium-plated smile. I have an iron will, a steel determination, and in case you need help handling your tough customers. When I snap my stainless steel teeth together they click like a meat cleaver on an anvil.

I'm only ten months old but I'm learning fast.

Almost any sort of job will do, just so it's something amazing. I'm a pretty versatile hunk of ore-refined, of course, and highly polished. When I haven't anything else to do, I shine my ankles and knee caps with silver polish for the sheer pleasure of feeling bright. I'm very strong for my size, in case you wish me to lift your car up and grease it or move your front porch around to the other side of the house.

I stand six and a half feet tall and weigh nearly six hundred pounds; nevertheless I'm light on my feet, and speedy. I have rollers built into my soles so I can keep pace with the traffic on any pavement. In some ways I think I'm quite an improvement over the ordinary flesh-and-bone human being, but since there's only one of me, I don't often find anyone that agrees with me.

My metal fingers are swift and clever. You'd be surprised at how clever I am at filing cards. Or running the typewriter, if you need a stenographer. I can also chew gum and giggle, and I suppose I could sit on your lap, though I'm rather heavy. V. V. Blackridge, my recent boss, never cared for that sort of thing anyway.

If you need an errand boy, I can run nights as well as days. The Williams Brothers, who manufactured me, equipped me with headlights. Also a parlor reading lamp, built into the visor around my forehead. Also a taillight, which glows doubly bright whenever I'm embarrassed.

Speaking of the Williams Brothers, you'd probably like to know how they happened to manufacture me in the first place. So I'll tell you all about it, and also about my first job. Then you'll know whether we can do business.

CHAPTER I
Out of My Crate

FOR me, life began when I began to realize that Madge LaGrange was a very lovely girl who worked—much too hard—over a desk in a real estate office. She was blond, beautiful (so everyone said), a trifle plump and quite soft (as judged by my metallic standards). It was her nature to be cheerful and good-humored. But she had a boss, V. V. Blackridge, who was too stupid to appreciate her.

Blackridge was a grouchy old bear, not a bit like his two nephews, the Williams brothers. They're the inventors, you understand, who gave birth to me.

The ink flew one day in Blackridge's real estate office.

"You can't talk that way to me!" Madge LaGrange exploded, and suddenly she picked up an ink bottle and hurled it straight at her boss.

Kerspat!

Blackridge caught it right on the crest of his bald head, and those three pet hairs stuck up like three black wires. The ink rolled down over his nose, and I thought to myself, "Blackridge!"

At the moment the name fit him perfectly.

He grabbed for his handkerchief and began smearing. At the same time he took three swift strides toward Madge, and I saw there was going to be trouble.

Yes, I *knew* it. *I understood. I was thinking.*

Time out, please. It sounds impossible for a mechanical man to think, doesn't it? Time out, while I make a few little explanations.

All credit to the Williams brothers. When they manufactured me, they supplied me with some special thinking equipment, bless their hearts; otherwise I wouldn't be able to write this story. They put their very best genius into me, and that's the reason I've got to make good. I'm their number one all-around robot.

Actually, I'm number thirty-three among their robot experiments. But the first thirty-two were specialized mechanisms. Some could cook. Some could music. Some could do statistical operations. I was different because I was created as something flexible and adjustable, not specialized.

Moreover, I had one revolutionary improvement over the other thirty-two. I was given a cupful of *brain tissue.* This was experimental, of course, not standard equipment. And it was destined to cause plenty of trouble for me. But you can see how highly important this could be as an instrument for organizing all my other gadgets. It gave me a storehouse for my experiences—a protoplasmic base for my memory. It gave me a means of reflecting upon all the ideas that came my way, and of sifting them, so that I could meet my new troubles halfway.

To look at me, you might guess that my cupful of brains resides in my head, the same as a man's or an elephant's. Not so. The Williams brothers sealed this bit of treasure *inside the gleaming brass case which hangs in my chest.*

Where you have a heart, I have a brain. My brain weighs about a fifth as much as your heart, but it is surrounded by a case full of mechanisms that weigh all of seventy-five pounds.

This brass case is shaped like a thick watch. It's, as big around as a plate, and the mechanisms within are at least a million times as complicated as a watch. And along with the mechanisms, tuned to catch impulses from the brain tissue, are the provisions for sustaining life in that same precious bit of tissue.

A few ounces of life and hundreds of pounds of machinery—that's me.

T HE real me is, more accurately, that inner part of the mechanical man—that giant brass watch case which has the fun of directing this man-like metal shell around me. Most of the time it's great sport. Even when I get into trouble—like on that day when Madge threw the ink bottle. I'm coming to that in just a minute.

You wonder how I happened to be there?

Two weeks earlier, the Williams Brothers had told me I was all done, stamped and tested, and ready to go out into the world. My feet were ready to walk. My arms were ready to lift. The headlights, looking like two eyes in my metal head, with moving yellow rings around them, were ready to cut a path of light through the darkness.

But the Williams brothers had a certain corner of the world that they wanted me to fill, and a certain duty for me to perform.

"Obedience is the first lesson of life," Herb Williams would say to me over and over. "One who does not know about this world *must obey* until he learns to make his own judgments."

Waldemar Williams, the older of the two brothers, would shake his iron gray head and say, "I doubt if he understands what you're saying. He'll have to make his own mistakes."

Waldemar was right, I understood very little of their problem. They wanted to trust me to use my own powers, but they were afraid.

"First you'll have to get your bearings," Herb Williams went on, lecturing me very earnestly."

I responded by waving an arm as smoothly as a breeze. Then I tapped the silent mechanism of the elbow.

"I'm not talking about your roller bearings," Herb said patiently. "I'm not worried about that part of you. It's your mental bearings."

"Too complicated," said Waldemar, shaking his head.

They wrapped me in brown paper all around and crated me, then gave me a ride in a truck. All the way to Blackridge's real estate office Herb kept talking to me.

"You're not to move. You're just to stand like a statue, for days and days, until we come again. That's our first lesson in obedience. Just stand. Stand. Stand. Do you understand?"

Stand. Stand. Understand. Get my bearings. Not roller bearings. Mental bearings.

Waldemar took from his pocket a dark object that might have been a pocket camera.

"If you forget—if you get into trouble—we'll know. This instrument will tell us. We have a way of *freezing* you if you forget and start to make motions."

"There'll be people around you," Herb continued. "Later, after you've got your bearings, you'll work with these people. They are my uncle and a friend. They are very busy. They'll need your help. You must watch them to see how they work."

They unloaded me, rolled me on a little cart into the real estate office, and placed me near the front door, quite upright.

"Here's some new equipment, Uncle," Herb said. "I want to park it here for the present."

V. V. Blackridge said, "A file cabinet? We've got plenty." His voice was low and guttural, like the grind of a machine that is being choked with the wrong kind of raw material.

"N O QUESTIONS now, Uncle," said Herb. "We'll explain later. Don't open it yet. We'll come back one of these days."

"Ah! A mystery!" Madge said, looking up from her typewriter with an interested smile.

"Ugh! Those letters, Miss LaGrange!" This surly growl from Blackridge caused the girl to turn back to her work. Her expression was odd and it stayed with me, so that later I understood more clearly just what it implied. That half amused glance she shot at Herb Williams showed that she knew, and he knew, that her boss' hard command was out of order. She was obeying simply to humor him.

"Take it easy, Uncle," Herb said. Then he and Waldemar left me.

I was to stand. I was to obey by remaining motionless. I was to watch and listen and get my bearings. Later I would work here. Meanwhile, neither the boss nor the pretty girl working for him knew anything about me. All they knew was that a wooden crate containing something wrapped in brown paper had been parked against the front wall of their office.

They were curious, of course. But the Williams brothers had asked them not to open me. And as I later learned, the Williams brothers owned this real estate office. They had bought it a long time before and turned— it over to their Uncle Blackridge to give him something to do.

So V. V. Blackridge and Madge LaGrange both obeyed and left me alone.

And I, in turn, obeyed, and stood perfectly still for two weeks, absorbing what I could of their business. Until *that day*—

There were openings in the coating of brown paper, so that some of my ten little eyes could see out.

Yes—ten. Does that seem so strange for a mechanical man? I find them all very useful. Probably you wouldn't guess they are my eyes. They look like little jeweled, blue, five-pointed stars, and they are located at various points *not* in my head (remember, those two dark orbs in my face are my headlights) but rather *in the brass brain-box that is really me.* Brain, eyes, ears, and mechanisms of smell are all a part of this big brass watch—this inner me. Light waves reach me very readily through my dark Plexiglas chest and shoulders.

For two weeks I watched the customers come and go. I heard the telephone ring several hundred times a day, and listened to the irate voice of the boss, picking up the receiver, listening a moment, and shouting, "No vacancy!"

In contrast, I was pleased by the soft answers of Madge when she answered the phone. "I'm sorry, there's no vacancy at present. Would you care to call back in a few weeks?" Or, "Will you please leave your number. I may have something of interest later in the week."

Through the nights I stood in solitary reflection, listening to the gentle hum of night traffic.

At noons, on sunshiny days, I would cease to be a statue for just long enough to shift the position of my ten star-like eyes. The flicker of shadows from what I later learned was an elm tree directly in front of the door, out on the parking, provided a fascinating show through the openings in my paper covering. I would turn just a trifle to get the full benefit. But if I rustled the paper, Blackridge would look up sharply and growl.

"Now what did that?"

But Madge would go right on working, knowing that if she answered, he would snap at her to get back to work.

Then one noon the rattle of my paper brought Blackridge up with a start.

"I'm going to see what's in that damned box."

"Please, Mr. Blackridge," Madge protested. "You know they asked you not to." She was smiling, trying to put it politely.

"Who asked your opinion?"

Her smile faded. "I respect the Williams brothers," she said firmly.

"Meaning what? You don't respect me? Is that it?" His eyes blazed anger. He was as touchy as dynamite. "You might as well say it. *You don't respect me!"*

SHE returned his glare. "Sometimes I wonder."

"Shut up! Get your nose back in that ledger and don't let me hear another word out of you today—ugh—UGH!!"

That was when he got it. The ink. Right over the topknot. Black ridge! *Black ridge,* indeed!

"You can't talk that way to me!" she had retorted, and wham, zowie, kerspat, splatter! She had let him have it.

His hands smeared at his face, his eyes flashed fire through ink. He was going toward her, and he drew back a hand to slap. A brutal swing.

Smack!

His inky fingers left marks on her cheek. She gave a little cry. And that was when I burst out of my crate.

CHAPTER II
They Freeze Me in the Nick of Time

T HE very rattle of paper would have been enough, no doubt. It doesn't take much to stop a man like Blackridge. Especially when he's in the wrong, and knows he's caught.

The paper rattled, the wood ripped, and my shiny steel arms came bursting out into the noonday light. I bumped my elbows outward, the crate splintered, and I pushed out, free, into the room.

Clunk...clunk...clunk. My steel feet thumped across the linoleum floor. I caught a flash of my bright steel fingers reflected from the surface of a polished desk. I thought I saw the reflection of my bright metal head in V. V. Blackridge's eyes. Or maybe it was terror. I heard him give a deep-throated, "Uuulp!"

I didn't mind that. He had it coming. My left hand jammed out like a piston rod, and my extended fingers snapped over his throat. His head went *ker-bump* against the wall, so hard that the nearby picture jumped sideways.

There I held him. For just an instant I pulled my punch, to save knocking his head straight through the wall, as I certainly could have done with one moderate blow of my right fist.

It was the scream of Madge LaGrange that stopped me.

"Don't! Don't do it!" she cried. Then her hands went limp, and her eyes went shut, and she slumped down over her chair.

That scared me. I didn't want her to go to sleep. I wanted her to see me return that brutal slap to this hardboiled old growler.

Knowing what I know now, I guess it was lucky for me she fainted. It just goes to show how little a fellow knows when he gets angry and starts to use his fists. I was really *thinking,* now, and I could feel the thousands of little wheels turning.

Madge was coming to life, breathing slowly, opening her eyes a little. I looked at Blackridge, caught in my left hand, trying with his puny little hands of flesh and bone to pry my steel fingers free. He was kicking at my steel shins, too, with no effect whatever. His face was pink, so I eased up on my one-handed grip. Just a trifle.

Then, making sure that Madge saw me, I administered my punishment. Her eyes widened curiously as I did the deed.

With the finesse of a surgeon performing a delicate operation, I reached over with my free hand and removed one of those three pet hairs from the top of Blackridge's head.

"Yeee-ouw!" he shouted. "That's mine!"

I glanced at Madge. She was sitting up, now, watching me very intently, and I fancied there was a one-thousandth part of a smile showing through the sternness of her lips. So I deposited the inky hair on the desk, still holding my prisoner, and reached slowly, surely, in the same direction again.

"No. No, don't take any more!" the inky-faced boss yowled.

He shook his head violently, so that his eyes wobbled like ball bearings in a test tube.

But I nodded my head just as decisively, to warn him I wouldn't be stopped. I saw that my response was understood by Madge. There was at least a tenth of a smile visible now, in her parted lips. So nothing could stop me. I would remove those other two pet hairs.

Or would I?

Clink! Something snapped. Something went wrong inside me.

I was paralyzed!

THERE must have been a master switch somewhere within my inner mechanism. Someone had stopped me cold. I was frozen. I could see, I could smell, I could hear. But I couldn't so much as move a little finger.

The Williams brothers! They had done it, of course.

Yes, they had warned me that their pocket instrument would notify them if I became active. So they had received the alarm, at their laboratory, or at lunch, or wherever they were, and they had understood. I had disobeyed. I had broken out and gotten into mischief. And so they had snapped the freeze on me, and here I stood.

Here I stood, holding a struggling fretting businessman against the wall so firmly he couldn't possibly escape. He yowled for mercy, rolling his eyes up toward my right hand, poised above his bald head, pleading for me to spare those two pet hairs.

Then Madge began to plead, too.

"I don't know what you are, or where you came from. I don't know whether you can understand what I'm saying. But please, if this is a gag, you've gone far enough. Please—"

I couldn't have moved if there had been a flag to salute.

Madge called for the police, and I was still in the same position ten minutes later when they arrived. I was motionless, and Blackridge was still kicking.

CHAPTER III
Dead or Alive?

THE police consisted of Sergeants O'Malley and Cohen. I was impressed by their blue uniforms and their strong handsome faces, and I would have gladly smiled at them if my smile hadn't been paralyzed. My all-around eyes caught a reflection of my ludicrous pose from their silver badges. It looked bad, all right, the way I had Blackridge by the throat.

"What's the gag?" O'Malley said, gulping and staring. "Break it up, there. Break it up."

"*You* break it up!" Blackridge snarled, looking fierce and inky.

"Don't get sassy," said O'Malley. "How did you get into this mess. What have you got here? A Christmas toy? Where do you wind the darned thing?"

"Careful, O'Malley," Cohen warned. "It's some kind of booby trap. We'd better get the fire department."

"It came out of that box, Officer." This from Madge, who was in the act of putting on her hat and coat. "I think I'll step out for lunch."

"Lunch, is it?" O'Malley growled. "You'll sit right down and tell us what this is all about. You say it come out of that crate? A sort of grown-up jack-in-the-box, huh? Where did the crate come from?"

The questions and answers flew back and forth, with O'Malley and Cohen exchanging suspicious looks. O'Malley tapped me with his club. I didn't budge.

"Now let's get to the bottom of this," O'Malley said. "You say this crate has been here for two weeks, and just now this collection of hardware bounced out of it for the first time. *Why?* Why not *yesterday?* Why not *tomorrow?*"

"S-s-sh!" Blackridge said under his breath.

"I don't get it," said O'Malley. "Was there something in the air today that caused this tin demon to spring loose?"

"There was ink in the air today," said Madge. "If that creature knows anything—"

"S-s-sh!" Her boss tried to hush her. "Stop the argument and get me out of here."

"I told you don't get sassy," said O'Malley, walking over and thumping him lightly on the knee, but keeping well out of range of my upraised arm. "What's this about the ink in the air?"

"Shall I tell?" Madge asked. Her boss gave a threatening growl. She smiled at him sweetly. It was plain that I had him and the police weren't anxious to pry him loose. "It's like this," she began.

My alert eyes caught sight of the two Williams brothers, then, as they peered in at the side door. You could tell they were getting an earful, all right, the way they listened to Madge's speech. They heard and they saw. The ink marks were on her cheek to prove her story. Of course, she didn't realize they were listening.

When she finished, O'Malley and Cohen went into a huddle. They came out of it shaking their heads.

"We don't swallow that," said O'Malley. "Maybe he sprang out of the box, like you say. But ink didn't have nothin' to do with it. He just happened to tear loose at that time. You know how these mechanical toys are."

"That's right," said Cohen. "Just get on the phone and get those Williams boys over here to take care of their haywire gadget."

"Just as you say," said Madge, going to the phone.

Then Blackridge fairly screeched. "Ye gods, will you get me out of here!"

COHEN placed his fists on his hips and studied me skeptically. He said finally, "I wouldn't touch the thing myself."

O'Malley walked around to view me from all angles, his cautious eye ever watchful of my upraised hand.

"Just a dead chunk of metal, Cohen. There's no reason why we shouldn't pry him loose. Come here with your club."

They went to work on my arm. They could see that it was jointed. Apparently, it should fold back like a carpenter's rule. But it wouldn't. I could see that the Williams brothers, spying from the side door, were immensely amused.

While the two cops tugged, mystified because I couldn't be budged, Madge returned from the telephone. The Williams boys were both out to lunch, she reported. Now she looked at me with an air of discovery.

"Oh, his eyes aren't spinning any more," she said.

"What's that?" said O'Malley.

"When I first saw him, those yellow rings around his eyes were moving around like cogwheels around lightbulbs," she said. "That's what made me think he was alive. I mean, the way the outer rims of his eyes kept turning. But now they're stopped. I think he must be dead."

"*I'll* be dead if you don't get me out of here," Blackridge groaned.

O'Malley tapped my metal head with his club.

"He's dead all right. No question about that."

Cohen nodded. He was growing less afraid of me, at last. He tapped his club against my chromium-plated mouth. No effect.

Clink. The master switch! I saw the Williams brothers snap it. I was free. But the cops didn't hear it, and they went right on examining me. For a moment I held my pose.

"Dead as a string of doorknobs," O'Malley said. "Tell the Williams boys to get a new spring—"

"Look! His eyes! They're spinning!" Cohen pointed at my headlights with his club. O'Malley pointed too. My rigid form suddenly snapped into action. I ducked forward, like a serpent striking, and bit the ends of their clubs off.

Before I could spit out the pieces, my eyes were treated to the sight of two blurry blue streaks whizzing out of the room. One was Sergeant O'Malley, the other was Sergeant Cohen.

CHAPTER IV
Blackridge Takes Me to Lunch

V. V. BLACKRIDGE staggered to his desk like a convict who has just missed an appointment with the hangman. He glared daggers at the Williams brothers, who now walked in and sat down.

"Darned sorry this had to happen," Herb Williams said, trying not to smile. He was a bit slow of speech always, but quick with his eyes. He held the automatic switch box, ready to freeze me if I misbehaved.

"I don't get the idea," Blackridge said stonily. "I try to run a real estate agency. I try to make money for you. You come in with a mysterious crate and I let you park it. Two weeks it haunts my front door. And what does it come to? Practical jokes!"

"Practical *chokes,*" said Madge.

"I say it was a mistake, Uncle," Herb repeated. He turned to Madge. "Did it do any harm to you?"

"On the contrary," she said, arching an eyebrow at Blackridge. She touched her cheek where the slap had struck a few minutes before. She knew, evidently, that I had deliberately come to her rescue. That made me feel strangely happy, and I started to do a mechanical jig. Clank-clankety-clank.

"Stop it!" Herb ordered. "Quiet. You've done damage enough."

I obeyed, becoming as motionless as a steel statue. Herb walked around to make sure my metal feet hadn't cut any marks in the linoleum floor. Madge must have decided from Blackridge's angry glare, that there was too much tension in the atmosphere for her. It was time for her to go to lunch.

"I think I'll go with you," Herb said.

"You can handle things, Waldemar."

An hour later, Waldemar Williams, Blackridge, and I loafed in a restaurant booth, sipping coffee and talking. I sat in the corner as inconspicuously as possible. (Waldemar had put a folded newspaper under me so I wouldn't scratch the seat.)

"If he's such a useful servant, why doesn't he stir my coffee for me?" Blackridge was saying.

Waldemar turned to me, "How about it, Buzz-Bolt?"

I took the spoon in my steel fingers and began to stir. Blackridge watched me skeptically. How did he know that I wanted to pour that coffee down his neck?

They went on talking, and I went on stirring. The more I watched Blackridge, the more mischievous I felt. I didn't know it at the time, but it was that bit of human brain tissue that was wanting to get me into trouble. Such devilish impulses! What sort of tricky person had my brain come from anyhow?

"He wants me to cool his coffee," I thought. "Instead, I'll heat it, just to fool him."

So I began sending electrical heat down through my steel fingertips into the spoon. Meanwhile, the older Williams brother continued to explain to Blackridge that I might be trained to become a very useful assistant.

"We've named him Buzz-Bolt," the inventor said proudly, passing his thin fingers through his silvery hair. "Buzz-Bolt Atomcracker. In time he may develop a sort of personality. We'll see."

A number of people passing by would stop and stare at me for a moment and say to each other, "What is that thing?" or "Am I seeing things? It must be something I ate."

Waldemar would whisper to me to pay no attention—that was something I'd have to learn, he said, and he was right. I went right on stirring.

"ENOUGH," said Blackridge, trying out his orders on me. "That coffee ought to be cool—ugh!" He gulped. "Look, Waldemar. The darned stuff's boiling!" He reached for my hand. "Give me that spoon. Ye-ippp!"

The spoon fell to the floor, and Blackridge jammed his fingertips to his lips.

Waldemar frowned. "Buzz-Bolt, did *you*—"

Blackridge came to his feet, snorting clenching his fists. "That thing and I aren't gonna get along, I just know!"

Waldemar Williams must have felt pretty dubious about me then. He gave me one of those "I'm disappointed in you" looks. He was a pretty stern old fellow, and you couldn't help feeling he was a square shooter. For all my mischievous desires, I'd never have overheated his coffee.

"We'll go now," Waldemar said coolly. He paid the bill, and we all walked back, amid the surprised stares and laughing wisecracks of the passersby. When small boys stop and point at you, you can't help but feel a little self-conscious. But already I was becoming used to it. There was a much bigger worry on my mind.

What sort of person was I going to be? Was I to go through life playing tricks on people like Blackridge? I *had* wanted to pour coffee down his neck. Why?

The natural answer was that this slice of brain they had given me to bring me to life had carried over some habits and impulses from its own mysterious past. I wanted to play tricks. I wanted to *clown.* And I *would,* in spite of anything.

"Don't jump to conclusions," Waldemar was saying to Blackridge. "He may turn out to be a good machine, not a bad one. If he does, we can manufacture his kind on a wide scale. Don't you see, Uncle, we hope to relieve overworked men like you of a lot of drudgery."

"I don't question your good intentions," said Blackridge, again touching his bruised neck.

"Do you realize, Uncle, how you've been grinding yourself down?"

"I wasn't aware that I'm over-worked."

"That's just it. This overstrain has crept up on you. You're so busy, you don't see yourself as other people see you. They think you're becoming an automaton."

"Me?" V. V. Blackridge walked a little faster, looking straight ahead. "Who says so?"

"Some of your friends. They say you don't have time to be human."

"Who says? Madge LaGrange, for instance? Let her talk. I'm not impressed."

At the office Herb was fixing up a desk for me. Madge, hard at work, looked up with a quick smile.

"I hear we're to have some assistance," she said.

"I am not impressed," said Blackridge, hanging up his hat and going to his deck. I followed him, for now he was to be my boss.

"Mr. Williams tells me," Madge said, "that this mechanical man can become quite efficient at the telephone—if he can learn to talk."

"I am not impressed." Blackridge said coldly.

"You'll see," said Herb.

"I am not impressed. *I am not impressed. I am not—*"

I PINCHED Blackridge's left ear with my steel fingers. I think he was impressed. He turned pale, in fact, and reached for his throat protectively. But I didn't mean to harm him. Just then his telephone rang, and my long steel arm reached out and picked it up.

Would I answer it?

Everyone was eyeing me, now. Up to this moment I had not spoken a word. There had been some off-sides debate as to whether I could talk. The Williams brothers had urged me to make use of that fine mechanical voice box they had given me.

"Buzzzzz!" I said into the phone.

"Answer it!" Herb shouted excitedly. "Answer it!"

Through my head diaphragm, the sound of the speaker on the other end was vibrated down into my "interior." It was someone asking for a furnished apartment.

"Buzzzzzz!" I replied.

"No, no, no," Herb cried. "Let Blackridge answer."

It was then that I gave them a surprise that Blackridge and Madge would never forget. I answered—in *Blackridge's voice.*

"No vacancy!" The words were perfect Blackridge.

Immediately I added—in Madge's voice, very sweetly, "I'm sorry... Would you care to call back later in the week?"

Then I hung up. Blackridge's own voice! And Madge's!

You can hardly imagine what that did to my four observers. Madge was so dumbfounded she couldn't speak. Blackridge went red with a blustering sort of rage. "He's a damned phonograph!"

The Williams brothers were suddenly incandescent with happiness. This was their hour of triumph. They pounded each other on the shoulders, laughing and shouting like a pair of cheerleaders after a Thanksgiving victory.

Both of them tried to explain at once. It was funny, two fellows so slow of speech trying to talk so fast.

"You see, it *was* your own voice, Madge." That was *you,* Blackridge—your words."

"No, *not* the mechanical man's voice. *He* couldn't imitate that way. *His* voice was that *buzz.* It's still raw. He hasn't learned to use it. But he can *record.*"

Their jabbering was pretty excited, and I was recording it, too, because I was so interested. The brothers did their best to explain that I carried a goodly spool of magnesium wire, upon which I might record any of the numerous sounds that fell upon my mechanical ears.

Blackridge was aghast. "Do you mean—do you mean that this compound gadget might have picked up any words I've said here in the last two weeks?"

"It's possible," said Herb, and his older brother nodded.

For some strange reason, Blackridge went quite white.

Then the phone rang again, and Herb gave me the sign to go ahead.

It was another request for a furnished apartment. I answered with the first recorded words that happened to come up. Blackridge's ugly voice: "Shut up. Get your nose back in that ledger and don't let me hear another word out of you today."

That was it. I said it and hung up. And what an icy silence there was all around me. The brothers weren't looking at me, now. They were staring at V. V. Blackridge. They had heard his own words. Words he must have flung at Madge.

"Uncle," Waldemar said slowly, "Sometimes I wonder if you don't need a long vacation."

Blackridge didn't say anything, but somehow I knew he was impressed.

CHAPTER V

A Mysterious Client

OF ALL the passers-by who stared at me and asked curious questions during the next few weeks, the man who impressed me most was a hard-faced man with a silent step and a noisy necktie.

"Well, buddy, you're quite a creature, ain't you? Just like the newspapers said."

He had edged up to me as if to talk in private while no other customers were around. He had evidently seen some of the newspaper photographs and the newsreels that had shown me at work answering telephones.

In a very suspicious manner he whispered, "How'd you like to take a walk with me some night?"

I didn't answer. I couldn't. Not with my own voice. All I could do with my own voice box was to make that senseless buzzing sound. Other than that, my speech consisted of playing back the recordings from my wire spools.

When he repeated his question, insistently, tapping my steel head in a very friendly manner, I croaked back to him, in Blackridge's voice, my old standby answer.

"No vacancy."

His name, as I later learned, was Joe Moberly. But for the present I thought of him simply as the man with the purple and yellow polka-dot tie, the strong brown cigar and the sinister eyes.

He turned to Madge. "Where'd you get the walking machine, sister?" He saw that she was very busy, so he gestured with his cigar that it made no difference. "Don't mind me. I just dropped in to see your boss about some Simpson holdings on Q Street. Go right ahead with your work, sister."

He proceeded to eye me up and down, back and forth. Many people were doing that there days. But not so thoroughly as Joe Moberly.

He strolled across to the window and pretended to read a magazine. He was watching my reflection in the glass. Presently he saw Blackridge coming down the street. He tossed his cigar in the ash stand and walked out.

When Blackridge came in, Madge told him there had been a Mr. Joe Moberly here to see him.

"I don't know any Moberly. What did he want?"

"Something about some Simpson property on Q Street."

"Never heard of it."

So Moberly's first visit was forgotten by everyone but me. I remembered—why? Because the man's eyes took in details of my make-up that the average person would have missed. He appeared to be measuring my dimensions and making mental calculations.

I had a hunch Moberly would come again, and he did.

"The newspapers said you might learn to talk," he said, quite guardedly. "How'ya doing?"

"Buzzz-zzz." I replied. Madge turned, and I winked one of my headlights at her. She went on working. Again Blackridge was not there. So Moberly tried to get next to me again, but I disappointed him, because I couldn't talk.

Madge saw that he wasn't satisfied with the recorded answers I gave him, so she tried to help. He asked about some mythical property, and when she went to look up the information in the files, he went to work on me. With a carpenter's rule. He took a half dozen measurements before she got back. Arms, legs, feet, hands, chest, and head.

Two days later he was back again, and this time, while no one was looking, he managed to open the Plexiglas doors of my chest. I could have snapped him, but I was curious to see what he was up to.

"Inner pockets…hmmm," he mumbled to himself.

He WAS fascinated by my insides, all right. I had two rows of card cases built into what should have been my ribs. He could see that I was full of the telephone numbers and addresses of our clients, but this made little impression on him. Again he was more concerned with taking measurements.

"Take it easy," he whispered. "I won't mix up your files. Just looking around."

I didn't answer. But the second time he blew a puff of that black cigar smoke in at my ten interior eyes, I gently removed the cigar from his mouth and took a puff. For a moment this got his goat, and he drew back, half afraid of me.

"Take it *easy.* Take it *easy,*" he muttered.

I jammed the cigar back in his mouth, and soon he was on his way. I had made him nervous, and I thought he might never come back again. If he should come back, I thought, I'd have to play a gag on him that he wouldn't forget. I'd poke that burning cigar down his collar and echo back to him, "Take it easy."

There it was again—that craving to play mischief! Where did it come from? Did the Williams brothers know they'd planted a strain of the practical joker in me?

Later that day, when Blackridge was about to close up shop, he opened my Plexiglas chest to check up on my day's work, and sure enough, the cigar smoke puffed out at him.

"Where'd *that* come from?" he growled. "I hope you haven't taken to smoking with the customers."

There was a touch of jealousy in what he said. Poor old hardboiled Blackridge had been finding me hard to take. I had been growing much too popular with the clients. They liked to deal with me, just as they liked to deal with Madge. For one thing, I talked with them in her voice whenever possible. For another thing, there was my chromium-plated smile—but I'll come to that in a moment.

Blackridge pressed me for an answer about the cigar smoke, and I did the best I could. I came back at him with Joe Moberly's voice:

"How'd you like to take a walk with me some night?"

Blackridge uttered some profanity. My recorded maunderings meant nothing to him. Just as a warning, I gave his profanity right back to him, and at that he locked his lips. Since that first awful day, when I had exposed his harsh talk and given the Williams brothers an earful of his bawlings-out to Madge, he had guarded his words like stolen pearls. About all he ever said to either of us was, "Get to work."

Can you imagine what effect it had on a hardboiled old boss like Blackridge to discover that I, a mechanical man, was becoming far more popular than he? Was he burned up? You know it!

PART of it, as I mentioned above, was my use of Madge's voice. The other factor was my smile.

What a stroke of genius on the part of my inventors to give me a smile! Herb Williams had patterned the curves of my metal mouth after his own. Madge didn't know that, but right from the first week I could tell that she was strangely fascinated by the pleasant form that my metal lips took when anyone smiled at me.

There was a secret here, all my own. Something I had discovered, watching her and Herb Williams. She didn't dare show him how much she liked him, because he didn't pay any particular attention to her—or at least, so she thought. But back of her fascination for my smile was her secret interest in Herb Williams.

"How's your friend Blackridge?"

Herb would say to her casually whenever he'd drop around at lunch time.

"No change," Madge would say. "At least none for the better."

"I'd hoped that Buzz-Bolt would take enough weight off the old boy's shoulders that he'd have time to be human. Hasn't he taken up golf or bowling, or gone to the movies, or read any books, or attended any baseball games?... No?... Has he cracked any jokes?"

"Blackridge couldn't crack a joke with a sledge hammer," Madge would say. "I wish Buzz-Bolt could talk. I'll bet he'd crack jokes. That smile of his—" She stopped, and I'm sure she didn't guess what a compliment she was paying to Herb.

"It's all tin," said Herb.

"Anyway the customers like it."

"Just a mechanical trick," said Herb. "You know, everyone smiles when they first see Buzz-Bolt. And what happens? His electric eyes gauge their smile and he automatically matches it with his own. If they smile wide and handsome, so does he."

"I *like* it," said Madge.

I was smiling broadly then, the same as Madge. It must have been contagious, for Herb was smiling too, just a little. Madge added, "I wonder if he would be bashful if he could talk. It's a sort of bashful smile, don't you think?"

Then, for some reason, she and Herb were looking at each other and they both grew quite red in the face. Whatever it was about, their embarrassment was contagious too, for my tail light came on with a doubly bright red glow. Thank goodness, the telephone rang at that moment. I got back to work.

CHAPTER VI
Night Visitors

THEY had me give a demonstration in one of the display rooms in the city's finest office building. Two hundred and seventy-five business men looked me over and discussed my merits. Would mechanical men be a good investment as a substitute for their present employees?

They put me through the paces! They had me add and subtract, do bookkeeping, answer phone calls, deal with customers.

And while they sized me up, and marveled at my abilities, I was thinking to myself, "What a serious gang of men! Why don't I cut up a little, to liven up the party?"

"How much does he cost to operate?" "Can parts be replaced?"

"Can you depend upon him to obey orders?"

"Does he have to sleep at nights, or will he keep right on running?"

"Do you have to have a boss over him?"

The Williams brothers did their best to answer all questions. It looked to me as though they might make a fortune, if I didn't make some break and spoil everything.

"Can he sweep the floors? Can he scrub? Can he polish all the office furnishings, including himself?"

I swept for them. I scrubbed for them. Every time they put a broom or a mop in my hands, I wanted to take a swing at someone, just for pure mischief. But I refrained. Madge was there, and she and the Williams brothers were very proud of the way I was conducting myself.

"Can he wash windows?" someone asked.

They gave me a sponge and a dryer and I went to work on a patch of plate glass. Then—trouble.

I swear it wasn't mischief. It was that reflection I saw in the glass. The waiter. He was moving through the crowd, serving drinks. But mostly, he was watching me. It was Joe Moberly.

He moved close, and I saw that he held a small camera under the tray. I didn't see the flash, but I heard the click. He had caught a shot—maybe an infra-red of my inside workings.

Click-then-crash!

I pushed with too much force against the plate glass and, darnest luck! The window went out.

PANDEMONIUM! A whole swarm of officials of this swanky display room pushed up through the spectators and demanded to know what on earth was going on, and what kind of a stunt was this. There'd be damages aplenty!

They were pretty angry with Herb Williams, even though my break hadn't actually hurt anyone. If the glass had fallen over the street, it might. Have been bad. But it fell on a roof. Nothing serious.

"If you can't handle your iron monster, Mr. Williams," the dress-suited manager said severely, "we'll have the police help you."

That insult was uncalled for, in my estimation, and I picked up the surly fellow in the dress suit, turned him upside down, and stuck his head in the handiest wastebasket. The crowd made way for me, and I reached for another official in a dress suit.

Click!

Waldemar Williams had his little switch box ready, and he suddenly put the automatic freeze on me. That did it. I was as paralyzed and motionless as any cornerstone, and so I remained until the crowd went home.

The last man to take his eyes off me, that night, was, as you might imagine, Joe Moberly. He had kept out of Madge's path, so that no one recognized him. But this I knew. He hadn't missed one important bit of information from the Williams brothers' sales talk. And he had'nt missed much of the dressing down the brothers gave me after my break....

It was to happen just three nights later.

Somehow I felt it coming, though there were no very definite indications.

The office work was clacking along as usual. New clients came, always to be disappointed because of the general shortage of available apartments. Old clients came in to collect their rent, to buy, to sell, to discuss their problems. Occasionally someone would tell of making several hundred thousand dollars, and Blackridge's dark and gloomy mood would brighten for a few moments.

Then the mood would pass, and he would scowl deeper than ever.

The exterminator came, and Blackridge had him spray the inside of my chest, along with the other dark corners of the room. Just one of the boss's reminders that I was no more important than a filing cabinet.

Herb Williams came in on some pretext, and decided that he and Madge had just as well have dinner together. When they returned to the office, I learned that they had decided to make an evening of it and go to the movie.

"Sorry we can't take you along, Buzz-Bolt," Madge said, but I don't think she meant it.

They went, and I was left to the silence of the night, as usual. Those long nights with nothing to do! The worst of it was, they made a habit of locking my feet to the floor every evening after work hours, just to be sure I wouldn't go off on a spree. It was a wise thing to do. They knew it, too, because I had shown a tendency to climb the chandeliers and juggle the furniture and dance all night to the radio during my first unguarded nights. If I had been left completely to my own devices, I'd certainly had taken a streetcar for a ride on some lonely night.

This was a lonely night until the office clock struck three.

The night's traffic had spent itself. Most of the neons had blacked out. Everything was quiet.

A truck drove along the alley and stopped at the rear door. Its quiet purr choked off. Who could that be? And why?

Presently a key turned in the lock and the rear door opened softly. Two shadowy figures moved into the front office-two men, whispering.

"You sure he's locked?" one of them said.

I had never been more resentful of my paralysis.

"Don't worry, Steve. They freeze him every night. I've checked on that."

I *knew* that low, guttural voice. It was Joe Moberly's!

CHAPTER VII
Presence of Mind, Absence of Body

MOBERLY moved in a wide circle around me. A shaft from the street light passed over his strong face, revealed his unlighted cigar and his polka-dot tie. He was chewing the cigar nervously.

"We've got it all our own way, Steve." He was managing to be pretty cocky and self-confident.

"If somebody don't bust in on us."

There was an apprehensive whine in Steve's voice. From his slight stoop, I guessed him to be one of the waiters I had observed at the demonstration a few nights before. He was skinny, yet strongly muscled. His face was pointed and toothy like a rat's.

The two men paused in the dim light for a moment. Moberly moved close to me, tapped my arm, and satisfied himself that I was helpless. Then he gave some crisp instructions.

They returned to the truck at the rear door. I could hear them unloading a heavy weight. Soon they wheeled it into the front room—a blanketed something as large as a man. When they unwrapped it and inspected it by flashlight, it was revealed to be *another mechanical man.*

It might have been my twin brother.

"I can just see old Blackridge when he tries to make *this* hunk of steel behave," Moberly said. "He'll have apoplexy."

The skinny fellow looked from me to the substitute and breathed a satisfied, "Gee!"

"Not bad huh?"

"Spittin' image. You're a genius, Moberly."

They had trouble moving me out of my place at the desk. You see, the power was off, and I was paralyzed. The wheels in my feet wouldn't even turn.

Finally they decided the thing to do was lighten my load. They removed everything they could from my full chest-cards and files and shelves, tools and gadgets. Eventually they unhooked *me—the inner me—the* big watch-shaped brain case with my ten star-shaped eyes and four sensitive ears.

This being the heaviest removable part, they placed it—that is, *me—* on the desk, and went on about their business. The outer part of me—my metal body—was now lightened sufficiently that they were able to struggle with it. After improvising some rollers, they moved it to the rear door and loaded it onto the truck.

Next, they moved this new mechanical man into my place at the desk. They opened its Plexiglas chest.

"Darned if I remember how to pack this stuff back," Steve said, looking over the scattering of equipment. He started with the files.

"Wait, you dope," Moberly said. "Give me the light. This thing goes in, whatever it is."

"A water cooler, maybe." Steve gave me a shake.

This new metal body was a very crude thing, really. It didn't contain any of the necessary fixtures to fit around me. Of course it lacked the thousands of pin-point triggers through which my brain impulses operated. While Moberly held the flashlight, Steve took pains to wire me in place. They replaced my accessories and then stepped back to study the effect.

"Perfect. Perfect." This from Steve. "Nobody'd ever know the difference."

"The Williams brothers might know at ·a glance," said Moberly. "But Blackridge won't."

That completed their operations. A moment later I heard them drive away in the truck.

There I hung—an encased brain with no workable body. I was hung up! I was as helpless as a turtle hung by the tail. More helpless. A turtle could at least wink his eyes and kick. All I could do was watch and listen.

And wait....

CHAPTER VIII
Sit-Down Strike

T HE theft of my metal body occurred at about three o'clock Sunday morning. I waited impatiently for Monday. It was a long wait, and if I could have talked aloud I would have said some bitter things. You can imagine that I felt pretty savage toward the whole world, even the Williams brothers, my makers.

If they had only known! If they had only trusted me enough to leave me in possession of my powers through the night. What a proud victory it would have been for them if I could have grabbed a pair of thieves and walked them into the police station!

Monday morning came at last.

Blackridge entered in his usual humor. He barked an order at what he thought was me and went on back to the next room to hang up his coat and hat.

Madge came in on the stroke of nine, looking very lovely in her pink dress and fresh pink cheeks.

"Good morning, Buzz-Bolt."

I didn't answer. She raised an eyebrow in my direction. Through this fake creature's Plexiglas shoulders I watched her.

"Are you in a mood this morning, Buzz-Bolt?" she asked as she hung up her coat. "It's a lovely morning—or doesn't the weather make any difference to you?"

I didn't answer.

She added, giving a little laugh, "I'll bet you'd rust in the rain."

She kept on with her one-sided chatter while she watered the plants. Usually I would buzz some sort of response, or draw some appropriate words out of my store of recordings. Usually, too, I would make a few courteous gestures with my metal arms.

Suddenly disturbed, she came over and faced me.

"Buzz-Bolt! Your eyes aren't turning. Has Herb Williams forgotten to turn you on this morning? Or are you ill?"

She went to the phone and called. Her worry deepened. Evidently the Williams brothers insisted that they *had* turned me on.

Blackridge came in on the last of her conversation. He turned his sullen eyes on me and gazed for several minutes. "What is this, a sit-down strike? Give us a buzz, there.... You won't, eh? Stubborn! Madge, get those inventors on the phone again. Let me—"

He stopped abruptly, for someone had just walked in the door. It was Moberly. He sauntered up to my desk as brazenly as a counterfeit dollar.

"Morning, neighbors. Fine morning. Oh, pardon me. Go right on with your telephoning."

Blackridge, momentarily disconcerted, turned his back on the newcomer and proceeded with his conversation.

"LISTEN, Herb, this cursed compound gadget has gone on a strike. Now I don't want the damned thing cluttering up my office if he won't work.... You'll come over? Both of you?... Sure, the sooner the better...."

When he finished and turned, Moberly was already going out the door. "Be back later," he said.

Blackridge shrugged. Strange clients were always changing their minds.

There was not a thing in the world that I could do but hang in there and watch and listen and *think*.

"What," I thought to myself, "did that brazen thief mean by walking in here first thing this morning?" And right away I thought I had the answer. "Of course! He came back looking for the part he missed last night—me."

I could imagine their chagrin—his and Steve's—upon discovering that the mechanical man they'd stolen wouldn't work. What would they do?

I wasn't sure of all my answers, but I guessed, for one thing, that they had made a discovery. They had found that their stolen metal man contained a few thousand tiny triggers that needed to be touched off by some thinking mechanism before the metal man would perform.

So Moberly must have concluded that I, the circular brass case they had discarded, was something more than a water cooler.

But did he mean to steal me here in broad daylight? Or was he planning to come back tonight? Did he understand that the Williams brothers were on their way? Did he realize that they would take one look at this crude metal substitute and know there'd been monkey business?

It was nearly noon, and Blackridge was fuming.

"Why in heaven's name don't they come?" he sputtered. "Look at the work piled up on Buzz-Bolt's desk. All because there's a loose connection somewhere."

He and Madge tapped around on all corners of my substitute frame. Clank-clank-clank. Blackridge took a tack hammer to the metal head, and once he thought the eyes began to roll. Madge tapped the knees with a ruler.

"That's the trouble with these damned gadgets," Blackridge said, passing his hand over his barren topknot of two pampered hairs, "A million dollars worth of experimenting and what do you get? A dead machine on your hands...ugh. What are you sniffling about?"

Madge looked up with a curious tenderness in her pretty face. "Suppose he is dead. Really and truly, I mean. Poor guy, he's been a real friend."

"Stop that sniveling. He's just a chunk of metal."

"He was kind to me," Madge said quietly, "He never acted cross."

To Blackridge her words evidently were a backhanded thrust. "Stop drooling. You were quite the chums, weren't you? If he's dead, maybe it's a good thing.... Stop that sniveling."

But Madge wasn't sniveling, she was just sniffing.

"Do you think he smells all right, Mr. Blackridge?" she asked." Well, I *don't*. There's something phony. He doesn't look quite like himself, today, and be doesn't smell right."

The phone rang, and Madge took the message. She turned white and began to stammer. She hung up and turned to her boss. "Get me a taxi."

"What is it?" he demanded.

"Accident. Someone crowded the Williams brothers into a ditch. It wrecked their car and they're both in the hospital. Herb's in a critical condition."

CHAPTER IX

ON THE instant I knew what had happened. What I couldn't have done if I had been free! And here I was, stranded in a metal body as dead as a stovepipe.

Madge taxied off to the hospital. Blackridge called a couple times, and his usual gloom deepened.

Late that night the rear door opened again. I was not surprised. I had known it was coming. It was Moberly and Steve. They had come back for the rest of me.

"Here it is," Moberly said, holding the light on me. "We should have known this was the brains of the gadget."

"Hs-s-sh!" Steve whispered. "Someone's at the door."

"Nightwatchman, probably." Moberly sounded brave, but he ducked for the deep shadows, right along with Steve. For a long moment there was nothing but tense silence. The clock ticked off the seconds. Presently the night watchman went on his way. I knew his step.

The two men, hiding near the desk beside me, whispered of their plans. What they hoped was that this morning]s accident would take my inventors out of circulation for several week's time enough for them to take me apart and learn all of the secrets of my construction.

"There's millions of dollars in this deal," Moberly kept saying, *"Millions*—and all we have to do is beat those boys to the punch before they recover."

"One of 'em may not recover, from what I read in the paper," Steve said.

"That's the least of our worries."

"But the other one may get out in a couple days."

"If he does, we'll get him again," Moberly said. "Sometimes I think we'd be wiser to make a clean job of it. Then we'd have clear sailing, with no competition."

They removed me with utmost care and were all set to leave. But again they ducked for cover. There were footsteps at the front door. A key turned. By the street light I saw the man that entered—a tall man with a bandaged forehead and one arm in a sling. It was Waldemar Williams.

If I had had a heart it would have stopped beating during the next few moments. Everything happened so fast.

My inventor had evidently just come from the hospital. Probably he had slipped away without permission. Although it was still the dead of night, some burning worry had brought him straight to this office. He had come to see about me.

He snapped on the light. He came straight toward me, his eyes ablaze with suspicions.

What happened then was dreadful. I knew it was coming. I couldn't stop it. I heard the two hidden men exchange whispers.

Waldemar held a hand out toward me. "Are you free to move, Buzz-Bolt? I took the switch off. But I hear something's wrong. Do you hear me?"

He took the left hand of my left body and shook it. He was surprised at how loosely it dangled.

"Why, you're not Buzz-Bolt!"

Those were his last words. For at that instant the right steel band struck. It swung like a hammer. Waldemar caught the blow on the side of the head. It staggered him.

Moberly's elbow grease was back of that blow.

Steve leaped to the light switch and put the room in darkness. But I could still see. My inventor was down. He was being mauled by an arm of steel, blow after blow.

When, a few minutes later, I was carted away, my ten eyes were full of the horrible sight—Waldemar lying murdered, his bandaged head crushed, and that senseless statue of steel hovering over him with a bloody steel fist.

"They'll get Herb out of the way for sure, now," I moaned to myself, "and then the world will never know. They'll always believe that I did it—that I murdered my own inventor."

CHAPTER X

IN A basement laboratory in another part of the town Moberly and Steve reassembled me.

Again, for the moment, I was complete. But they had chained and bolted my metal body to a steel girder imbedded in concrete. About all I could do was wiggle my steel fingers and blink my headlights.

They brought in three technicians, and made ready with the drafting equipment. They set up a schedule for demounting me, bolt by bolt. I watched them empty the shelves and pigeon holes along the wall, to make space for my various parts.

Their plans were interrupted by the noon headlines.

MECHANICAL MAN PULVERIZES INVENTOR.

They read aloud all the gory details. It was dreadful, to think that the man who had worked so hard to create me was gone. And as I heard them chuckle over their success, the very molecules of my steel seemed to fill with fighting anger.

The next day the technicians were ready to go to work on me, when Moberly and Steve came in and stopped them.

"Postpone it, boys. We've got to get him out of here."

They chained me with three hundred pounds of chains and rolled me out to the truck. Steve drove. Moberly talked.

"Just a precaution, Steve. The younger brother in the hospital is talking."

"The papers said he was raving," said Steve.

"All right, raving. But at the rate he's recovering, they may decide to listen to him. And what he says might make sense."

Moberly admitted he was worried. It seemed that Herb was asking the cops to investigate. He was sure that I wouldn't have committed murder.

"Some smart cop might drop into our lab for a friendly visit," Moberly said. "If he does, there mustn't be any signs of Buzz-Bolt around."

They hid me in the loft of an old barn, and covered me with hay. I was chained so tight I could hardly turn. I watched them climb down the ladder.

As soon as they were out of hearing my struggle began.

It was awful. I knew that the news of "my" crime would spread like wildfire. It would go rough on Herb—if he lived. And poor Madge! I must fight free and tell them the truth. I strained at my chains.

Somewhere in the deep recesses of my cupful of human brains was a memory. In my previous life—my human life—I must have watched an exhibition of a man freeing himself from such a trap.

In this dim memory he seemed to be tied to a ladder. It was in a huge tent, and a crowd was humming with excitement, watching him try to free himself. And I was running around him, making jokes.

Where did these memories come from?

I struggled, not like a mad man, but like a clever stunt man. As if there might have been an audience. As if I had to prove that I could work myself free, without injuring myself.

I struggled, but I got nowhere. That stunt man I remembered had been tied with a rope. Three hundred pounds of chain was something else.

I COULDN'T turn. I could barely shake my head. I could barely move my steel fingers. They weren't made to serve as files, but I tried to use them that way. No good. After working for hours, through the night and into the next morning, I was able to estimate my rate of progress.

At best, it would take me 768 hours to cut through four links. Over a month! By that time Herb Williams' laboratories would be ruined. If I worked any faster, the heat of friction would burn up my fingers and very probably set the barn on fire.

This was the most deserted hiding place you could ever imagine.

Through the hay I looked out of the open door of the barn loft toward a little feed lot to the north, and on to a curving country highway and distant hills.

For the next three days I lay there, a prisoner, languishing in chains. Twice a day I tried with my recorded voices to attract the attention of the farm hand who came to feed a few cattle. The sounds never reached him.

I buzzed with my own untrained voice box. I buzzed as tirelessly as a locust. No response. That farmhand had an ear for bawling calves, but not for buzzing machinery.

"It's hopeless," I finally told myself. "It may be weeks or months before anyone else comes this way. If Moberly is thoroughly scared over what he's done, I may be left to rust my life away."

You do a lot of tall thinking at a time like that. But how useless my thoughts were when my body couldn't function.

As always, I came back to that old tantalizing question, where had my bit of brain come from? What had the fellow been like who had possessed this living part of me before his death?

He had been prankish, that I knew. He had been generally happy and gay. He liked color and noise and crowds—

It was high noon and I was looking through the musty hay toward the highway. A traveling circus came into view, its gaudy red and gold wagons blazing in the sunshine. Ten sluggish old elephants plodded along with their trunks swaying. Animal cages, a calliope, a clown wagon—

Then and there I knew! I remembered my dark past! It all flashed back in a wave of thought that was like a flame.... Painting my big red mouth on my white face. The red diamonds on my cheeks. The gay red and white clown suit.... The night I saved the little girl from the fall and met my own sudden death....

A circus clown—that's what I had been.

The traveling circus passed out of sight, and my memories dimmed. I was a machine, now.

Even the chemical-nurtured brain of a mechanical man must sleep sometimes. These fires of thought had tired me. Although my voice box went right on buzzing at full volume, and my automatic fingers went right on filing at the chains, my thoughts at last blacked out and I went to sleep.

CHAPTER XI
Familiar Voices

WHEN I woke up—I have no idea how many hours or days later—familiar voices were falling on my ears.

I was instantly on the alert. Yes, hearing my old friends Madge and Herb. A radio was playing very softly, so I knew that they were in a car. They had driven up and parked just below my hayloft.

By mere chance? Hardly. I didn't guess at first how they had found their way here. Somehow I thought they had come to look for me. I tried to croak a loud buzz to them.

I couldn't buzz! My voice box had played out.

I listened.

Right away I gathered from their conversation that there had been strange developments since my disappearance. An investigation was going on, and some of the star witnesses were missing.

Poor Waldemar, the victim of some mysterious outrage by a fake mechanical man, had been buried.

But the courts wouldn't believe that the fake was not Yours Truly, the one and only Buzz-Bolt.

Herb's testimony should have been good, but since his injury he had been out of his head a part of the time, and the court was reluctant to believe him. They were also turning a deaf ear to Madge's testimony. At first I couldn't understand why. Then—

"If you hadn't admitted you were in love with me," Herb said softly, "they would have listened. But now they believe you're prejudiced."

"I had to tell them the truth," Madge said quietly.

"It was the nicest thing I ever heard anyone say in court," said Herb, and now he made her say it again. For a little while there was silence, and I wouldn't have interrupted it for anything.

Piecing together what I had overheard, including some remarks about Joe Moberly, I understood that they had come here hoping to find him, not me.

They didn't know they were looking for a murderer. They only knew that Moberly had been in the office on a certain morning when I had failed to work. Madge thought he might testify. She had not found him at his address, but had gone to great effort to dig up some old addresses. Somewhere, she learned that he had once been interested in this piece of farm property. Herb, just out of the hospital, had agreed to ride out with her, just on a long hunch. So here they were, parked below my hayloft window, talking the whole thing over. And here I was, containing all the answers, yet unable to rattle my chains.

My buzz wouldn't work, my recorded voices were too weak to carry. What was I to do?

Once I had over-heated Blackridge's coffee by sending electrical heat to my fingertips. I looked at the dry hay that surrounded me. I started the heat down through my trapped arm, full blast, and waited.

They turned the radio higher to listen to the part of the news that concerned them.

"Here it comes," said Herb.

THE radio announcer droned: "Sensational developments in the investigation of the robot murder case today. Herbert Williams, co-inventor, testified that the metal monster with the bloody fist is not his invention, but a cheap imitation. Miss Madge LaGrange supported this opinion. The court is weighing their words against other factors. It is well known that the Williams brothers laboratories looked to make a fortune from the mass production of these Buzz-Bolts. That vision will collapse like a punctured balloon if Mr. Buzz-Bolt is a creature that turns on his own friends in the dead of night and murders them. A call has been issued for a certain Mr. Joe Moberly, whose testimony may be valuable. Meanwhile, the decision apparently hinges upon Mr. V. V. Blackridge, who will testify tomorrow. Mr. Blackridge is the real estate man for whom the mechanical monster worked, and it is believed that Mr. Blackridge and Buzz-Bolt were never on highly congenial terms...."

Herb snorted, "As if Uncle was ever on congenial terms with anyone! Let's get back to town."

They started the motor.

The wisps of hay at my fingertips grew red and began to curl up and begin to smoke.

The car was leaving. Its headlights cut a path along the lane beyond the fence. If they had looked back, then, they would have seen a small blaze in my barn loft.

The hay was dry. The flames leaped up around me. If they would only look back now! I disregarded the heat. My eager eyes followed that pair of headlights. They had reached the highway, there they were hesitating. Now my heart, so to speak, leaped like fire. They had seen! They were debating whether to come back. I'll bet they were mystified, all right. What had they done that could have started a fire in a deserted barn?

CHAPTER XII
A Fall Through Flames

IT WAS hard to see what was going fastest, the hay or the roof. But right away the floor was burning too, and along with the terrific heat I began to feel the quiver of the building.

From beyond the feed lot, the spectators watched from their cars. Ten or twelve had driven in from the highway to watch the sight and wonder what could be done.

I could see Herb, now, wearing bandages on both arms. He sat in the car, calling to Madge. She had gotten a bucket of water from the watering tank, probably without knowing what she was doing. A bucket of water was no match for these flames. She looked beautiful, standing there, bewildered and half frightened over something she couldn't understand, the high flames lighting her face.

Suddenly there was a ripping of black timbers beneath me, I was thrown to one side, my weight crushed down through fire-eaten floor, and I fell.

The clank of that fall was not loud, compared to the crackle of flames. My chains were too tight to make much noise. The sound I remember most was a scream from Madge.

"It's a person!" she cried. "Somebody's there, I saw them."

And she ran right to the burning edges, peering in at my dark form. Then suddenly she saw me clearly, and recognized me.

"Buzz-Bolt! *Buzz-Bolt!*"

The men from the other cars were quick to come to my rescue—not because they understood what they were doing, but because they wanted to help Madge—who certainly knew what she was doing.

Someone had a log chain with a hook, and he threw it in among the falling timbers, hooked my chains and threw a hitch around the car's rear bumper.

"Haul away," he shouted, and out I came.

I was dragged out on my tin pants, so to speak, straight across the cowlot. The affair was pretty rough on my dignity at the moment, but anyway I was out. There would be plenty of time to repair and polish myself afterward.

Well, Mr. Palmer, this has turned out to be a rather long-winded application for a job, but I think I've given you a fair sample of my experiences and I have implied, quite honestly, that I do have my limitations and need the help of human beings now and then, even though I'm a pretty robust and self-sufficient robot, as robots go.

You may imagine, and you're right, that, once I was unchained and given a chance to testify in court, I was able to clear up things for Herb and Madge.

But there was one tense moment in that court room scene when I took an awful chance. My old clowning instincts got the better of me.

Was I the true Buzz-Bolt? Was this other creature with the bloody fist a fake that had been substituted for some malicious purpose?

This was the contention of both Herb and Madge. The court wondered.

MY TESTIMONY, which I would have gladly written in full on a typewriter, they refused to accept. All my recorded voices, as well as my buzz, were out of order. That fire was going to cost me some repairs.

And now a sour-faced boss by the name of Blackridge took the stand and I saw that whether we won or lost depended on his whims of this one crucial moment.

"Mr. Blackridge, will you please examine these two metal creatures and tell us which is the one that the Williams brothers manufactured and placed in your office as your assistant?"

Blackridge gave me his darkest scowl. He turned slowly to that dead metal form whose free swinging arm had been made to commit the murder.

If he identified it as Buzz-Bolt, I realized that Herb and Madge would lose everything they dreamed of. Moreover, the murderer of Waldemar would go free.

But if he admitted that I was his servant, he might have to put up with me again. I don't think he wanted more of me. I had brought him too much trouble.

He started past me. A whim, an ornery whim, an act of spite. He was going to cut me cold.

I marched over to him so suddenly that he backed up against the wall in surprise, just as he had done once before. You should have seen his eyes pop at me. And he reached—you guessed it—right for those two pet hairs that struck up from the top of his bald head.

"Don't pull them out, Buzz-Bolt!" he yelled. "You promised me, Buzz-Bolt!"

I stopped and smiled. Then Blackridge saw the absurdity of his words, and, believe it or not, he smiled, just for one rash moment.

That did it, and nobody in court had any doubts about it.

I'm still working for Mr. Blackridge, Mr. Palmer, but gradually I'm learning to talk, and I know V. V. Blackridge doesn't like it, that's why I'm looking for a better job.

Daytimes preferred. Herb Williams lets me go out at nights, by the way, and just at present I'm hot on the trail of a murderer named Joe Moberly. Would you like to hear about it?

Well, maybe some other time.

THE BATTLE OF THE
HOWLING HATCHET

The Battle of the Howling Hatchet signaled a change in both style and attitude for Wilcox. Its sobering ending remains as powerful today as when it was first published in 1952. This psychological war tale was one of Don Wilcox's final stories for Amazing Stories *magazine.*

YOU COME out of your daze slowly, trying to remember. You know they've forced you into this machine, this tank that isn't a tank. You know the guns of war are roaring around you and you're supposed to do something about it. All you want to do is get to your typewriter, knock out your daily story, and go back to sleep.

A shell rips in front of you!

Your tank jumps like a pebble. Your head bumps the iron works above you, and your helmet crunches down over your face. The blast of fire outside your windows blinds you.

Voices are yelling at you through the phones: "Full speed ahead! This is it! Move it, move it!"

As if you know how to operate this *contraption!* There's been a mistake. You've never been in one of these things before. All these gadgets are meaningless. You can stare at them, but you can't do anything about them.

But they're yelling at you to give her number ten, and in your bewilderment you reach out with a gloved fist and strike a button-shaped lever with the number ten on it. The button plunges in about four inches, and the lighted ten turns from green to red. And suddenly you're moving forward, right square into the big shell hole.

"GREAT gory guns!" I yelled, trying to break out of this ghastly nightmare. Only it wasn't a nightmare. The big machine was clanking and roaring all around me as I sat in the driver's seat. My action had set the thing in motion, and I was in a state of utter confusion.

"That's right. That's perfect!" they yelled at me through the earphones. "Hit her hard, Steve. You can't miss."

And another voice, an older, heavier voice, called: "Good luck, Stevie boy. We'll see you in a few days—we hope!"

I shouted, "Hey, who do you think—ye gods! Where'm I going?"

"Right into the earth, Steve—right on your course, boy. Don't fail us. Everything depends—"

I didn't hear any more. The roar of the accelerating motors fairly deafened me. I was thundering over the embankment…into the shell hole. The dust and smoke were blinding.

My monster tank roared down into the depths of the pit, and *plowed in!*

My windows showed me the inner edges of the massive circular stonecutting equipment that surrounded the front end of the machine. The atomic-powered augurs howled as they moved into the bank of earth and rock. I was riding into a hurricane of dust and flying stones, right into the earth!

Blackness engulfed me. Then headlights came on, and I could see the dizzy spinning of the augurs up ahead. My big cigar-shaped tank was eating its way into the mountainside like a redhot spike burning into a wall of soft pine. Daylight was already left behind. I was cutting a tunnel into the blackness of solid earth.

So this was the "Howling Hatchet" I had heard about. A secret weapon for underground warfare. Atomic-powered and geared for disintegrating solid granite, it was supposed to be able to walk through mountains, leaving back of it a sealed tunnel of smoothly coated walls.

But how did I happen to be here? I, Bill Barth, the fledgling war correspondent. All I wanted out of this war was a chance to write up stories of the daily fighting, so the folks back home could know what the boys were going through. There'd been some mistake chucking me in here, calling me "Stevie!"

AGAINST the howl of the machine I tried to reassemble my thoughts. The last I could remember before they'd slammed this door on me, was an explosion, then a hospital bed. But that was a long time ago…and my memories seemed so dim….

Against the howling, screaming noises of the machine, I kept shouting into the transmitter. But, those voices that had yelled orders at me were out of reach. I might as well try to outshout a volcano. I calmed down and glared at the intricate instrument board before me. Its glinting little polished buttons and colored lights mocked me as the machine drilled deeper into the rock.

"They said I was *on my course!*" I mocked myself. *My* course! As if I had anything to do with it!

Suppose I should experiment with the controls and fail! I'd find myself stuck deep inside the earth with no way out. The temptation was to stop everything before I'd gone any farther. I could walk back, couldn't I? A backward glance showed me beyond the long, dark, cylindrical, machinery-filled shaft, a spray of fire at the rear, blasting circular wails into rigid shape in my wake. Yes, if I could cut off the power, I might be able to get out and walk back through that freshly made tunnel—go back to them—tell them they'd made take—I was the wrong man.

I snatched the little packet of papers that dangled from a knob. By the light of the flashing instrument board I could read the names on the credentials. Steven Thomas Sanders. Henry Longworth.

There were pictures of both men. The photo of Steven Sanders looked exactly like me!

So that was it. They'd ushered me out of the hospital into this. There must be an urgent errand ahead. It must all have been timed. Something was coming up that couldn't wait. What?

All at once I was watching the arrow on a certain dial. It shone with narrow parallel lines four inches long, red and green lines, three lines. The arrow was rising very gradually: The colors were jumping rapidly.

A SLIGHT shadow came over my hands. I couldn't look to see what caused it. I was fairly hypnotized by that one nervous arrow, creeping slowly toward a red illuminated zero. The great machine was grinding forward steadily, cutting its path out of that hard rock, so that a steady procession of raw cut circular walls glided back. Horror gripped me. I was riding into nowhere, yes, I must be riding toward something. The arrow was rising, pinpoint by pinpoint. An audible signal was sounding with a series of notes, each a little higher pitched than the last.

The shadow over my hand trembled. I reached to lever number ten and drew it back. Just a little. The scream of the grinding lowered to a sickening whistle. And I instantly regretted my action, with a vision of jamming to a stop amid a heap of broken rocks under the mountain. Rocks were bursting out into my headlights. I struck number ten again and plunged forward with renewed fury.

Then it happened. And I saw, in a glimpse, what I was plowing into was not rock or dirt, but a great horizontal barrel of steel. It was moving square across my path—another "howling hatchet" like the one I was driving.

I crashed in through its sides. My motors whined and groaned, but I bored right in. The walls of steel tore open. The lighted interior was revealed for a split second before it all went dark.

In that flash I saw two men in helmets and tank suits, their arms flying up in terror.

I was bearing down on number ten, and my howling hatchet with its thousands of screaming teeth ate through the other machine—steel fiber, flesh and bone. In the whirl of dust and fire I saw helmets, arms, straps of steel—everything flying, darting through the area of suction into the path of disintegration.

That was all. The mad tank carried me on into the blackness of the earth. The singing signal silenced, and the flickering arrow rode away from the red zero and blinked off.

"I've killed a fellow prowler," I muttered to myself. "Who or what, I'll never know."

AND THEN I was aware, suddenly, that the shadow across my hands was someone back of me, standing crouched, watching the instruments over my shoulder. I looked up and saw the face of a young man, framed in a tank helmet.

I had never seen him before, and I had never seen anyone so white, in such a cold sweat. He looked at me as if he wanted to speak and couldn't. He pushed his helmet back and pressed his hand against his face.

"Well, Stevie, you did it. You've got through the first barrier and we're still alive."

I stared at him. "Have you been there all this time?"

"I was back in the bunk when we started."

"And you knew I was sitting here, helpless...."

"Nothing helpless about you, Stevie." He tried to grin, but the scared look made his lips quiver. "I've been watching you ever since you saw him coming."

"I was too paralyzed to talk. I figured it was all up with us. I didn't know what in the world you could do. He was dead on our path. He figured on a suicide smash—a small price to pay to prevent him from getting there first. At first I thought you meant to outrun him—and that's what he thought, too. But then I saw it couldn't be done. And it was too late for a dodge. It sure looked like death for all of us. But you had a trick up your sleeve, Stevie. I might have known."

"A trick, you call it?" I thought I would faint.

"The way you suddenly throttled down. More perfect timing I never hope to see. But the real trick was the way you played the grain of the rock in your favor. He tried to retard, too, but the way the rock lay, he ate right on ahead like a drill through rotten wood. By the time he'd retarded, you'd slashed on, full speed, and caught him broadsides. So—well, he's now neatly molded into our walls, what's left of him."

"So—"

"So—I congratulate you, Stevie." My hand was so limp I couldn't lift it. But he gripped it for a handshake and ended by saying the sweetest words I ever heard: "Now that that's over, Stevie, I guess I can take over the controls for awhile."

FOR MANY minutes I watched over his shoulder. I followed the movements of his clever fingers and swiftly memorized his every move. Then I began to ask him questions.

"Can you stop the machine and start it again with no danger of stalling?"

"If I can't I ought to be shot, as many times as you've shown me."

He thought I was questioning him to test his knowledge. To him I was Stevie.

"I'm asking for information," I said bluntly.

He gave me a look that said, "Tell that to the Marines." He went on ploughing through the earth, and a long black tunnel formed back of us. The howl and whine of the drills' screwing into solid stone filled the inside of the machine with a ceaseless uproar. Most of the time he kept going full blast.

"I don't figure we've got much time to waste," he said. "You certainly don't mean to put me through all those tests again, Stevie."

"Excuse my embarrassment," I said, "but I'm not Stevie. I've never been in one of these cussed things before, and I'm asking for information."

"My lord, Steve!" He gave me a look of disgust.

"But I'm telling you, Hank, it's all new to me."

"Steve, you've pulled some dillies in your day—"

"I'm not Steve!"

"You've pulled some sharp ones, but this takes the cake. Not Steve! I'd know you in hell. I'd know you by your voice. I'd know you by the way you move that right shoulder. Not Steve! Oh, yeah?"

"I tell you I'm not! Dammit, what do I have to prove to show I got in here purely by accident?"

"How did you know my name was Hank?"

"You've got it printed across the back of your jacket. Besides I looked into that batch of identifications in the envelope. Your photo is there with the name Henry Longworth."

"Did you overlook your own photo?"

"I found someone by the name of Steven Thomas Sanders. I will say this: he looks like me. They must have got us mixed in the hospital."

Hank Longworth turned and glared at me, his eyes narrowed. "Did you ever hear of Banalog?"

"What's a Banalog?"

"It's not a whatsa, it's a who. It's the person that helped you invent this howling hatchet. Only Banalog, unfortunately, happened to belong, to the enemy, and when this cussed war began, you and Banalog found yourselves on opposite sides. And now, Stevie, you've got the painful duty of fighting your fellow inventor. Does that ring a bell?"

"It might to Stevie, whoever he is. But it's all Greek to me. I'm Bill Barth, the war correspondent."

Hank LONGWORTH groaned and bore down on the number ten lever. We had removed our' helmets and earphones during our talk. Now, the increased speed and higher screams of the rocks against our metal teeth caused us to put on our gear again. Our conversation through the intercom was brief and brittle. Hank was angry. He thought I was trying to play some hoax on him, and he couldn't understand it. We were pressed for time, our assignment ahead would mean· life or death. How could we fritter away our energies playing games?

"How do you operate the guns on this thing?"

"I wouldn't know," he bit back sarcastically.

"If I'm going to be any help to you, you'd better teach me."

"You don't know what a gun is? You never heard of a gun?"

"What's this compartment marked *eggs?*"

"I suppose you never heard of an egg?"

"I never heard of one in a tank."

"Eggs are something you put in a nest. At the proper time they hatch."

"Is that why they call this the howling hatchet?"

"You ought to know. You named it. Banalog wanted to call it the boring bazooka, and I guess that's the only time you and Banalog ever quarreled, isn't it?"

"I never heard of Banalog."

"The military big-shots took up your quarrel, if you remember," Hank said, giving me the deep drill of his eye. "They finally agreed with you. It's not a bazooka. It doesn't blow through the earth. It has to hack its way with its battery of mechanical hatchets. As fast as the mass breaks up, it disintegrates, except—"

"Go on, I'm listening."

"You're testing me."

"I'm asking for information."

"The elements needed are automatically retained. The machine automatically takes in what it needs to form a concrete tunnel back of it. The water supply is continually replenished—"

"Out of dry rock?"

"Of course. You and Banalog, in making your tests, never found any rock so dry that it didn't yield quantities of water on an average run."

"What is an average run, an hour or a day?"

"On your tests you made twenty seven miles in nine hours, but you claim you're good for three days, non-stop."

THE INSTRUMENTS were acting up in a way that absorbed Hank's attention, and I was left to think things over. I recalled something that had been shouted at me when it all started. One of the voices had yelled, "We'll see you again in a few days—we hope." The more I thought of it, the more I was certain this howling hatchet was off on a job too big for its britches.

Through the several hours that followed, I tried to observe everything Hank did. I began to know, from the whine of the machinery, that certain granite formations gave us a bad time. At other times we struck soft spots, and a few times, between mountains, we nosed up for a glimpse of daylight.

That was dangerous business. The enemy has sharp eyes. Once, right after we had caught a flash of sunlight, we felt the earth rock, and knew that a shell had exploded not far off. That, Hank muttered, was a bad break. We had been spotted, and the enemy nest was sure to be warned. They would know that their own underground tank, sent out to intercept us, had muffed its job.

We quickly gored him. Our emergence had occurred in the depths of a steep V-shaped valley. We plowed into the bank of the stream, and the river waters came hissing in after us, rushing against the blasts of fire that streamed back from our rear.

"The river will follow us right in," I said.

"For a hundred feet, yes." He turned our boring boat upward a moment later. "There—in case anyone tried to follow us, let them find their way through that water trap."

"If we ever get back, it won't be on foot."

Hank muttered something scornful. "You seem to have the optimistic notion we're going to get back."

That remark rattled around in my head like a spiraling bullet. I moved back into the narrow passageway and found the compartment Hank had called the bunk. I examined, in this privacy, the toe tag I was wearing, and discovered that it bore the name of this fabulous character Steven Thomas Sanders. I couldn't help wondering what would happen to the real Steve if I never came back. Would he, an inventor, find himself rudely forced into my role of newspaper correspondent?

No—he'd never allow the exchange to go that far. Not if he was in his right mind.

Probably by now, I told myself, he was already raving at the doctors for causing such a mix-up.

"By now the jeeps are racing down our tunnel trying to overtake us," I muttered to myself, seeing it all in my mind. "I'll bet Steven Thomas Sanders is in the front jeep yelling at them to step on it. All he wants is to overtake his howling hatchet and get back in the driver's seat."

T HEN I THOUGHT, "They'll come to the river. That devilish river will stop them, and an enemy shell will blast them to dust, and that will be the end of Stevie. And here I am, stuck with his job."

I tried to take a quick nap. I was still weak from the hospital experience, and this terrorizing hatchet ride had tied my nerves in knots. I came out of a brief rest, however, with new strength. We shared a meal while Hank stayed on at the controls. Again I watched him, trying to pick up everything. And it was well that I did, in the light of what followed.

I was beginning to like Hank. It troubled me to see that he was so deeply fatalistic. "It's like I told you two months ago—"

"I'm afraid I wouldn't remember."

"I'd remember if you remembered anything," he said. "I'm beginning to think you're not Stevie—"

"I've been telling you. I'm Bill Barth."

In a moment he went on glumly, "It's like I told you two months ago. I had a hunch from the start that I'll not come through alive."

We roared on, watching our maps, making routine checks from our dials.

"All I hope is that I live to see the enemy's nest mussed up. If we can once break into the central cavern and score one direct hit, three-fourths of their radio-controlled warfare will go berserk."

The charts and maps showed it all plainly enough, and I knew, front the dials, that the subterranean headquarters we meant to blow up were now less than an hour away.

"Another hour will do it," I said.

"If we don't smack into any mines."

"Won't our instruments warn us?"

"You should know." He traded places with me now, and said he guessed he was entitled to a few minutes' rest before the action started. "I don't exactly trust myself to dodge the web of tunnels when they come too thick."

I drew back on lever number ten, and cut the speed almost in half. Our big growling tank ploughed on into the wilderness of stone at a dogged pace. My eyes flicked back and forth from dials to maps and across to the little three-dimensional chart that warned of our approach to any underground openings.

STEERING BECAME more difficult. I could see from the map that the enemy "Underquarters"—the subterranean headquarters we sought—was like the hub of a wheel. It was charted as a big natural cavern, larger than a football gridiron, into which artificial tunnels had been built in several directions. The enemy's top brass motored in and out of those Underquarters at high speed, according to the description that went with our orders. We weren't to spill any hints of our approach until we broke in on the real nest.

"How are we going to help it?" I asked. "Don't they have the same instruments we have?"

"That depends on how much Banalog knows."

"Banalog. That's the other inventor."

"You're the only one who knows how many of your inventive secrets you shared."

"I wouldn't remember," I said blankly. "Banalog. I never heard of him."

"Cut it out!"

"What's wrong? I just stated a fact."

Hank squared around as if to tell me off once and for all. "Stevie, there's a soft spot in you. You know it's a hundred to one that you'll have to kill your friend Banalog on this mission. You've guessed that he'll be there, in the middle of their nest of equipment, and it'll be your ugly job to blow him to hell. You can't face it, can you?"

"Hank," I said coldly, "You're a good joe and I like you. But you're so far off your base—"

"Look!" Hank interrupted. "We're about to bust into a path. Hold up." I struck out at the levers, and number ten bounced back toward me as we groaned to a stop.

"The eggs!" Hank said, whirling to the bomb compartment. "If we're going to give their seismographs the proper jitters, we'd better do it fast."

He fed fifteen of the metal baseballs into a chute. There was a patch of darkness ahead, off to the right, which might have been a crevice or a break into a natural tunnel. The transparent chute projected forward at the touch of a lever, and turned off into the crevice like an elephant's trunk as Hank manipulated the direction levers. The "eggs" rolled down the plastic pathway and deposited themselves somewhere outside the path of our light.

But one of those loaded baseballs came rolling out into our immediate pathway, and we didn't care to take the chance of running over it. What it contained would make TNT seem like a small firecracker.

"That was my own fault, damn it," Hank said, perspiring as he worked at the levers. "I can't seem to pick it up, and there's no time to waste. Those eggs are ticking—so here goes!"

"Where are you going?"

"Out!"

H E OPENED a forward door that I hadn't remembered seeing. He crawled out through the geometric pattern of rock-cutting teeth, temporarily at rest. He walked into the glare of the headlights toward the uncut wall ahead of the foremost augurs. He held a pistol, ready for possible trouble from the dark opening off at the right. He bent to pick up the "egg".

His body suddenly twitched. He turned painfully, sinking to one knee.

His pistol spat fire into the unlighted cave. The he dropped the gun and with both hands lifted the egg and threw it—pushed it, like a track man putting the shot. It rolled off into the blackness, and Hank crumpled to the floor.

I reached him as soon as I could climb out the door. I flashed a light into the narrow cave and saw a single fallen guard, no one else. I bent to lift Hank into my arms.

He groaned a little as I bore him back into the interior of the hatchet. "Keep going! Don't bother with me, just keep going."

I ripped his jacket open and tore at his bloody shirt.

"No time," he cried. "They're set. Keep moving!"

He made a mad struggle, freeing himself momentarily from my grasp, so that he reached forward and struck lever number ten. The big machine growled and roared into action, and on we moved, past our planted explosives into the wall of stone.

"The controls!" he moaned. "You've got to put this job over, Bill

Barth. Whoever you are, you've got to...."

And that was all I heard. The life had gone out of Hank Longworth.

LEVER NUMBER ten shifted between full speed and half speed during the next twenty or twenty-five minutes. I moved on a course of my own choosing not identical to the one mapped out on paper. Part of my weaving about was the result of my state of mind. Then there were other factors.

On a straight shot, where the three-dimensional chart assured me I wasn't coming close to any underground traffic-way, I set the controls and took time to move Hank back to the bunk. I still had a wisp of hope there might be life in him, but the hope was a vain one. I plastered a bandage across the bullet hole in his chest, closed his jacket and spread a towel over him. Looking at his white face for the last time, I couldn't help thinking of the last words he had spoken. Now the job was mine. He had called me by name, and charged me with my responsibility.

"So it's up to me," I whispered to myself, drawing the towel up over his face. The knowledge of this machine that dwelt in his brain had passed away into the nothingness of death. I hurried back to the instruments. "So it's up to me. It's up to Bill Barth!"

I had the strange feeling that I was another person, looking in at myself from these walls of rocks I was moving through. I was seeing myself as the inventor Steven Thomas Sanders might have seen me. And I thought what he might have said to me.

"You've inherited our machine, Bill Barth. By a trick of fate it has fallen into your hands. The victory is tied up in this machine, Bill Barth. Keep it going; keep your head, and destroy the enemy Underquarters. Do that, and the howling hatchet will be worth the investment. Fail, and our lives—Hank Longworth's and mine—have come to nothing."

"Can I do it?" I kept asking myself. "Can I do it?"

"Find the nest, plough into it, and get one direct hit," the voice of my unseen observer seemed to be saying through the roar of the machine. "Find the nest.... Find the nest.... Kill the enemy...."

It was only the roaring, howling screeching noises of steel against stone. Walls of stone, grinding away under the impact of the hatchet. Noises screaming through my brain, prodding me, knifing me, electrifying me with the one challenge to keep going—to do the thing that must be done.

I moved on a course of my own choosing, not identical to the one that had been mapped out. I was now going over the top of the enemy nest, according to the little three-dimensional chart, the dials, the auditory signals....

Every source of information convinced me that this was the nearest I had come to the Underquarters. And the nearest that I would come *until I came up from underneath!*

That was my own chosen strategy.

This was my job now, and I would take my own chances doing it my own way. Only sometimes, through the screeching howling noises of the rock drills, I tried to hear that imaginary voice again, the voice of Stevie, calling to me through the roar of rock and wind and steel, telling me to keep going.

And telling me *how to go.*

Was it I who had thought of looping over the nest and then drilling back from the underside? Or had that mysterious invisible companion been whispering to me again?

Or was it the spirit of Hank Longworth, saying, "Go to it, Bill Barth. It's up to you!"

I was moving over the nest, to the west of it. The ceiling of the cavern I hoped to blow up was less than a hundred feet below the path I was cutting.

Now, I knew, the "eggs" we had planted somewhere back yonder would soon start exploding. I dodged all areas that showed signs of containing paths into the central nest, and planted number ten down solid, cutting as fast as I could go.

T HEN, GETTING well to the west of the nest, I did something I hadn't tried before. I made a straight cut. I stopped. I backed away, leaving a spur of perhaps thirty feet.

Into that spur I poured the remainder of my supply of eggs, with the time triggers set.

I pressed the forward lever, veered to the right again, and started on a downward path. Now there were two well-planted pockets full of timed eggs, set to go off in series. I held the machine down to a slow pace and watched everything.

Was I close enough to the nest for the enemy's seismographs to have picked me up?

If not, I soon would be. I was now of battle came.

F IRE RIPPED across the cavern in a straight line of instant death. Fire sprayed up through the wires that overhung the cavern walls. Flashes of electricity jumped from instruments in every corner of the room. Showers of rocks came tumbling down. Flame. Men and uniforms and weapons were thrown about in mangled heaps in all directions.

The third blast went wild. The jump of the howling hatchet had sent the gunfire in an indiscriminate direction. A tank of gasoline must have been struck. The yellow flames boiled out and ran in streaks, illuminating the room. Smoke billowed out, and I could see the figures of uniformed men chasing across in front of it.

They were coming toward me.

"Why didn't you get out!" Those words were roaring through my head again. "You've missed your chance!"

"I couldn't leave!" Was it the thought of Hank's body, back there in the bunk, that had held me here? A senseless thought, perhaps, in the light of what was happening. But he was still a friend, still with me, still giving me moral support, somehow, even though he was dead.

"Hank has played his part. You've got to leave him. Get out if you can. No—it's too late now. They're coming in on you. You're too late, Bill Barth!"

"Get out of my head, you damned roar—how can I think what to do? This is all new to me. I'm only a war correspondent. I wasn't meant for this. I ought to be back at my typewriter. This was a mistake, putting me in here."

"All right, Bill Barth," the voice seemed to say.

"What do you mean, all right?"

"I'm through trying to tell you what to do. Anyway, it doesn't make too much difference now. You've crippled their nerve center. That's the important thing."

"Yes," I thought. "That's the important thing."

"You've done it, Bill Barth. Hank and I have seen our purpose accomplished through you. It's all right now. Only, don't you think you ought to try to save your own life?"

"Zeeeeng-BRRRROOOM!"

The fire was still synchronized. The eggs were still going off at regular intervals. And that meant that all this fury of conversation had taken place in my head in a matter of seconds. They were coming toward me across the room. But the new blast of death caught the front of their line. The foremost man, running in a circular path, escaped the blast of fire. The next six or seven must have got their everlasting. Another dozen or more bolted off in another direction toward a gleaming piece of artillery.

As I HAD guessed, the artillery that guarded the many entrances to this Underquarters was trained on directions determined by the hoax explosions. My appearance by way of the cavern floor had caught everyone off guard. It was a suicidal attack, that fact was bearing down upon me with every vibration of the howling hatchet's motors.

Now I wished the voice would come back and tell me what to do. I looked for something across the room that might serve as a shield—something they would not want to destroy—something I could take refuge behind to avoid being blown to hell by the big guns.

A heavy shell suddenly smashed across the upper side of the hatchet's cylindrical frame.

"Hold it!" Someone screamed. "Give me a chance! I'll get him." It was the shout of the one man who had outraced my last shell. He was somewhere around the hatchet, trying to break in.

Another *Zee-eng!* And another blast of my own artillery, smashing across the fiery way to catch a row of jeeps racing down into the circus of destruction. Wheels flew in all directions, and a section of stone wall came ripping down with clouds of smoke and dust.

At the same time another blaze of fire struck out from one of their guns. The shell struck hard, and the big steel framework around me jumped and staggered. My head was struck as I fell back sidewise. I clutched at my helmet.

"Help me get out of this damned—help me! It's smashing my damned brain! Help—Ugh! Who are you?"

I was talking in a daze for a minute. I had the impression that the side door had flown open and an enemy soldier was standing there pointing a pistol at me.

"Who are you? Or are you just something I'm seeing?"

That last hard jolt had fairly knocked the seams out of this steel monster. And now it was all up, I saw. The flames threw light across the edge of the open door, and clinging to it was this soldier's hard hand, the knuckles white. His eyes glittered in the glare of the light. I thought he must be breathing smoke.

I couldn't move, I was too dazed. The pistol was aimed squarely at me. If I could have dodged back three inches I might have had a chance to shoot it out with him. But my head was just clear enough to know that if I moved a fraction of an inch he would shoot.

Yet he didn't shoot, and this made me think he wanted something from me. Did he think he could capture this hulk of steel? It was little more than a wreck now.

I began to count. In another second, surely, there would be one more explosion up yonder, and this steel boat would give another jump. Or had the last one already happened?

One, two, three, four. No explosion. It was all over. My howling hatchet had made its last automatic jump. And all I would have to do to enter another world would be to try to reach for lever number ten.

"All right, you've got me. Do you want me dead or alive?"

I doubted whether he could understand my language, but it was worth a chance. "If you think I can reveal the secrets of this machine, you're all wrong. Well, what are you waiting for?"

He didn't blink an eyelash.

On a bold impulse I reached for the handle that would swing the door closed. He didn't shoot. I touched the door handle, the door moved an inch, and he fell forward. As he fell I saw that the back of his head was shot off. That last shell from his own comrades had caught him, and he'd frozen in his tracks against the door.

I tried lever ten, then, and the jolted, shaken hulk of steel slowly moved into action. I set it to make a wide circular swing around the big room, and I got out and ran for the shadows.

M Y ONE and only chance to make a getaway was to go back the way I had come.

It may sound slightly bloodthirsty for me to admit that during the next twenty minutes I killed more than twenty men. I look back upon that deal as the most exhausting and nerve-wracking twenty minutes of my life. And I only wonder that I had the good fortune to come out alive.

As I see it now, my nerve to kill the enemy would have given out, and I would have lost my last slender grip on life if one particular person had confronted me. For the tenuous hold on life which was mine in those twenty minutes was simply the will to keep on killing, nothing else but that.

The one direction I looked for, through all the smoke and flame and flurry, was *down*. I remember dashing across from one shadow to another, ducking back whenever a new light flared up, and at last spotting the pit in the floor where the tank had brought me up.

The fireworks were still going hot and heavy. The tank was limping around a wide circle, and every few yards, responding to the automatic mechanisms that I had left turned on, it fired another shell. Seven or eight more blasts must have burst from its inner guns before the flow of ammunition ran out, and by that time I had won my first and easiest battle. In a quick contest of fists, I knocked out someone who blundered into my path.

He fell with a grunt of surprise, and I pounced on him. He was in no shape to argue, and whatever it was he muttered, I paid no attention. All I wanted from him was part of his uniform, for whatever protection it might offer. A moment later I donned his coat and borrowed his pistol and went on my way.

THE NEXT step might have been right down in the pit, but my eye caught sight of something on the floor that I needed badly—a flashlight.

Luck was with me, no doubt about it. Someone's scream from across the room was my warning to duck another shell. The artillery was getting into gear in reality, at last, and the poor old howling hatchet, sturdy as it had been through miles of earth-cutting, was at last in for an awful beating. The enemy nest was already a complete shambles, and from then on it was up to everyone to look out for his own life. Those flying shells were no respecters of anyone.

I rolled over the floor under a spreading cloud of smoke. I snatched the flashlight, and rolled again.

I climbed down into the pit with care. It presented an inclined surface, and I might have bounded down if it hadn't been pitch dark. Then a streak of fire came running across toward me and I saw the way clearly. Right up to the surface the big machine had laid its smoothly plastered walls a neat cylinder, large enough to drive a small tank through.

"Fire! Fire! Fire!" The wail rang through the room. If any of those chasing, frenzied soldiers still believed I was in the tank, the shout dispelled the illusion. Rifles began to crackle.

I was down in the depths, sprinting.

Until the shadowy cylindrical walls curved away from the light, I sprinted.

I paused long enough to glance back at the emptiness. I flashed on the light for an instant, caught a glimpse of the wide open path ahead, and ran as fast as I could go.

They would follow me, I hadn't the slightest doubt of that. I thought ahead to one point of safety. All I could hope for was to make my way up the long fishhook curve to the spur where the tank had cut a path and backed away.

Racing up the grade, I heard the sputter of jeeps. They were coming after me on the tear. My moments were numbered, unless—

The path curved, then curved back. I almost missed the spot I was looking for, it was so well concealed. A quick flash of light revealed it—the spur that led off the upward route. I darted into it. With a pistol in each hand I waited.

The first jeep that came swinging up through the curve had two occupants. I aimed carefully and with two shots I put an end to both of them. I held my breath for a tense moment waiting to see whether the jeep would come coasting back down the grade. Luck was with me. It rolled on ahead, over the hump. There would be no dead men coasting back down the path to warn of my hiding place.

Two more jeeps followed over the same course and I took care of both before the soldiers on foot followed up the path. The game was a tense one now. One slip could be fatal. The roar of my pistols must have echoed down through the tunnel. But there the roar from below was still booming through the hollow passages.

ABOUT A half hour later the pathway had grown quiet enough so that I ventured out, stepping carefully over the men I had had to shoot down. Ahead, blasts had broken the floor of the tunnel. The jeeps had fallen through.

Through the darkness I plodded for what seemed miles before I got away from the smoke-filled air. The fumes must have circulated like compressed gas. I was gagging for a breath of fresh air when at last I came to the place where Hank had been murdered. I paused, standing in the darkness, listening, breathing. What a luxury to breathe clear air.

I wondered where the narrow natural cave might lead, but I knew I dare not take a chance. My one way back to home territory was by the route I had come. I trudged on.

At length I reached the descent that was filled with water from the river. I flashed my light around, hoping against hope that there might be some break in the ceiling that I could climb through.

I rested for several minutes, then stripped down to my shorts. The one way back home was through the tunnel. The one way through the tunnel at this point was to swim about a hundred feet under water and find my way up into the river.

Maybe I tried it the hard way. I plunged in and pawed through the watery blackness until my lungs grew tight, and then turned back. I reached my starting point, and crawled back up onto the dry surface, panting hard. Something told me it was a longer underwater swim than I would ever make. I had estimated more than fifty feet of forward progress, and my open eyes had failed to see any hint of light ahead through the clear water.

It was more than an hour before I tried again. I tried to estimate how much time had passed during the battle at the Underquarters. Perhaps it was night outside. If I dared to sleep for a few hours, would my next trial find daylight?

The low muffled sound of a motor brought me up with a start. Were they coming? Placing my ear down on the surface of the tunnel I could hear the steady hum.

I rolled my clothing and possessions into a ball and hid them in the only possible place—under the edge of the water where the tunnel inclined downward. And again I dived in to try the swim for freedom.

I swam with the roar of motors in my ears, and when I had gone until my lungs were bursting—when I thought this was surely the last moment of life—my hands caught onto an object that was moving through the water under me.

IT TOOK me back to the side I had come from. I clung tight. I was dragged up onto the inclined tunnel floor more dead than alive.

I heard the voices of men as they clambered out of a rubber-enclosed tank. They pumped water out of me and soon had me breathing in good style.

"Stevie!"

"What on earth were you doing in that water trap, Stevie?"

"Stevie, don't you remember me? I helped you and Banalog build that cave-cutting go-cart. Lemme shake your hand, boy. You've put the deal over."

They helped me dress and got me into the rubber-sealed underwater tank and we went through the water and up to the dry tunnel entrance on the other side of the river.

As we motored back through the smoothly banked tube, they talked in satisfied terms. The Underquarters of the enemy had been blasted to hell.

I said, "You've got the wrong man in me, fellows. I don't happen to be Stevie. The fellow Stevie you've got me mixed up with must be back in the hospital."

One of the soldiers looked at me and nodded. "I think so. Would you like to go back and see him?"

That's where they took me. From then on for a couple of days a doctor had me in charge. He had me go over my story several times. Each time he would mention one particular detail.

"You didn't come in contact with Banalog, did you?"

And I would always ask, "What's Banalog? I don't think I ever heard of it."

"I told you yesterday, it's a person. It was the partner of Steven Sanders—his fellow inventor. Banalog happened to be on the other side in this war, and it would have been Stevie's painful job to kill him if they had met."

"I killed several men."

"But you didn't kill Banalog."

"I don't know Banalog. I never heard of Banalog. I wouldn't know whether I killed him or not."

That was the way our conversation ran until late the second day, when the doctor added, "I'm sure you didn't kill Banalog, because he's been taken prisoner. He's alive. He'll remain a prisoner until the end of the war. Which means he won't be harmed."

Something inside me let go, then, and I began to sob like a child.

"You're going to be all right now," the doctor said. "Our minds can play tricks on us sometimes."

I listened, and what he said seemed to dislodge a lot of darkness from somewhere in the front of my brain.

"You see, the cruelties of war sometimes give us jobs to do that are simply too painful to be faced. And when two men have been very close friends and have high admiration for each other, their minds might choose a devious path of escape from reality—even a mental blackout— rather than admit that they can kill each other. Do you understand what I am saying?"

"I—I think so."

"Good," the doctor said gently. "You're going to be all right. And just who are you, if you don't mind telling me?"

I drew a quiet breath of deep relief, swabbed the tears of distress and shock from my eyes, and said what I knew to be true, "I'm Steven Thomas Sanders, the inventor—Banalog's best friend."

BLUEFLOW

When the "pulp" magazines faded away in their losing battle against paperbacks and television in the 1950s, an era of more sober and sedate near-future science fiction was in style and the old one of galaxy-spanning adventure and colorful, distant worlds was out. Don Wilcox could have continued writing in the new style, but it didn't appeal to him. So he turned to other writing and teaching challenges and left his former career far behind. Years later in retirement Don opened an art gallery in Florida, fulfilling another lifelong passion.

When well into his eighth decade Wilcox was persuaded to write two stories, Trip to Yo-Yo Falls *(1989) and* Blueflow *(1992), which merged the modern polished style with the dream imagery of his early work. Historian Mike Ashley asked Don to write an Arthurian story featuring the magical talents of a painter for his anthology book* "The Camelot Chronicles". *Wilcox's ingenious tale,* Blueflow, *touches upon the storm brewing over Genevieve's relationship with Lancelot and proved to be the final published work of his 53-year writing career.*

CHAPTER I

$\mathbf{A}$ WANDERING artist who loved walking by moonlight strayed through a strange forest from midnight to dawn with no certain destination. At daylight, reaching the edge of a meadow, he removed the packets of paints and brushes from his shoulders, placed them on the ground, and lay down to sleep. He awakened when the noon sun was beating down on him, warm and friendly.

He looked up to see an old man standing near, gazing at him. What a long white beard. What bright eyes, gleaming through the wrinkles of the mysterious old face.

The old man spoke. "Good noon, my friend." Low, gentle voice. "Are you not a stranger here? Are you lost?"

"Never lost," the artist replied. "Just roving through forests to explore more of this beautiful world." He rose up on one elbow and brushed his ruffled hair.

"I see that you have brought paints and brushes. An interesting way to travel."

"I am a painter, as you have probably guessed. Some people believe I am a great artist. They call me Master Artist Blueflow."

He sat up while explaining his name. Friends had given it to him when he was a child. "It's a fitting name because I flow, mentally, with the skies of ever-changing blue." He came to his feet and gestured toward the sky. "Always flowing blue. Sunset, sunrise, noon. Peaceful days and storms. I have made a list of eighty blues. I even have names for them—and of course there are many more."

The old man looked down at the display of paints: twenty-one colors arranged in three rows of little leather cups.

"I hope to watch you paint someday. Permit me to ask, doesn't the sun make your cups of paint go dry? You must have to mix fresh fluid daily."

The artist smiled. "You have guessed one of my problems. You yourself must be a painter."

"I happen to be a magician, as the people of this land will tell you. My name is Merlin. I have many powers. If you wish, I could freshen your paints at this moment." His upraised hand suddenly held a container of liquid. "I feel sure you would like the results, Mr. Blueflow. If you wish—"

The master artist was cautious. "Your offer has the sound of a gift. I should return the favor somehow. Perhaps you wish me to paint your portrait."

"A portrait of me?" The old man laughed. "I am quite a complex subject. Do you think you could do me justice?"

The artist smiled with amusement. "Quite honestly, no. I would probably paint your beautiful beard in five minutes. You may have taken fifty years to grow it. Indeed I would not be doing you justice."

"A generous answer, my friend. However, portrait painting must be expensive. Let's try to reach a bargain. Have you observed yonder brown building at the edge of the trees? It's a travelers' lodge. There you could sleep, eat, bathe and rest to suit your needs for a day or two. I will gladly pay for your lodging. Later, you may undertake to paint me if you wish."

The plan sounded agreeable, and Master Artist Blueflow immediately went to the lodge.

The following day he asked the people where he could find the elderly man with the white beard. They answered that he had left early on business. To return soon? No one knew. He was never predictable.

Blueflow said, "I must find him to paint his picture. I owe it to him." Then someone brought a slab of wood, finely polished, ready for painting. The lodge keeper explained, "The old man left this for you in case you want to start the painting in his absence."

"I'll start at once," Blueflow said.

He began. The paints were surprisingly fresh and responsive and the brushes moved fast. Some of the people at the lodge gathered near, watching, guessing that he might start the background during the subject's absence. To their surprise he did more. He painted, with a few touches, the shape of the head; with a few careful strokes he suggested the features; then with amazing delicacy came the mysterious wrinkles around the burning bright eyes. Soon the slightly bent shoulders appeared. And finally the magnificent white beard with its tinges of blue shadows began to take form. In less than half an hour the painting was almost complete. The colors of the garments were, at the start, a reminder of the clothes the old man had worn the previous day.

How did the artist do it? He explained briefly. This was a skill that he had acquired with years of self-training. To memorize a face. To hold it in his mind and paint from the mental image.

Suddenly he did something that puzzled the onlookers. He began changing the color of the shirt. One of the watchers spoke.

"Excuse me, Mr. Blueflow, but I recall he was wearing a yellow shirt last evening. Did you forget? I see you're now changing it to green."

The artist turned to glance across the room. "Your memory is correct, my friend, but I just now caught the strange feeling that the old man has returned and has asked me to paint it green. Am I mistaken?"

Someone else spoke up. "The fact is, he did come in, just two minutes ago, and paused for a moment to watch."

Blueflow nodded. "That was the feeling that I caught through the air. Where has he gone?"

"Into his room, but—pardon me—in truth he was still wearing the same yellow shirt from yesterday."

"Strange," Blueflow said. "These mental messages—" He broke off, for at that moment the old man returned from his room. And now he was wearing green. The viewers pointed, puzzled. "Look, he's changed." It was something the artist had felt!

Old Merlin came up briskly, saw the completed painting, and exclaimed in celebration. "Mr. Blueflow! Mr. Blueflow! You've already done me. And I like it! Every detail! Even my clothing!

How on earth could you do it?" Merlin whirled with a grand gesture; he spun with such excitement that his flying beard created a small whirlwind. He was laughing, lifting his arms in tribute to the artist's victory. "I'm going to give a banquet for you tonight—and all of you are invited!"

CHAPTER II

BEFORE Artist Blueflow left the following morning he had been treated to many stories about the greatest, most noble king. And the Round Table where the most valorous knights came together. And the oath of knighthood that was lifting this part of the world to new levels of excellence. This was a morning for such a wandering artist as Blueflow not to talk but to listen. To listen in admiration. These good words had filled him. He would not forget the hospitality of these friendly people.

While walking along the paths beyond the meadow he saw many knights in armor riding out in various directions. Not toward combat, he was told, but for practicing their skills across the open lands. One rode near to offer him a ride to the castle, which was over the hills. No, thank you, it was pleasant to walk. Others volunteered to help him with his luggage. "No, thank you, I always carry my paints personally."

"Will we see you painting sometime? We have heard about your painting of Merlin."

"Will you paint the king or the queen?"

Their praise-filled conversation revealed a very favorable circumstance: it was well known at Camelot that the great King Arthur wanted a painting of himself and his queen. It should be as tall and as wide as necessary to represent the two of them, life-size, sitting together.

Blueflow asked, "Are there no artists in King Arthur's domain?"

The answer was, yes, a few. Two, especially, were honored for their skills. These were two friendly rivals. Each had been requested to do the double portrait, but somehow the plan had languished. Blueflow was puzzled over it.

Hiking up the long slope, he now caught sight of the vast castle against the sky. The towers of pink, gold and blue were like a great fantastic mountain molded into architecture. "I am arriving," he said to himself. "Will I indeed have a chance to paint some of the royalty?"

Portcullis and drawbridge were ready; the way was open. At once he was inside, following mazes of walkways among the sand-colored walls. His path led him outward into a long curving balcony. From various doorways came voices of people at work.

To his left he looked down on the wide parade grounds that extended to the east. Again the knights on horseback could be seen, sometimes racing, drilling in formation, practicing their skills. On his right, a few spectators were looking down from tower windows. Fragrance filled the air, flowing over the open lands. Blueflow paused, resting his arms on the railing, enjoying the scene.

Someone was walking toward him, calling to him. He was a slender young man dressed in an ill-fitting outfit of light green. He was not in knight's clothing but was perhaps in the service of some castle department. He gave a pleasant wave and introduced himself. He said he had been asked to find this stranger and guide him.

"My name is Breunor. I believe you are the artist who has gained fame for himself by painting Merlin the Magician. Your reputation has arrived ahead of you. Some of the knights who were at the lodge yesterday while you were painting came back to the castle and told King Arthur about you."

"The great King Arthur? He knows about me?"

"He is interested in your abilities. He has long wished for a portrait of himself and his beautiful Queen Guinevere. Last night at the lodge, after you retired following the banquet, the two best-known artists at this castle, hearing of your portrait of Merlin, rode out to the lodge and saw—"

"Saw the portrait that I painted?"

"Saw and were enthusiastic. They came back to talk with our king about you. As a result, the king has been making plans this morning. He is a man of action. He has decided to put you to work at once."

"Are you leading me to his throne? Am I to have the privilege of meeting him?"

"Unfortunately he is very busy at this hour. He is administering oaths to the newly selected knights. It's a very sacred and emotional ceremony—but I see you have your painting equipment at hand."

"Always."

"This is good. You will begin painting at once. The scene is being arranged on this east balcony, on the curve a few steps ahead. But first we'll pause for a bit of food and drink, and by that time the queen will be ready."

"Do you have the panel on which I'll paint?"

"Fortunately, yes. The perfect size for the two subjects, king and queen, life-size, sitting together. It's the panel that was previously prepared for one or the other of the two artists. Quite ready but untouched."

Blueflow gave his guide a questioning look. "Tell me what happened, Mr. Breunor. Was there a conflict between the two of them? I'm a man of peace. Am I about to walk into a fight?"

Breunor laughed. "Peace, I assure you. These two artists defer to each other like a couple of comedians. When the offer of the job was in the air, each preferred that the honor go to the other. They would have done the painting jointly if it could have been done. The block was that the king himself was always too busy. He could never find time to stop and pose. And Queen Guinevere herself realized that her hope was futile. But now, suddenly, following the reports of your success with Merlin, the king feels sure. Are you now ready to go to the scene and set up your paints?"

"Ah—didn't you mention—"

"Oh, forgive me. Food and drink before you start. Of course. This way, please."

CHAPTER III

BEAUTIFUL Queen Guinevere, protected from the glare of the early afternoon sun, sat in a cushioned chair, waiting for the artist she had been promised. She was dressed in pink, white and lavender, and adorned with jewelry. She was slightly ill-at-ease, as some of her friends may have noticed. Not from the task of posing, however, but because her usual lady-in-waiting was not with her, having gone on a short vacation. This abrupt event had been planned only this morning. All of which explained the presence of a "substitute" lady-in-waiting, a tall, nervous one who was adjusting the queen's clothing.

"She's visiting here this week—the tall one in the dark purple and green. She came from a distant village. Her name is Mellicent. Years ago she was Guinevere's companion, and this week she's reenacting her old role of self-importance. It was her idea to bring three guards with her because she doesn't trust knights. If she worries over imaginary dangers, try to overlook it."

Blueflow hardly noticed what was being said. For the moment he was transfixed. Guinevere's beauty held him. The descriptions that he had heard were not exaggerated. Yes, she was stunningly beautiful. All right, stop acting paralyzed, he scolded himself. She is already posed, waiting. He lined out his paints and brushes in the order he liked.

More explanations from Breunor? Something of secret importance that should be confided to him?

"Her beauty has such drawing power—"

Low voice. Was this something that Blueflow really needed to know?

"—such drawing power that one of our great knights—the very popular knight named Lancelot—highly skilled—yes, and handsome—but that's another story. I'll not burden you—"

The half-whispered words were left unfinished. Blueflow gave complete attention to what he was doing. No more digressions. The queen was sitting perfectly. His paints were fresh and the brushes were swift. Start where? With the cascade of golden brown hair that framed her face? He was beginning. Several people were gathering too close. That substitute lady-in-waiting, Mellicent had promised to hold them back. She started to scold them—yes, they began to respond. Good, some free working space around him now. The brush was in action. The panel had been well mounted, the surface was smooth and clean. With a light purple stroke Blueflow drew a nearly vertical dividing line, a guide to his separation of the space. Here was where the shoulders of the king and the queen would touch, and where the king's hand would reach over to touch hers as they sat close together. All the space on the left side would remain untouched until sometime when the king would come and pose.

When would that be? Optimistically, Breunor had said that possibly a small party of knights, together with the king himself, might ride along the parade grounds within view of the balcony sometime this afternoon. If so, the king might be persuaded to stop for a few minutes. A stairway of eighteen or twenty steps led up from the parade ground level. This visit could give Blueflow at least a passing glance at the great man himself.

Were the onlookers coming too close again to Blueflow's paints and brushes? Should he speak to the lady-in-waiting? No, better not. It might bruise her feeling of authority. He sensed that this whole occasion was felt by her to be an imposition, and he was the cause of it.

Who were these gathering spectators? Some were bringing chairs, crowding up around the area of action. Those ladies dressed in finery were probably the wives of knights, turning the event into a game. There were quieter onlookers too, by now the people on the left, dressed in dull brown and gray. They were some of the palace workers. Their chores had brought them to this east porch and here they had stopped to watch.

At the other side were three uniformed guards who stood stiffly by the stone railing. From Breunor's words, Blueflow knew they were not a part of Camelot, but were Mellicent's private protection, her three-man army from her distant village. Their presence gave Mellicent self-importance, no doubt.

Blueflow was painting now with a swift hand. The crowd was attentive. Whispers but no talking. Paint, paint, paint! Catch quick glimpses of his subject, perfectly posed. What his eyes saw his skilled hand converted into brush strokes.

For nearly an hour the spectators were entranced. Even Mellicent. She hovered near, frozen in fascination.

Finally Blueflow stepped back to see the picture from a little distance. He added a few touches and the work was done. Mellicent gave a slight gesture to the onlookers. Yes, he was finished. "But don't crowd. Make way for Her Highness."

Queen Guinevere rose, radiant with pleasure, and stepped forward. To Artist Blueflow she smiled and nodded. He bowed. Now all began to speak soft words of praise. Breunor tapped Blueflow on the shoulder and whispered, "Wonderful, my friend."

QUITE abruptly the praise was cut short. Mellicent spoke with a tone of command. Enough of confusion. She ordered the onlookers to stand aside.

"Back to your seats, everyone. This artist is only half done. Give him room."

What was going to happen next? Everyone wondered. "All right, Mr. Artist." Mellicent assumed the role of a general commanding the battle to continue. "Go ahead. You're wasting time."

Blueflow gave her a puzzled look. "What are you trying to tell me?"

Pick up your brushes and go on with the job—the second half—the portrait of the king."

Blueflow frowned. "Miss Mellicent, don't you realize we need the king himself to be here, to pose? We must wait. He may come sometime this afternoon."

Mellicent's voice was edged with suspicion. "Are you trying to dodge us? We know about you. We've heard how you painted Merlin the Magician while he was absent. They say you did it from memory. Let's see you do the same for our king."

Blueflow was shaking his head slowly. "Miss Mellicent, I was able to do that only because Merlin's face was fresh in my mind. But I have never seen King Arthur."

"You're dodging. You're lying. Everyone has seen King Arthur."

"You're quite mistaken, Miss Mellicent. I arrived only this morning."

She turned her sharp glare on Breunor. "Do you know anything about this artist scullion?"

"He's telling the truth. He has never seen King Arthur. He came over from the lodge this morning."

The substitute lady-in-waiting was about to break into rage, being defied. Blueflow spoke quietly. "Miss Mellicent, your queen has been sitting beautifully for a full hour. Posing isn't easy. We might ask if she'd like a drink. Perhaps someone—"

He glanced at Breunor and the friendly guide motioned to one of the attendants. At once a cup of wine was brought to the queen. With a thank-you she accepted and drank. Then other courtesies were extended. The artist was pleased to accept a cup of water.

Refreshed, he turned to Mellicent and the others closed around him in a mood of natural friendliness. "As to my going ahead in the king's absence, there may be a way. Listen closely, please. There is a sort of miraculous method that only a few artists know how to use."

"Do it," Mellicent said.

"I will try, but only on certain conditions. Our Mr. Breunor who is kindly guiding me must be given command of everyone. The others must obey him and there must be no mistake. You, Miss Mellicent, must cooperate. And all of those around you. If you agree, I will try."

"Do it," Mellicent repeated.

CHAPTER IV

THE scene was changed and Blueflow was ready to start the lefthand side of the panel. The queen's chair had been moved close. She understood that she must be blindfolded to help her concentrate.

Three screens larger than doors had been brought from another part of the balcony. They were placed to stand upright in triangular arrangement, to enclose the artist and the subject at work.

At the start, Breunor and Mellicent were detained for a moment beside the queen and the artist inside the enclosure. It was Blueflow's wish that they listen while he explained his method. The crowd was closed out.

"As you know," Blueflow said, "I tested our Queen Guinevere moments ago with a few questions. She has proved to me that she is able to close her eyes and see a clear mental picture of his majesty King Arthur."

"What is that supposed to prove?" Mellicent asked. Breunor gave her a sign that said, "Hush and listen."

Blueflow continued, "Am I quite right, Your Highness? Can you see the king clearly in your mind."

Her reply was, "Of course. It's easy."

"Good. That's the whole secret of the miracle-art that I'm about to undertake. This means that your mind is able to hold the dear picture that I want to paint on this panel. Do you understand?"

"I understand."

"All right. We are now blindfolding you to help your concentration, and at once you will begin seeing his image. Your mental picture will enter my mind and guide my art. We are now almost ready. The crowd is outside these screens and will be kept silent. Miss Mellicent and Master

Breunor are going out to join them. Now they have gone. You and I are alone within this triangle so that no one can see what I'm painting. Are you ready?"

"Ready."

"As you look at his majesty in your mind I want you to notice the shape of his forehead. Straight? Slanted? Wide? Narrow? You are not to answer me in words. My mind is taking the image from your mind. Your mental images guide my hand. And now I am painting."

"You are painting!" the queen repeated. "I don't know how you can do it. And I can't see through the blindfold, but I believe you, Mr. Artist. *My mind is telling you what to paint.*"

"Your Highness, you are understanding perfectly. Keep your mind working. We won't have to talk. You keep watching your visions closely and my hand will keep working."

"And no one is watching us? No one?"

"No one."

The work went on quietly. Blueflow breathed slowly with a feeling of gratefulness. He spoke only an occasional word of guidance... "Eyebrows...cheekbones...flesh colors...shadows under the brows...highlights on the bridge of the nose..." The details were coming through to him faster than he could speak. Now he was catching the color areas on the face, a design that surely matched the lines of a helmet that had been worn in the sun...on and on...the upward tilt of one shoulder adjusted to the weight of the armor.

Faster than human speech could have described the numberless details, the picture kept coming through. She was breathing slowly, almost as though she had gone into a trance...a trance of visualizing the features she knew so well....

Blueflow thought, would Mellicent suddenly appear around the corner of a screen and break the spell? No, no such trouble. Breunor was in control, over there on the other side of the enclosure. All was well. The master artist worked on at lightning speed. Paint, paint! More images. More details. A profusion of colors from paints that were doubly alive from some of the magic the magician had once given them. Paint, paint! Keep catching the images that came through like a chain of fire. Shoulders, chest, form of the masterful body, sturdily armored; reflecting shafts of sunlight, shadows of the arms... Almost finished? More to be done on the background, yes, but that could wait until the full resemblance had been captured. Almost finished? He heard a sigh of the queen's breathing.

At last, break the spell. "Your Highness, you may remove the blindfold and see the painting."

"Thank you, Mr. Artist." She removed the blindfold. As if awakening, she saw the painting. Spontaneously she called her joy to the artist. "He's beautiful! He's handsome! So natural!" She jumped up as if to embrace the picture.

"Don't touch, please! It's wet! It will smear!"

Suddenly something changed her manner. She was stepping back from the painting. She touched her hands to her lips, her eyes went wide. She cried out as if in pain.

Mellicent and Breunor must have heard her cry and thought she was hurt. They dashed in, looked, and stood stunned by what they saw. Mellicent's arms flew out in shock. *"Oh, no—NO!"*

And Breunor called in a tight, coughing voice. *"What happened?"*

Again, Mellicent's shriek. *"That's not King Arthur, that's Sir Lancelot! Your artist has gone wild! This is tragic!"*

The queen was shocked. Artist Blueflow couldn't possibly understand what had gone wrong. It seemed as though something was crushing her. He caught her terrified words. She was moaning, "How did I do it? I was supposed to think of the king. But I slipped. How did my thoughts get mixed?"

Mellicent shouted, "Your artist did it! I'll have him executed! This is a high crime!"

"I did it!" the queen protested with weeping in her voice. "I—I—"

Mellicent cut in. "Not you! That mad painter! He's a criminal! This is blasphemy! Guards, guards, step up! Take this man."

Her uniformed guards came up, confused but trying to obey. At her order they batted down the screens and crowded in on Blueflow to seize him as their prisoner. Not understanding the situation in the slightest, Blueflow yielded. This must be a mistake. Whatever the matter was, let Mellicent and the guards play their game. But now her commands sounded dangerous.

"Crush him! Crush him! Smash the bones of his hands!"

The people were surging forward. What was the commotion all about? Suddenly they saw and were choked with surprise. Somehow an awful thing had happened. The new picture which the artist had added to the panel was not King Arthur, it was Sir Lancelot!

Sir Lancelot! The queen's favorite! What a terrible mistake! No one could understand. No one had time to think. The substitute lady-in-waiting was storming, calling wild orders to her guards.

The tall Number One Guard, however, was slow to obey. He stood back while the other two seized Blueflow and pulled him over to the ledge. They placed his hands on the stone surface as Mellicent had ordered. She repeated, "You, Number One, I order you to crush his hands."

The tall guard had taken a battlehammer from inside his coat but he held back. He stared at Mellicent in disbelief. "If we break his fingers he will never paint again."

"I command you."

"I heard." He had moved a step closer.

"Strike!" Mellicent shrieked. "This artist is a criminal. Strike for the sake of the queen!"

The voice of the queen called, *"No!"* A single clearly spoken command. The tall Number One guard turned and bowed to her. He returned the weapon to his coat. The bewildered group surrounding the scene watched in awe. She was their beloved queen; whatever the situation, her words were sacred.

Now Breunor's voice shouted a surprising discovery. "Look! They're coming across the parade ground—some knights—and the king is with them!"

The queen's voice called, "His Majesty! He's coming this way. He'll see. He won't understand!"

Breunor was on the alert. "Can we hide the second picture?"

For an instant Guinevere looked helpless. She covered her eyes with her hand. "Oh, what have I done? Why did I—"

Mellicent screamed at her. "You didn't do it! You didn't! It was that wild artist!" She lurched forward, slipped and fell; she sank to the floor in a tantrum, beating her fists. Again Guinevere was controlled. She stood, hand upraised, and called a sharp order. *"Mellicent,* go! Go *back!* Go *now! Someone help her!"* Two friends nearby came to the rescue and led the distraught woman off toward a shadowed aisle.

Breunor was asking, "Shall I erase the second painting? Shall I tear off my shirt and mop off the paint?"

The queen's glance darted around. "Where is the artist?"

Blueflow stepped forward, gave a slight bow. "Your Highness."

"Mr. Artist, do you understand what's happened? If my husband the king comes he'll see—he'll see—how shall I explain?"

Blueflow nodded. "Do you want me to remove the man's portrait? I have a wide brush. With your permission I'll brush away the entire left side of the panel." He went to work. The queen urged him to hurry. He worked at all possible speed, and the people around began to whisper in tones of relief. All of the second portrait was disappearing.

For a moment the pressure of time eased, for it appeared that the knights were riding on past. Maybe they would move on at a distance. Blueflow had heard that they were starting on a trip westward which the king had planned. But now the king turned to look back across toward the balcony scene and suddenly he came galloping straight toward the stairway. Two knights came with him. They stayed below to attend his horse. He marched to the stairway and ascended. When he reached the balcony there was only one portrait showing on the panel, and all was serene.

CHAPTER V

T HE revered King Arthur stood before the crowd. Everyone bowed.

For a moment he was a proud statue. Motionless, taking in the quiet scene. Handsome in blue with a design of purple and gold across his chest. With fine dignity he lifted his plumed gold and blue cap in a gesture of greeting. Another deep bow from the crowd. They stood applauding. Guinevere, however, continued to bow. When she looked up, King Arthur was before her, arms open, to take her into his embrace.

She gestured toward the painting. The left side of the panel contained no figure, only a light gray smudge that might be a background for the new painting yet to be done. But on the right side was something wonderful: the life-size portrait of Queen Guinevere.

The king was deeply pleased.

He held an arm around her and together they gazed. The king's expression, as seen by the onlookers, was deep adoration, a prayer of devotion to his queen.

Guinevere said, "You are liking it. I see it in your eyes."

"Yes, my dear queen, and I will be doubly pleased if the artist can complete the portrait. But where is he?"

She gestured to Master Artist Blueflow. The artist bowed. He felt the king's gaze on him. The king offered a handshake that was more than the pressure of a strong hand. It was an entrance into Blueflow's heart of the spirit of a great and noble leader.

The king spoke to him in the tone of a friend. "We are grateful. I have heard about your skill from my own two top-ranking artists of Camelot, and also from our Merlin. They have given me the description of your remarkable ability to paint from memory. You know I wish I could take time to pose. But let me ask, Mr. Blueflow. During these minutes could you study my features—my expression—my clothes—my stature? Could it be done by you from memory during my absence? Or am I asking too much?"

Blueflow replied with a slight smile. "Your Majesty, what you are asking me to observe I have now already observed and memorized. I am now prepared to start at once."

"Indeed?" The king studied him with admiration. "Sometime within a few days I will return, looking forward to seeing the completed double portrait."

His farewell embrace with the queen was prolonged, as though her heart compelled her to hold him, as though she could hardly let go. Then he gave the crowd a quick wave and bounded down the steps. He and his knights galloped away.

"At once" had been Blueflow's words to His Majesty, and without hesitation the artist, with spirits lifted, started the new painting, with the warmth of the king's handshake giving tone to his work. The image in his mind was clear and strong.

At the completion of the portrait several of the spectators spoke words of praise. Were they becoming friendly to him, an itinerant artist? Blueflow wondered. He began packing his equipment and a good friend joined him, an old man with twinkling eyes and a long white beard.

"Do you think you've reached a happy ending?" Merlin asked. "How easily we may be self-deceived by the appearance of success. We must always be prepared for surprises. However"—momentarily changing his mood—"here come a couple of your admirers—those two corpulent fellows in the orange costumes. No deceit from them, I promise."

"I knew they were back of me, watching. I don't know who they are."

"They're the two most highly esteemed artists in Camelot. And I'd better warn you, they're a couple of clowns. I was afraid they might bother you with their jokes while you worked, but you evidently had them hypnotized."

The two orange-clad ones introduced themselves and extended congratulations. One asked, "How do you paint the whole picture out of your head?"

The other said, "We've come over to examine your head. How can you look so normal?"

Again, "What we really want, Brother Blue, is to sign our own names to your paintings, as though they are ours."

"When the king pays us, we'll give you a slice."

"And take you out to a banquet."

Blueflow laughed. "Keep talking. We artists like to be rescued from starvation." He relaxed, listening to their banter.

As they departed they called back. "Save some time for us. We want to take lessons."

"Don't run away, but keep out of trouble."

Keep out of trouble? There it was again, a hint of something puzzling, similar to Merlin's remark. Just now, all that Blueflow wanted was to take a long walk away from this balcony. Walk where? Down the long slope away from the castle, across the meadows, back to the lodge where this long day had begun.

"Could I carry some of your luggage?" Merlin asked, joining him. But no, the artist never thought of needing help. Just now his brain was still spinning with images.

"Everything we see along the way," Blueflow confessed, "turns into faces waiting to be painted. These flowers look up at me like a garden of Guineveres. And those tree trunks resemble the one you call Lancelot, loaded down with armor. Or if with branches, they're kings reaching out as if to embrace their beloved queen."

Merlin added to the game, guessing that the plants with prickly spines might recall someone named Mellicent.

"Mellicent," Blueflow laughed. "I had almost forgotten. I hope she doesn't come back with more commands."

Apparently no such thought was in Merlin's mind. The queen had stilled her shrieking voice. But there was a real threat for Blueflow to look out for: the portrait he had painted that had to be erased.

Deep in the night this thought would break in on Blueflow's sleep through a strange circumstance.

CHAPTER VI

DEEP in the night the owner of the lodge tapped on Blueflow's door. "Sorry to awaken you, Mr. Artist, but someone is asking to see you. A friend named Breunor."

As Blueflow knew, Breunor was one of those who had volunteered to keep watch over the painting through the night. Now here he was, standing breathless on the lodge porch in the moonlight.

"Forgive my disturbance, Mr. Blueflow, but something very mystifying has happened to your double portrait."

"Has someone damaged it?"

"No one has touched it. Only the moonlight touched it. It changed."

"Possibly some slight change in the color effects?"

"A complete change in one of the faces," Breunor said. "Several of us were watching as the moonlight began, and—you must believe me— as the moon rose, the king's face melted away. It faded out and changed to the face of Lancelot, the queen's lover—just as you had painted it originally from the mental transfer."

"Unbelievable! There was nothing in my paints to account for this kind of thing. I'm trying to comprehend. Is this part of Camelot? Some mysteries are beyond my understanding." As he read Breunor's countenance he realized that no one should doubt this friend's honesty. "Is the change continuing? And no signs of the king's face visible? Of course I'll be blamed."

"Come back to the castle with me. You'll see for yourself."

They made the trip over the moonlit landscape.

As they approached the castle the moonlight over the scene was beginning to fade. Near the area of the east balcony Blueflow could see shadowy evidences of a crowd. No doubt many persons had watched through the night.

"We'll keep away from that mob," Breunor said. "For you it will be safer. Some of them may be angry over the way your painting has been changed by the moonlight."

"I want to see it for myself," said Blueflow.

"You will. I know a way. Follow me."

Instead of ascending the stairs from the parade ground to the balcony, he led Blueflow into a dark passage, through some heaps of storage in the understructure. He told Blueflow to follow closely through the darkness and feel his way. "There's a secret room up ahead. Here, we're coming into it. Catch sight of that vertical, narrow slice of sky, up, to your left. It's a slip in the architecture. It will be our window. No one sees it from above, but we'll have an upward view. See? A glimpse of the moon. And some of the people in front of your painting. Now, move your head slightly. Can you see it? Do you see how the moonlight has changed your painting?"

Blueflow concentrated his gaze. The night view could be made out. Yes, there it was. "The queen is just the same, but there's no king. What I see is the person I made from her mind, the one you call Sir Lancelot. It has come back!"

"Now you know why the night viewers are amazed—and some of them angry."

Blueflow's eyes took in the surrounding crowd and soon he discovered the queen herself. "Queen Guinevere. Over there to the left. She's acting sick. Does she dread what she sees? The very portrait that came out of her memory!" Blueflow studied the whole puzzling situation. "I don't see Miss Mellicent."

"Mellicent has been sent back to her own town. Now it's the queen's regular staff. That's the real lady-in-waiting trying to lead her away. But look, Blueflow, isn't something new happening to the painting?"

They watched in silence for several minutes. The crowd began to talk with excitement. "Look, look! The moonlight overhead is fading. The white light of dawn is changing the sky—and Sir Lancelot is fading out. His armor is growing dim. Now the lines of the king are coming back!"

Breunor whispered, "A miracle. Right before our eyes!"

Voices were sounding in astonishment. *"King Arthur—returning! His face—the blue of his shoulders—his strong hands—he's returning! The whole portrait! Daylight is bringing him back!"*

The lady-in-waiting was leading the queen forward to see, and everyone could hear her outcries of excitement.

Several minutes later the night crowd realized that the picture had come back to its daytime normality. Finally, eased in their minds, they began to depart. Some were quoting what they had heard the queen say before she left. *This was the picture that His Majesty must see when he returns!*

When would he come?

It was certain that the rumors of this magical happening would race through the castle and spread out across the land almost at the speed of lightning. And with what emotional overtones! Even as Blueflow and Breunor listened to the conversations that echoed down to them they realized that some incriminating words were being spoken. Breunor whispered, "You're about to get an earful of danger."

"I'm hearing it. Someone is saying that I'm to blame. They're calling me a trickster. Listen!"

The strongest voice declared, "It was a deliberate act of evil... Dastardly mischief... It could shatter the peace of Camelot. If it happens again tonight when the moon rises we shouldn't hesitate. We'll hunt that artist down."

"Where did he come from?"

"And where did he go? Didn't he walk down the slope toward the lodge after he finished? We needn't wait for the king's return..."

The voices moved out of hearing but Blueflow and Breunor had caught the sound of action.

Blueflow wasn't accustomed to being wrong in his judgments; however, now he began to ask, had he made a mistake, coming to this land? He should have packed up his luggage and hiked back into the forest as soon as his work was done. Breunor tried to counsel him, but one fact was obvious: he mustn't return to the lodge.

"You must stay here, Blueflow, until the air is clear. I'll bring food and water. And a blanket. Before the danger widens I'll go to the lodge and pick up your luggage. I'll go now."

CHAPTER VII

THE magic effect of the moonlight on the portraits each night would soon be known across the land. Of course the moon was an hour later each night but that didn't keep the crowds from coming. It was believed that Sir Lancelot himself, who was stationed with some other knights nearly half a day's ride away, had not only heard; but had come in disguise, on the second night and strolled along the balcony at the back of the groups of onlookers; that he had now seen himself and the queen pictured together enjoying the blessings of a moonlight rendezvous.

Of course everyone was curious to know when King Arthur himself would return and see.

Blueflow, secluded in the understructure hideaway, listened hourly to the passing conversations above. Not all pleasant. Occasionally those hard-voiced accusers could be heard repeating their rumor that the artist must be totally evil, and that his trickery would cause a moral earthquake.

By midmorning of the new day Blueflow saw that the skies were growing dark. Now he heard soft steps approaching and knew that Breunor was returning.

"Big storm coming, Mr. Blueflow. I may have a chance to get you away, out of danger."

The rain came down in blinding torrents, and Blueflow, covered in the blanket from the top of his head to his knees, was led by Breunor up the slope of the balcony, past the guard and out over a narrow walk that led across toward the edge of the forest. Here was a knoll, lost in clouds and rain, thickly covered with trees.

"There, Mr. Blueflow. Catch your breath. Get close under these branches out of the storm, have some food and drink, and I'll give you the news from the lodge."

"If I had only brought my luggage, especially the paints and brushes—"

"They're all right here, almost within reach. I went for them the other day, before those three or four went down to the lodge to look for you. The lodge keeper was on our side, and the searchers never learned anything. They believe you've headed out to the northeast through the forest, in case—"

"In case of what?"

"In case our king, when he comes back and sees the painting switching by night, wants to try you in court. Don't mind my gloomy talk. Go ahead and eat. You must be starved."

"Thanks for food, and for hiding me out. I've taken in hours of overhead conversations, daytimes and nights. Am I safe here until the storm passes? If I accidentally fall asleep, who will be first to find me here?"

Breunor gave him some sort of answer, but it was lost in the roar of the rain.

CHAPTER VIII

B LUEFLOW slept on a cushion of damp leaves for two days. He awakened to the sounds of men laughing and joking. He blinked his eyes at the sight of two corpulent fellows in orange costumes. Where had he seen these orange clowns before? At first he thought they were having a sword fight with paint brushes—no they were engaged in some sort of game which involved their slapping at each other with wet paint.

They saw that he had awakened. Good. Just in time to see the finish of a contest. The game was not complicated, once you understood.

"See the idea, Mr. Blueflow? The storm tossed us this branch full of leaves. We've hung it up by a cord—"

"And given it a few hundred twists so that it hangs here spinning—"

"So it's a game of speed—a contest—to paint the leaves whirling by—"

"To see how many we can paint with your brushes—"

"My brushes?" Blueflow was waking up. He came closer to watch.

"Don't worry, Mr. Blueflow, we're using our own paint.

"The idea is to slap paint on the leaves with lightning strokes. When the whirl stops, we'll count to see who wins."

"If he loses I'll push his face into the leaves. And paint his eyebrows orange."

"If I win, I'll paint him up with a blue mustache and a blue beard."

Blueflow walked over toward them. *"My brushes?* Where did you find my brushes?"

"Breunor brought all of your equipment up here. It's all hidden there under that fan-shaped bush at the foot of the big tree."

"When?" Blueflow asked. "When did you see him?"

"Two days ago, following the big storm. He assigned us to watch over you. It was easy. You've been asleep for two days."

"Trust us, Mr. Blueflow. We're going to keep you out of harm until you have your appointment."

"What appointment?"

"With King Arthur. He returned a couple of days ago and he wants to see you."

Blueflow backed away to give the two orange-clad clowns space to go on with their game, slapping paint at the leaves and accidentally smearing a few strokes on each other's faces.

When the battle wore itself out, the two artists settled down to give Blueflow a few of the details that he wanted to hear. Especially about the king and his first hours after coming back and seeing the painting. Suddenly, to Blueflow's surprise, the two buffoons talked like a couple of sensitive, serious artists.

The king had planned his return, they explained, for two afternoons ago, and the event was to be his viewing of the double portrait, accompanied by his queen. The rain that had gusted in before noon suddenly ended by mid-afternoon. The two, accompanied by her lady-in-waiting and a few others, walked down the balcony promenade in the golden afternoon sunlight that came through in dramatic brilliance following the rains. Guards had protected the painting with screens throughout the storm. Sunlighted afternoon clouds heightened the color effects as the screens were being removed. King Arthur and Queen Guinevere held each other in close embrace for many minutes. They loved the painting. Later there was a dinner party.

But of course there was another drama yet to come, the one of the appearance of moonlight that would play its magic. It occurred late in the night, the unannounced but fully expected visit of the king to the painted panels. Were many people waiting there to watch from a distance? Curiously, not the expected crowd. Public courtesy to his majesty was evident. He appeared, accompanied by four knights; he sauntered along the way within fifteen or twenty feet of the painting, a few errant clouds intruded on the view; then came a well illuminated moment. The work of art was before his eyes; the queen and her lover together. The king asked no questions of those walking with him. However, it was known that he made a point of returning just before the coming of daylight to see the mysterious changing of the picture back to normal. "As far as we know he made no comments."

"Thank you," Blueflow said when the two Camelot artists had finished their description. "Perhaps he is saving his comments for me. Did you mention there is an appointment in store for me?... Will the two of you kindly visit me in prison?"

CHAPTER IX

LATE that night it was Merlin who led Blueflow to the scene of the portraits. His brief words were, "I wish you luck, brave Mr. Blueflow." He conducted the quiet artist to the row of chairs where King Arthur was sitting, watching the moonlight version of Blueflow's art.

One of the knights sitting beside his majesty rose and moved aside, so that Blueflow could take his seat. The king's eyes turned from the painted panel to the artist. His expression was not unfriendly.

"Mr. Artist," he began in a low voice, "you may be surprised to learn that I am planning to build permanent seats on this part of the balcony, so that people may enjoy this art in comfort." He paused and watched the affect of his words upon Blueflow. The artist could not read the King's expression and was unsure what to say. The King continued.

"I was surprised to learn about this painting of Sir Lancelot. I felt sure that neither of my two court artists would have painted it."

Blueflow's throat was dry with nerves, but he gulped and said. "I did it."

King Arthur nodded. "That is the information which others have given me. However, Master Merlin tells me that you didn't know what you were doing."

"That is true."

"Are you in the habit of not knowing what you are doing?"

"I knew what I was doing, sire, but I did not realize my mistake."

The king nodded again and turned his eyes back to the portrait. "Had you seen Sir Lancelot before this painting?"

"No, I have never seen him. I attempted to work from mental images, not realizing—" Blueflow lapsed into silence.

The king had folded his arms, and it was hard to guess what he was thinking. His eyes were half closed. Then, more alertly, he began to watch the panel. The moonlight from overhead was fading and dawn was starting to transform the painting. The king watched in silent fascination.

Presently he returned to the unfinished conversation. "So you have never seen him. The portrait is quite a good likeness. If it continues to reappear by moonlight many people will come to see it, naturally. It will remind all of us that strange things can happen here at Camelot."

He lapsed into silence for a while, and then turned his eyes fully on Blueflow.

"You have done me a service, Master Artist, for which I thank you. I do not need to go into detail, but let me say that a king needs to always be alert. I shall encourage all visitors to come and see this portrait so that all may marvel at your art, and at the same time consider the world about them, and their part in it. Your talent is being greatly admired. My queen and I thank you deeply for the daylight glory of our portrait."

Blueflow looked into the king's eyes, where he saw a growing spirit overcoming a deeper sadness. The king smiled.

"I have a further idea. You must attune your mind to the mental images, as you call them, of this whole castle. I want you to paint a huge mural, capturing the entire city, bringing it alive. And," he added, as his eyes turned again to the portrait of himself and his wife, now gleaming in the morning sun, "I want it to be a true reflection of this castle, and all who are in it."

Blueflow did not know what to say, but bowed an acceptance to the King. After a while he realized that the audience was at an end, and he was ushered away. The king sat in silence, drinking in the portrait of himself with Guinevere, and dreaming a thousand dreams.

CHAPTER X

OVER the next few weeks Blueflow labored hard over the mural, using Merlin's enchanted paints. He worked with the two court artists, but while they painted the background and the buildings, it was Blueflow who looked into the hearts and minds of the people who came to watch his work, and captured them forever.

And if you come today, to Camelot, you may be guided from the castle to a nearby knoll. There you will stand among the trees to look back at the fantastic architecture against the sky. And there you will discover, near at hand, a magnificent mural on a wide panel built between two trees, which reflects that same scene. But in that mural are all the citizens of Camelot, and if you stay to watch the mural as the moon rises, you will look into the hearts of the citizens and see what they really desire.

There, among the swirls of blue and gray, stands King Arthur, strong of feature, radiating greatness of spirit. About him his knights, courtiers and citizens go about their business. Each night, Arthur comes and watches the mural, and the people know he is watching them. And there are those who fear for the thoughts that are in their hearts. The pattern of the future is set.

www.ingramcontent.com/pod-product-compliance
Lightning Source LLC
Chambersburg PA
CBHW02074250626

47155CB00003B/909